LELAY · AGUIRRE
ESPOSITO · COOKE

BLACK MASK

# WE ARE THE DANGER

CREATED BY **FABIAN LELAY**

WRITTEN AND ILLUSTRATED BY **FABIAN LELAY**

COLORIST **CLAUDIA AGUIRRE**

LETTERER **TAYLOR ESPOSITO**

LETTERING ASSISTANT **JAY CASTRO**

EDITOR **STEPHANIE COOKE**

★★★★

COVERS BY **LELAY**

★★★★

PRODUCED BY **MATT PIZZOLO**

BOOK DESIGN, PRODUCTION AND LAYOUT **PHIL SMITH**

BLACK MASK

Published By Black Mask Studios LLC

WE ARE THE DANGER trade paperback volume 1. First Printing. February 2020.
 Published by Black Mask Studios, LLC. Office of publication: 2798 Sunset Boulevard LA CA 90026. Originally published in single issue form as WE ARE THE DANGER #1-5 by Black Mask Studios.

# TABLE OF CONTENTS

# ISSUE 1

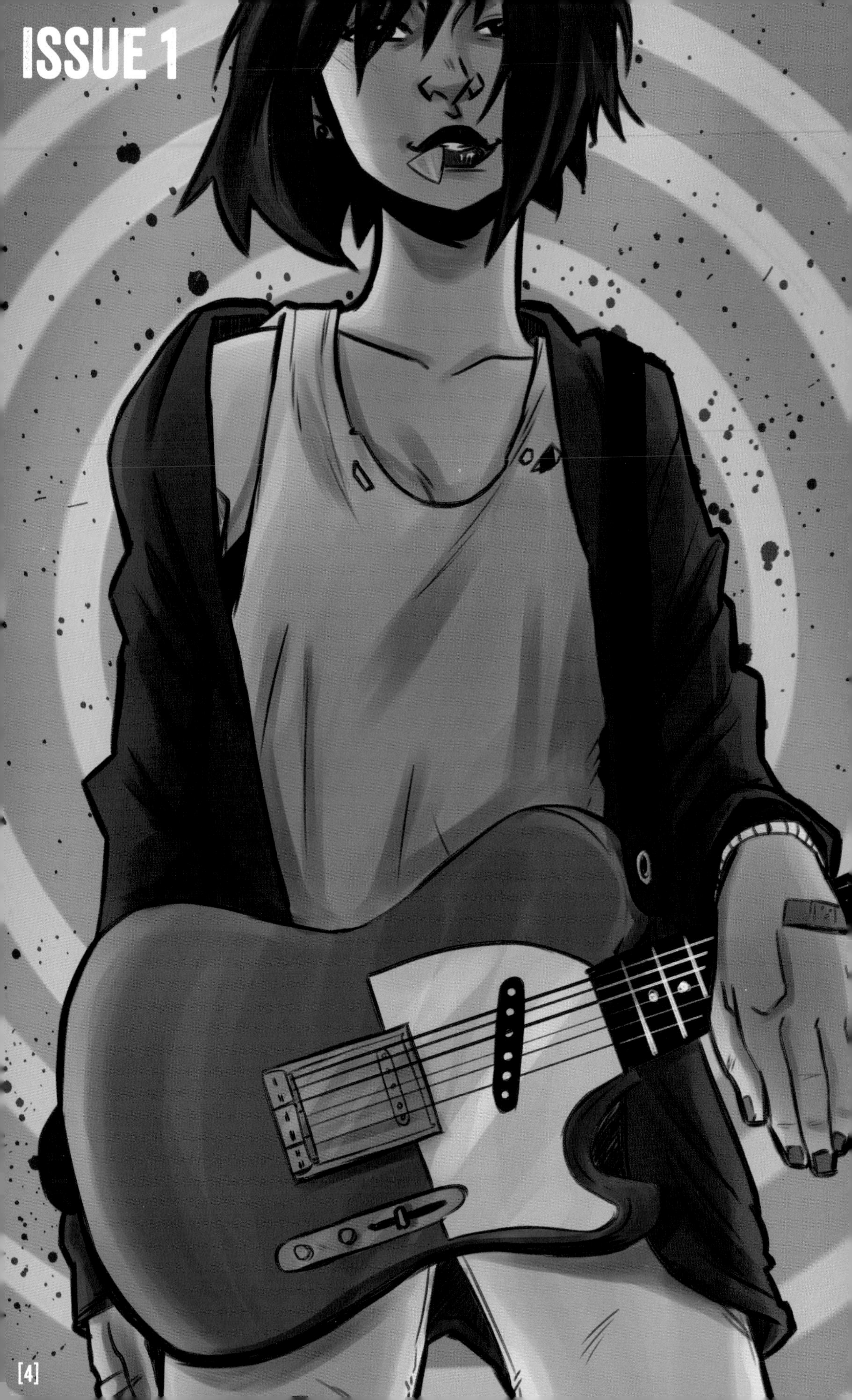

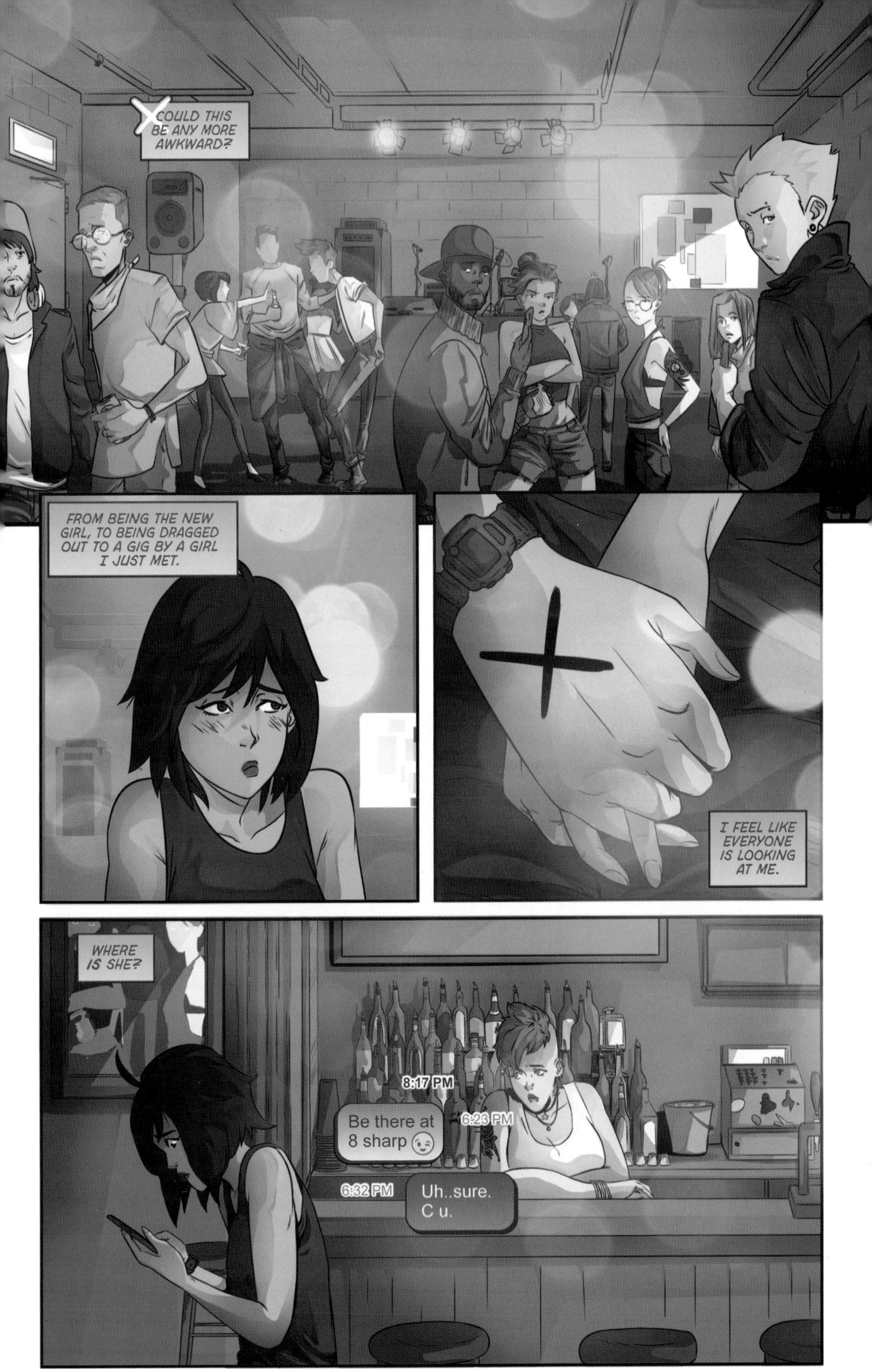
COULD THIS BE ANY MORE AWKWARD?
FROM BEING THE NEW GIRL, TO BEING DRAGGED OUT TO A GIG BY A GIRL I JUST MET.
I FEEL LIKE EVERYONE IS LOOKING AT ME.
WHERE IS SHE?
8:17 PM
Be there at 8 sharp
6:23 PM
6:32 PM
Uh..sure. C u.

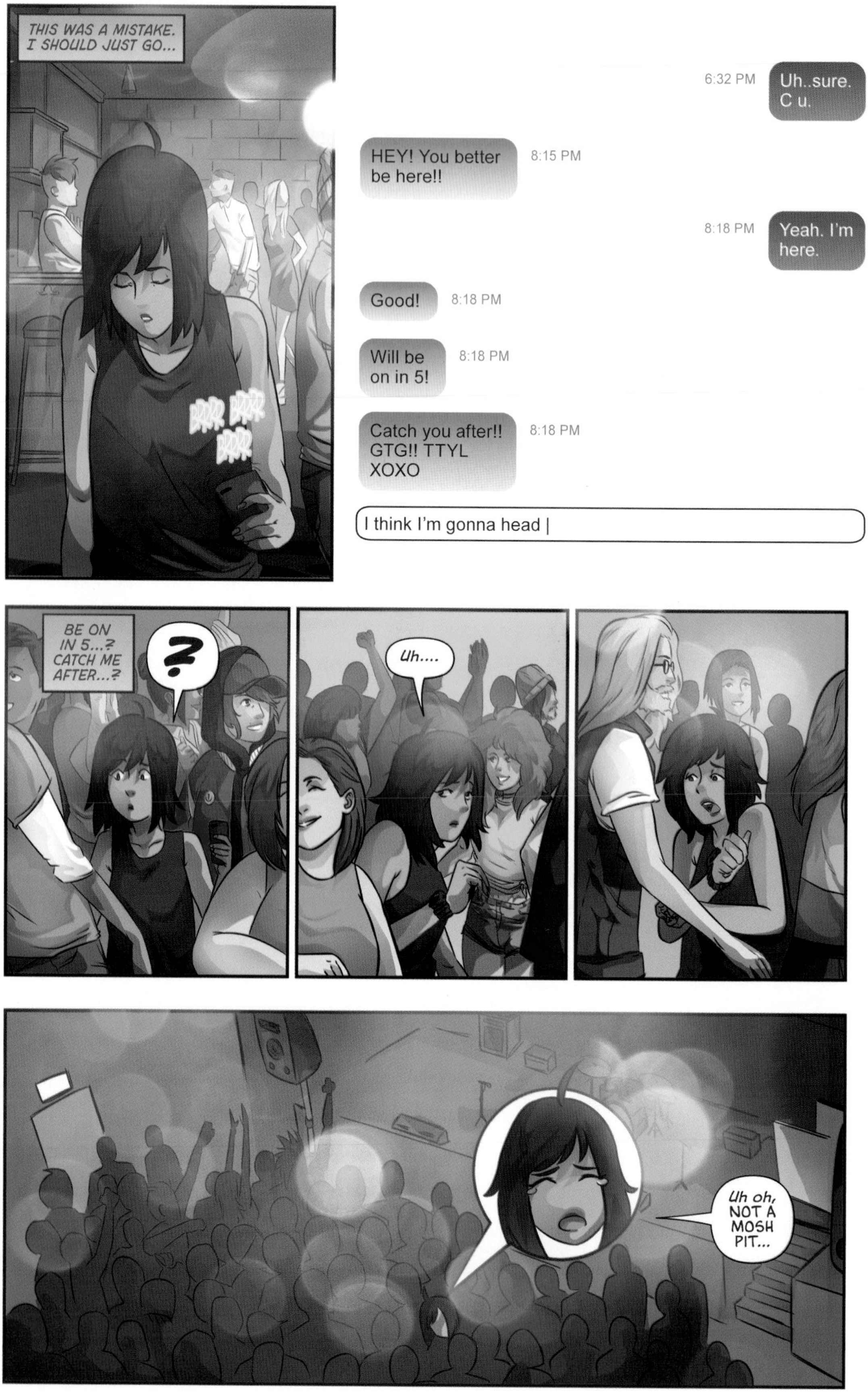
THIS WAS A MISTAKE. I SHOULD JUST GO...
BRRRR BRRRR BRRRR
6:32 PM
Uh..sure. C u.
HEY! You better be here!!
8:15 PM
8:18 PM
Yeah. I'm here.
Good!
8:18 PM
Will be on in 5!
8:18 PM
Catch you after!! GTG!! TTYL XOXO
8:18 PM
I think I'm gonna head |
BE ON IN 5...? CATCH ME AFTER...?
?
Uh....
Uh oh, NOT A MOSH PIT...

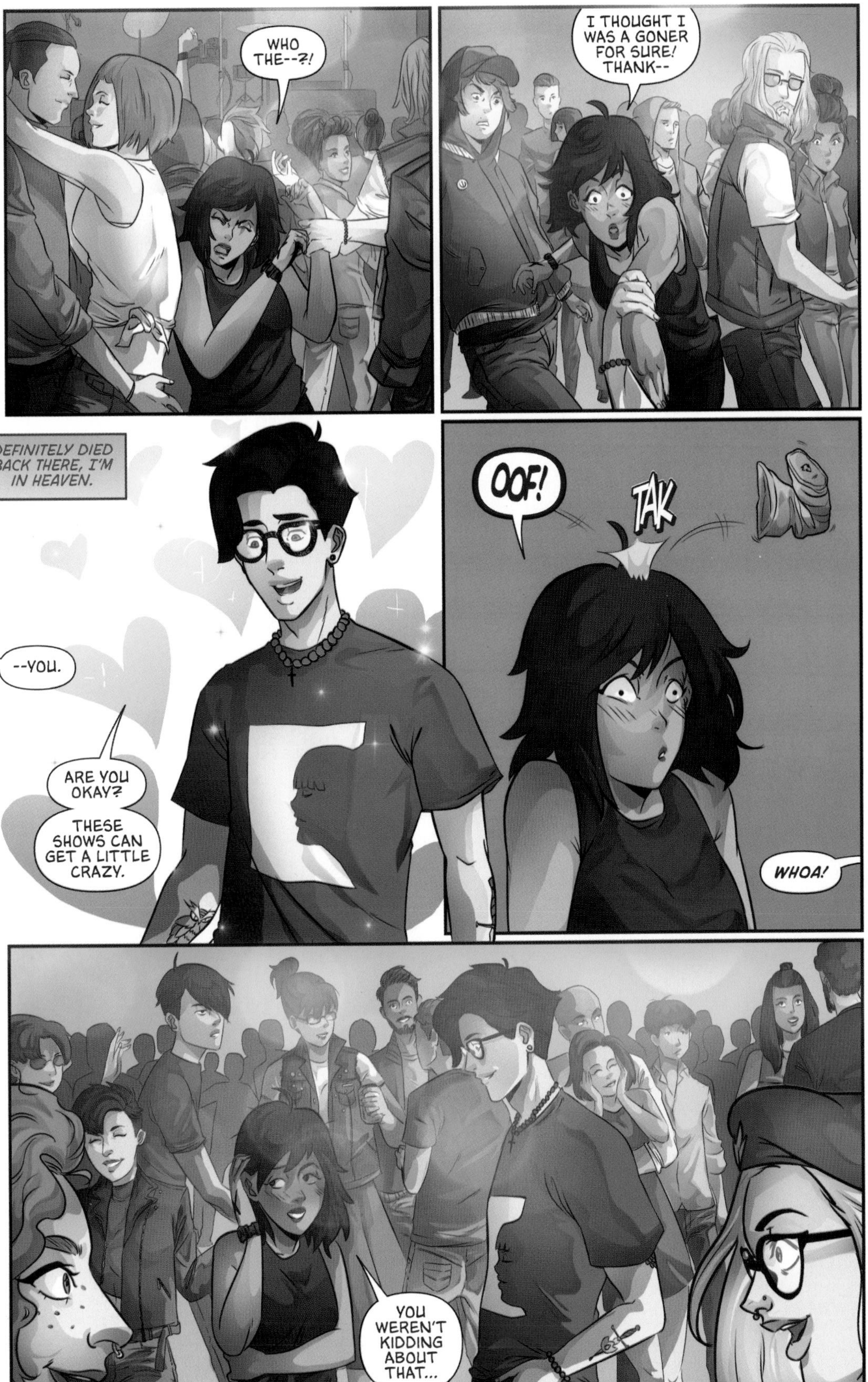
WHO THE--?!
I THOUGHT I WAS A GONER FOR SURE! THANK--
DEFINITELY DIED BACK THERE, I'M IN HEAVEN.
--YOU.
ARE YOU OKAY?
THESE SHOWS CAN GET A LITTLE CRAZY.
OOF!
TAK
WHOA!
YOU WEREN'T KIDDING ABOUT THAT...

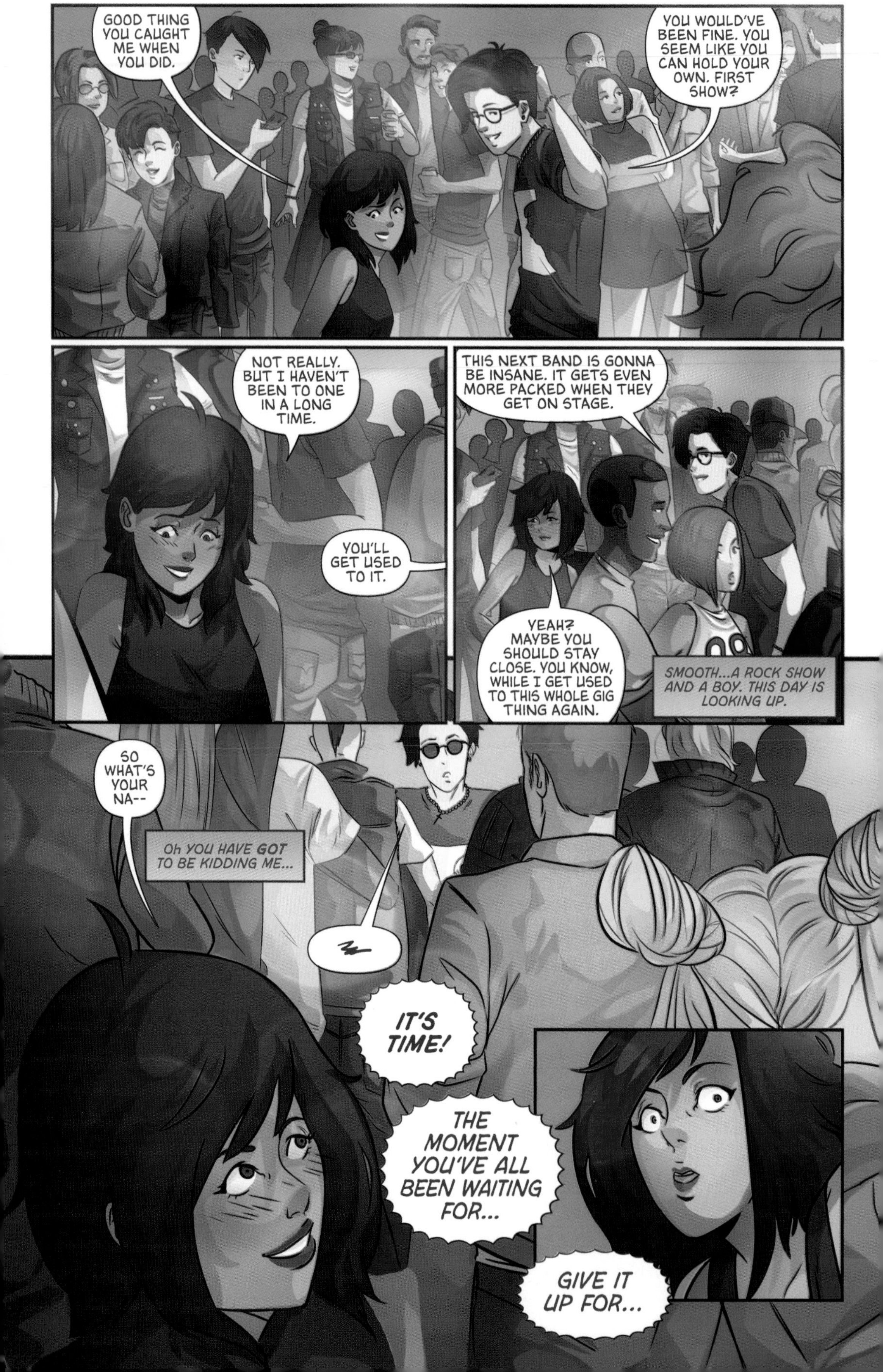
GOOD THING YOU CAUGHT ME WHEN YOU DID.
YOU WOULD'VE BEEN FINE. YOU SEEM LIKE YOU CAN HOLD YOUR OWN. FIRST SHOW?
NOT REALLY. BUT I HAVEN'T BEEN TO ONE IN A LONG TIME.
YOU'LL GET USED TO IT.
THIS NEXT BAND IS GONNA BE INSANE. IT GETS EVEN MORE PACKED WHEN THEY GET ON STAGE.
YEAH? MAYBE YOU SHOULD STAY CLOSE. YOU KNOW, WHILE I GET USED TO THIS WHOLE GIG THING AGAIN.
SMOOTH...A ROCK SHOW AND A BOY. THIS DAY IS LOOKING UP.
SO WHAT'S YOUR NA--
Oh YOU HAVE GOT TO BE KIDDING ME...
IT'S TIME!
THE MOMENT YOU'VE ALL BEEN WAITING FOR...
GIVE IT UP FOR...

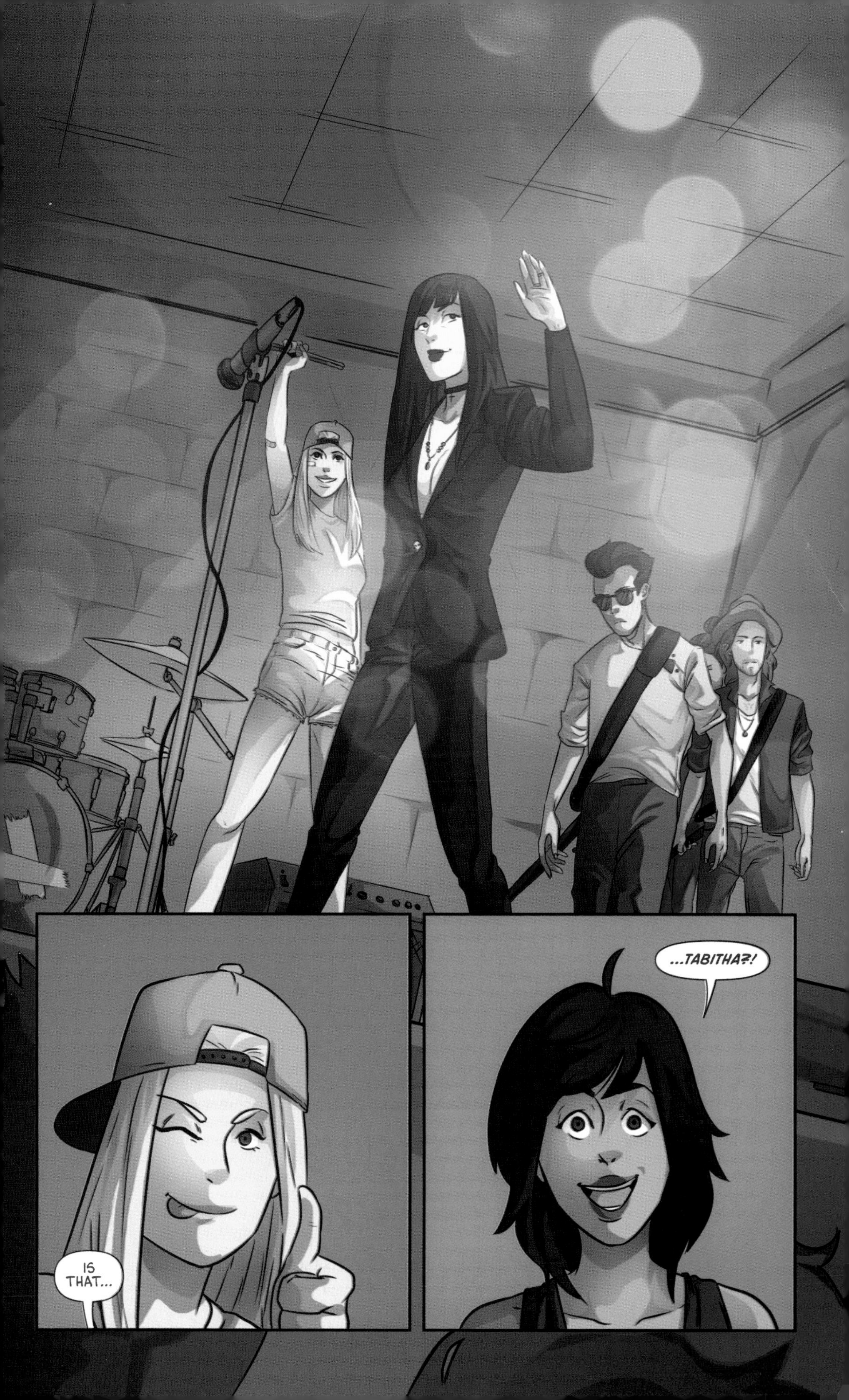
IS THAT...
...TABITHA?!

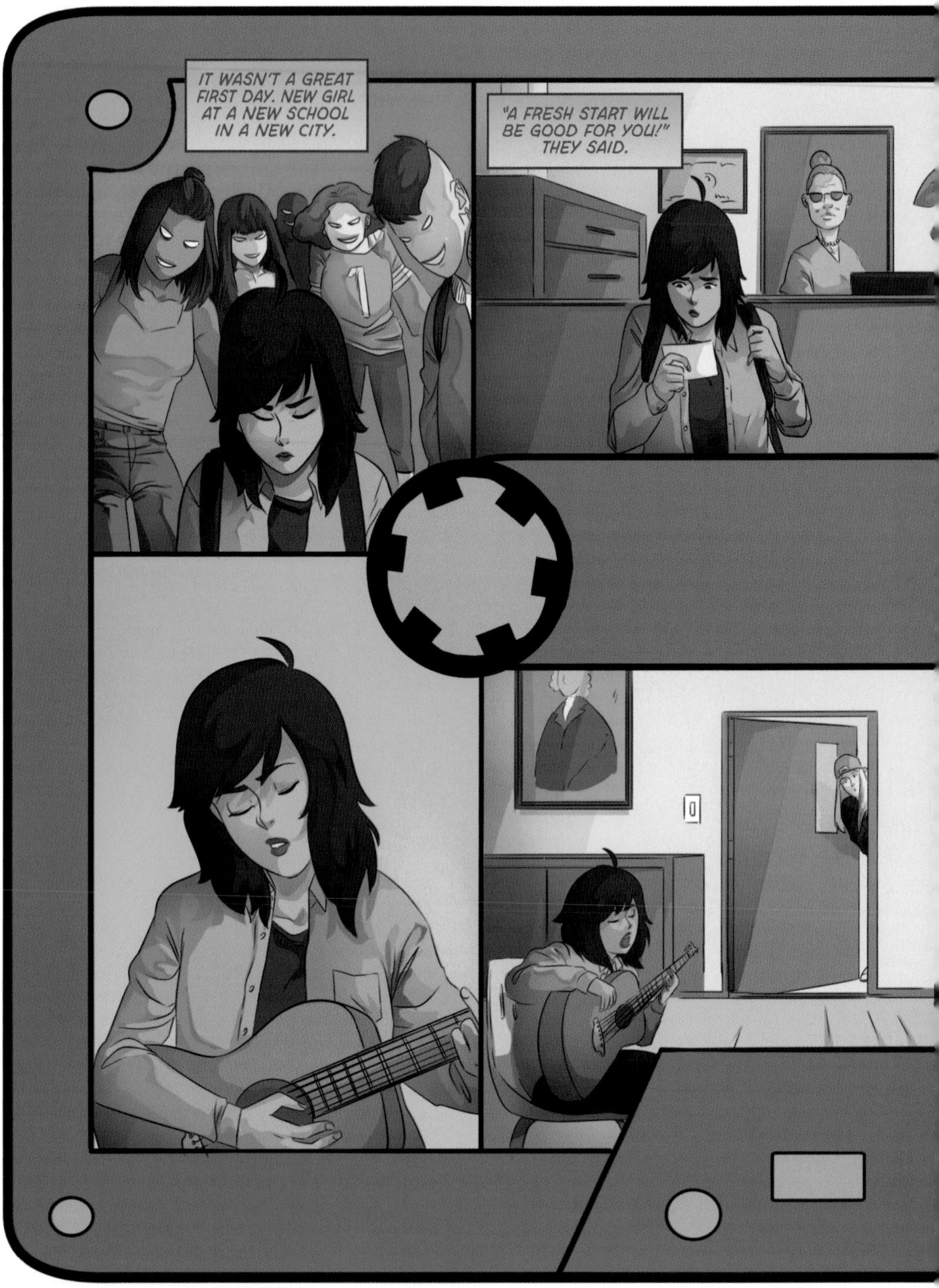
IT WASN'T A GREAT FIRST DAY. NEW GIRL AT A NEW SCHOOL IN A NEW CITY.
"A FRESH START WILL BE GOOD FOR YOU!" THEY SAID.

1 TRACK 1 - NEW GIRL

TRACK 2 - WHERE DO I GO FROM HERE

TRACK 3 - ARE YOU KIDDING ME?

TRACK 4 - SOLACE IN SILENCE

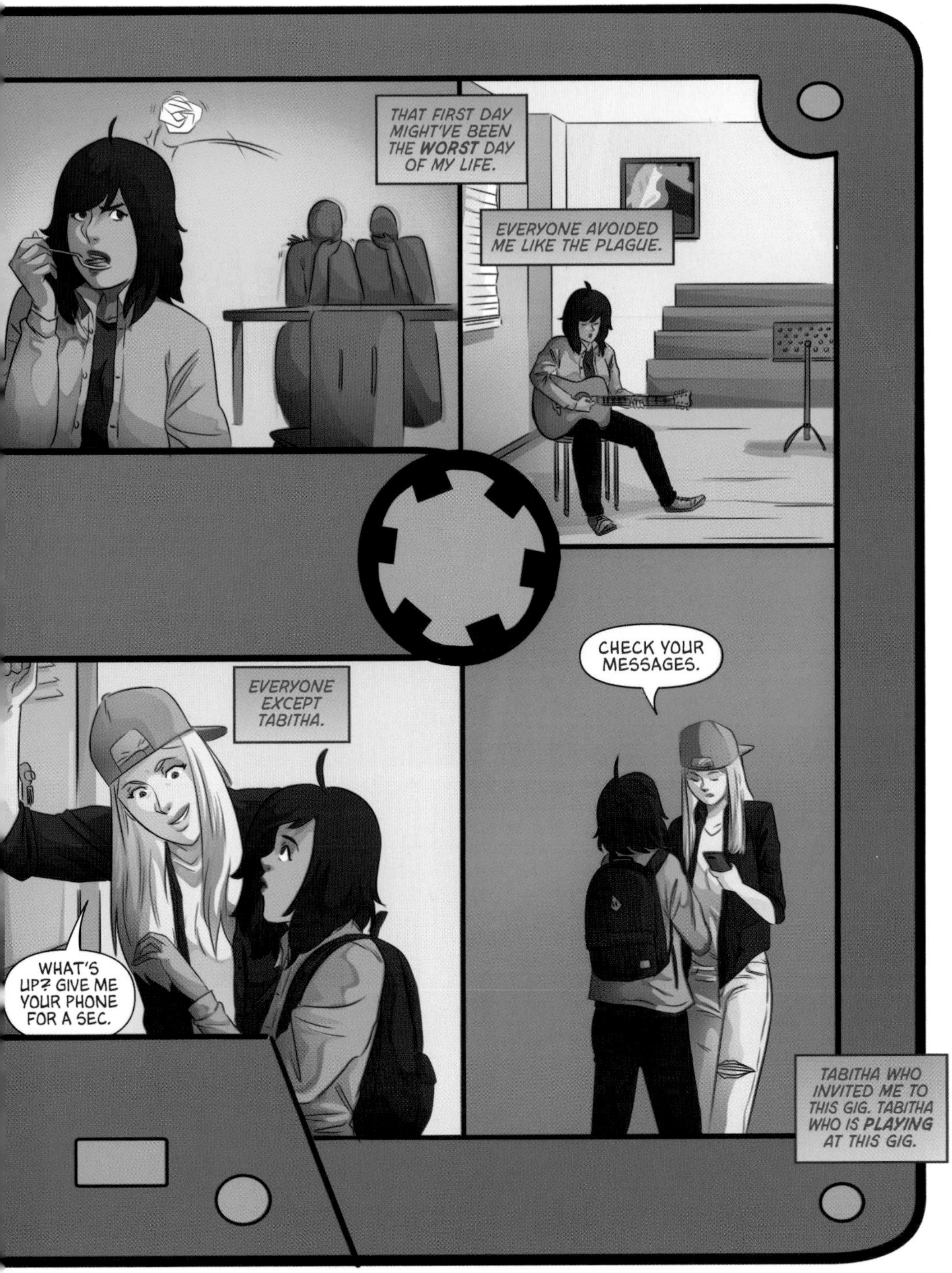
THAT FIRST DAY MIGHT'VE BEEN THE WORST DAY OF MY LIFE.
EVERYONE AVOIDED ME LIKE THE PLAGUE.
EVERYONE EXCEPT TABITHA.
WHAT'S UP? GIVE ME YOUR PHONE FOR A SEC.
CHECK YOUR MESSAGES.
TABITHA WHO INVITED ME TO THIS GIG. TABITHA WHO IS PLAYING AT THIS GIG.

TRACK 5 - MY SONG 2

TRACK 6 - HEAR MY HEARTBEAT

TRACK 7 - WHITE KNIGHT

TRACK 8 - TAKE ME WHERE I NEED TO GO

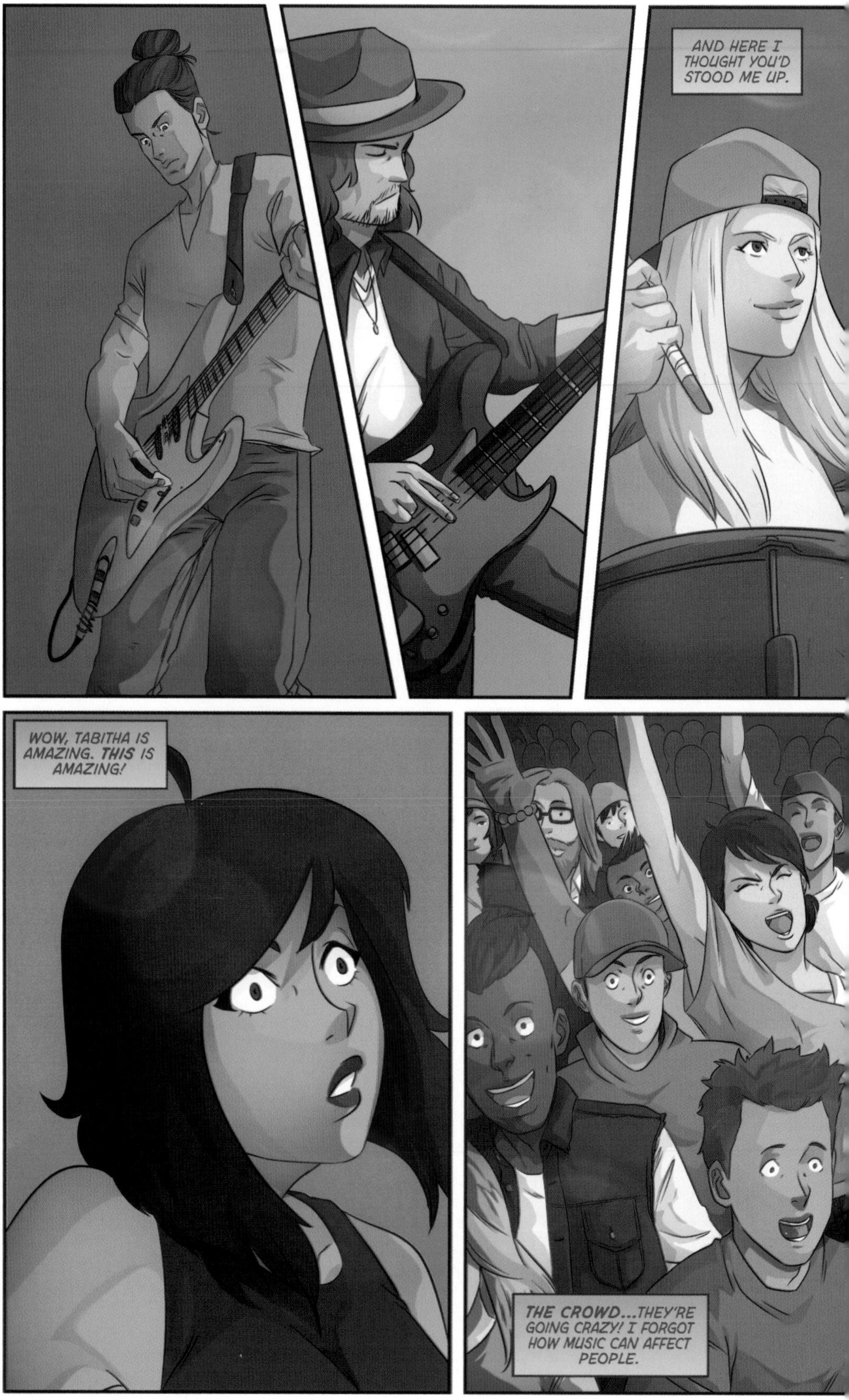
AND HERE I THOUGHT YOU'D STOOD ME UP.
WOW, TABITHA IS AMAZING. THIS IS AMAZING!
THE CROWD...THEY'RE GOING CRAZY! I FORGOT HOW MUSIC CAN AFFECT PEOPLE.

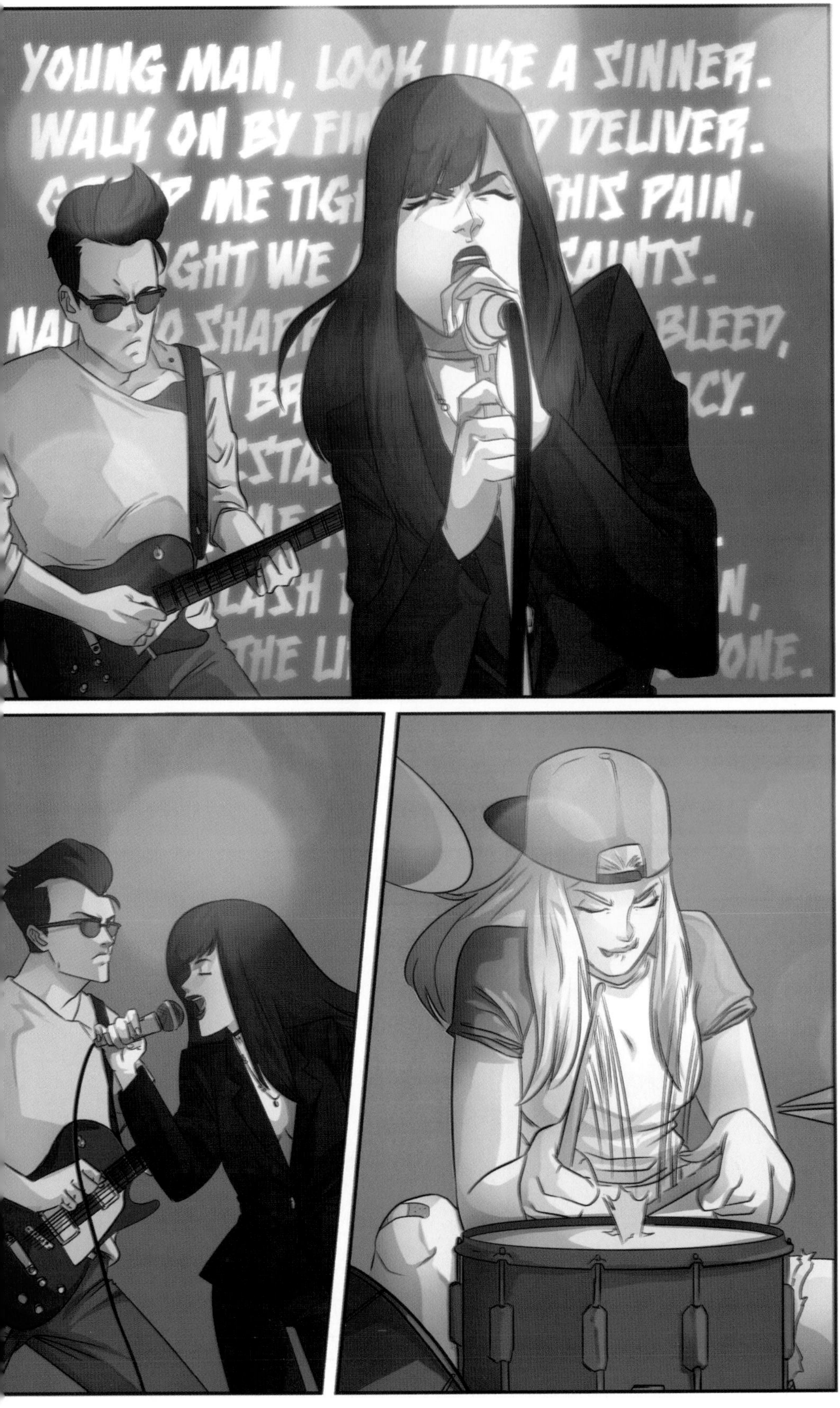
YOUNG MAN, LOOK LIKE A SINNER.
WALK ON BY
DELIVER.
ME TIG
THIS PAIN,
BLEED,
CY.

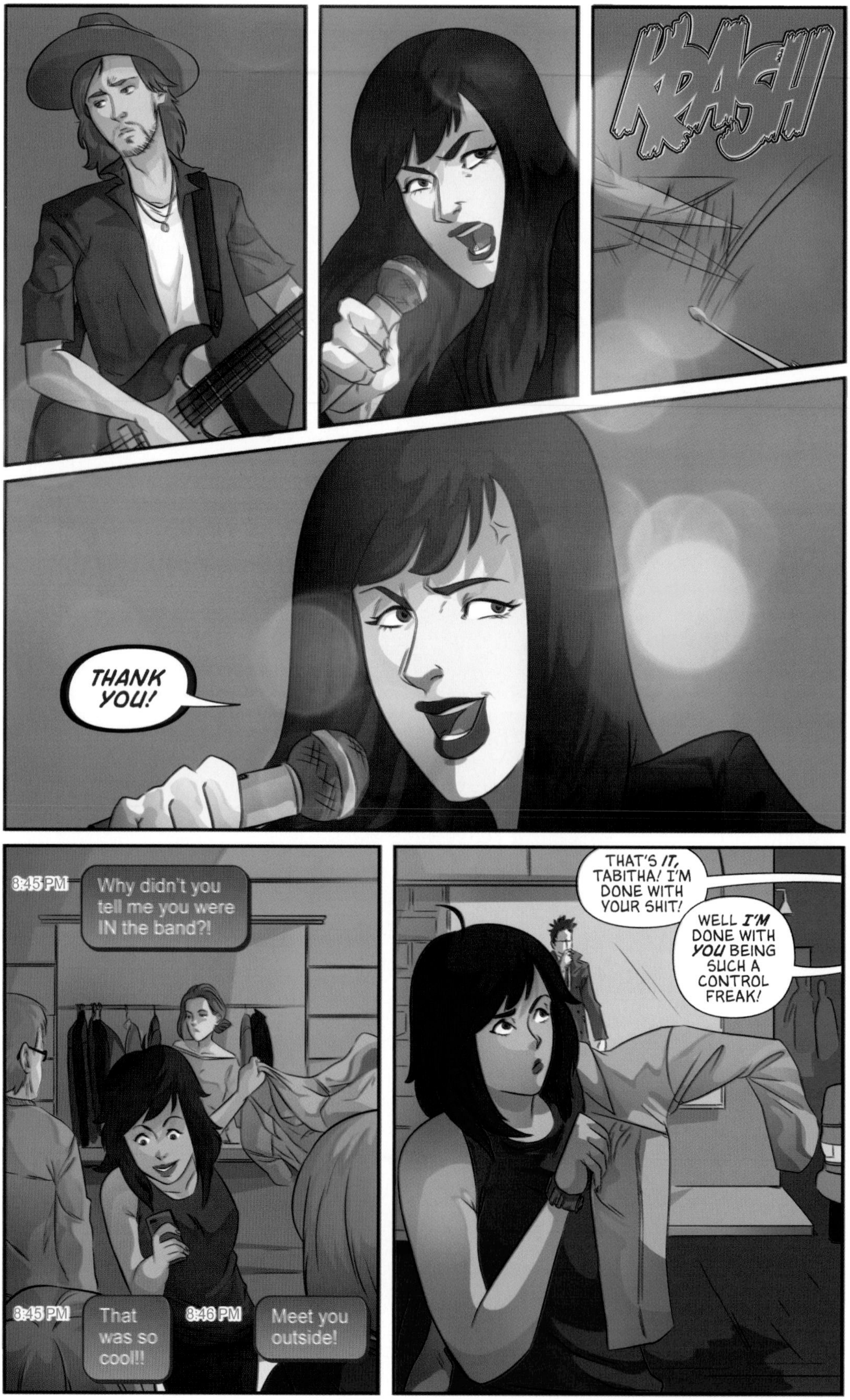
KRASH
THANK YOU!
8:45 PM
Why didn't you tell me you were IN the band?!
8:45 PM
That was so cool!!
8:46 PM
Meet you outside!
THAT'S IT, TABITHA! I'M DONE WITH YOUR SHIT!
WELL I'M DONE WITH YOU BEING SUCH A CONTROL FREAK!

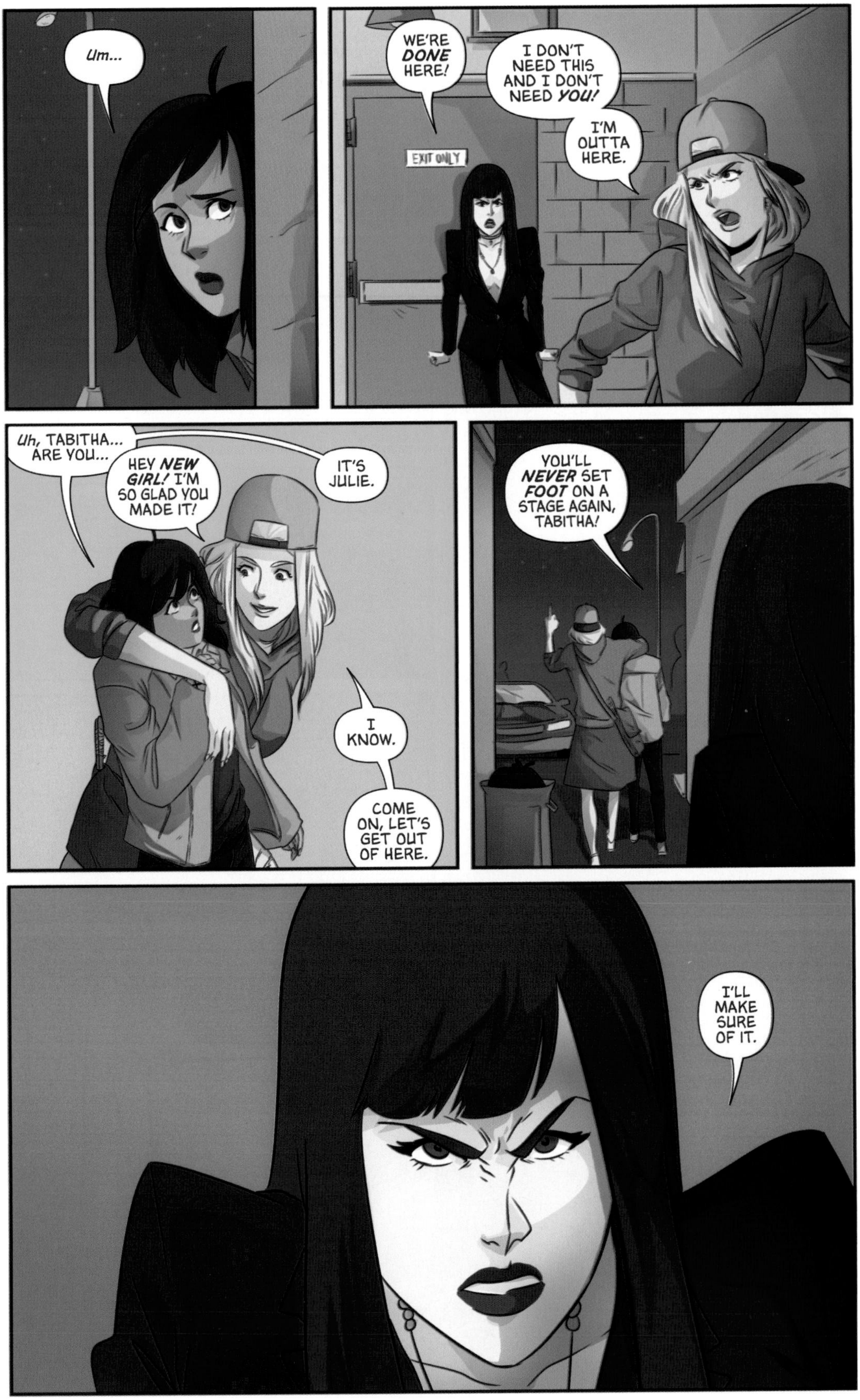
Um...
WE'RE DONE HERE!
I DON'T NEED THIS AND I DON'T NEED YOU!
I'M OUTTA HERE.
EXIT ONLY
Uh, TABITHA... ARE YOU...
HEY NEW GIRL! I'M SO GLAD YOU MADE IT!
IT'S JULIE.
I KNOW.
COME ON, LET'S GET OUT OF HERE.
YOU'LL NEVER SET FOOT ON A STAGE AGAIN, TABITHA!
I'LL MAKE SURE OF IT.

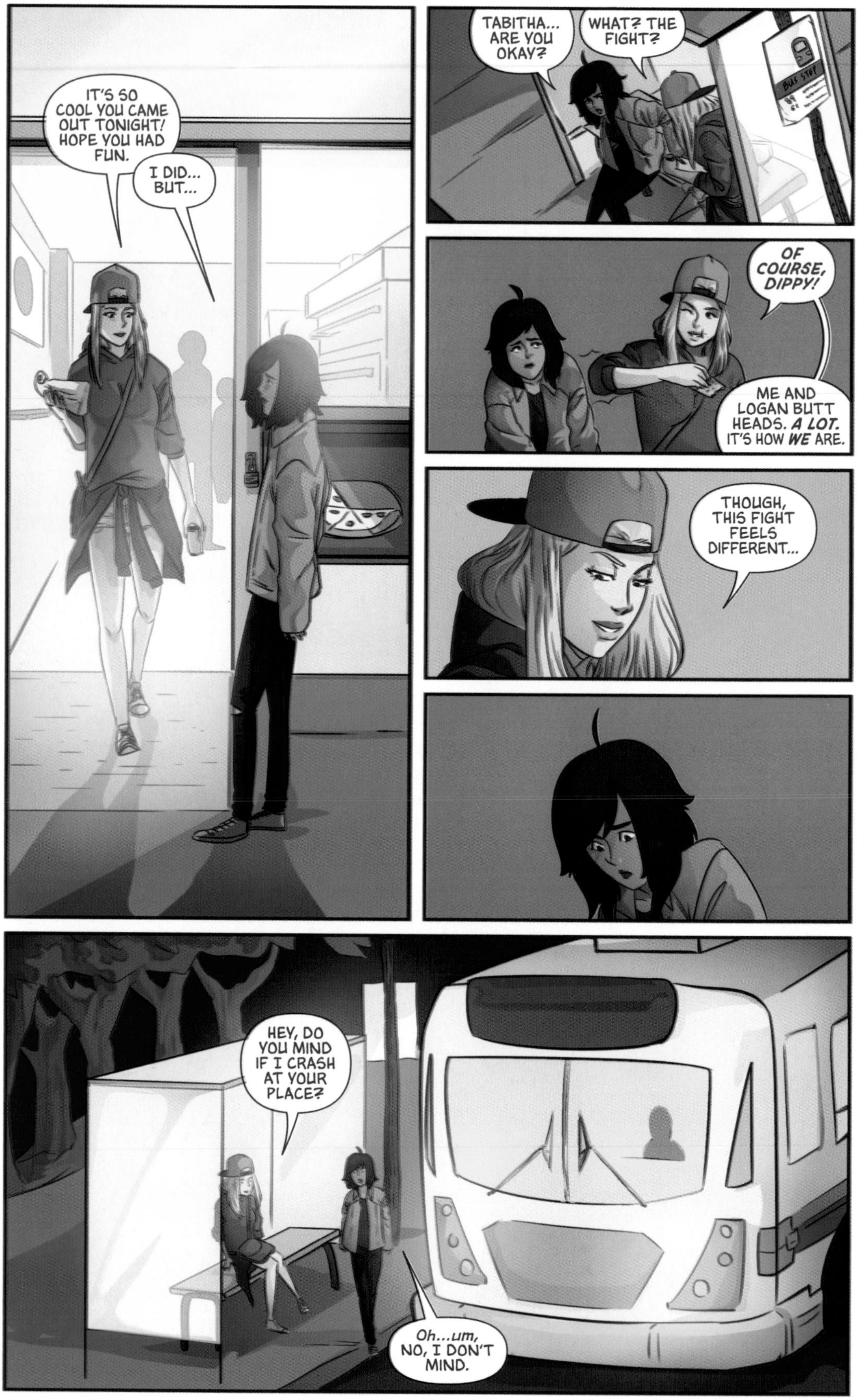
IT'S SO COOL YOU CAME OUT TONIGHT! HOPE YOU HAD FUN.
I DID... BUT...
TABITHA... ARE YOU OKAY?
WHAT? THE FIGHT?
OF COURSE, DIPPY!
ME AND LOGAN BUTT HEADS. A LOT. IT'S HOW WE ARE.
THOUGH, THIS FIGHT FEELS DIFFERENT...
HEY, DO YOU MIND IF I CRASH AT YOUR PLACE?
Oh...um, NO, I DON'T MIND.

I BARELY KNOW TABITHA BUT THERE'S SOMETHING ABOUT HER.

I WANT TO BE HER FRIEND. I WANT TO HELP HER.

SORRY MS. MALARI, I HOPE IT'S NOT A BOTHER THAT I'M HERE!

NOT A BOTHER AT ALL! STAY AS LONG AS YOU WANT.

HOW COULD I POSSIBLY HELP HER THOUGH...

REMEMBER THAT SONG YOU PLAYED BACK IN THE MUSIC ROOM? COULD YOU PLAY THAT FOR ME?

YOU HEARD THAT?!

Um...SURE. I CAN PLAY THAT FOR YOU.

Sa hindi inaasahang, pagtatagpo ating mundo. may minsan nagdugtong damang nagong nito.*

I WONDER IF THIS IS HOW TABITHA FEELS WHEN SHE PLAYS MUSIC...

*LYRICS IN FILIPINO.

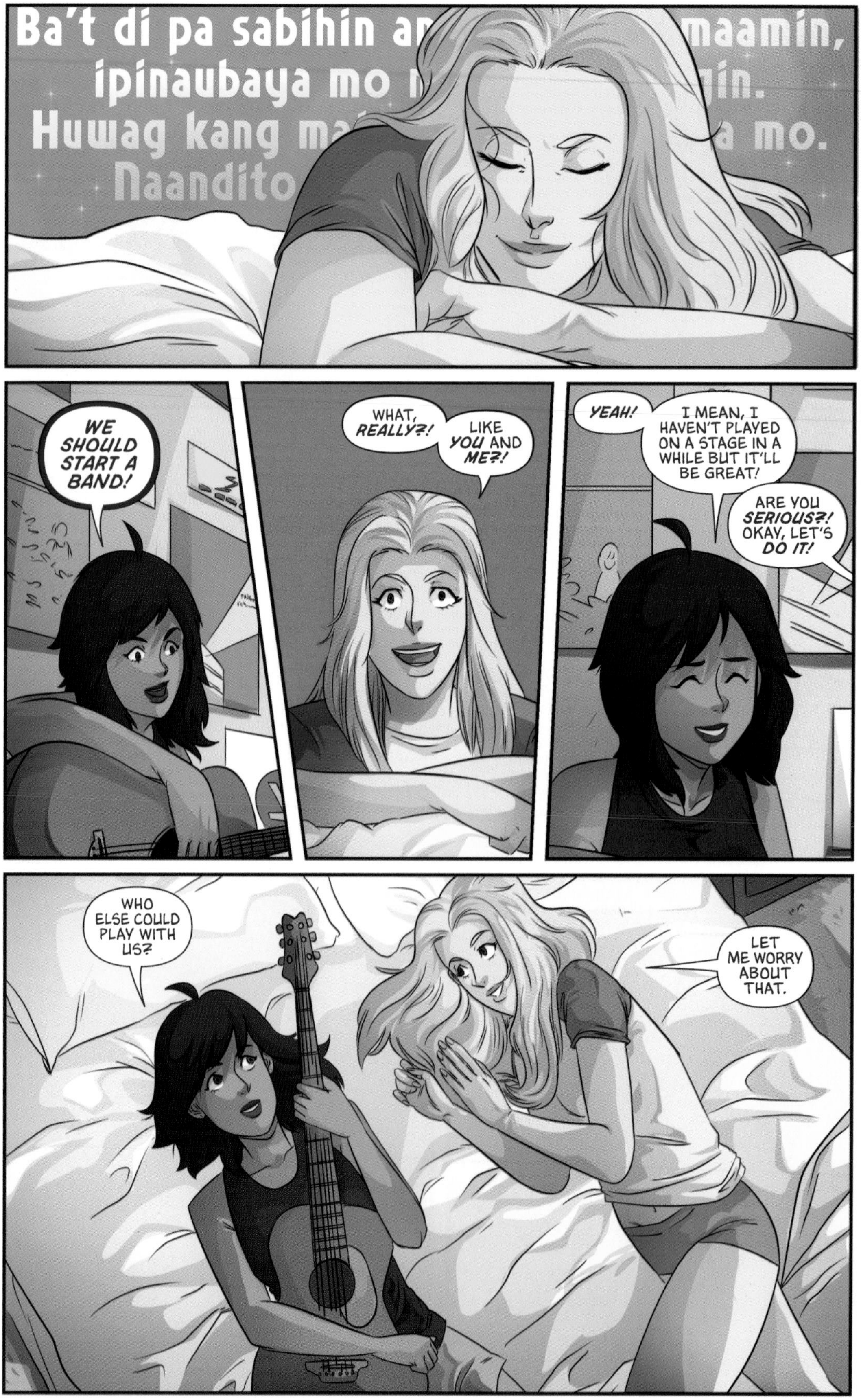

Ba't di pa sabihin an
maamin,
ipinaubaya mo n
in.
Huwag kang ma
a mo.
Naandito
WE SHOULD START A BAND!
WHAT, REALLY?!
LIKE YOU AND ME?!
YEAH!
I MEAN, I HAVEN'T PLAYED ON A STAGE IN A WHILE BUT IT'LL BE GREAT!
ARE YOU SERIOUS?! OKAY, LET'S DO IT!
WHO ELSE COULD PLAY WITH US?
LET ME WORRY ABOUT THAT.

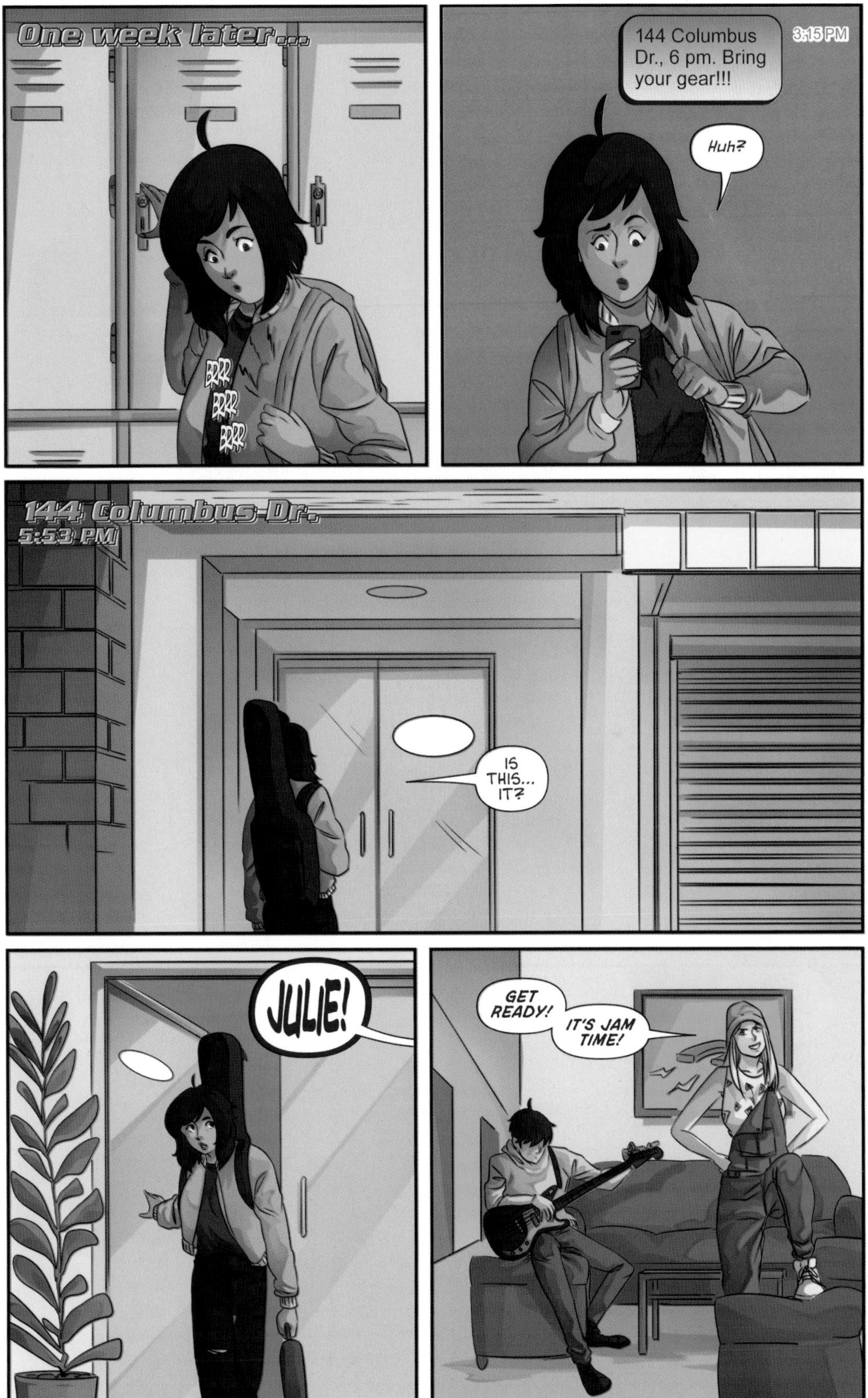
One week later...
BRRR
BRRR
BRRR
3:15 PM
144 Columbus Dr., 6 pm. Bring your gear!!!
Huh?
144 Columbus Dr.
5:53 PM
IS THIS... IT?
JULIE!
GET READY!
IT'S JAM TIME!

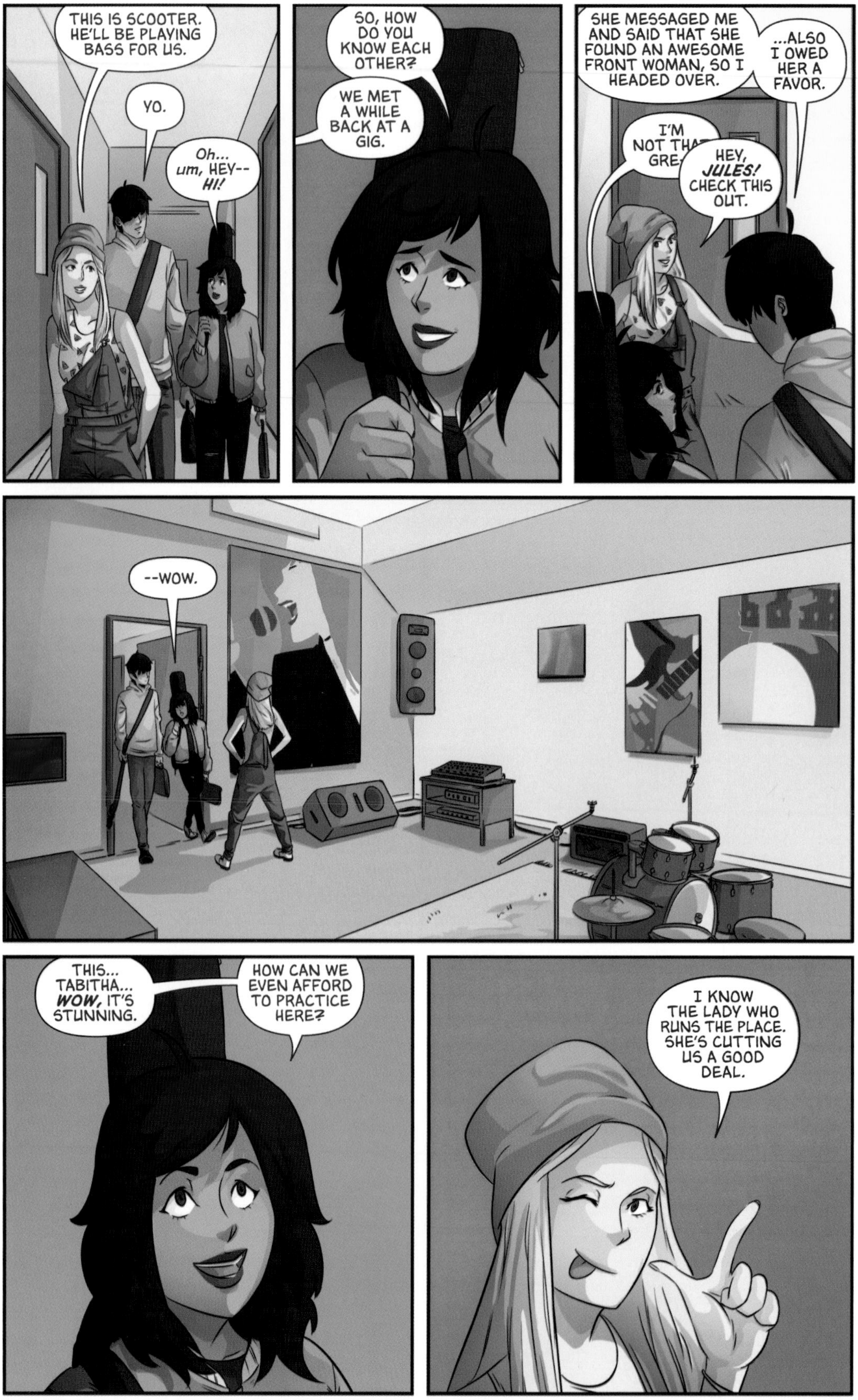
THIS IS SCOOTER. HE'LL BE PLAYING BASS FOR US.
YO.
Oh... um, HEY-- HI!
SO, HOW DO YOU KNOW EACH OTHER?
WE MET A WHILE BACK AT A GIG.
SHE MESSAGED ME AND SAID THAT SHE FOUND AN AWESOME FRONT WOMAN, SO I HEADED OVER.
...ALSO I OWED HER A FAVOR.
I'M NOT THAT GRE-
HEY, JULES! CHECK THIS OUT.
--WOW.
THIS... TABITHA... WOW, IT'S STUNNING.
HOW CAN WE EVEN AFFORD TO PRACTICE HERE?
I KNOW THE LADY WHO RUNS THE PLACE. SHE'S CUTTING US A GOOD DEAL.

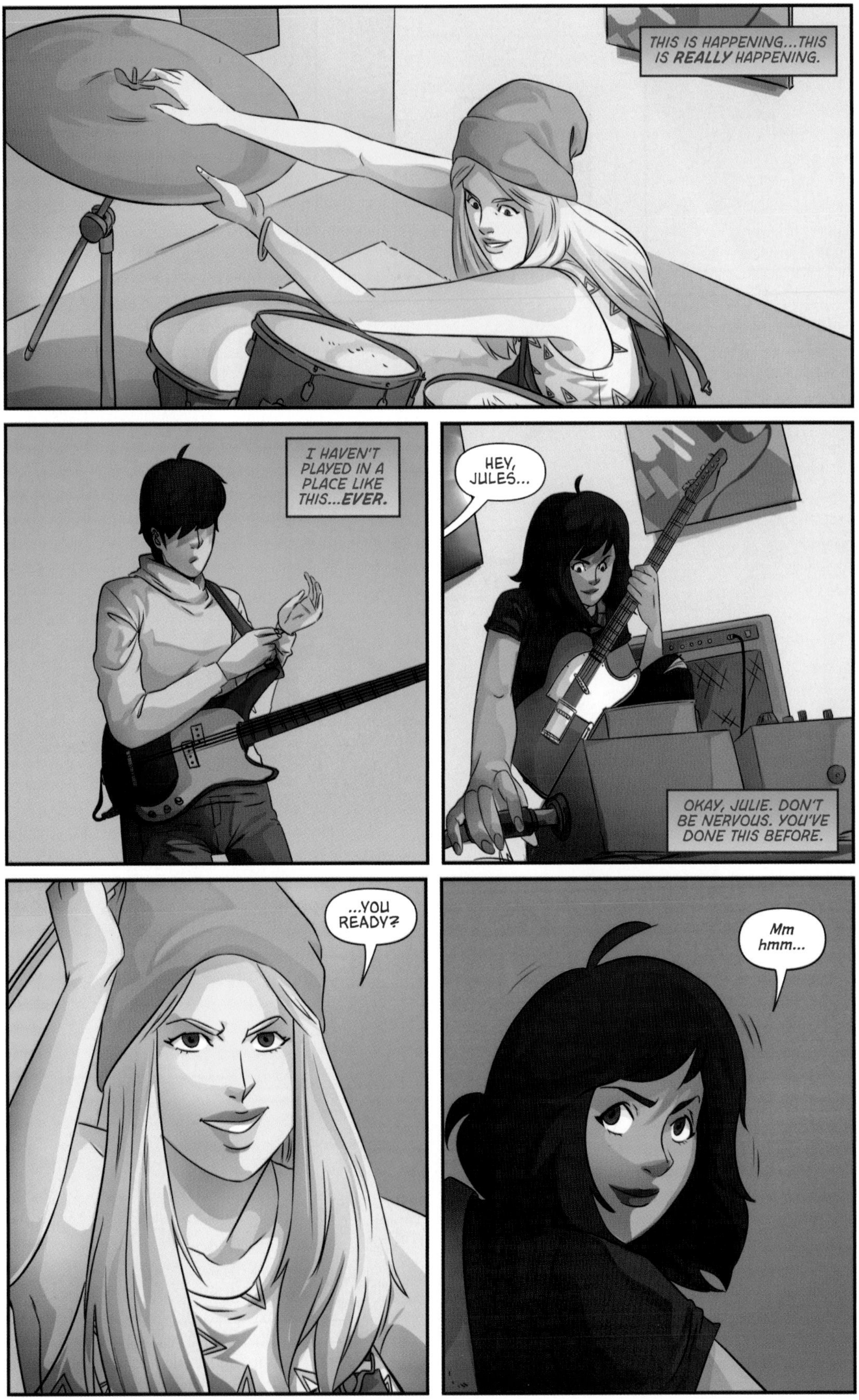
THIS IS HAPPENING...THIS IS REALLY HAPPENING.
I HAVEN'T PLAYED IN A PLACE LIKE THIS...EVER.
HEY, JULES...
OKAY, JULIE. DON'T BE NERVOUS. YOU'VE DONE THIS BEFORE.
...YOU READY?
Mm hmm...

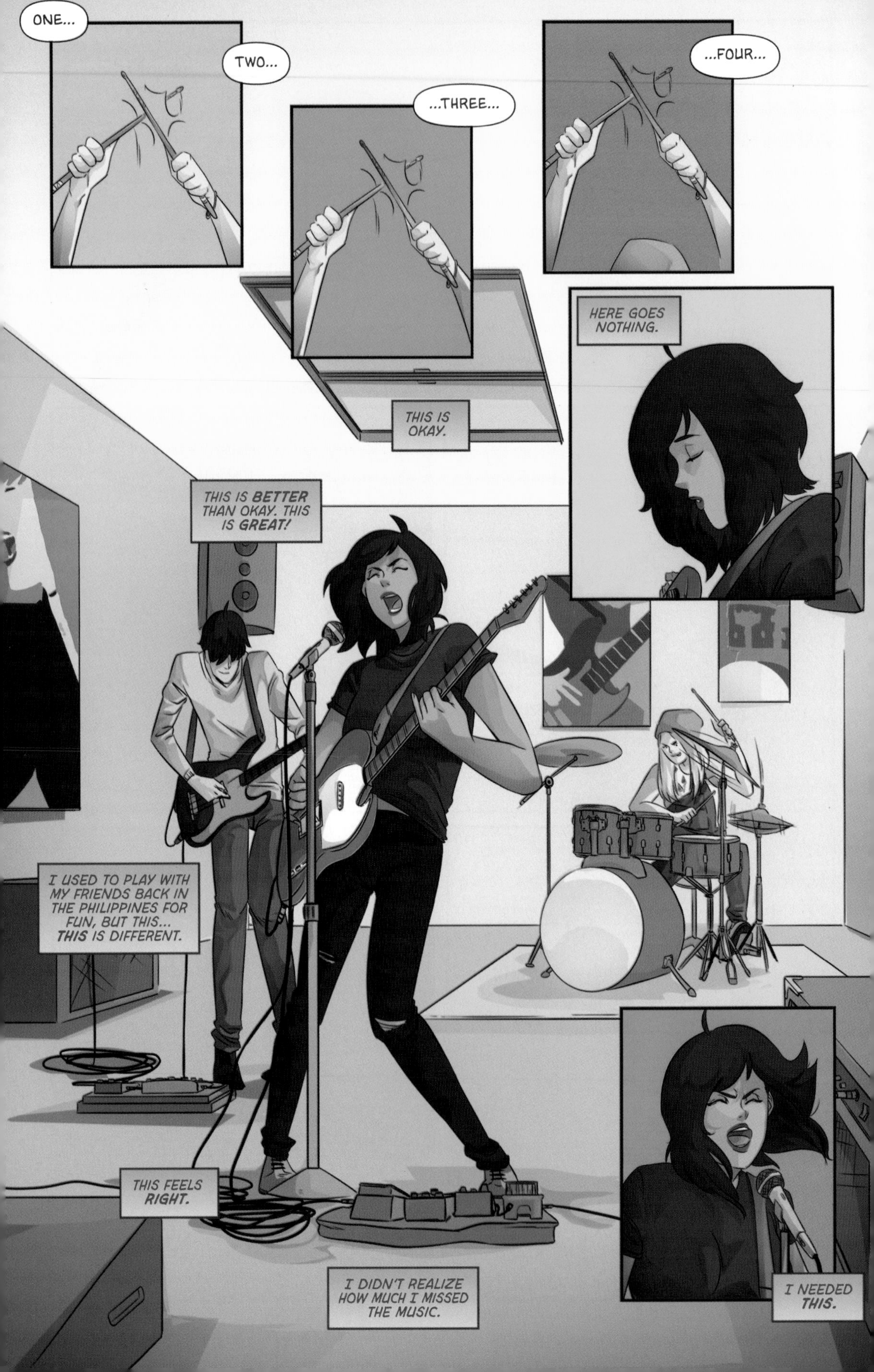
ONE...
TWO...
...THREE...
...FOUR...
HERE GOES NOTHING.
THIS IS OKAY.
THIS IS BETTER THAN OKAY. THIS IS GREAT!
I USED TO PLAY WITH MY FRIENDS BACK IN THE PHILIPPINES FOR FUN, BUT THIS... THIS IS DIFFERENT.
THIS FEELS RIGHT.
I DIDN'T REALIZE HOW MUCH I MISSED THE MUSIC.
I NEEDED THIS.

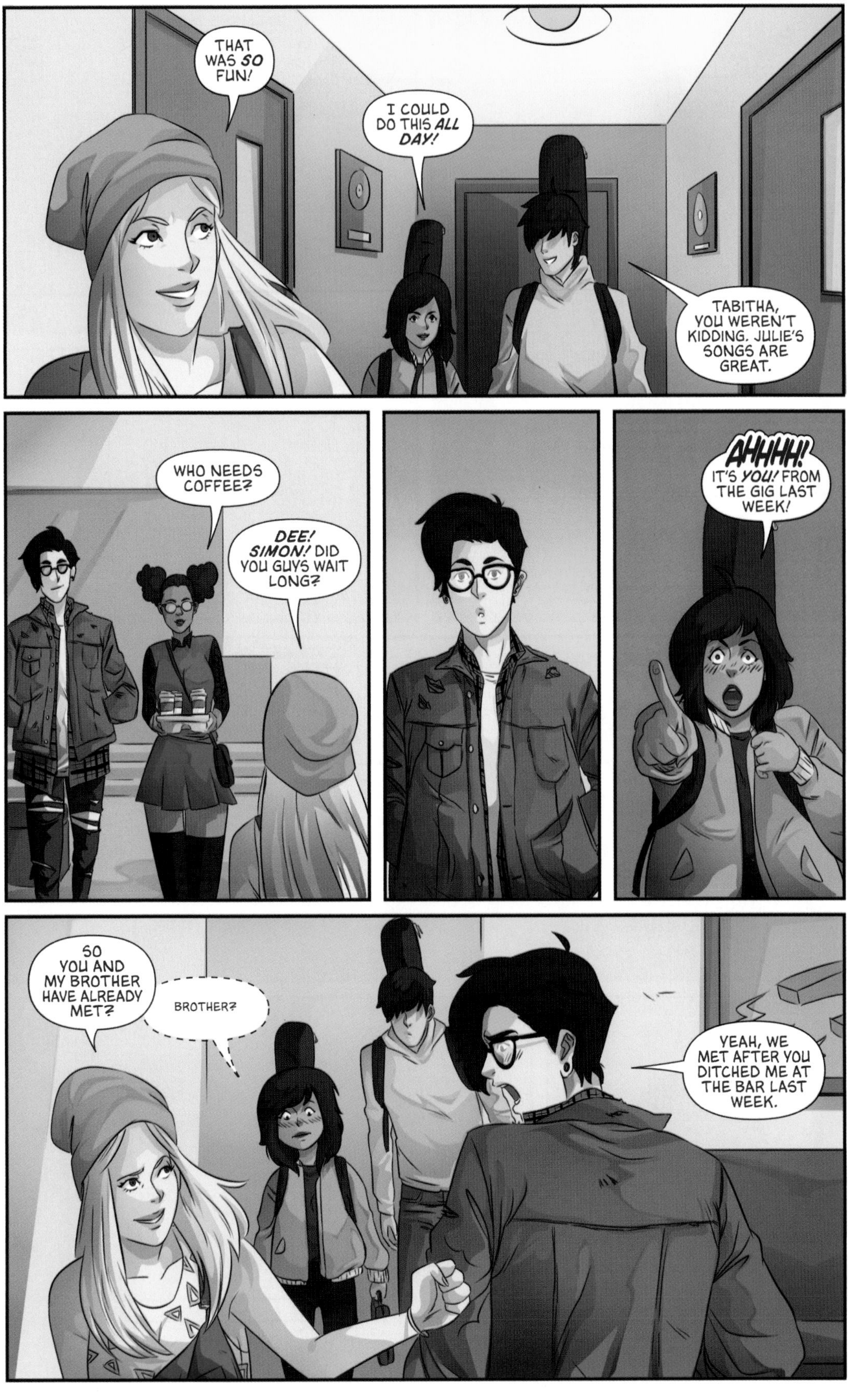
THAT WAS SO FUN!
I COULD DO THIS ALL DAY!
TABITHA, YOU WEREN'T KIDDING. JULIE'S SONGS ARE GREAT.
WHO NEEDS COFFEE?
DEE! SIMON! DID YOU GUYS WAIT LONG?
AHHHH!
IT'S YOU! FROM THE GIG LAST WEEK!
SO YOU AND MY BROTHER HAVE ALREADY MET?
BROTHER?
YEAH, WE MET AFTER YOU DITCHED ME AT THE BAR LAST WEEK.

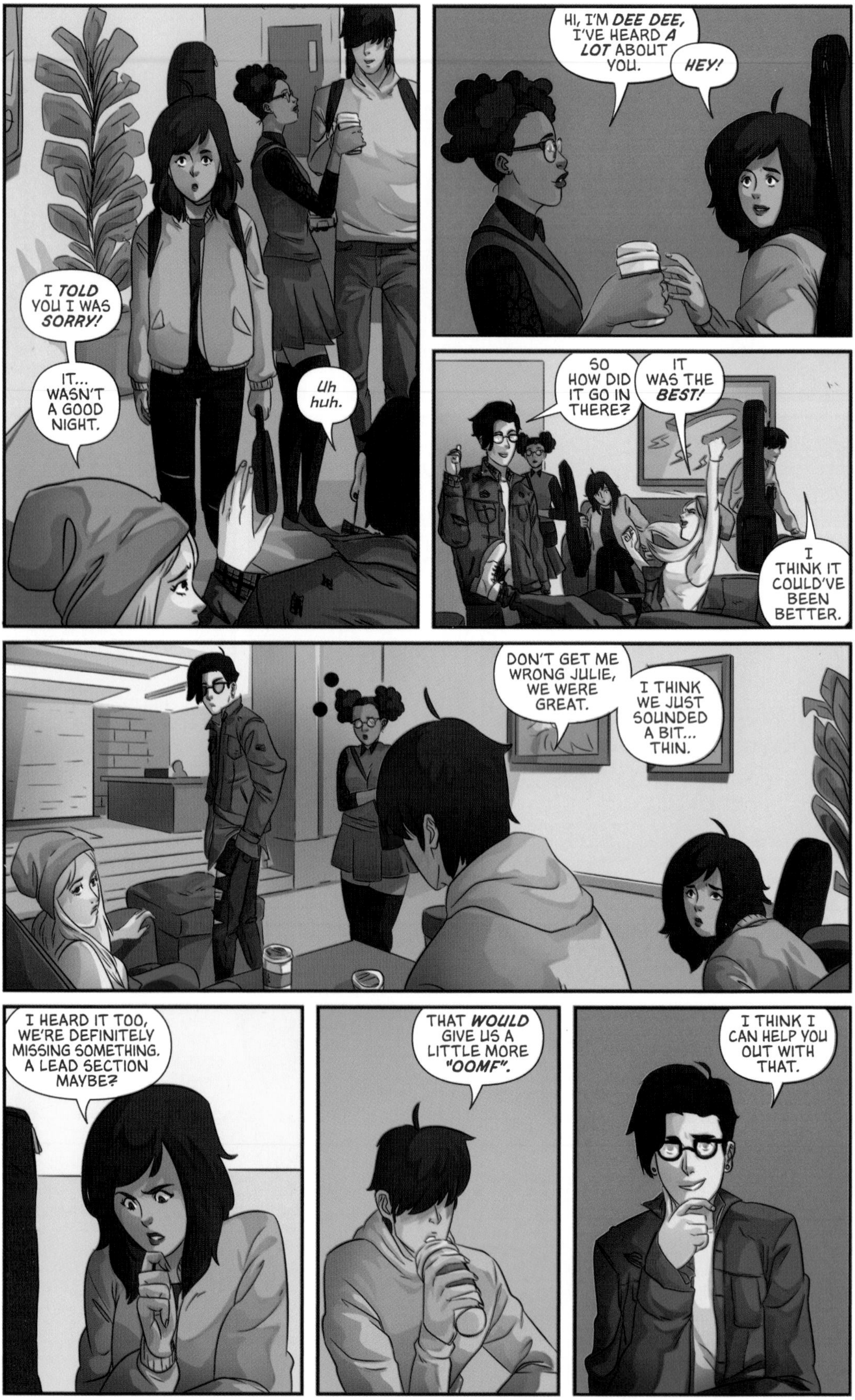
I TOLD YOU I WAS SORRY!
IT... WASN'T A GOOD NIGHT.
Uh huh.
HI, I'M DEE DEE, I'VE HEARD A LOT ABOUT YOU.
HEY!
SO HOW DID IT GO IN THERE?
IT WAS THE BEST!
I THINK IT COULD'VE BEEN BETTER.
DON'T GET ME WRONG JULIE, WE WERE GREAT.
I THINK WE JUST SOUNDED A BIT... THIN.
I HEARD IT TOO, WE'RE DEFINITELY MISSING SOMETHING. A LEAD SECTION MAYBE?
THAT WOULD GIVE US A LITTLE MORE "OOMF".
I THINK I CAN HELP YOU OUT WITH THAT.

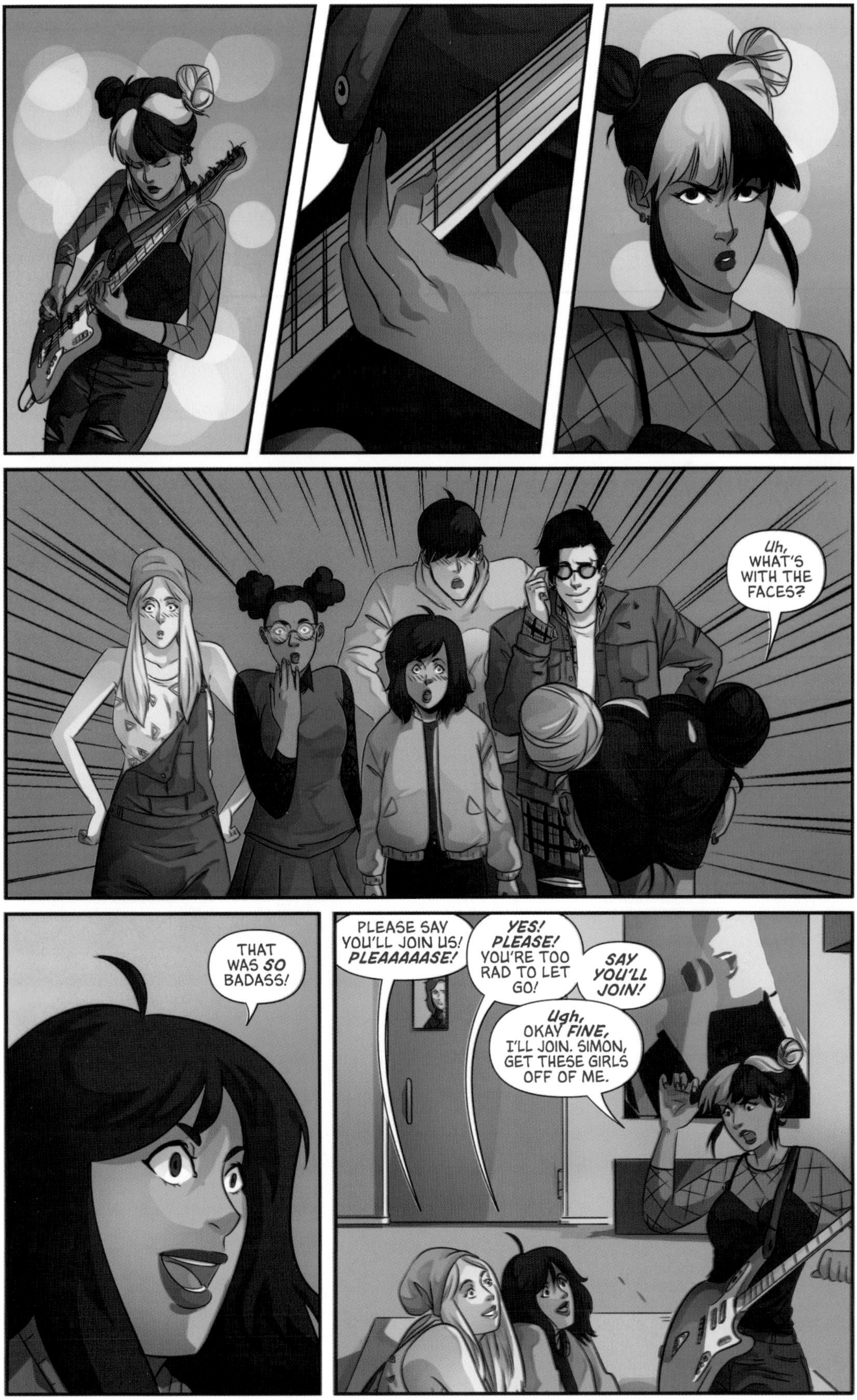
Uh, WHAT'S WITH THE FACES?
THAT WAS SO BADASS!
PLEASE SAY YOU'LL JOIN US! PLEAAAAAASE!
YES! PLEASE! YOU'RE TOO RAD TO LET GO!
SAY YOU'LL JOIN!
Ugh, OKAY FINE, I'LL JOIN. SIMON, GET THESE GIRLS OFF OF ME.

LOGAN'S NOT GONNA BE HAPPY ABOUT THIS.

PING

Hey, Logan...you'll never guess what I just saw. 7:32 PM

Tabi. With a new band. 7:32 PM

I'm watching them practice right now! 7:32 PM

7:33 PM New Band?!

7:33 PM This can NOT be happening.

7:34 PM Like I'd let her play anywhere...

Uhh...GANG, HOLD ON FOR A SECOND. THIS IS BAD.

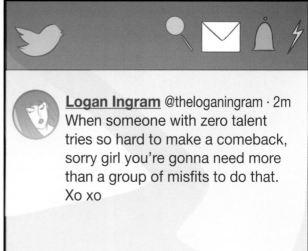

**Logan Ingram** @theloganingram · 2m
When someone with zero talent tries so hard to make a comeback, sorry girl you're gonna need more than a group of misfits to do that. Xo xo

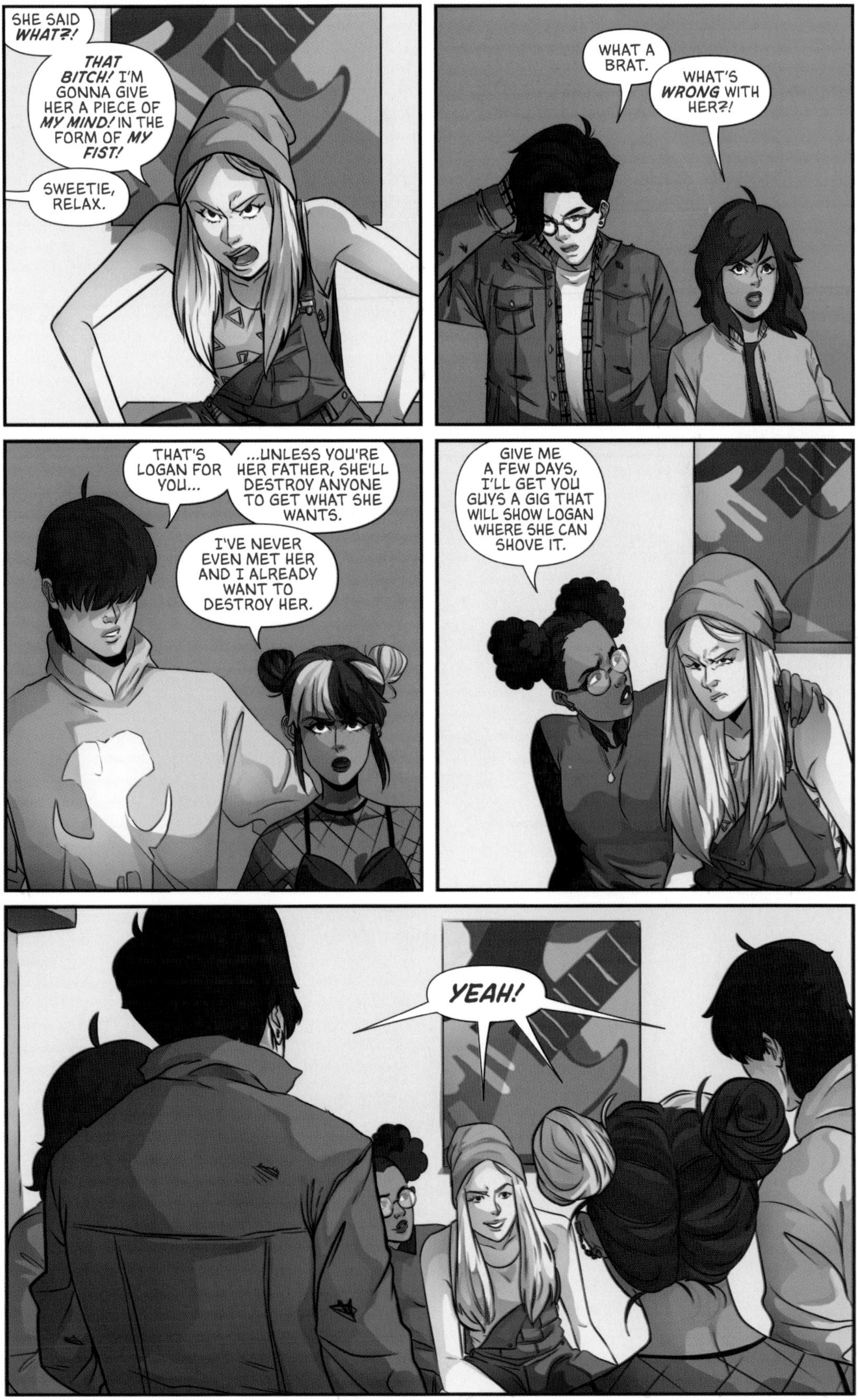
SHE SAID WHAT?!
THAT BITCH! I'M GONNA GIVE HER A PIECE OF MY MIND! IN THE FORM OF MY FIST!
SWEETIE, RELAX.
WHAT A BRAT.
WHAT'S WRONG WITH HER?!
THAT'S LOGAN FOR YOU...
...UNLESS YOU'RE HER FATHER, SHE'LL DESTROY ANYONE TO GET WHAT SHE WANTS.
I'VE NEVER EVEN MET HER AND I ALREADY WANT TO DESTROY HER.
GIVE ME A FEW DAYS, I'LL GET YOU GUYS A GIG THAT WILL SHOW LOGAN WHERE SHE CAN SHOVE IT.
YEAH!

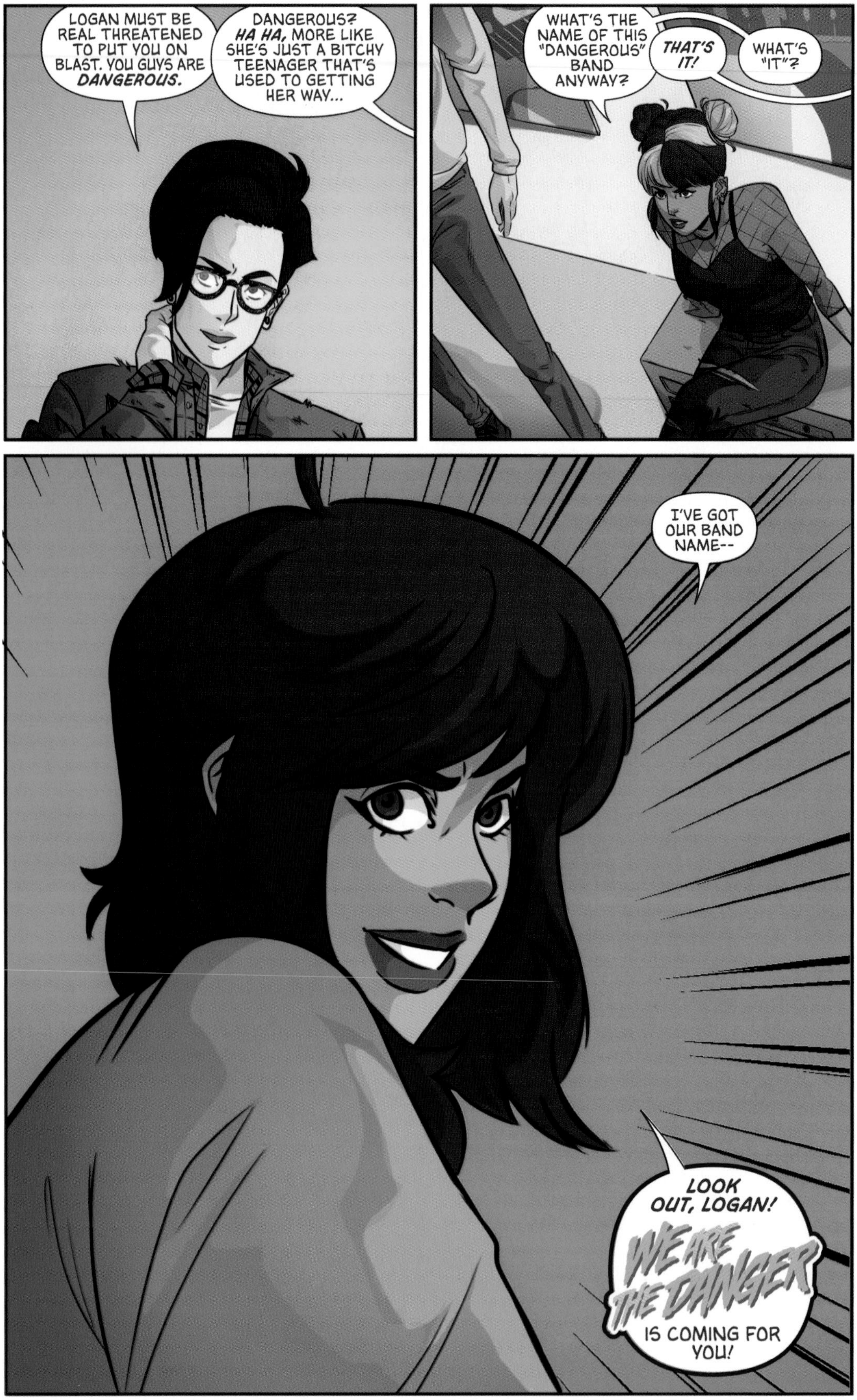
LOGAN MUST BE REAL THREATENED TO PUT YOU ON BLAST. YOU GUYS ARE DANGEROUS.
DANGEROUS? HA HA, MORE LIKE SHE'S JUST A BITCHY TEENAGER THAT'S USED TO GETTING HER WAY...
WHAT'S THE NAME OF THIS "DANGEROUS" BAND ANYWAY?
THAT'S IT!
WHAT'S "IT"?
I'VE GOT OUR BAND NAME--
LOOK OUT, LOGAN!
WE ARE THE DANGER
IS COMING FOR YOU!

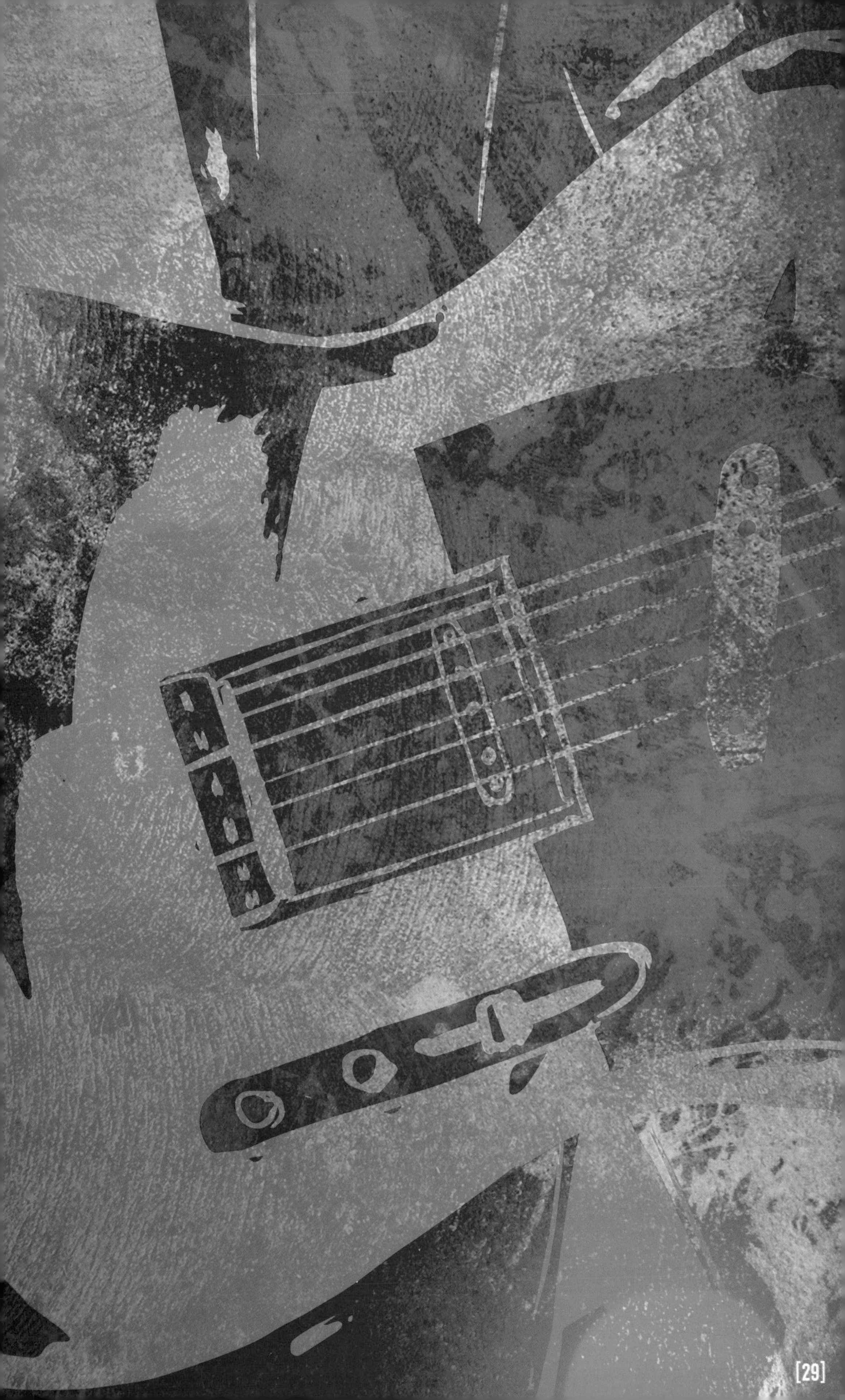

# ISSUE 2

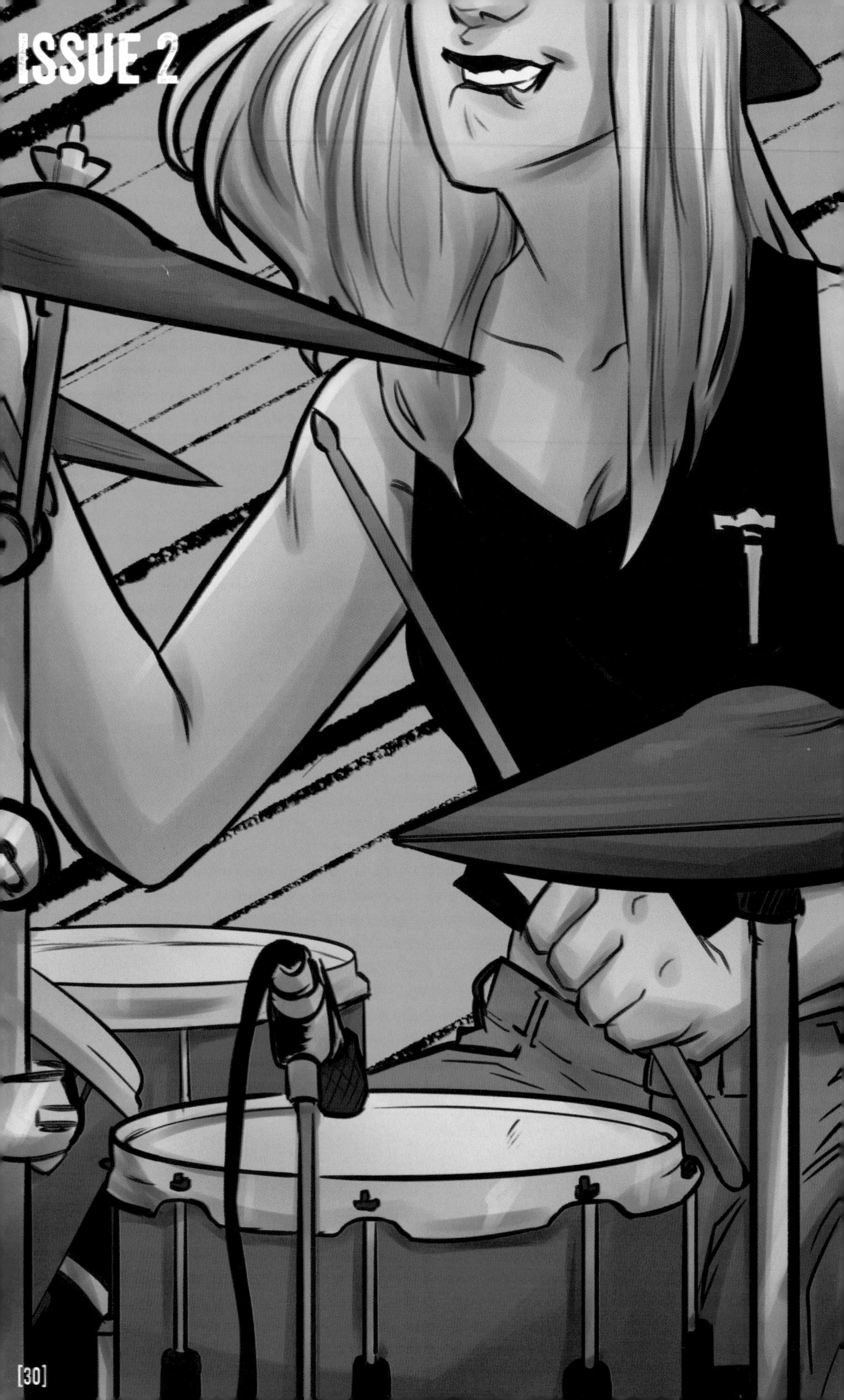

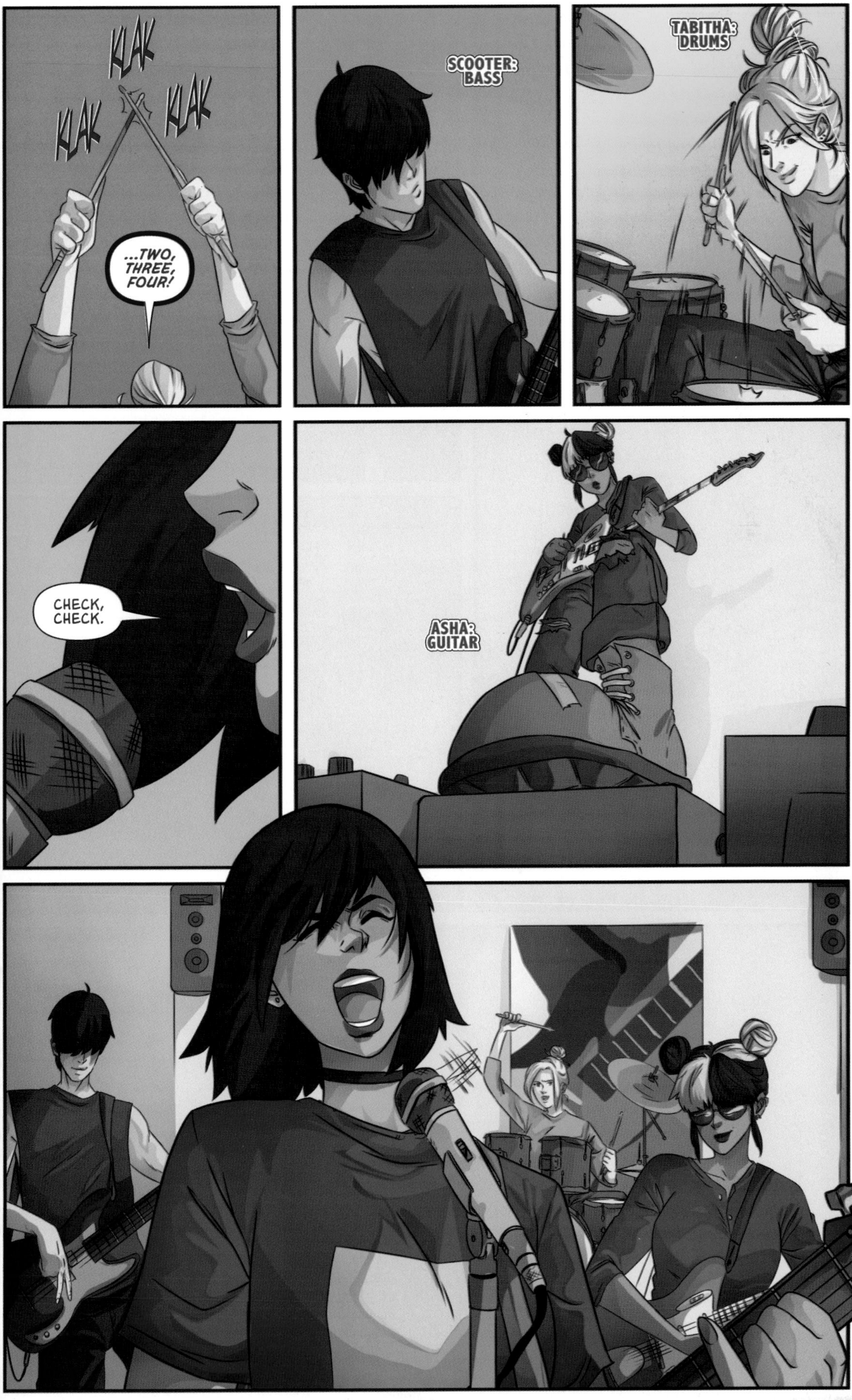
KLAK
KLAK
KLAK
...TWO, THREE, FOUR!
SCOOTER: BASS
TABITHA: DRUMS
CHECK, CHECK.
ASHA: GUITAR

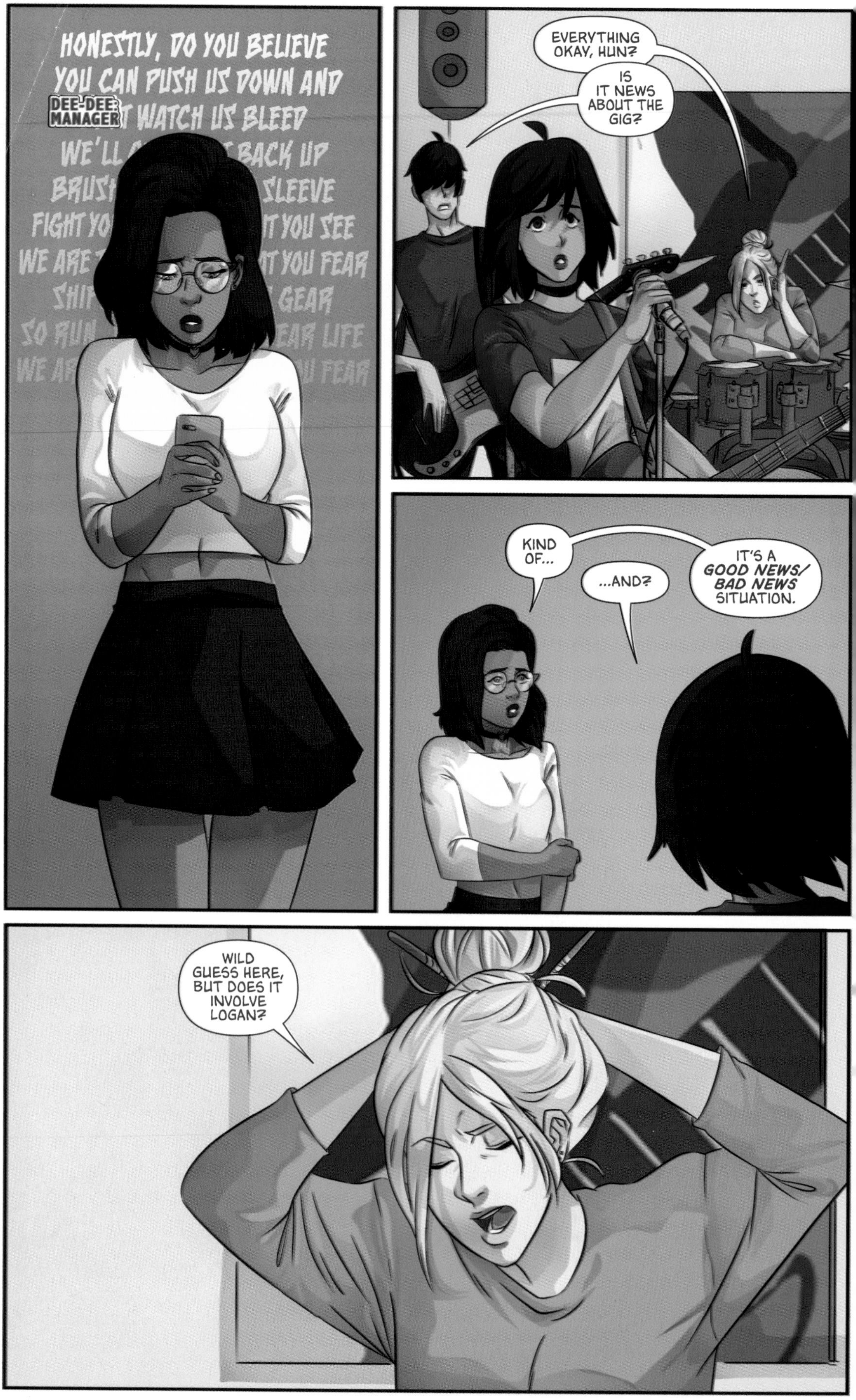
HONESTLY, DO YOU BELIEVE
YOU CAN PUSH US DOWN AND
DEE-DEE: MANAGER
T WATCH US BLEED
WE'LL
BACK UP
SLEEVE
FIGHT YO
T YOU SEE
WE ARE
T YOU FEAR
GEAR
SO RUN
EAR LIFE
U FEAR
EVERYTHING OKAY, HUN?
IS IT NEWS ABOUT THE GIG?
KIND OF...
...AND?
IT'S A *GOOD NEWS/ BAD NEWS* SITUATION.
WILD GUESS HERE, BUT DOES IT INVOLVE LOGAN?

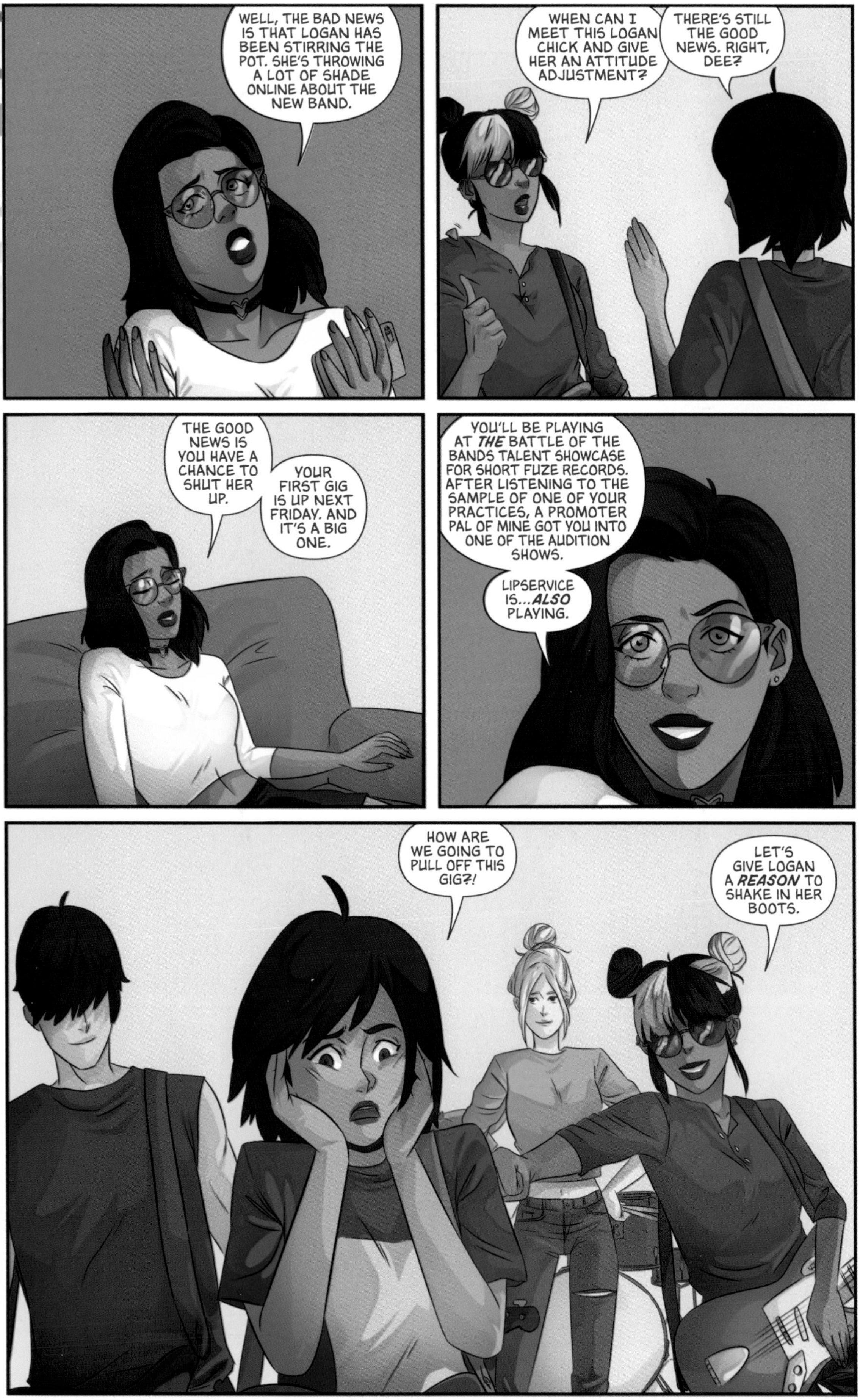
WELL, THE BAD NEWS IS THAT LOGAN HAS BEEN STIRRING THE POT. SHE'S THROWING A LOT OF SHADE ONLINE ABOUT THE NEW BAND.
WHEN CAN I MEET THIS LOGAN CHICK AND GIVE HER AN ATTITUDE ADJUSTMENT?
THERE'S STILL THE GOOD NEWS. RIGHT, DEE?
THE GOOD NEWS IS YOU HAVE A CHANCE TO SHUT HER UP.
YOUR FIRST GIG IS UP NEXT FRIDAY. AND IT'S A BIG ONE.
YOU'LL BE PLAYING AT ***THE*** BATTLE OF THE BANDS TALENT SHOWCASE FOR SHORT FUZE RECORDS. AFTER LISTENING TO THE SAMPLE OF ONE OF YOUR PRACTICES, A PROMOTER PAL OF MINE GOT YOU INTO ONE OF THE AUDITION SHOWS.
LIPSERVICE IS...***ALSO*** PLAYING.
HOW ARE WE GOING TO PULL OFF THIS GIG?!
LET'S GIVE LOGAN A ***REASON*** TO SHAKE IN HER BOOTS.

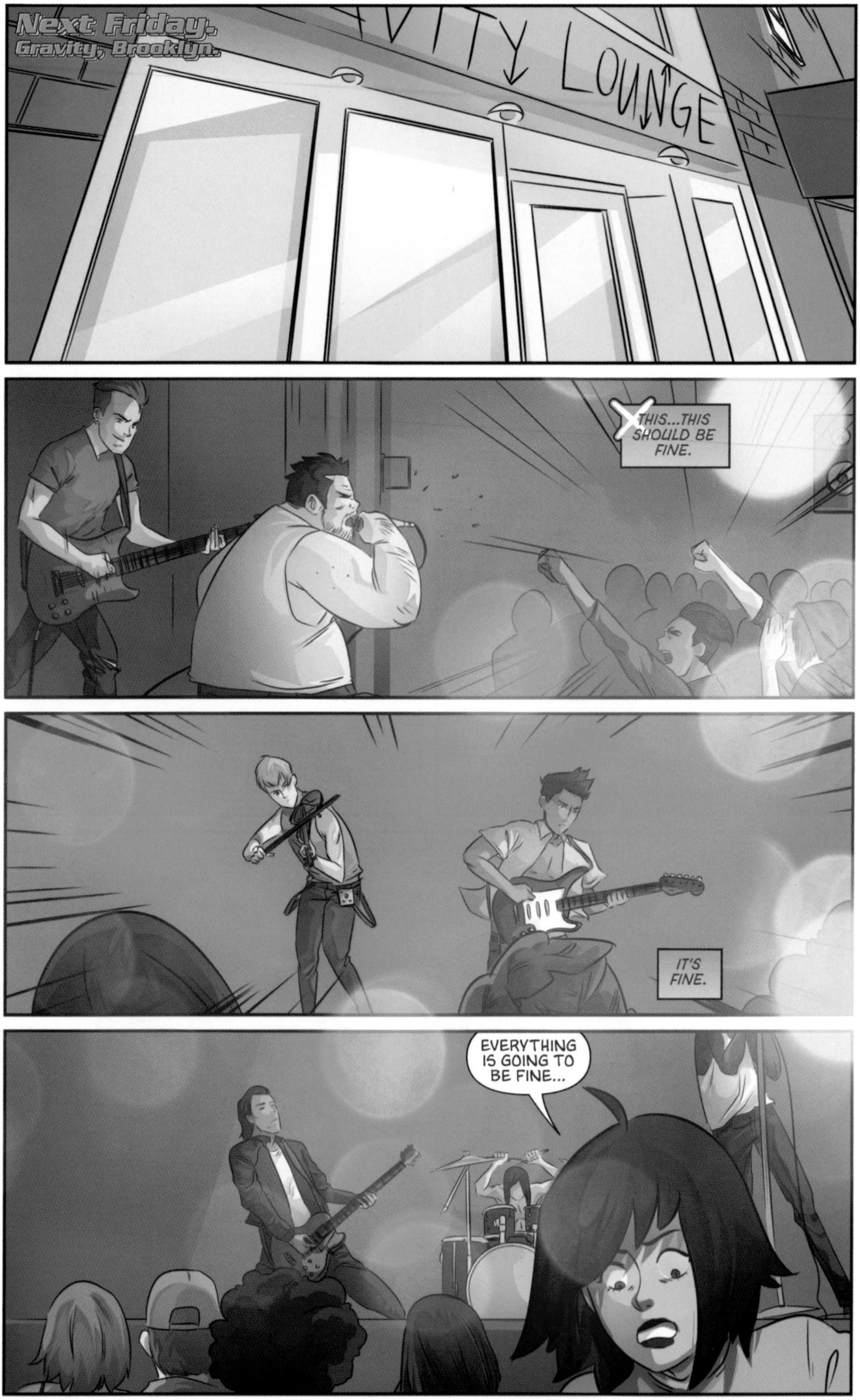
Next Friday.
Gravity, Brooklyn.
...VITY LOUNGE
THIS...THIS SHOULD BE FINE.
IT'S FINE.
EVERYTHING IS GOING TO BE FINE...

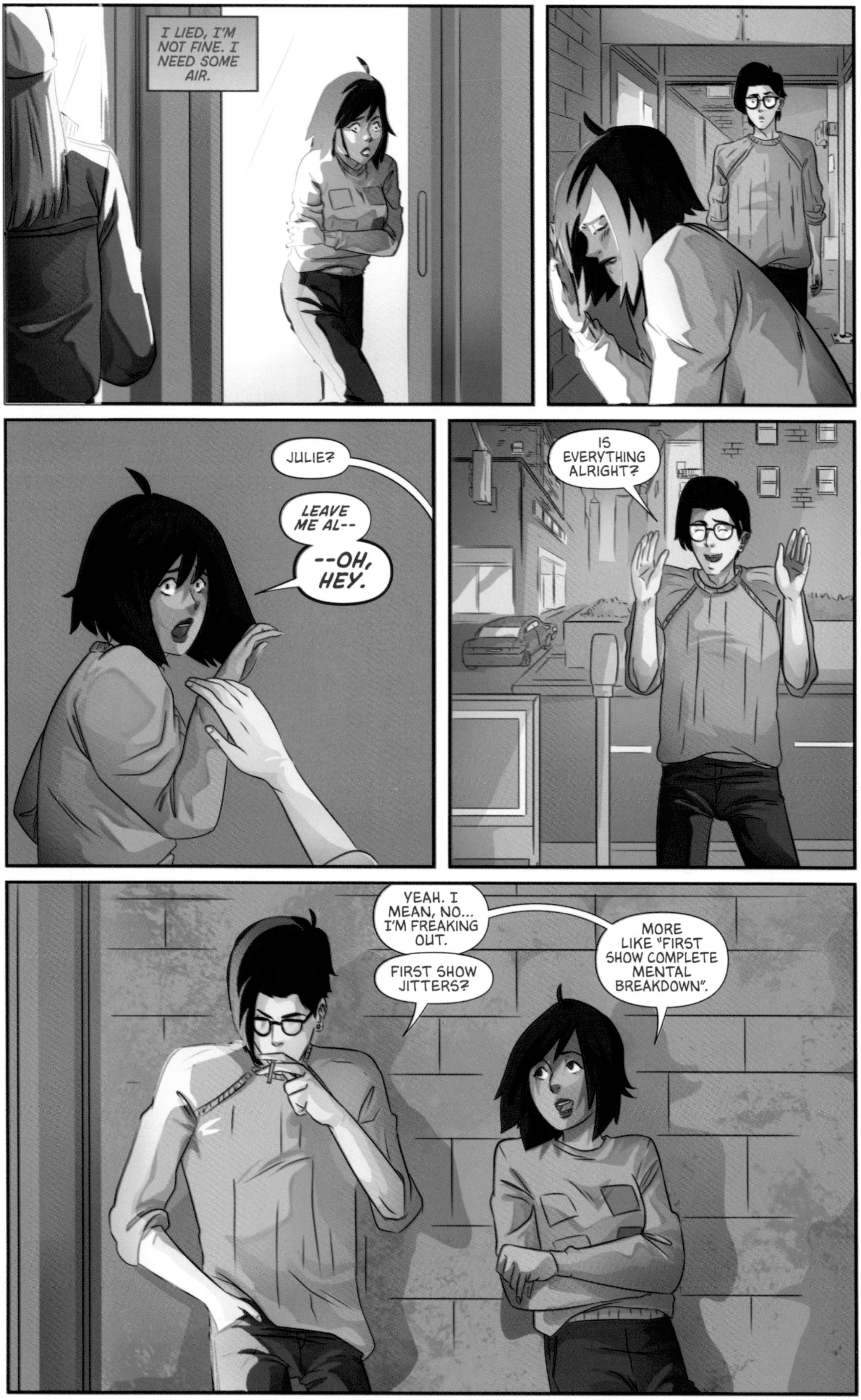
I LIED, I'M NOT FINE. I NEED SOME AIR.
JULIE?
LEAVE ME AL--
--OH, HEY.
IS EVERYTHING ALRIGHT?
YEAH. I MEAN, NO... I'M FREAKING OUT.
FIRST SHOW JITTERS?
MORE LIKE "FIRST SHOW COMPLETE MENTAL BREAKDOWN".

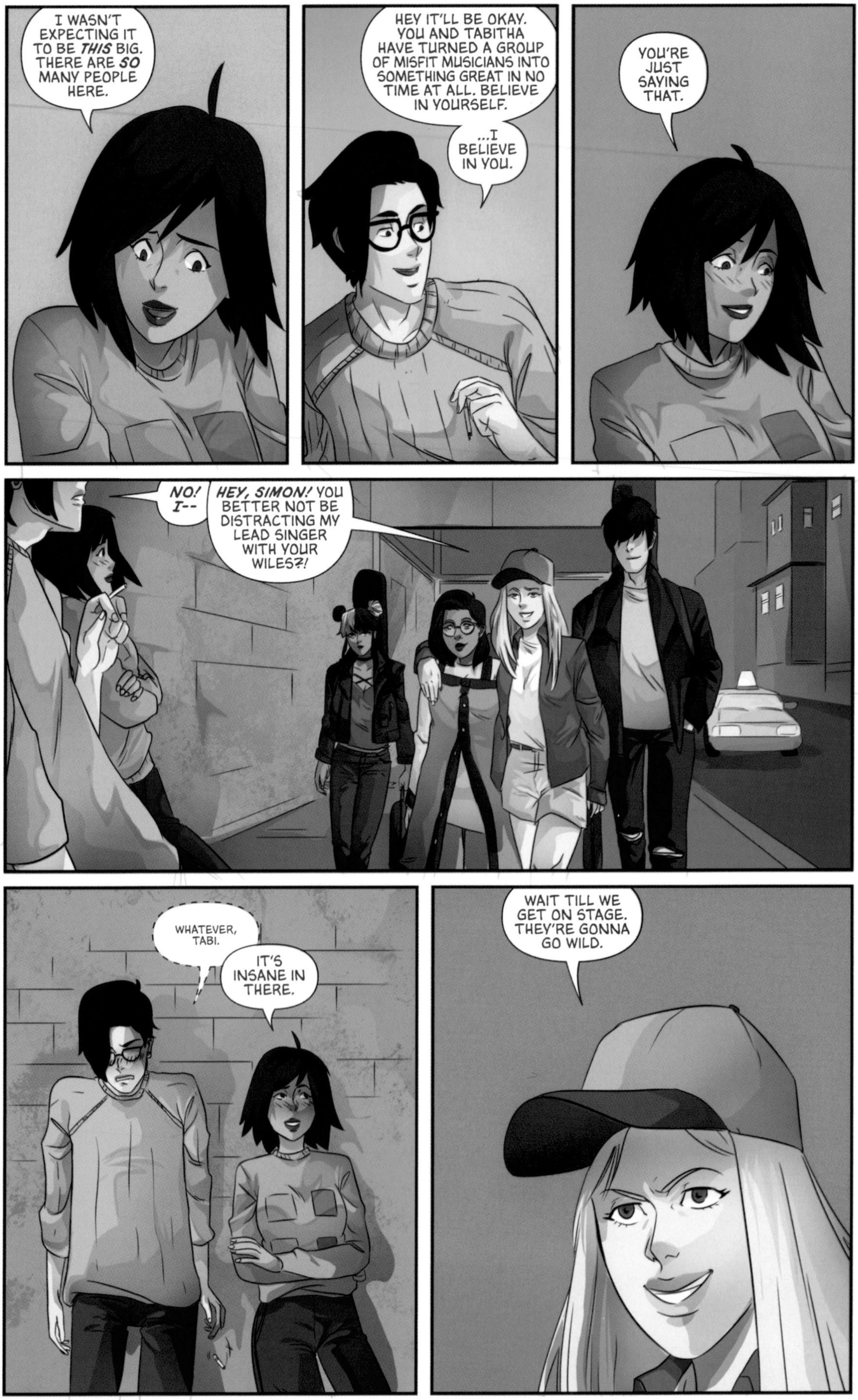
I WASN'T EXPECTING IT TO BE *THIS* BIG. THERE ARE *SO* MANY PEOPLE HERE.
HEY IT'LL BE OKAY. YOU AND TABITHA HAVE TURNED A GROUP OF MISFIT MUSICIANS INTO SOMETHING GREAT IN NO TIME AT ALL. BELIEVE IN YOURSELF.
...I BELIEVE IN YOU.
YOU'RE JUST SAYING THAT.
*NO! I--*
*HEY, SIMON!* YOU BETTER NOT BE DISTRACTING MY LEAD SINGER WITH YOUR WILES?!
WHATEVER, TABI.
IT'S INSANE IN THERE.
WAIT TILL WE GET ON STAGE. THEY'RE GONNA GO WILD.

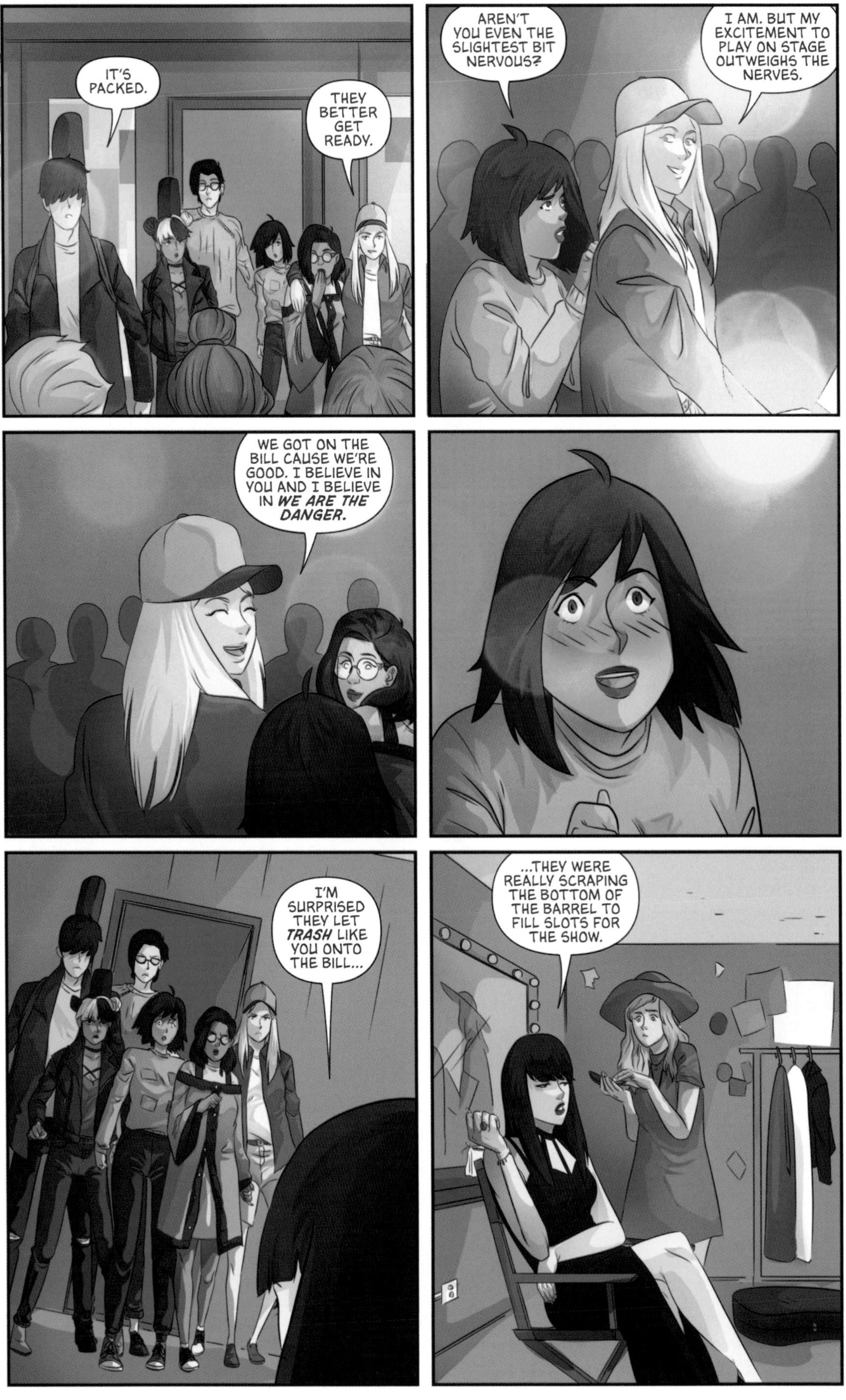
IT'S PACKED.
THEY BETTER GET READY.
AREN'T YOU EVEN THE SLIGHTEST BIT NERVOUS?
I AM. BUT MY EXCITEMENT TO PLAY ON STAGE OUTWEIGHS THE NERVES.
WE GOT ON THE BILL CAUSE WE'RE GOOD. I BELIEVE IN YOU AND I BELIEVE IN *WE ARE THE DANGER.*
I'M SURPRISED THEY LET *TRASH* LIKE YOU ONTO THE BILL...
...THEY WERE REALLY SCRAPING THE BOTTOM OF THE BARREL TO FILL SLOTS FOR THE SHOW.

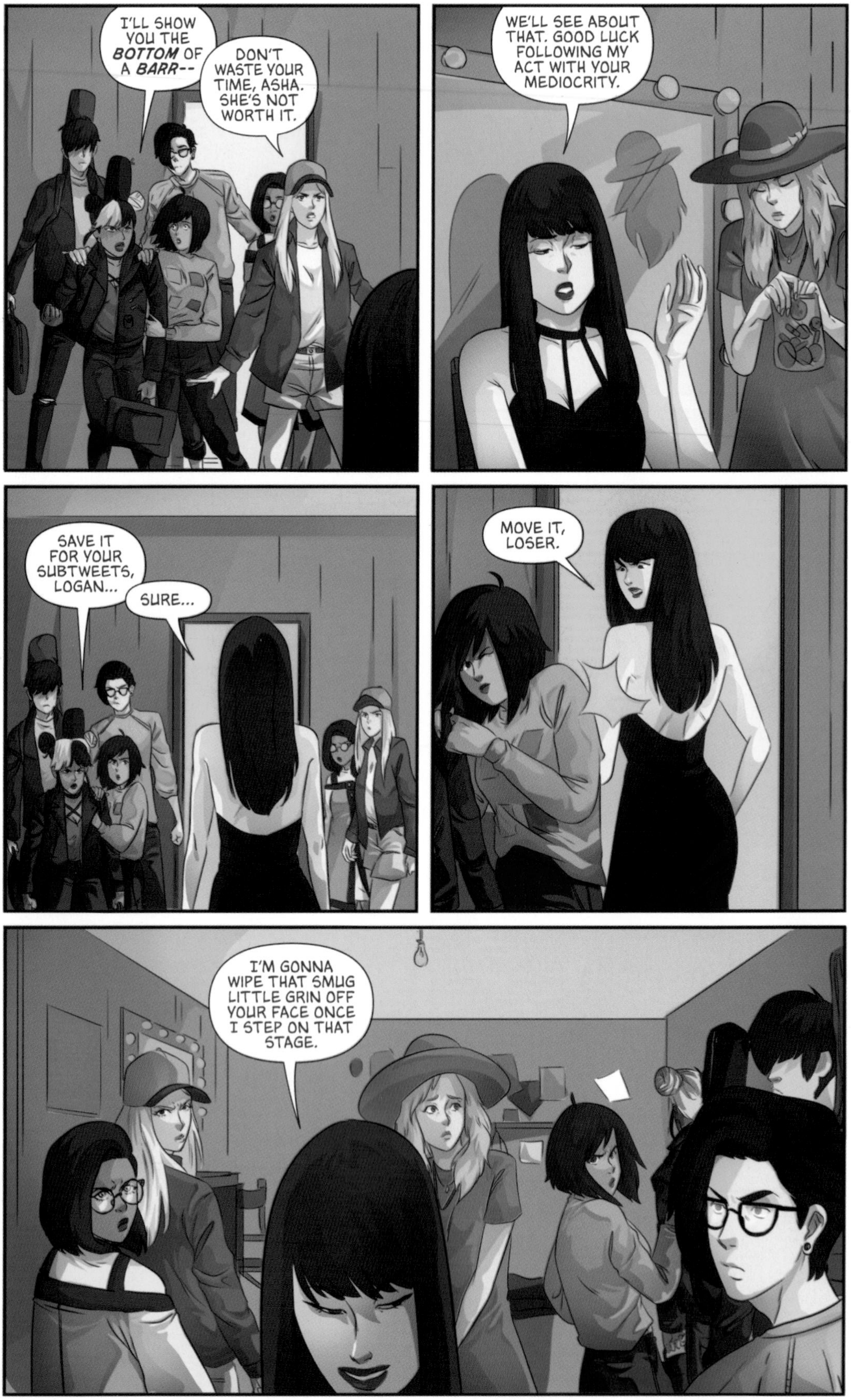
I'LL SHOW YOU THE *BOTTOM* OF A *BARR--*
DON'T WASTE YOUR TIME, ASHA. SHE'S NOT WORTH IT.
WE'LL SEE ABOUT THAT. GOOD LUCK FOLLOWING MY ACT WITH YOUR MEDIOCRITY.
SAVE IT FOR YOUR SUBTWEETS, LOGAN...
SURE...
MOVE IT, LOSER.
I'M GONNA WIPE THAT SMUG LITTLE GRIN OFF YOUR FACE ONCE I STEP ON THAT STAGE.

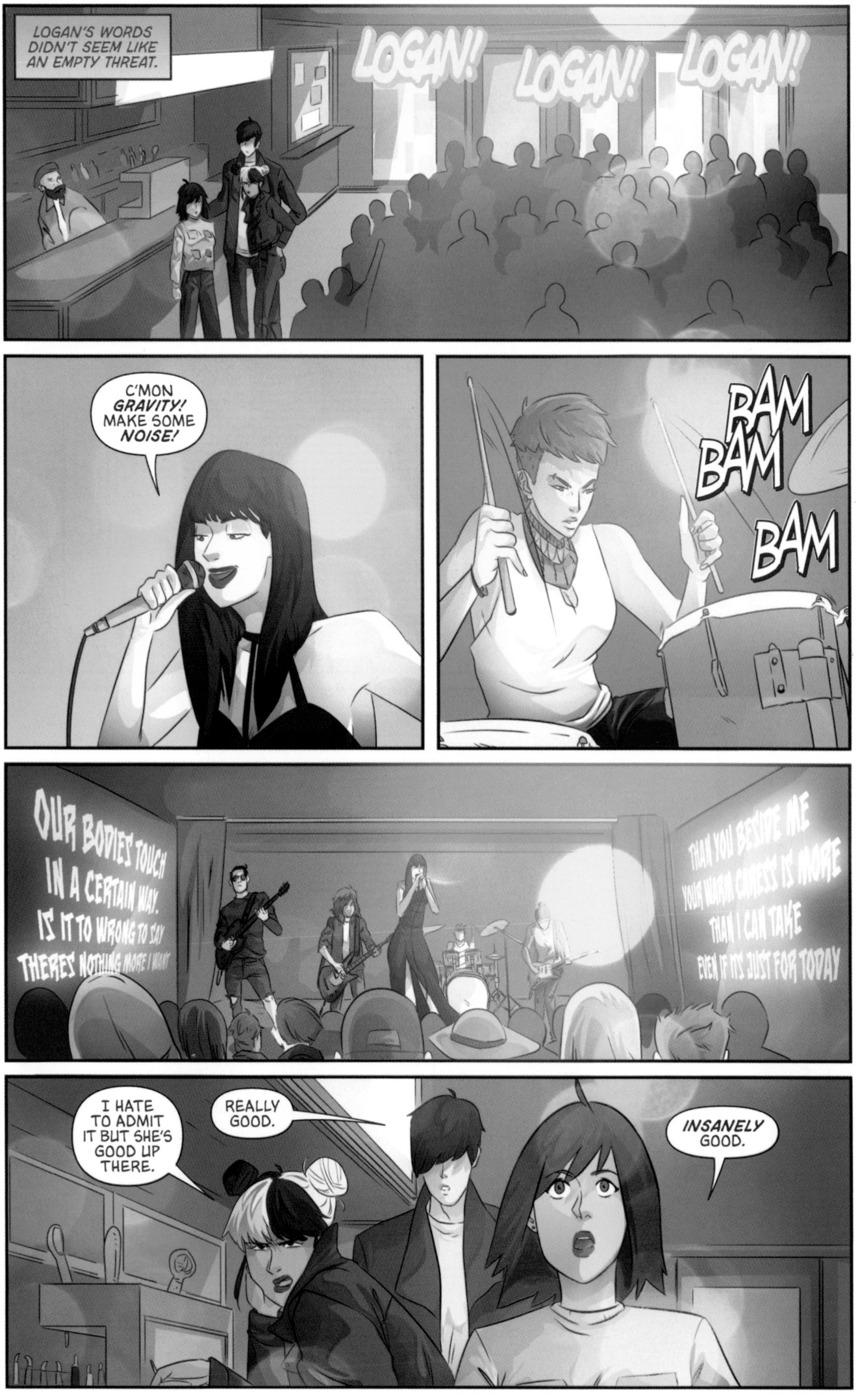
LOGAN'S WORDS DIDN'T SEEM LIKE AN EMPTY THREAT.
LOGAN! LOGAN! LOGAN!
C'MON GRAVITY! MAKE SOME NOISE!
BAM BAM BAM
OUR BODIES TOUCH
IN A CERTAIN WAY.
IS IT TO WRONG TO SAY
THERES NOTHING MORE I WANT
THAN YOU BESIDE ME
YOUR WARM CARESS IS MORE
THAN I CAN TAKE
EVEN IF ITS JUST FOR TODAY
I HATE TO ADMIT IT BUT SHE'S GOOD UP THERE.
REALLY GOOD.
INSANELY GOOD.

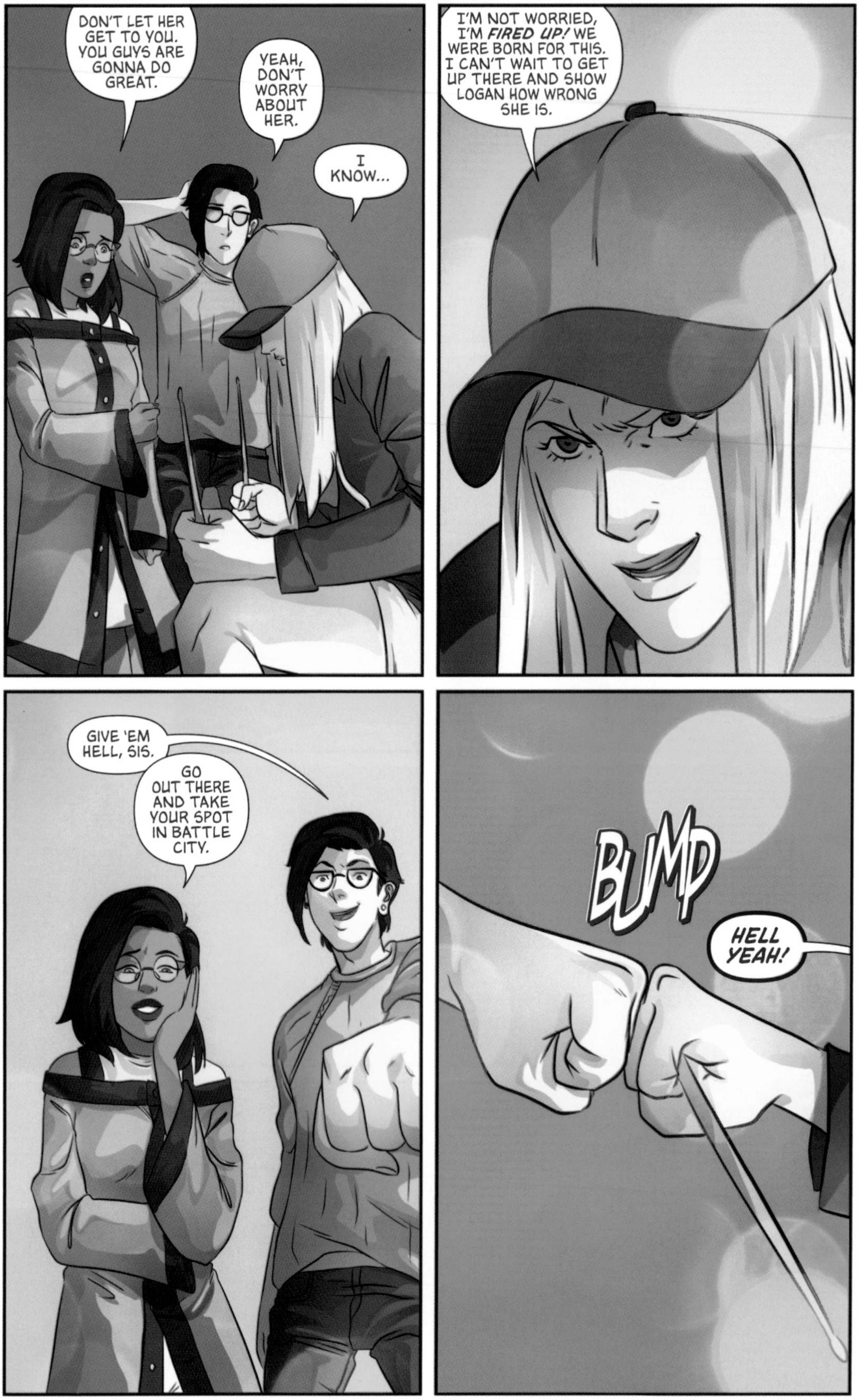
DON'T LET HER GET TO YOU. YOU GUYS ARE GONNA DO GREAT.
YEAH, DON'T WORRY ABOUT HER.
I KNOW...
I'M NOT WORRIED, I'M *FIRED UP!* WE WERE BORN FOR THIS. I CAN'T WAIT TO GET UP THERE AND SHOW LOGAN HOW WRONG SHE IS.
GIVE 'EM HELL, SIS.
GO OUT THERE AND TAKE YOUR SPOT IN BATTLE CITY.
BUMP
HELL YEAH!

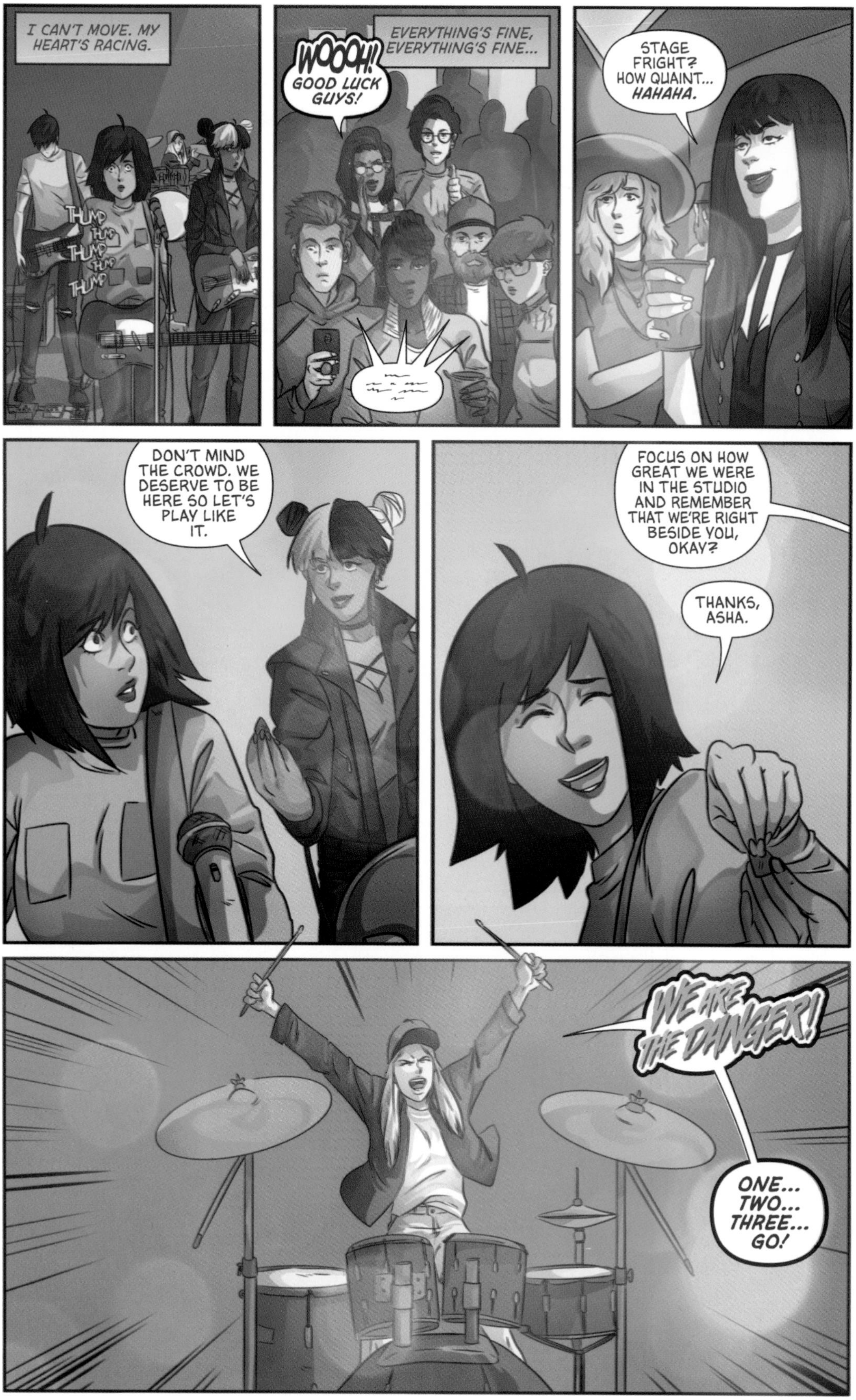
I CAN'T MOVE. MY HEART'S RACING.
THUMP THUMP THUMP THUMP THUMP
EVERYTHING'S FINE, EVERYTHING'S FINE...
WOOOH! GOOD LUCK GUYS!
STAGE FRIGHT? HOW QUAINT... HAHAHA.
DON'T MIND THE CROWD. WE DESERVE TO BE HERE SO LET'S PLAY LIKE IT.
FOCUS ON HOW GREAT WE WERE IN THE STUDIO AND REMEMBER THAT WE'RE RIGHT BESIDE YOU, OKAY?
THANKS, ASHA.
WE ARE THE DANGER!
ONE... TWO... THREE... GO!

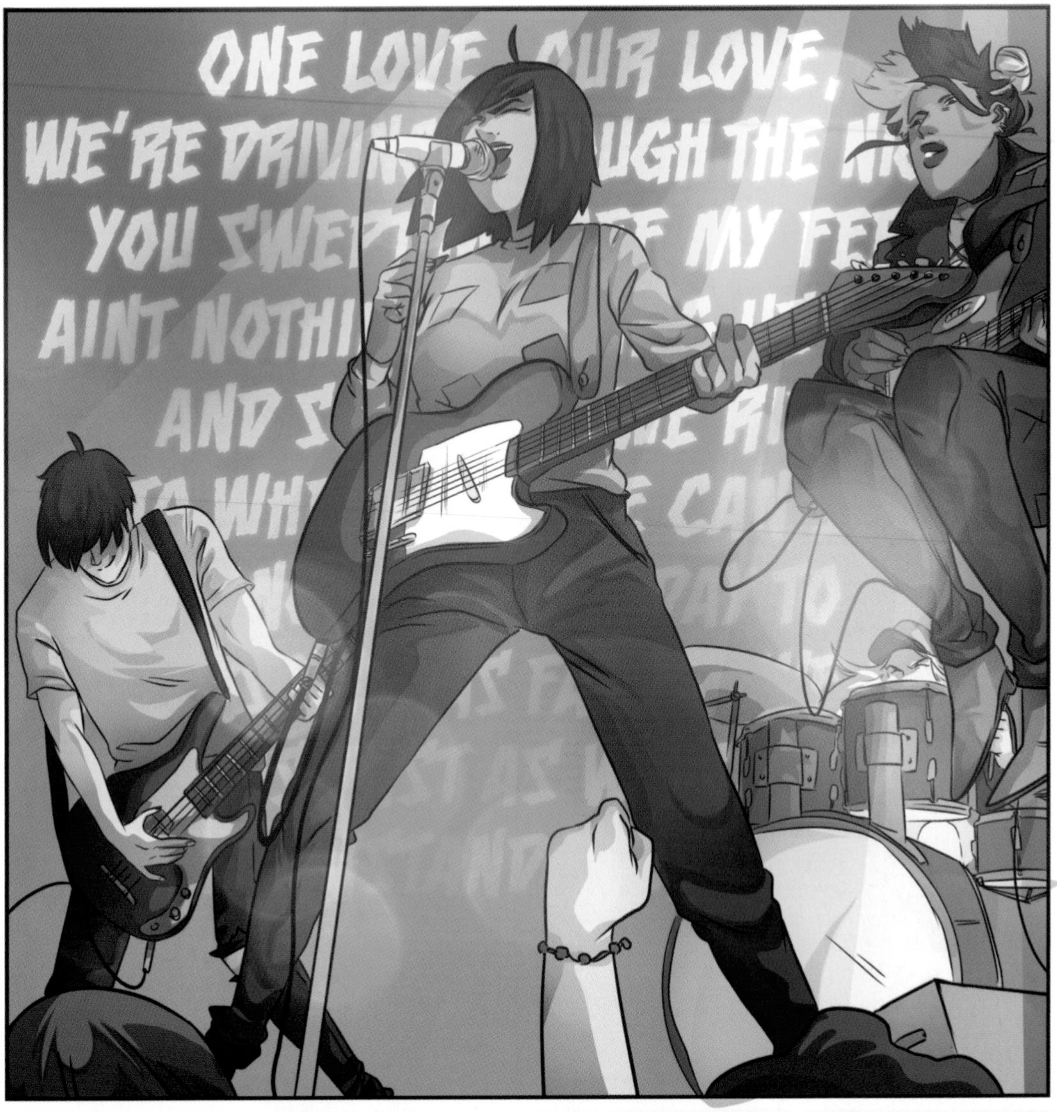
ONE LOVE
UR LOVE,
WE'RE DRIVIN
UGH THE
YOU SWEP
F MY FE
AINT NOTHI
AND S

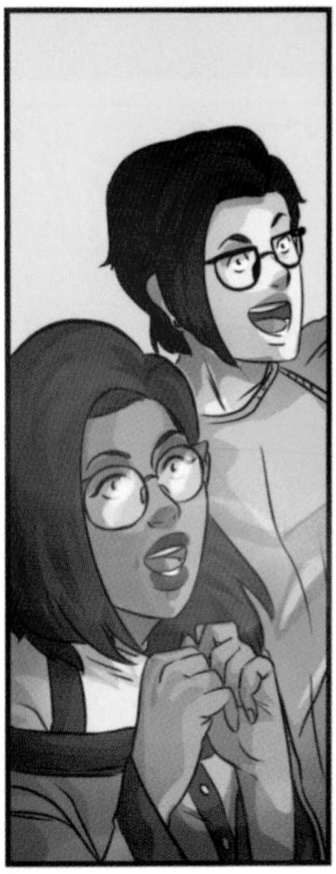

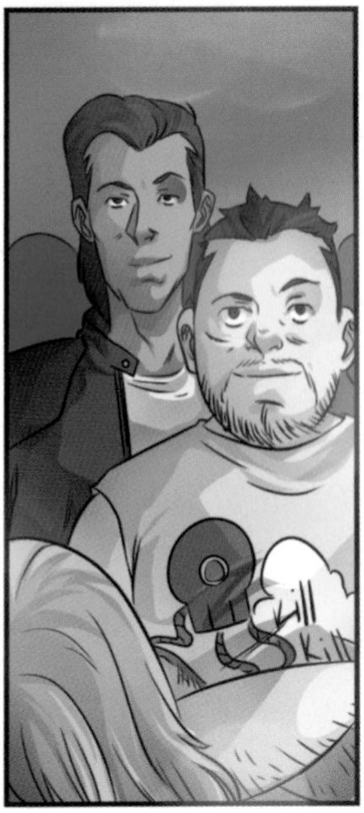

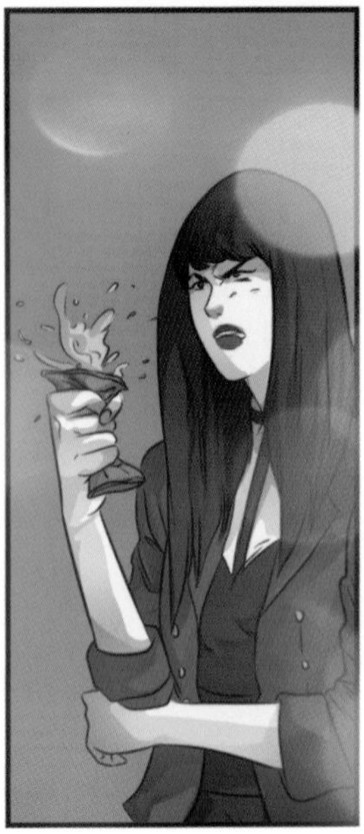

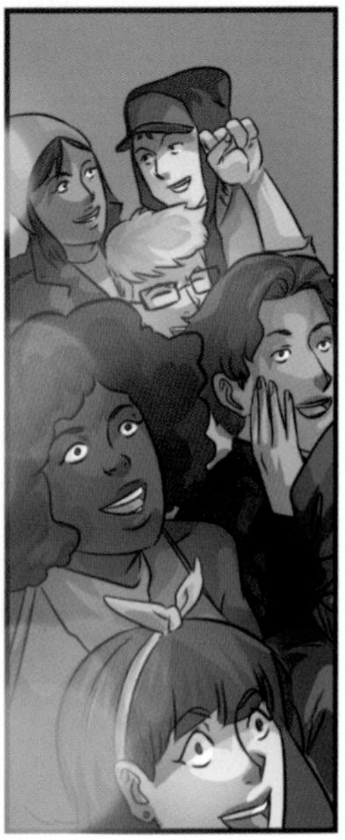

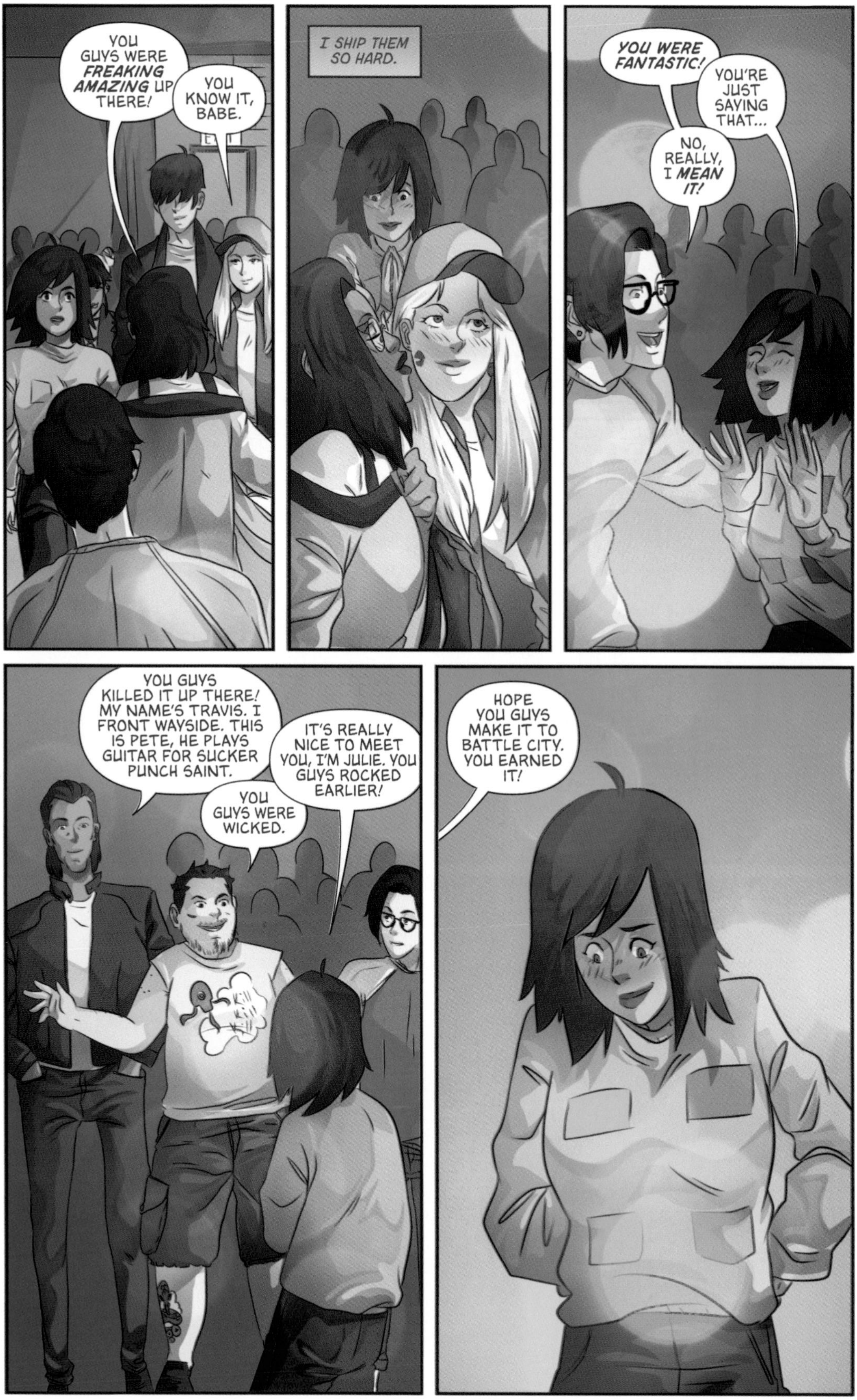
YOU GUYS WERE FREAKING AMAZING UP THERE!
YOU KNOW IT, BABE.
I SHIP THEM SO HARD.
YOU WERE FANTASTIC!
YOU'RE JUST SAYING THAT...
NO, REALLY, I MEAN IT!
YOU GUYS KILLED IT UP THERE! MY NAME'S TRAVIS. I FRONT WAYSIDE. THIS IS PETE, HE PLAYS GUITAR FOR SUCKER PUNCH SAINT.
YOU GUYS WERE WICKED.
IT'S REALLY NICE TO MEET YOU, I'M JULIE. YOU GUYS ROCKED EARLIER!
HOPE YOU GUYS MAKE IT TO BATTLE CITY. YOU EARNED IT!

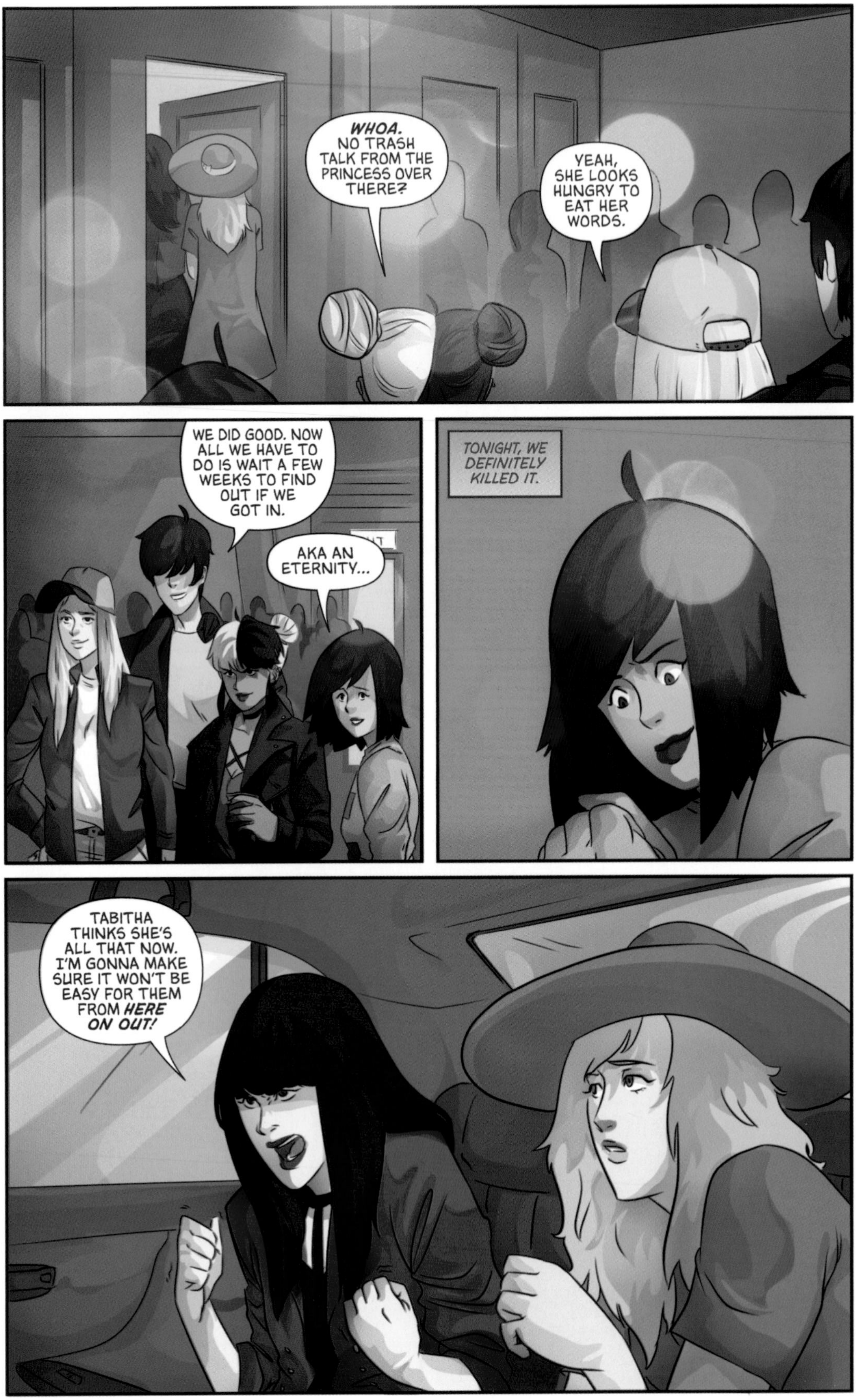
WHOA. NO TRASH TALK FROM THE PRINCESS OVER THERE?
YEAH, SHE LOOKS HUNGRY TO EAT HER WORDS.
WE DID GOOD. NOW ALL WE HAVE TO DO IS WAIT A FEW WEEKS TO FIND OUT IF WE GOT IN.
AKA AN ETERNITY...
TONIGHT, WE DEFINITELY KILLED IT.
TABITHA THINKS SHE'S ALL THAT NOW. I'M GONNA MAKE SURE IT WON'T BE EASY FOR THEM FROM HERE ON OUT!

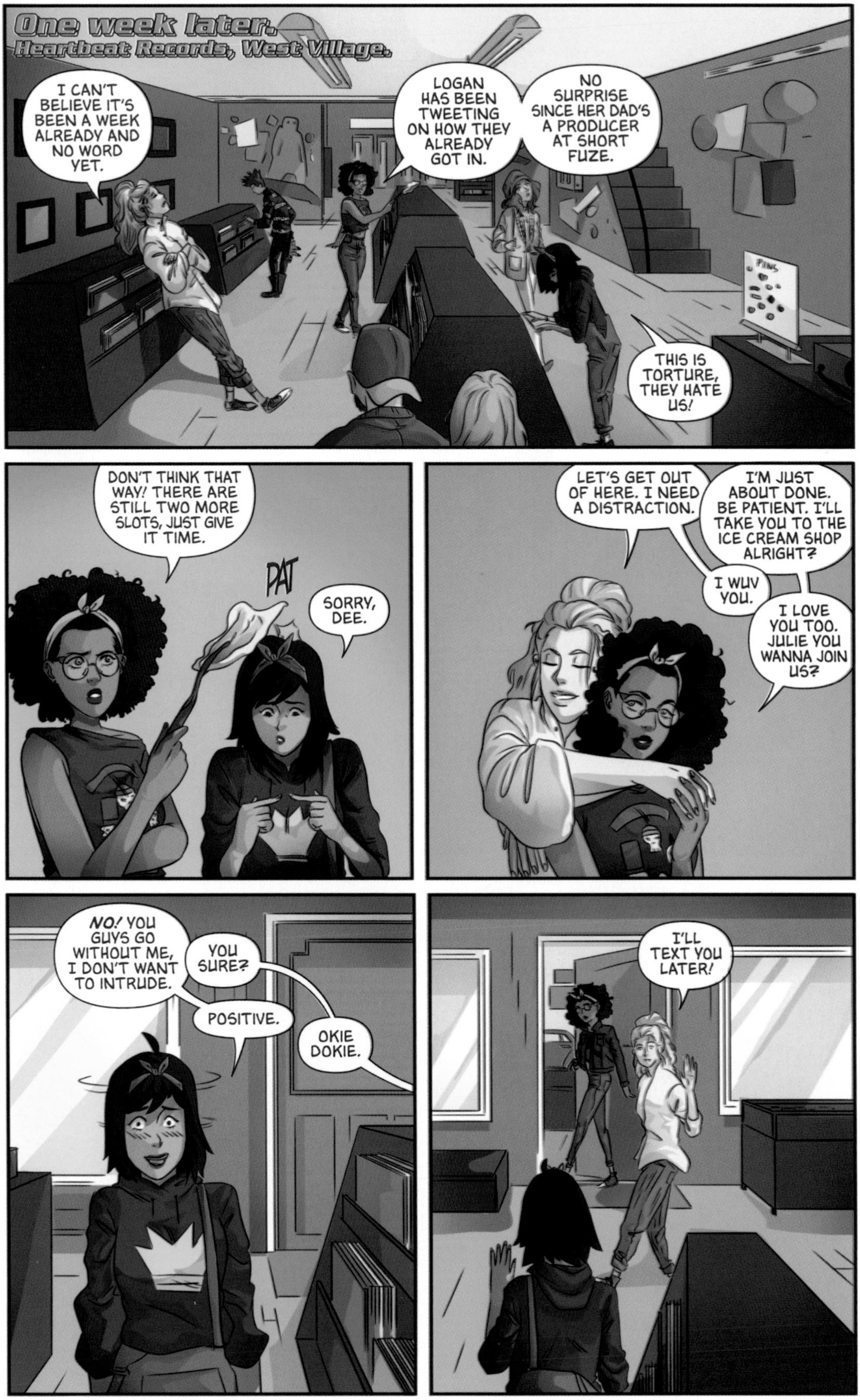
One week later.
Heartbeat Records, West Village.
I CAN'T BELIEVE IT'S BEEN A WEEK ALREADY AND NO WORD YET.
LOGAN HAS BEEN TWEETING ON HOW THEY ALREADY GOT IN.
NO SURPRISE SINCE HER DAD'S A PRODUCER AT SHORT FUZE.
THIS IS TORTURE, THEY HATE US!
DON'T THINK THAT WAY! THERE ARE STILL TWO MORE SLOTS, JUST GIVE IT TIME.
PAT
SORRY, DEE.
LET'S GET OUT OF HERE. I NEED A DISTRACTION.
I'M JUST ABOUT DONE. BE PATIENT. I'LL TAKE YOU TO THE ICE CREAM SHOP ALRIGHT?
I WUV YOU.
I LOVE YOU TOO. JULIE YOU WANNA JOIN US?
NO! YOU GUYS GO WITHOUT ME, I DON'T WANT TO INTRUDE.
YOU SURE?
POSITIVE.
OKIE DOKIE.
I'LL TEXT YOU LATER!

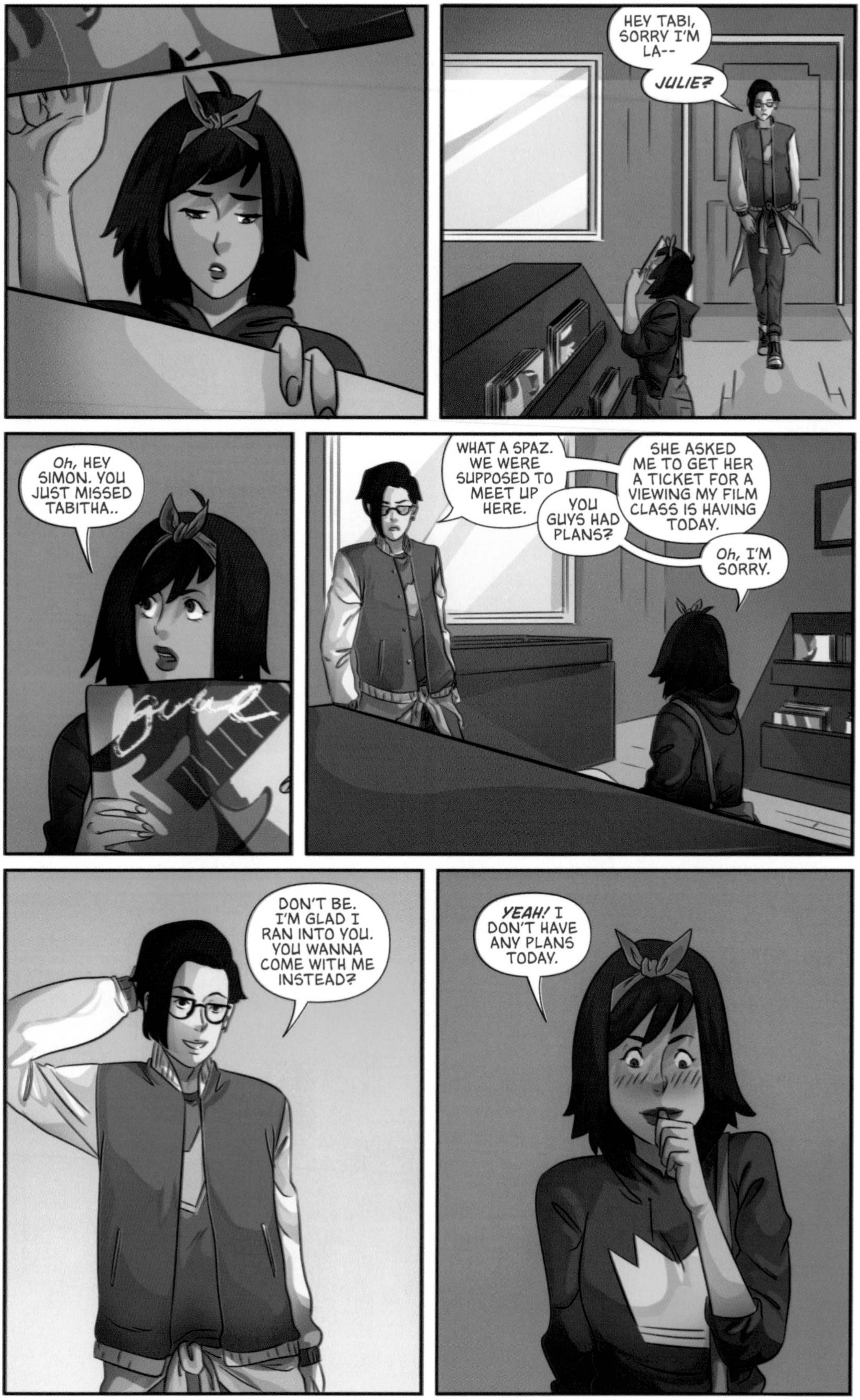
HEY TABI, SORRY I'M LA--
JULIE?
Oh, HEY SIMON. YOU JUST MISSED TABITHA..
WHAT A SPAZ. WE WERE SUPPOSED TO MEET UP HERE.
SHE ASKED ME TO GET HER A TICKET FOR A VIEWING MY FILM CLASS IS HAVING TODAY.
YOU GUYS HAD PLANS?
Oh, I'M SORRY.
DON'T BE. I'M GLAD I RAN INTO YOU. YOU WANNA COME WITH ME INSTEAD?
YEAH! I DON'T HAVE ANY PLANS TODAY.

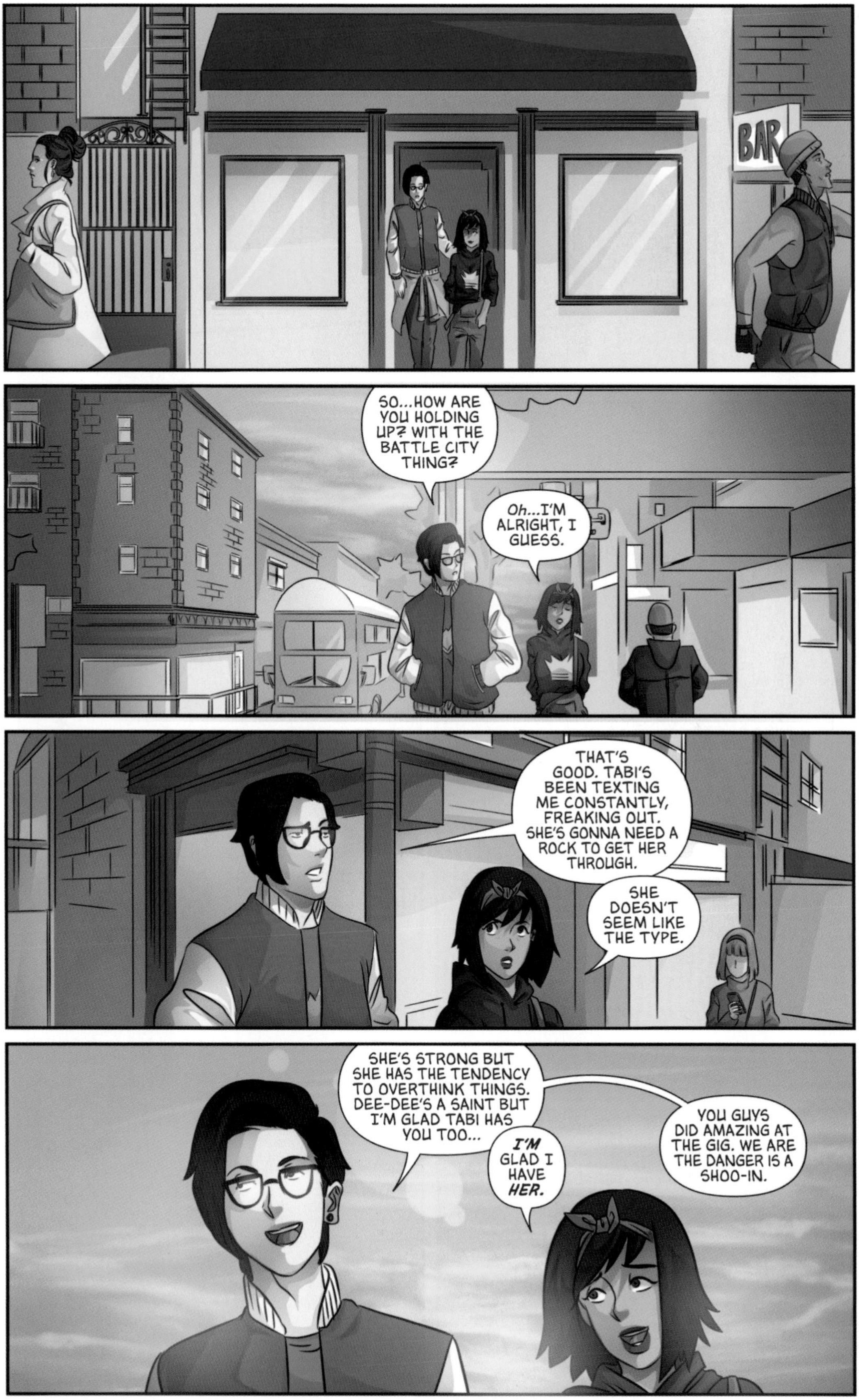
BAR
SO...HOW ARE YOU HOLDING UP? WITH THE BATTLE CITY THING?
Oh...I'M ALRIGHT, I GUESS.
THAT'S GOOD. TABI'S BEEN TEXTING ME CONSTANTLY, FREAKING OUT. SHE'S GONNA NEED A ROCK TO GET HER THROUGH.
SHE DOESN'T SEEM LIKE THE TYPE.
SHE'S STRONG BUT SHE HAS THE TENDENCY TO OVERTHINK THINGS. DEE-DEE'S A SAINT BUT I'M GLAD TABI HAS YOU TOO...
I'M GLAD I HAVE HER.
YOU GUYS DID AMAZING AT THE GIG. WE ARE THE DANGER IS A SHOO-IN.

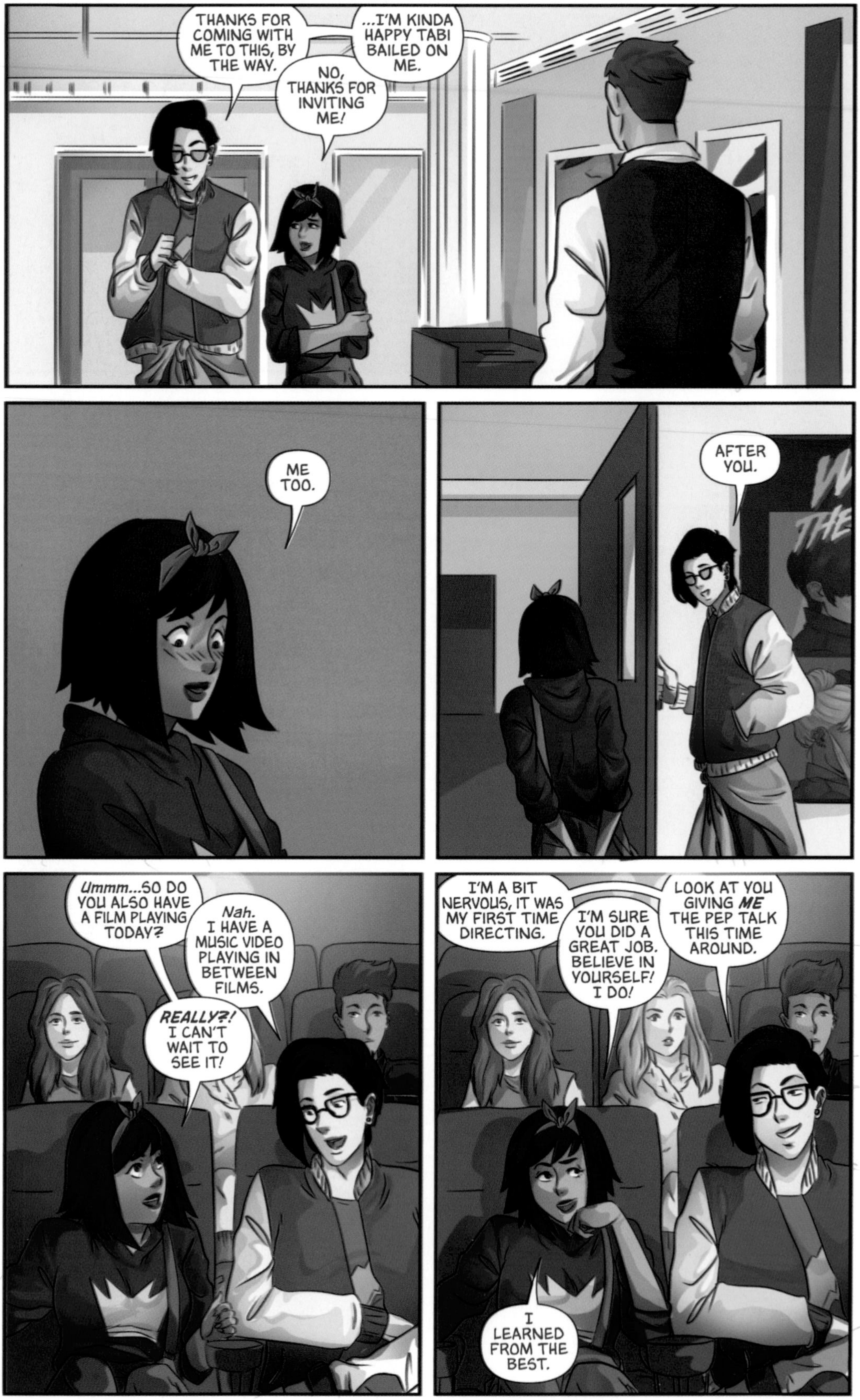
THANKS FOR COMING WITH ME TO THIS, BY THE WAY.
...I'M KINDA HAPPY TABI BAILED ON ME.
NO, THANKS FOR INVITING ME!
ME TOO.
AFTER YOU.
Ummm...SO DO YOU ALSO HAVE A FILM PLAYING TODAY?
Nah. I HAVE A MUSIC VIDEO PLAYING IN BETWEEN FILMS.
REALLY?! I CAN'T WAIT TO SEE IT!
I'M A BIT NERVOUS, IT WAS MY FIRST TIME DIRECTING.
I'M SURE YOU DID A GREAT JOB. BELIEVE IN YOURSELF! I DO!
LOOK AT YOU GIVING ME THE PEP TALK THIS TIME AROUND.
I LEARNED FROM THE BEST.

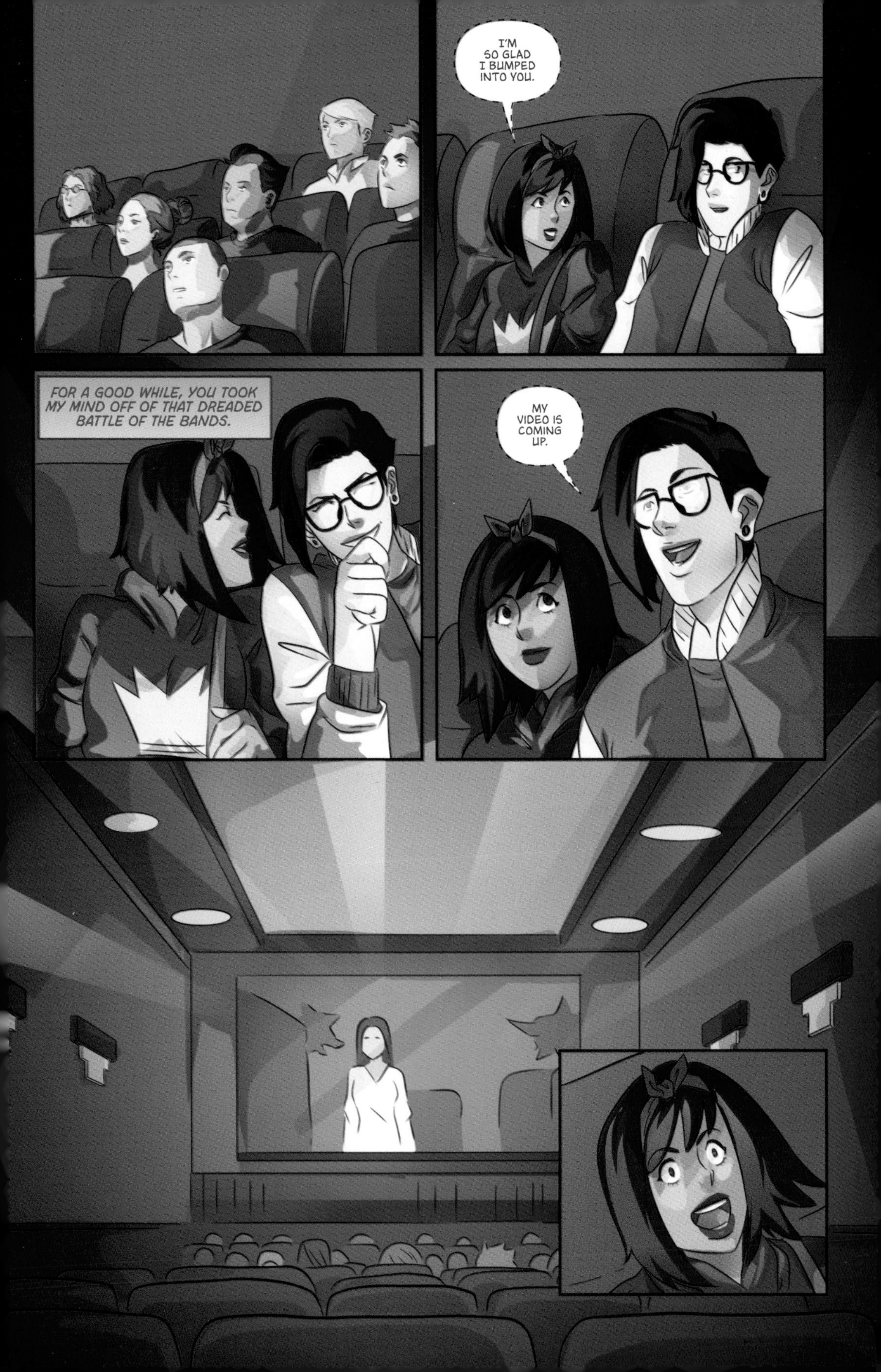
I'M SO GLAD I BUMPED INTO YOU.
FOR A GOOD WHILE, YOU TOOK MY MIND OFF OF THAT DREADED BATTLE OF THE BANDS.
MY VIDEO IS COMING UP.

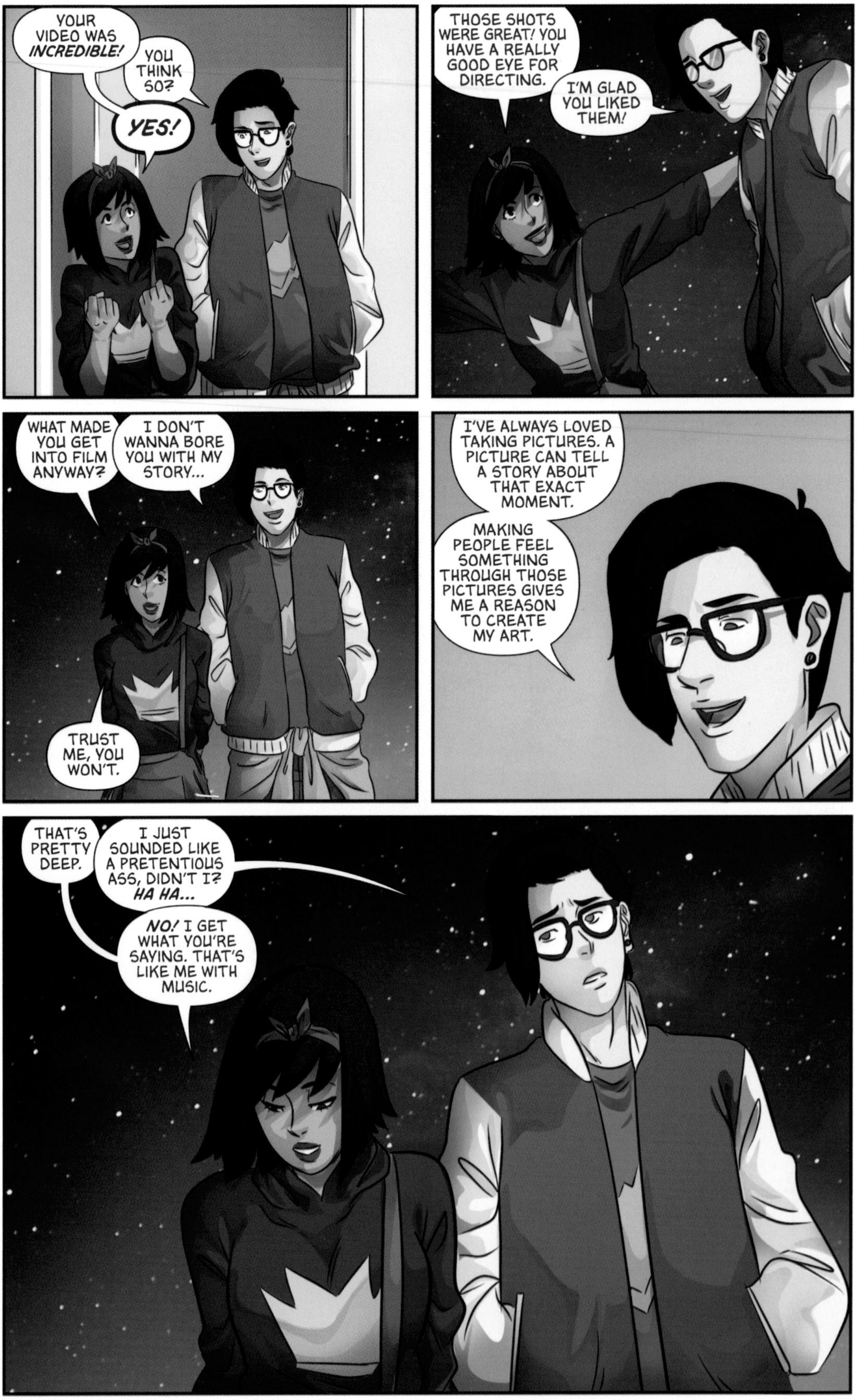
YOUR VIDEO WAS *INCREDIBLE!*
YOU THINK SO?
*YES!*
THOSE SHOTS WERE GREAT! YOU HAVE A REALLY GOOD EYE FOR DIRECTING.
I'M GLAD YOU LIKED THEM!
WHAT MADE YOU GET INTO FILM ANYWAY?
I DON'T WANNA BORE YOU WITH MY STORY...
TRUST ME, YOU WON'T.
I'VE ALWAYS LOVED TAKING PICTURES. A PICTURE CAN TELL A STORY ABOUT THAT EXACT MOMENT.
MAKING PEOPLE FEEL SOMETHING THROUGH THOSE PICTURES GIVES ME A REASON TO CREATE MY ART.
THAT'S PRETTY DEEP.
I JUST SOUNDED LIKE A PRETENTIOUS ASS, DIDN'T I? *HA HA...*
*NO!* I GET WHAT YOU'RE SAYING. THAT'S LIKE ME WITH MUSIC.

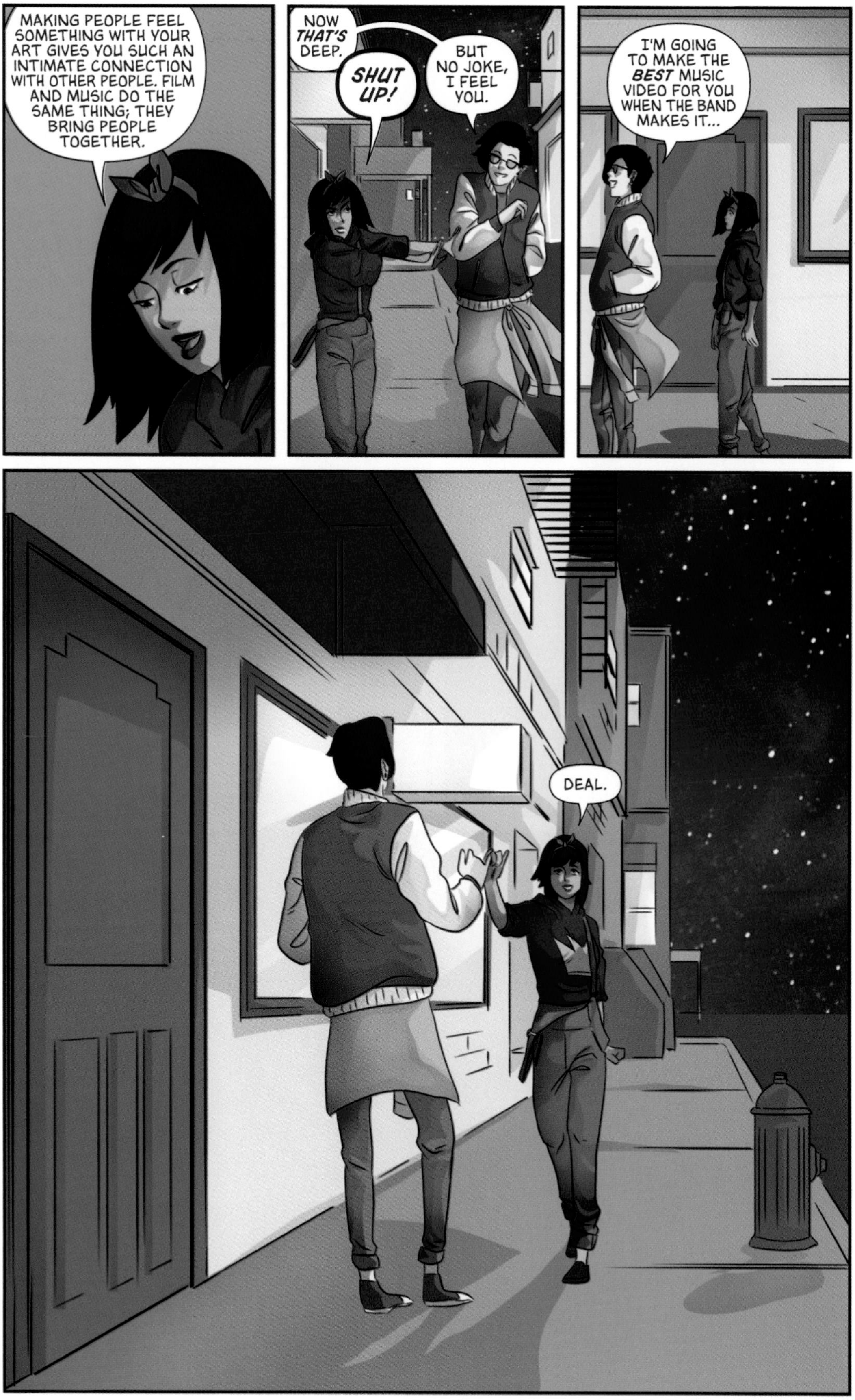
MAKING PEOPLE FEEL SOMETHING WITH YOUR ART GIVES YOU SUCH AN INTIMATE CONNECTION WITH OTHER PEOPLE. FILM AND MUSIC DO THE SAME THING; THEY BRING PEOPLE TOGETHER.
NOW *THAT'S* DEEP.
**SHUT UP!**
BUT NO JOKE, I FEEL YOU.
I'M GOING TO MAKE THE ***BEST*** MUSIC VIDEO FOR YOU WHEN THE BAND MAKES IT...
DEAL.

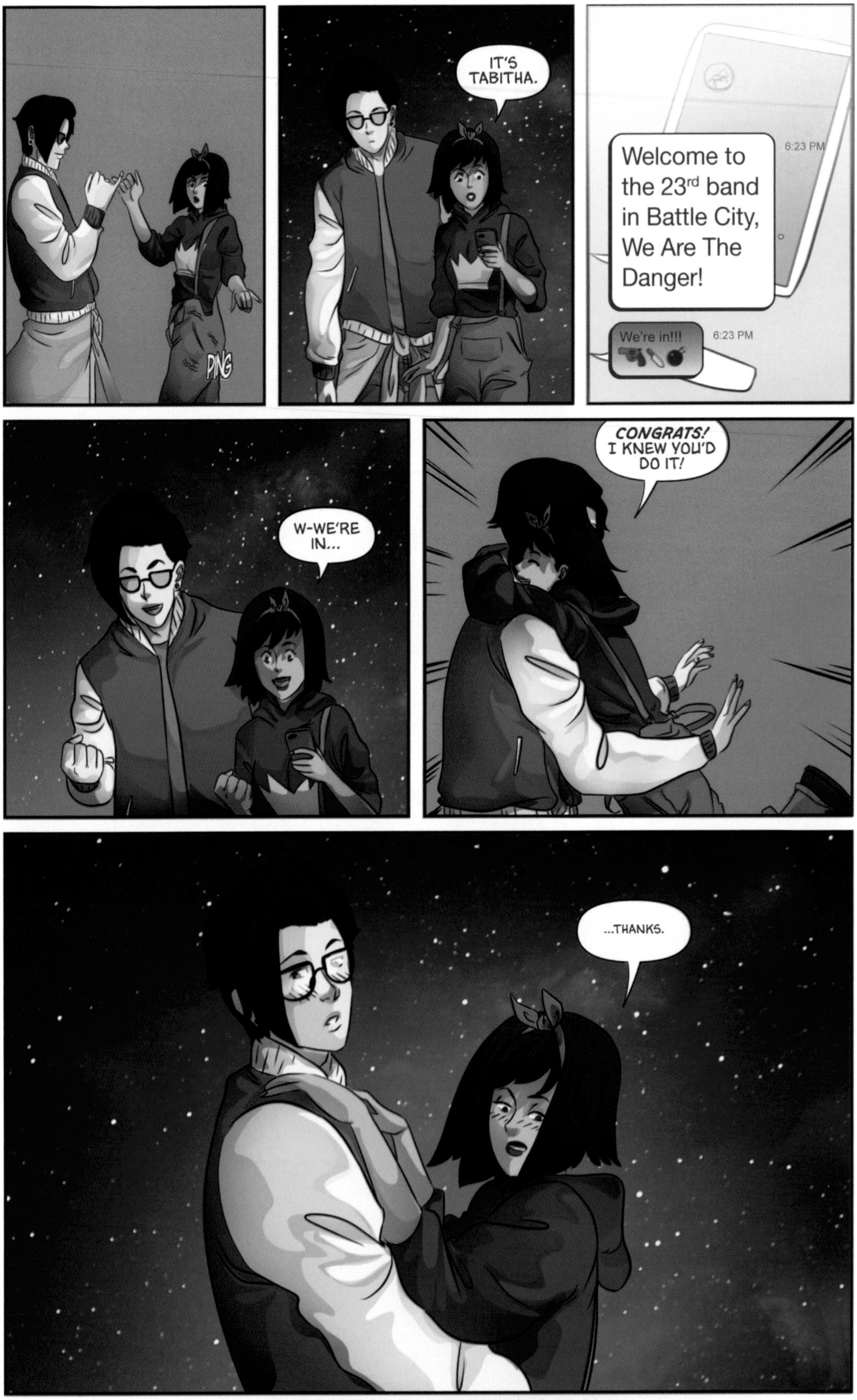
PING
IT'S TABITHA.
Welcome to the 23rd band in Battle City, We Are The Danger!
6:23 PM
We're in!!!
6:23 PM
W-WE'RE IN...
CONGRATS! I KNEW YOU'D DO IT!
...THANKS.

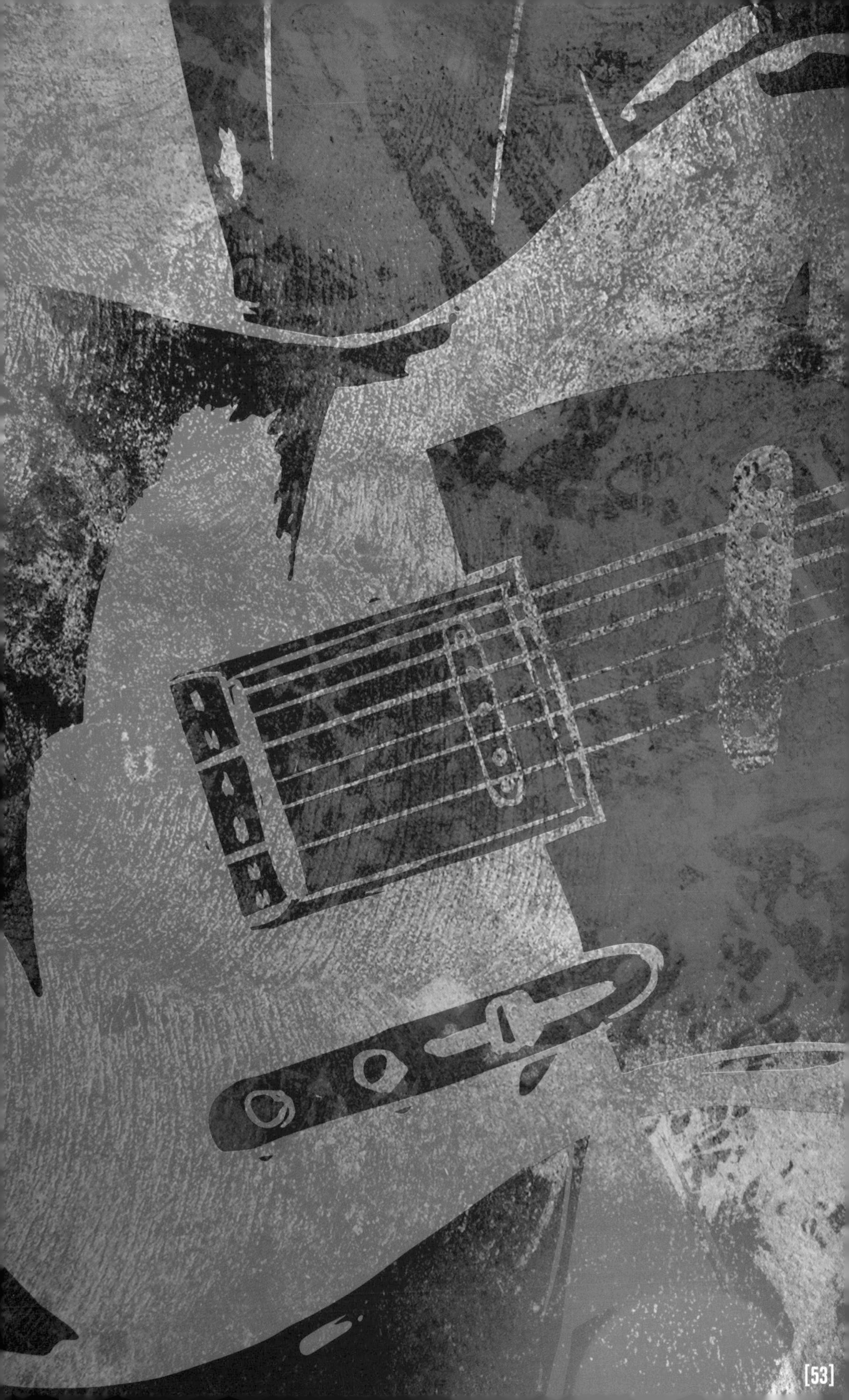

# ISSUE 3

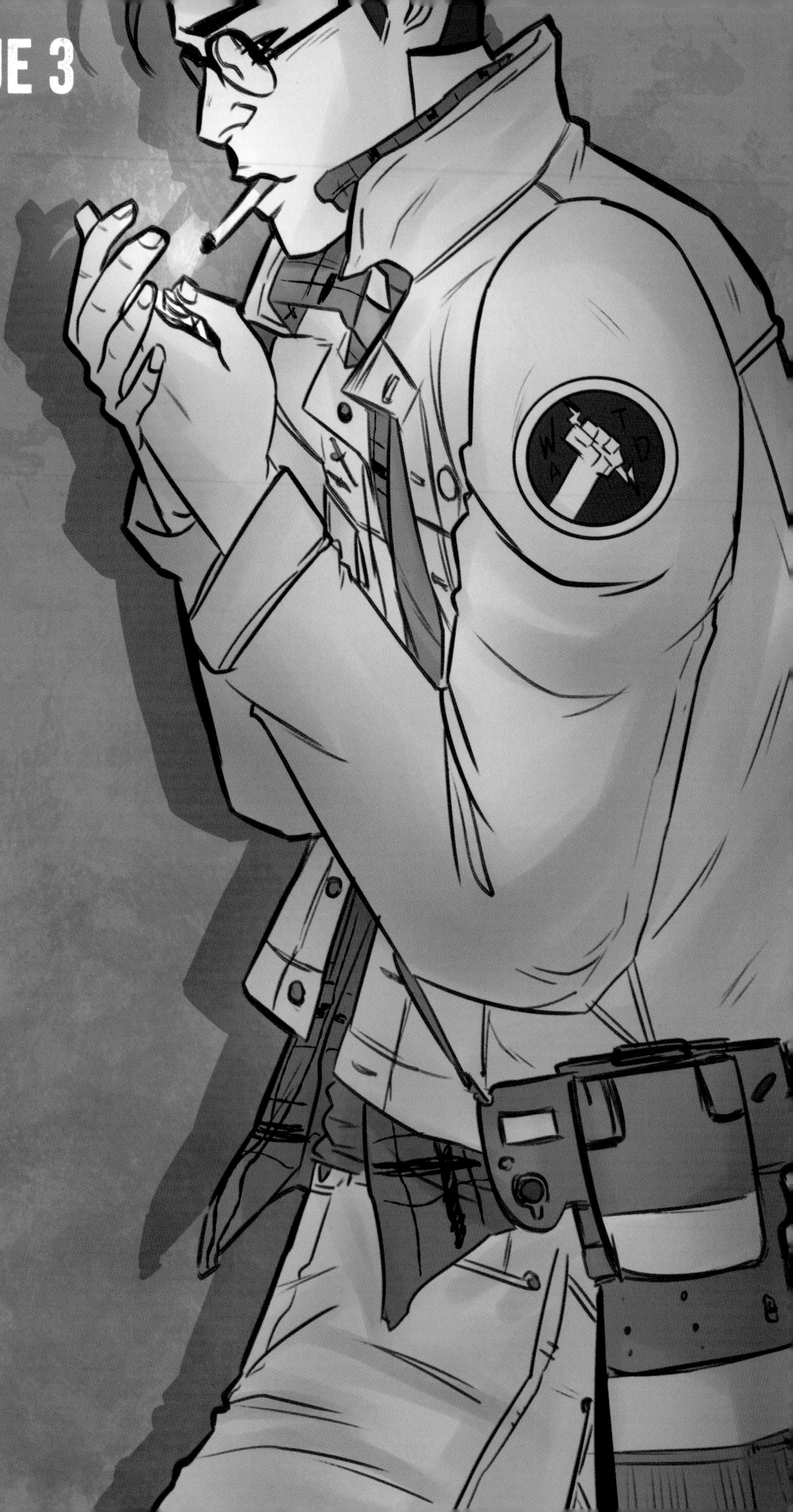

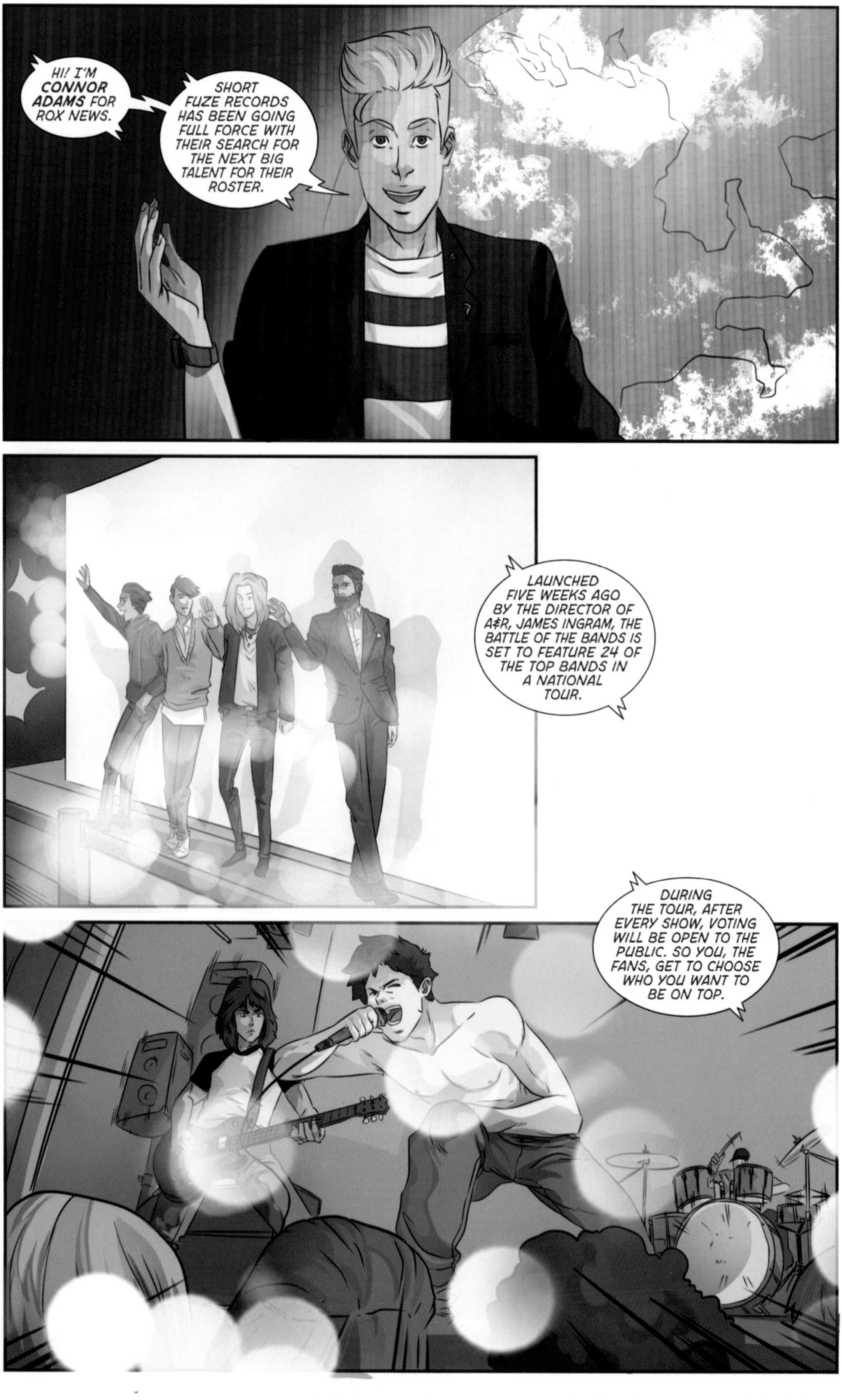

HI! I'M CONNOR ADAMS FOR ROX NEWS.
SHORT FUZE RECORDS HAS BEEN GOING FULL FORCE WITH THEIR SEARCH FOR THE NEXT BIG TALENT FOR THEIR ROSTER.
LAUNCHED FIVE WEEKS AGO BY THE DIRECTOR OF A&R, JAMES INGRAM, THE BATTLE OF THE BANDS IS SET TO FEATURE 24 OF THE TOP BANDS IN A NATIONAL TOUR.
DURING THE TOUR, AFTER EVERY SHOW, VOTING WILL BE OPEN TO THE PUBLIC. SO YOU, THE FANS, GET TO CHOOSE WHO YOU WANT TO BE ON TOP.

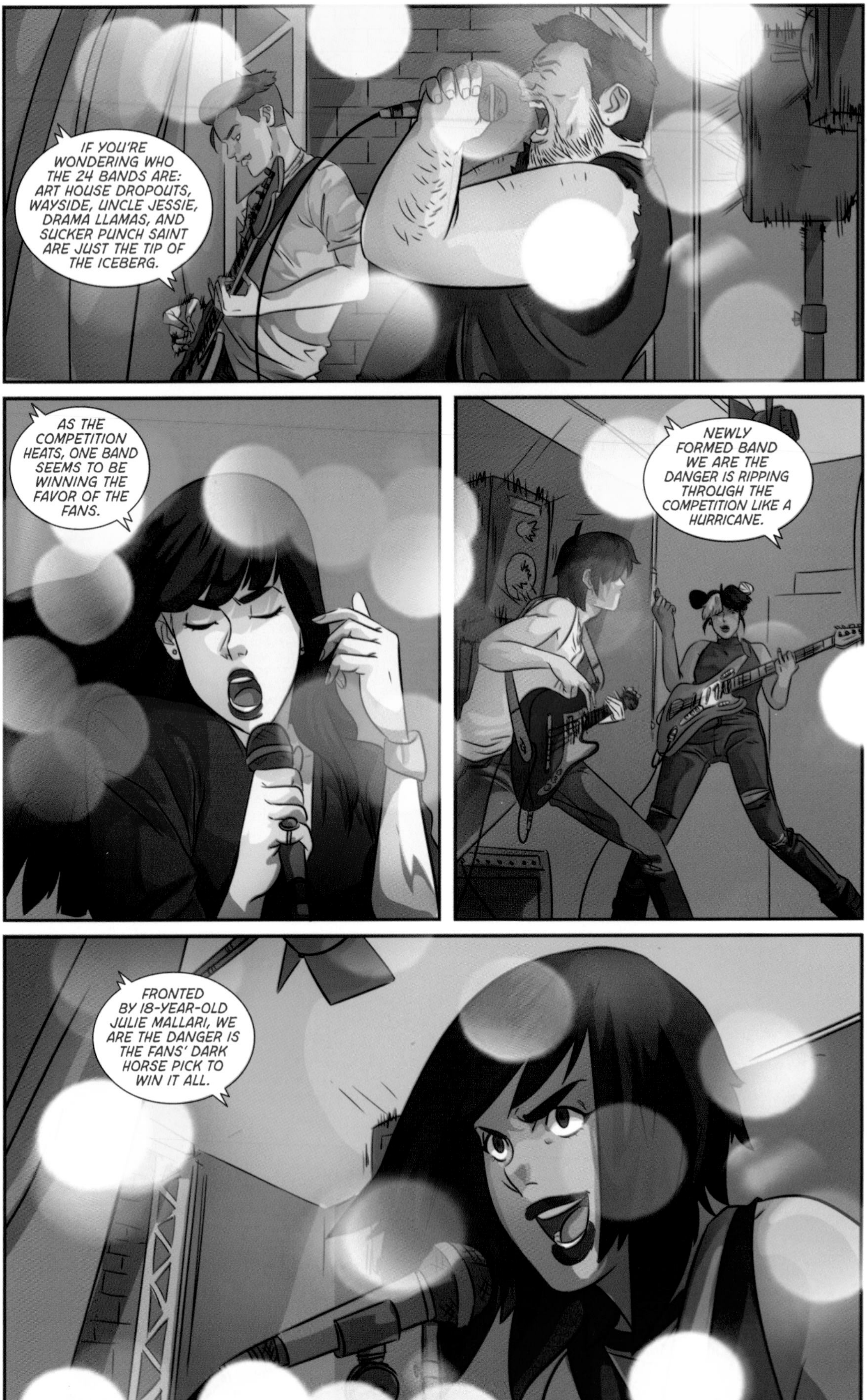
IF YOU'RE WONDERING WHO THE 24 BANDS ARE: ART HOUSE DROPOUTS, WAYSIDE, UNCLE JESSIE, DRAMA LLAMAS, AND SUCKER PUNCH SAINT ARE JUST THE TIP OF THE ICEBERG.
AS THE COMPETITION HEATS, ONE BAND SEEMS TO BE WINNING THE FAVOR OF THE FANS.
NEWLY FORMED BAND WE ARE THE DANGER IS RIPPING THROUGH THE COMPETITION LIKE A HURRICANE.
FRONTED BY 18-YEAR-OLD JULIE MALLARI, WE ARE THE DANGER IS THE FANS' DARK HORSE PICK TO WIN IT ALL.

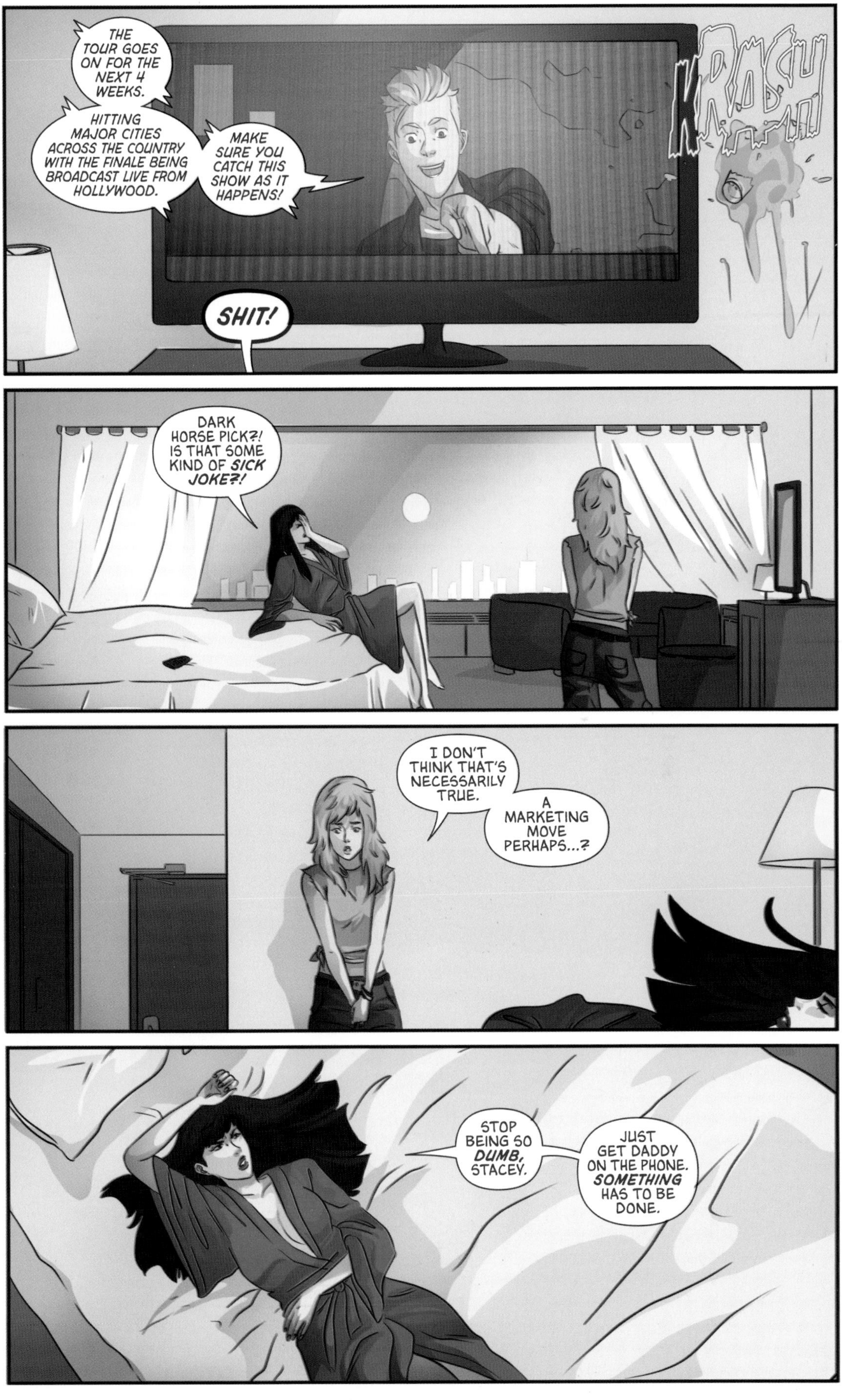
THE TOUR GOES ON FOR THE NEXT 4 WEEKS.
HITTING MAJOR CITIES ACROSS THE COUNTRY WITH THE FINALE BEING BROADCAST LIVE FROM HOLLYWOOD.
MAKE SURE YOU CATCH THIS SHOW AS IT HAPPENS!
KRASH
SHIT!
DARK HORSE PICK?! IS THAT SOME KIND OF SICK JOKE?!
I DON'T THINK THAT'S NECESSARILY TRUE.
A MARKETING MOVE PERHAPS...?
STOP BEING SO DUMB, STACEY.
JUST GET DADDY ON THE PHONE. SOMETHING HAS TO BE DONE.

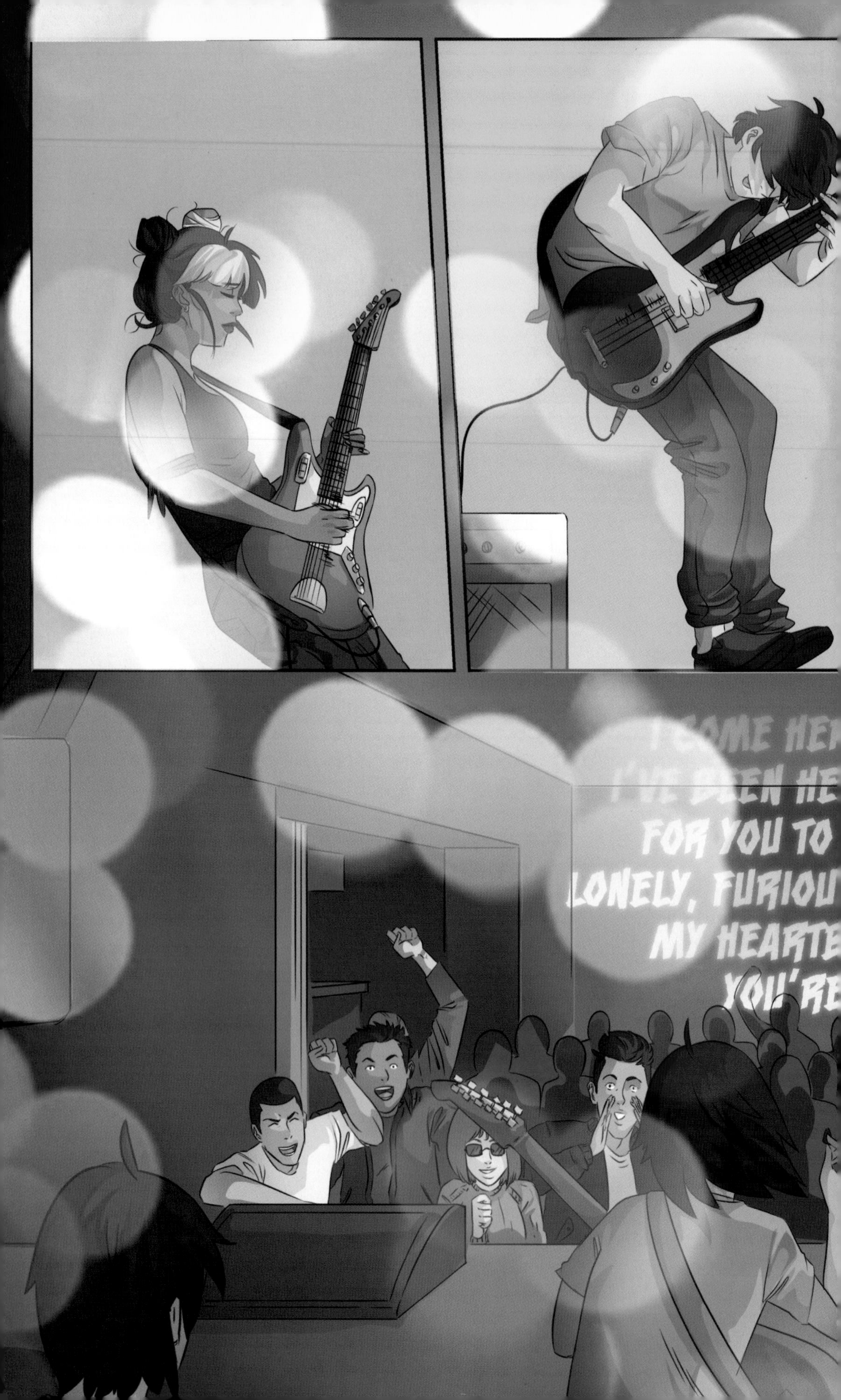
FOR YOU TO
LONELY, FURIOU
MY HEARTE
YOU'RE

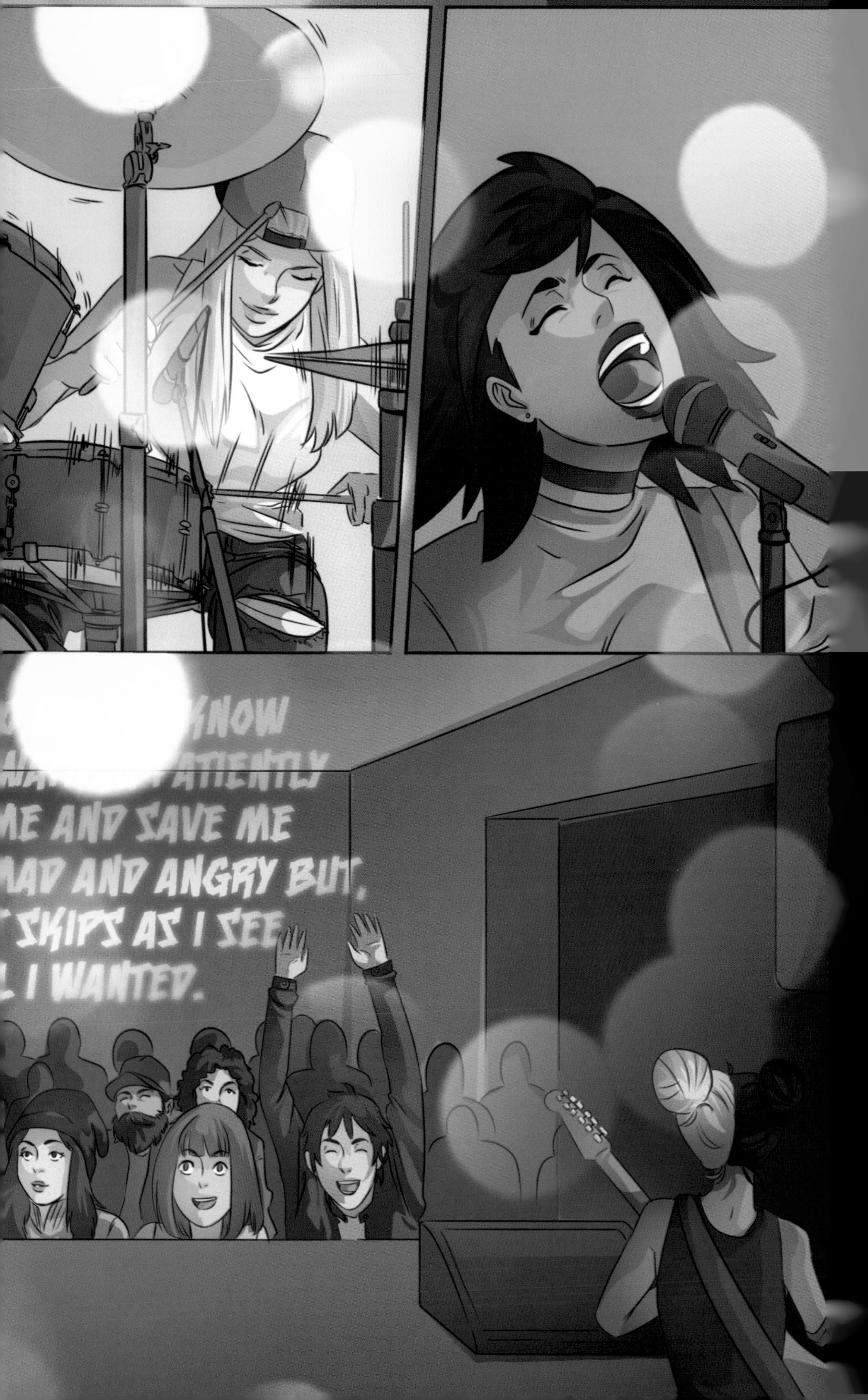
ME AND SAVE ME
MAD AND ANGRY BUT
SKIPS AS I SEE
I WANTED.

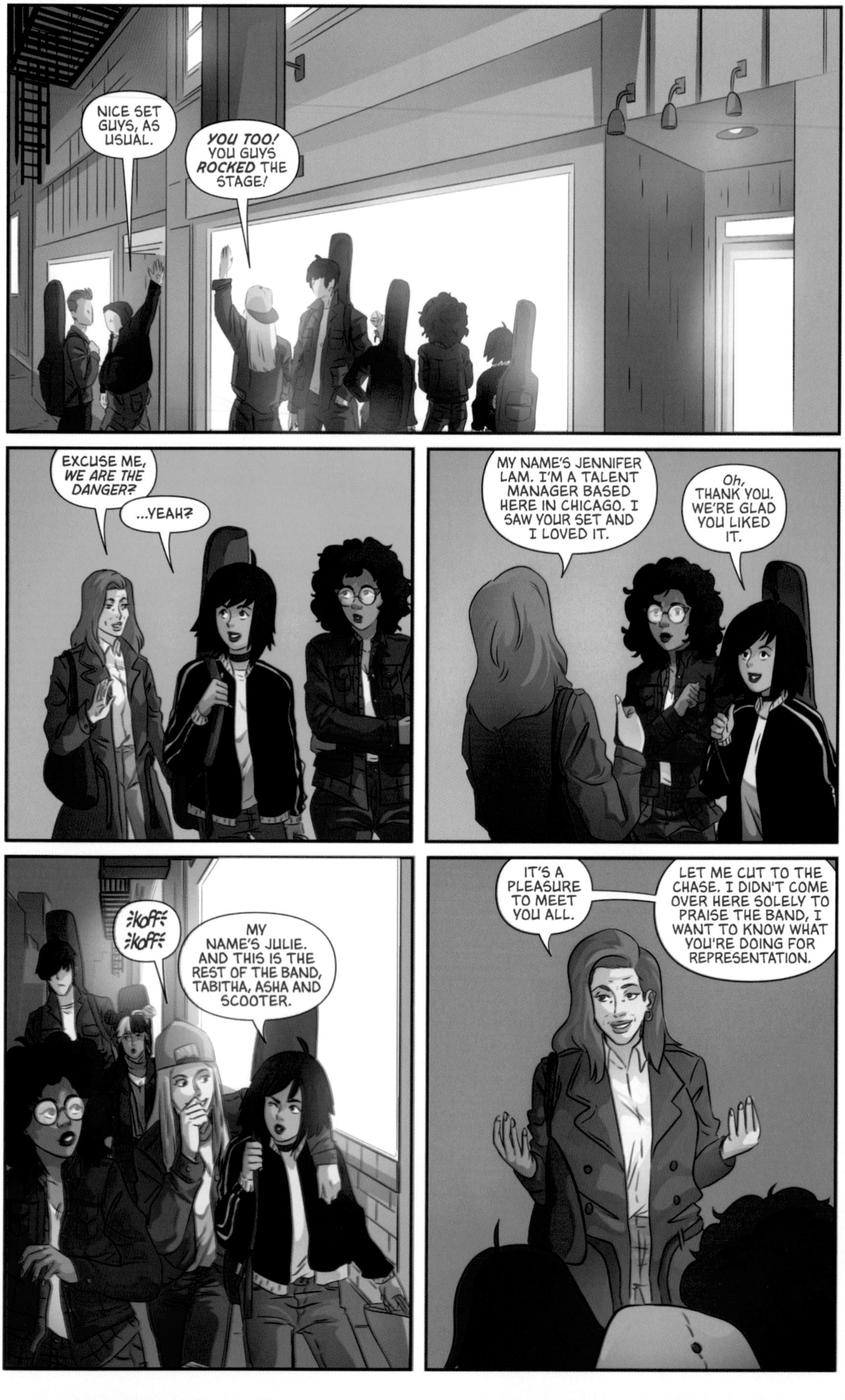
NICE SET GUYS, AS USUAL.
YOU TOO! YOU GUYS ROCKED THE STAGE!
EXCUSE ME, WE ARE THE DANGER?
...YEAH?
MY NAME'S JENNIFER LAM. I'M A TALENT MANAGER BASED HERE IN CHICAGO. I SAW YOUR SET AND I LOVED IT.
Oh, THANK YOU. WE'RE GLAD YOU LIKED IT.
*koff* *koff*
MY NAME'S JULIE. AND THIS IS THE REST OF THE BAND, TABITHA, ASHA AND SCOOTER.
IT'S A PLEASURE TO MEET YOU ALL.
LET ME CUT TO THE CHASE. I DIDN'T COME OVER HERE SOLELY TO PRAISE THE BAND, I WANT TO KNOW WHAT YOU'RE DOING FOR REPRESENTATION.

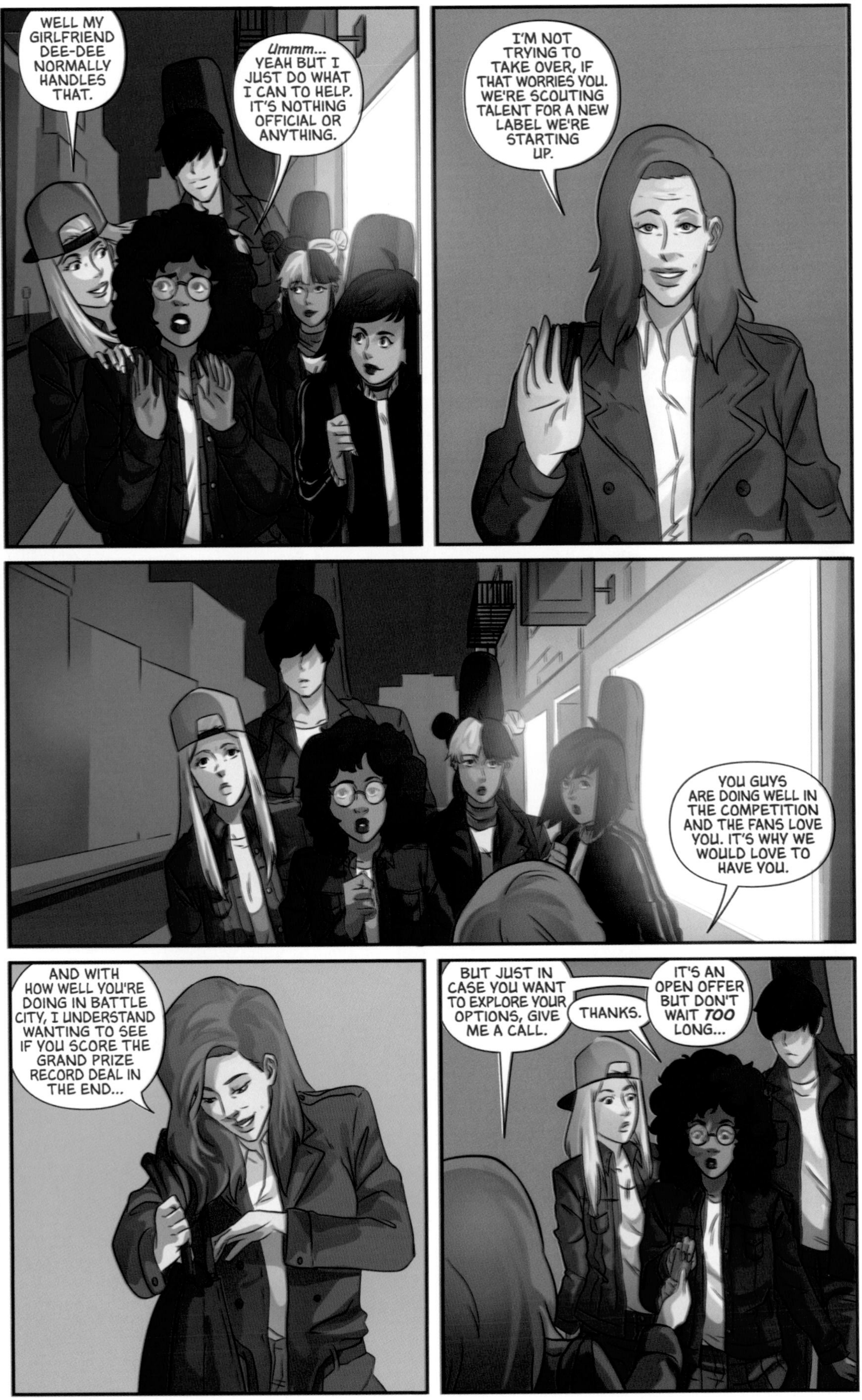
WELL MY GIRLFRIEND DEE-DEE NORMALLY HANDLES THAT.
*Ummm...* YEAH BUT I JUST DO WHAT I CAN TO HELP. IT'S NOTHING OFFICIAL OR ANYTHING.
I'M NOT TRYING TO TAKE OVER, IF THAT WORRIES YOU. WE'RE SCOUTING TALENT FOR A NEW LABEL WE'RE STARTING UP.
YOU GUYS ARE DOING WELL IN THE COMPETITION AND THE FANS LOVE YOU. IT'S WHY WE WOULD LOVE TO HAVE YOU.
AND WITH HOW WELL YOU'RE DOING IN BATTLE CITY, I UNDERSTAND WANTING TO SEE IF YOU SCORE THE GRAND PRIZE RECORD DEAL IN THE END...
BUT JUST IN CASE YOU WANT TO EXPLORE YOUR OPTIONS, GIVE ME A CALL.
THANKS.
IT'S AN OPEN OFFER BUT DON'T WAIT ***TOO*** LONG...

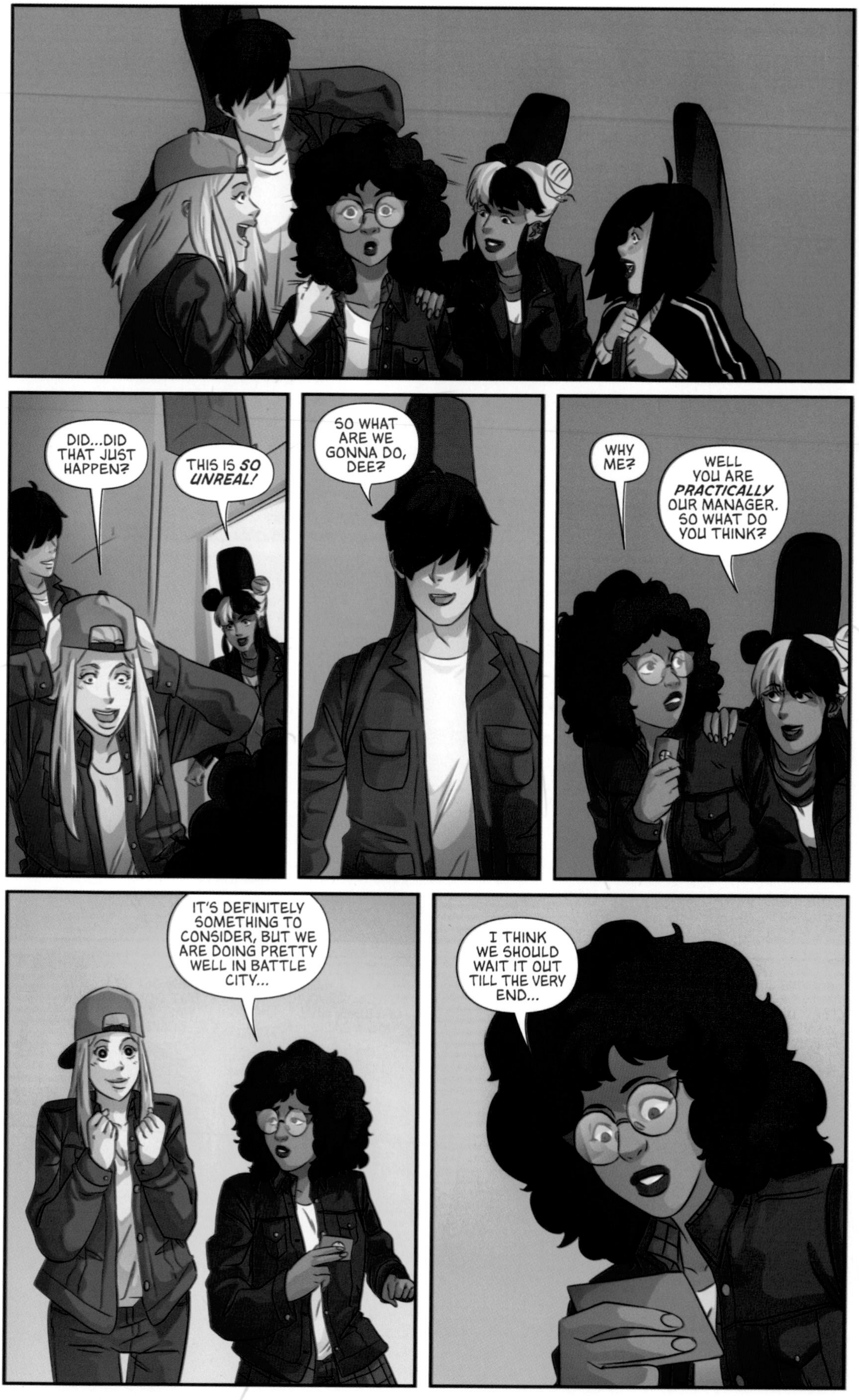
DID...DID THAT JUST HAPPEN?
THIS IS SO UNREAL!
SO WHAT ARE WE GONNA DO, DEE?
WHY ME?
WELL YOU ARE PRACTICALLY OUR MANAGER. SO WHAT DO YOU THINK?
IT'S DEFINITELY SOMETHING TO CONSIDER, BUT WE ARE DOING PRETTY WELL IN BATTLE CITY...
I THINK WE SHOULD WAIT IT OUT TILL THE VERY END...

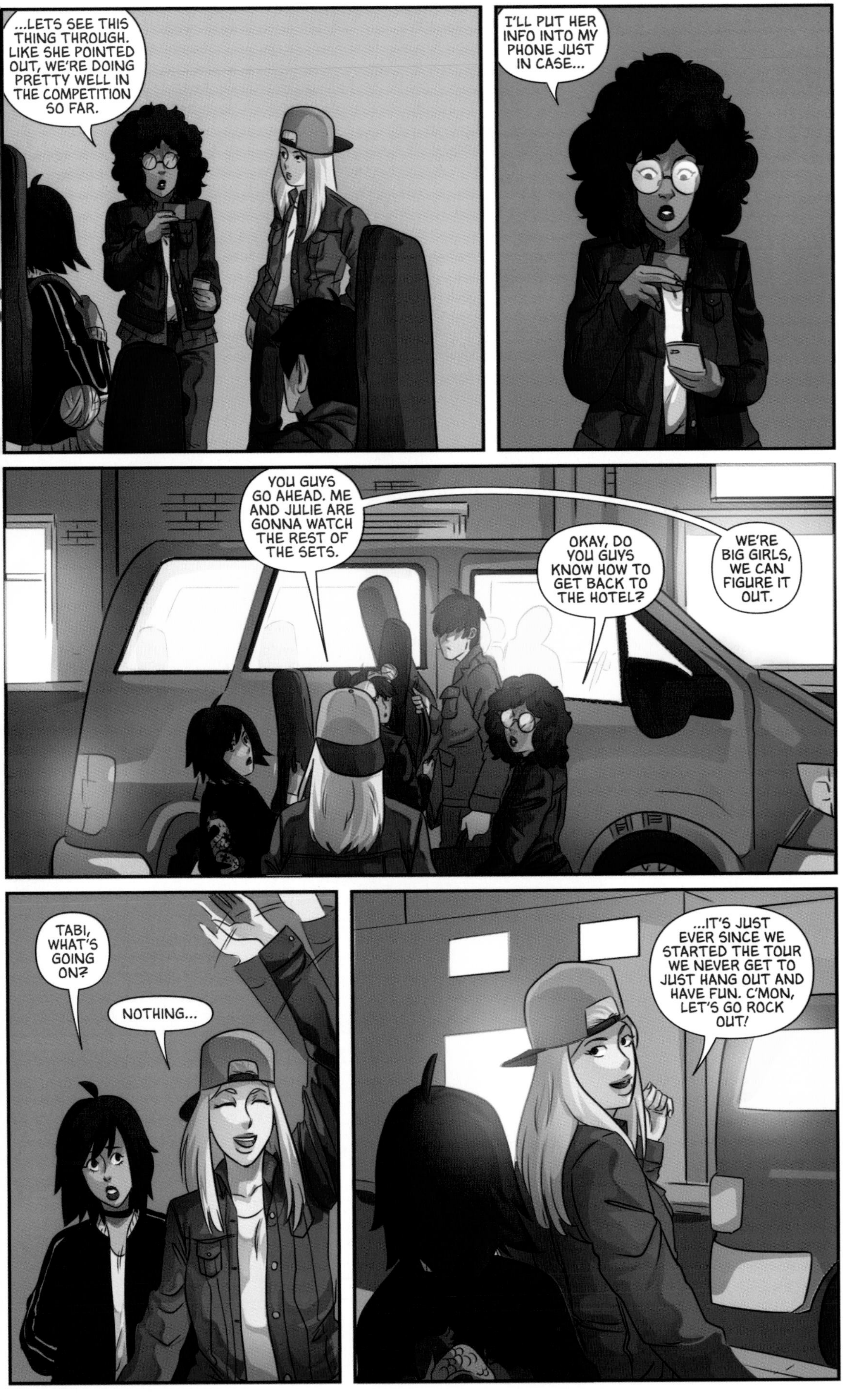
...LETS SEE THIS THING THROUGH. LIKE SHE POINTED OUT, WE'RE DOING PRETTY WELL IN THE COMPETITION SO FAR.
I'LL PUT HER INFO INTO MY PHONE JUST IN CASE...
YOU GUYS GO AHEAD. ME AND JULIE ARE GONNA WATCH THE REST OF THE SETS.
OKAY, DO YOU GUYS KNOW HOW TO GET BACK TO THE HOTEL?
WE'RE BIG GIRLS, WE CAN FIGURE IT OUT.
TABI, WHAT'S GOING ON?
NOTHING...
...IT'S JUST EVER SINCE WE STARTED THE TOUR WE NEVER GET TO JUST HANG OUT AND HAVE FUN. C'MON, LET'S GO ROCK OUT!

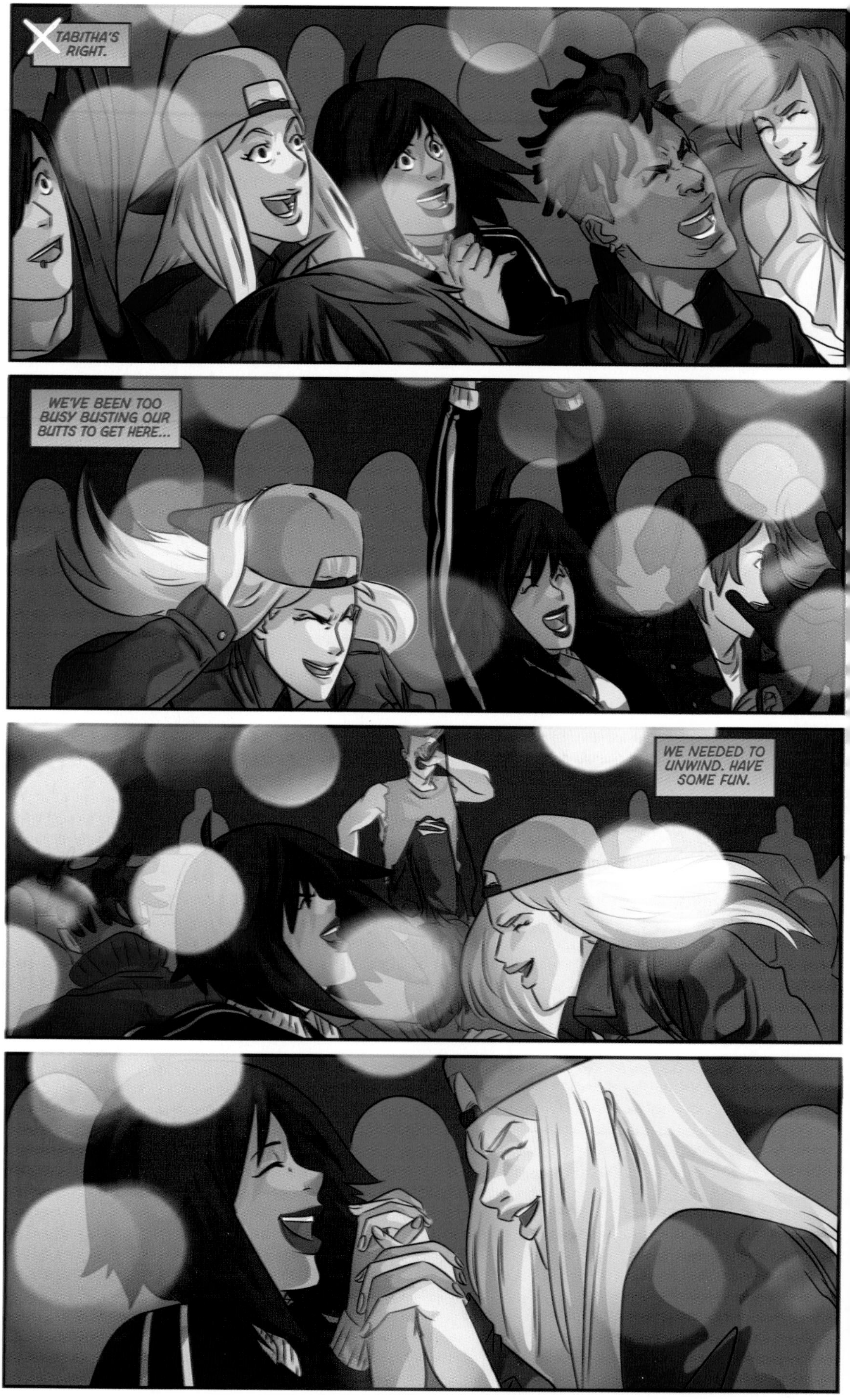
TABITHA'S RIGHT.
WE'VE BEEN TOO BUSY BUSTING OUR BUTTS TO GET HERE...
WE NEEDED TO UNWIND. HAVE SOME FUN.

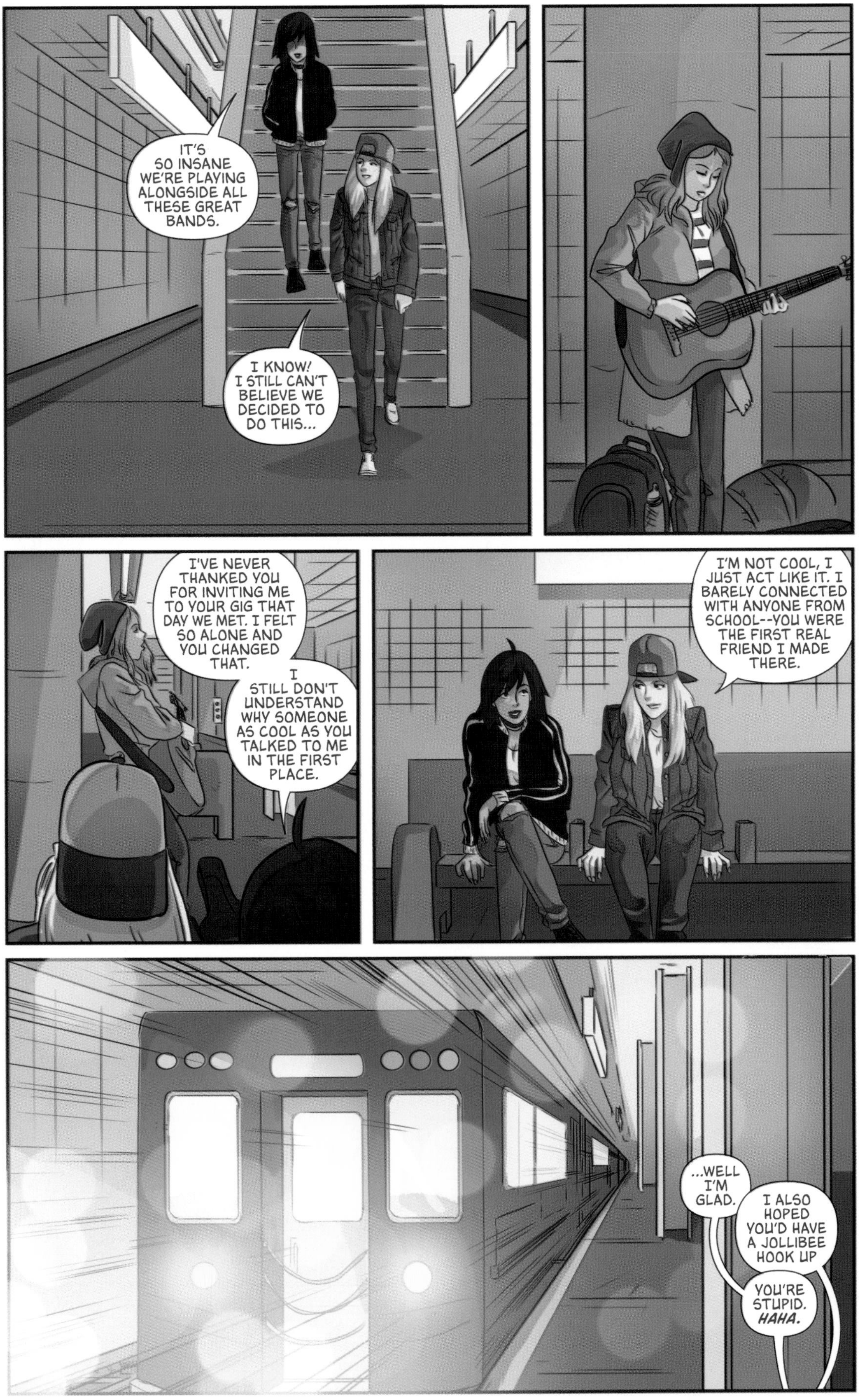
IT'S SO INSANE WE'RE PLAYING ALONGSIDE ALL THESE GREAT BANDS.
I KNOW! I STILL CAN'T BELIEVE WE DECIDED TO DO THIS...
I'VE NEVER THANKED YOU FOR INVITING ME TO YOUR GIG THAT DAY WE MET. I FELT SO ALONE AND YOU CHANGED THAT.
I STILL DON'T UNDERSTAND WHY SOMEONE AS COOL AS YOU TALKED TO ME IN THE FIRST PLACE.
I'M NOT COOL, I JUST ACT LIKE IT. I BARELY CONNECTED WITH ANYONE FROM SCHOOL--YOU WERE THE FIRST REAL FRIEND I MADE THERE.
...WELL I'M GLAD.
I ALSO HOPED YOU'D HAVE A JOLLIBEE HOOK UP
YOU'RE STUPID. HAHA.

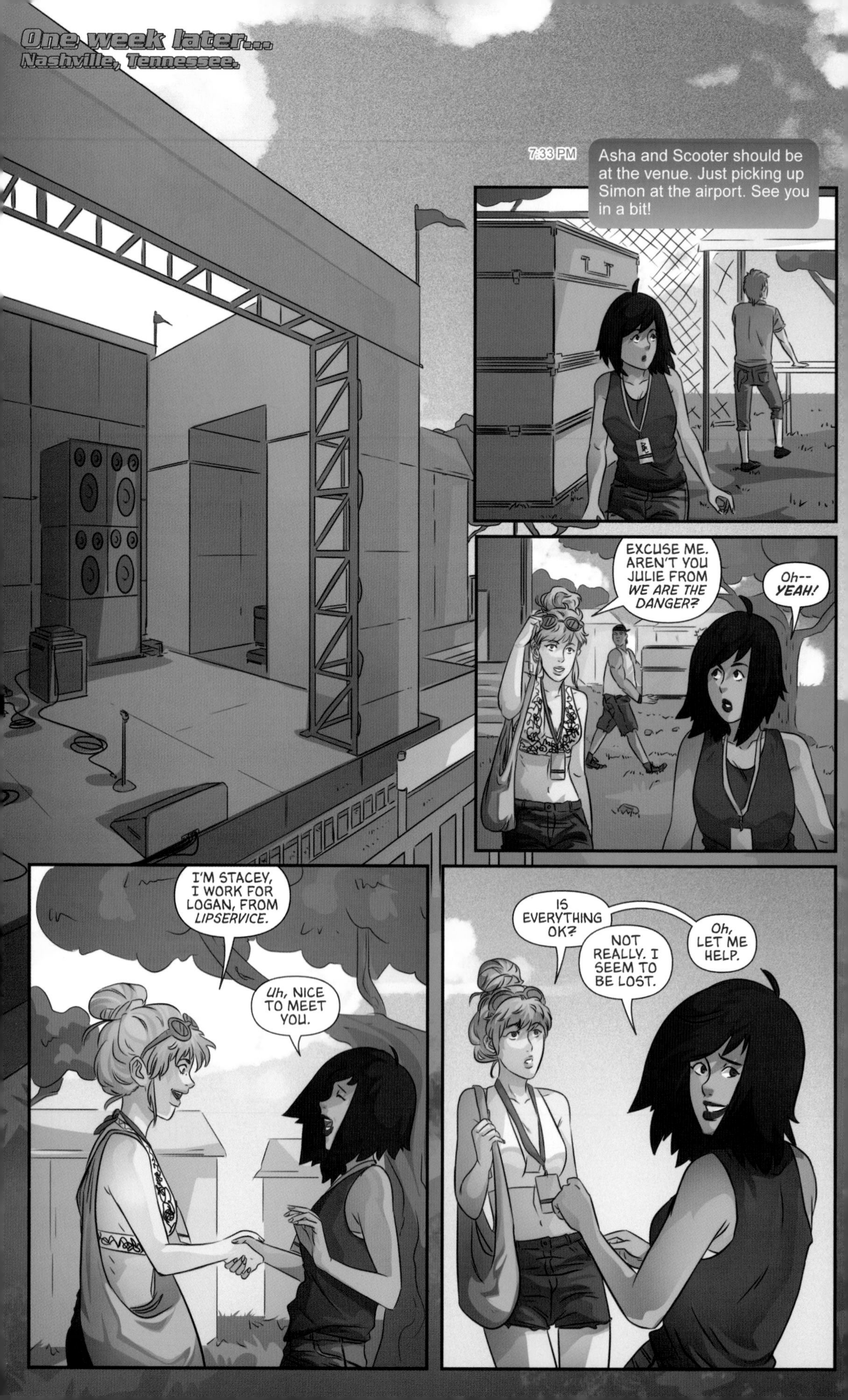
One week later...
Nashville, Tennessee.
7:33 PM
Asha and Scooter should be at the venue. Just picking up Simon at the airport. See you in a bit!
EXCUSE ME. AREN'T YOU JULIE FROM *WE ARE THE DANGER?*
*Oh--* ***YEAH!***
I'M STACEY, I WORK FOR LOGAN, FROM *LIPSERVICE.*
*Uh,* NICE TO MEET YOU.
IS EVERYTHING OK?
NOT REALLY. I SEEM TO BE LOST.
Oh, LET ME HELP.

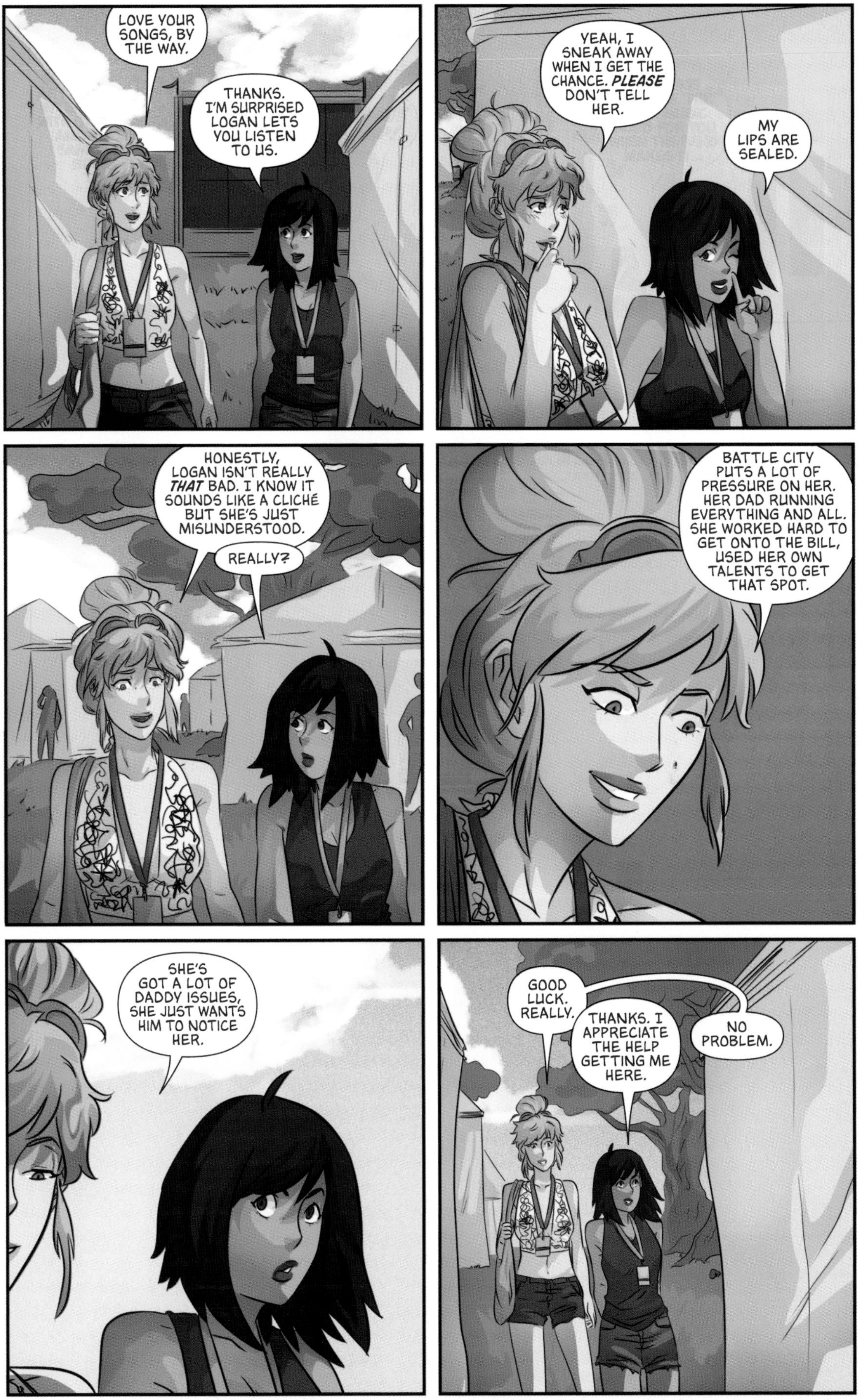
LOVE YOUR SONGS, BY THE WAY.
THANKS. I'M SURPRISED LOGAN LETS YOU LISTEN TO US.
YEAH, I SNEAK AWAY WHEN I GET THE CHANCE. *PLEASE* DON'T TELL HER.
MY LIPS ARE SEALED.
HONESTLY, LOGAN ISN'T REALLY *THAT* BAD. I KNOW IT SOUNDS LIKE A CLICHÉ BUT SHE'S JUST MISUNDERSTOOD.
REALLY?
BATTLE CITY PUTS A LOT OF PRESSURE ON HER. HER DAD RUNNING EVERYTHING AND ALL. SHE WORKED HARD TO GET ONTO THE BILL, USED HER OWN TALENTS TO GET THAT SPOT.
SHE'S GOT A LOT OF DADDY ISSUES, SHE JUST WANTS HIM TO NOTICE HER.
GOOD LUCK. REALLY.
THANKS. I APPRECIATE THE HELP GETTING ME HERE.
NO PROBLEM.

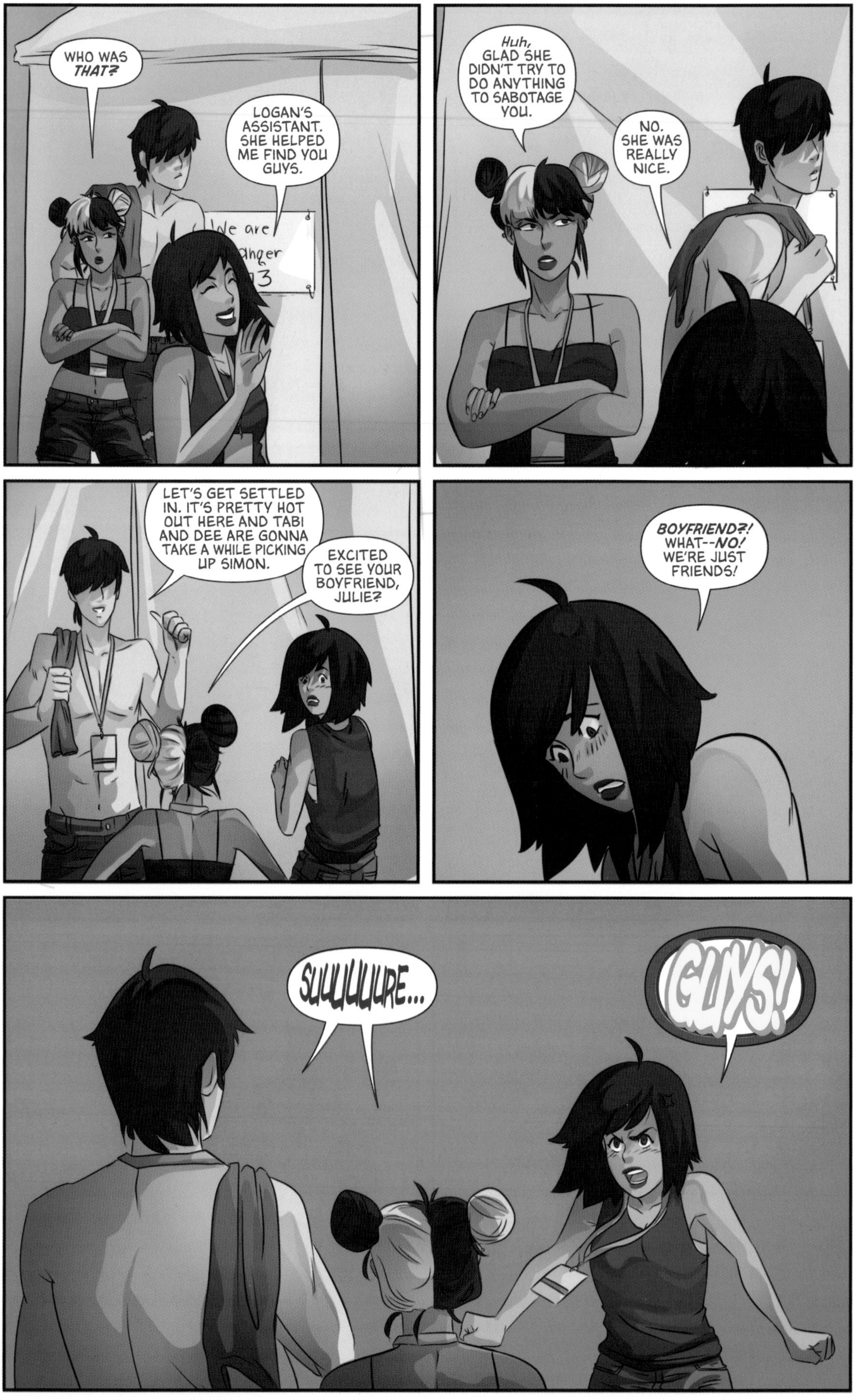
WHO WAS *THAT?*
LOGAN'S ASSISTANT. SHE HELPED ME FIND YOU GUYS.
We are
*Huh,* GLAD SHE DIDN'T TRY TO DO ANYTHING TO SABOTAGE YOU.
NO. SHE WAS REALLY NICE.
LET'S GET SETTLED IN. IT'S PRETTY HOT OUT HERE AND TABI AND DEE ARE GONNA TAKE A WHILE PICKING UP SIMON.
EXCITED TO SEE YOUR BOYFRIEND, JULIE?
*BOYFRIEND?!* WHAT--*NO!* WE'RE JUST FRIENDS!
SUUUUUURE...
GUYS!

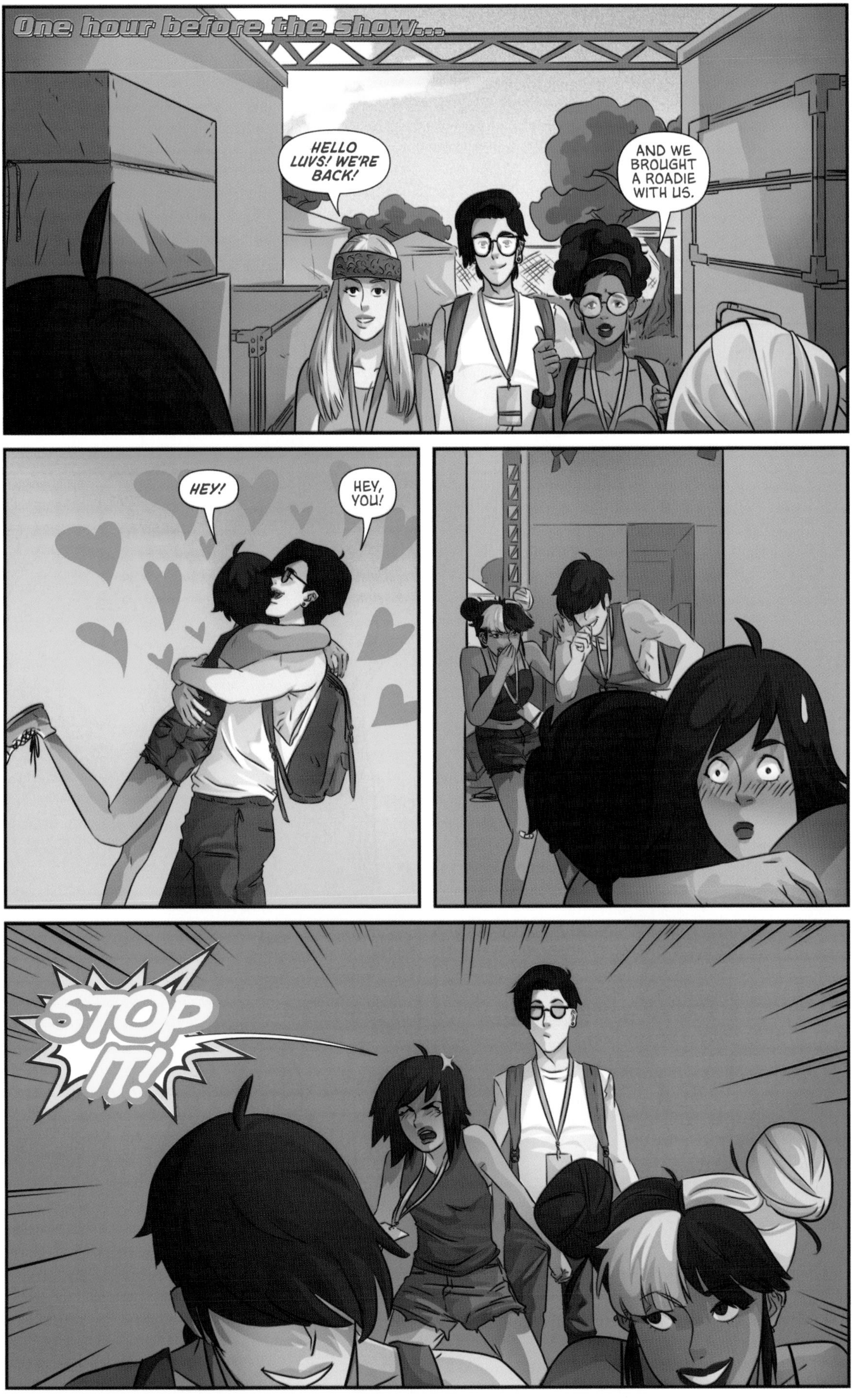
One hour before the show...
HELLO LUVS! WE'RE BACK!
AND WE BROUGHT A ROADIE WITH US.
HEY!
HEY, YOU!
STOP IT!

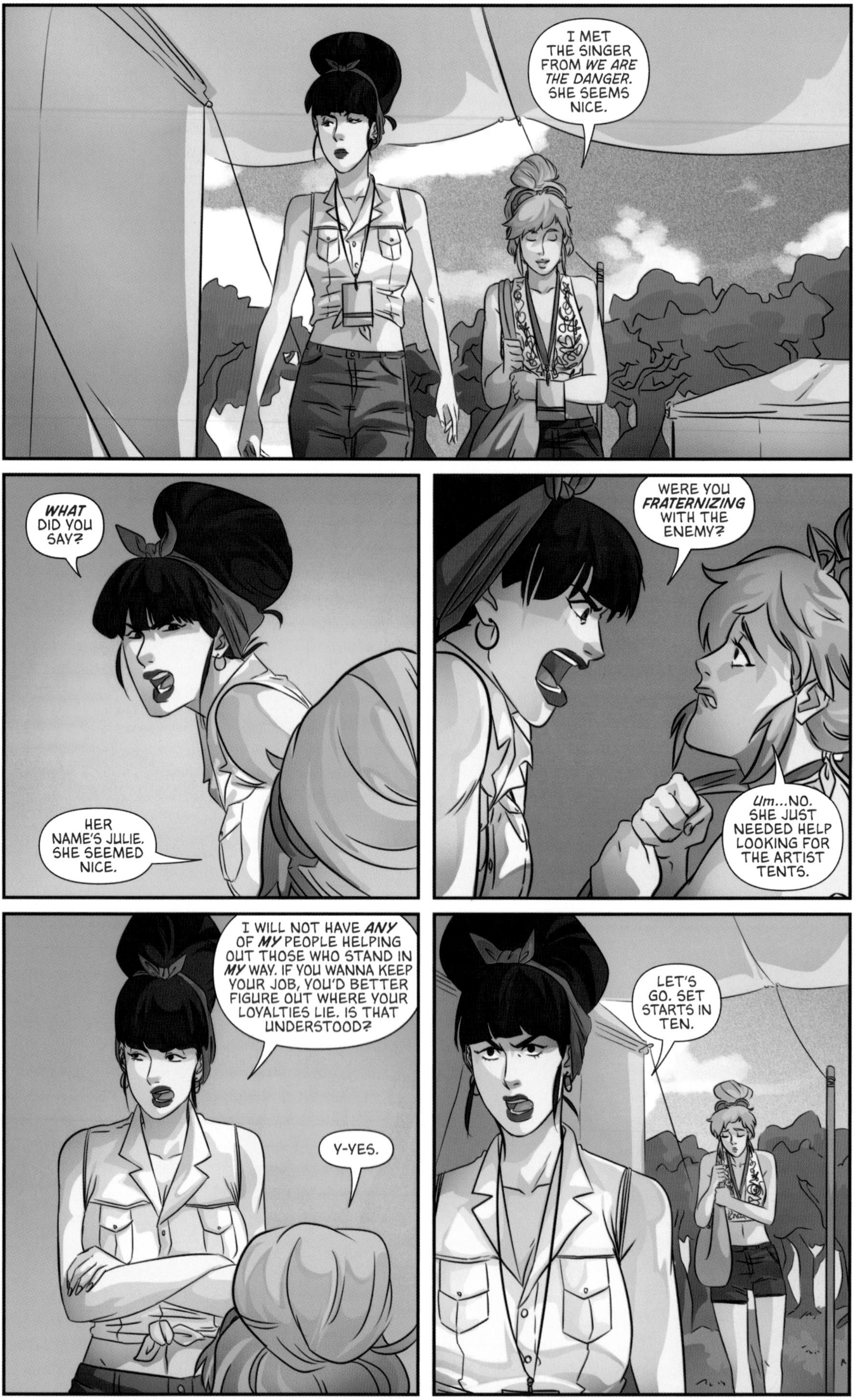
I MET THE SINGER FROM WE ARE THE DANGER. SHE SEEMS NICE.
WHAT DID YOU SAY?
HER NAME'S JULIE. SHE SEEMED NICE.
WERE YOU FRATERNIZING WITH THE ENEMY?
Um...NO. SHE JUST NEEDED HELP LOOKING FOR THE ARTIST TENTS.
I WILL NOT HAVE ANY OF MY PEOPLE HELPING OUT THOSE WHO STAND IN MY WAY. IF YOU WANNA KEEP YOUR JOB, YOU'D BETTER FIGURE OUT WHERE YOUR LOYALTIES LIE. IS THAT UNDERSTOOD?
Y-YES.
LET'S GO. SET STARTS IN TEN.

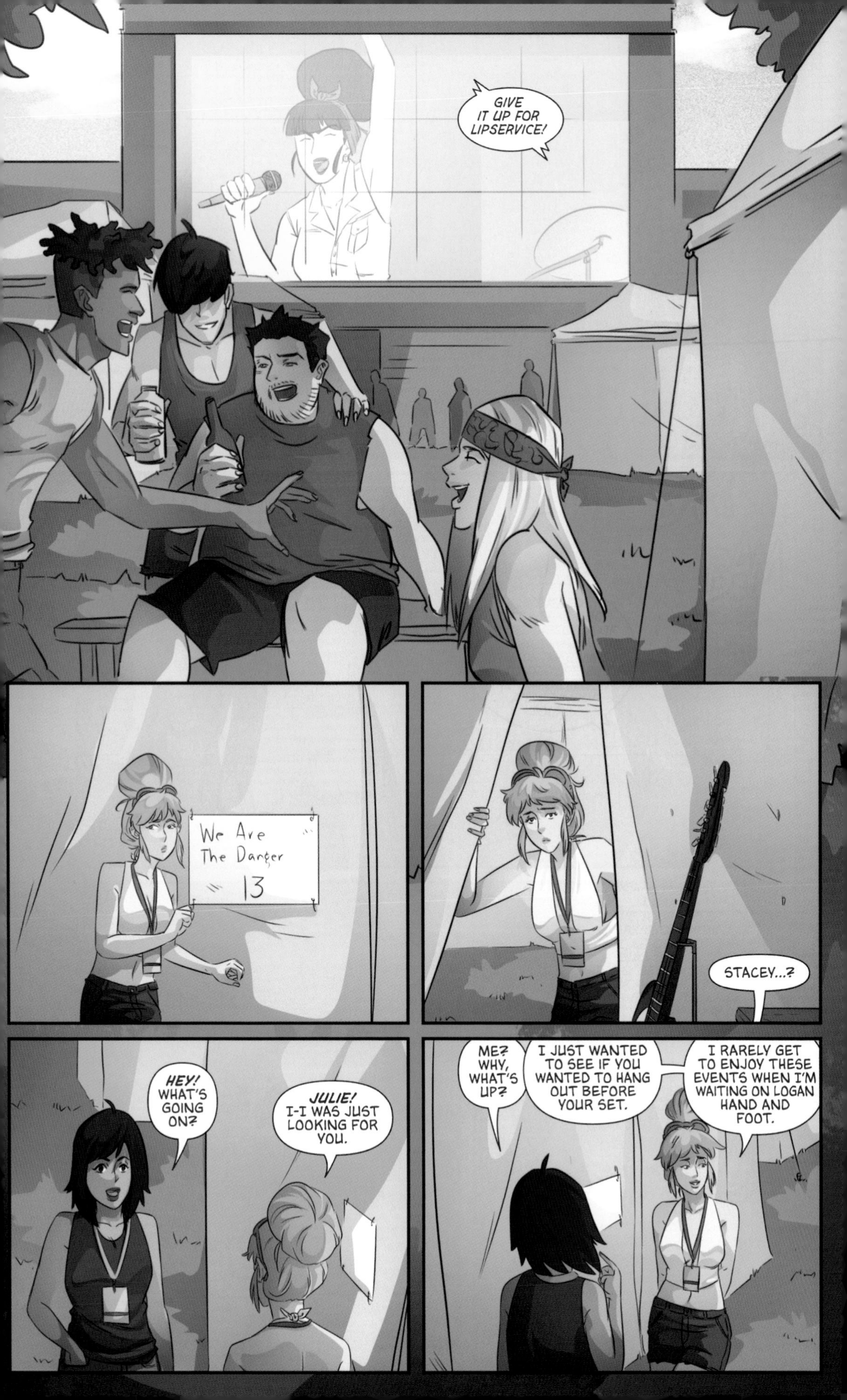
GIVE IT UP FOR LIPSERVICE!
We Are The Danger 13
STACEY...?
HEY! WHAT'S GOING ON?
JULIE! I-I WAS JUST LOOKING FOR YOU.
ME? WHY, WHAT'S UP?
I JUST WANTED TO SEE IF YOU WANTED TO HANG OUT BEFORE YOUR SET.
I RARELY GET TO ENJOY THESE EVENTS WHEN I'M WAITING ON LOGAN HAND AND FOOT.

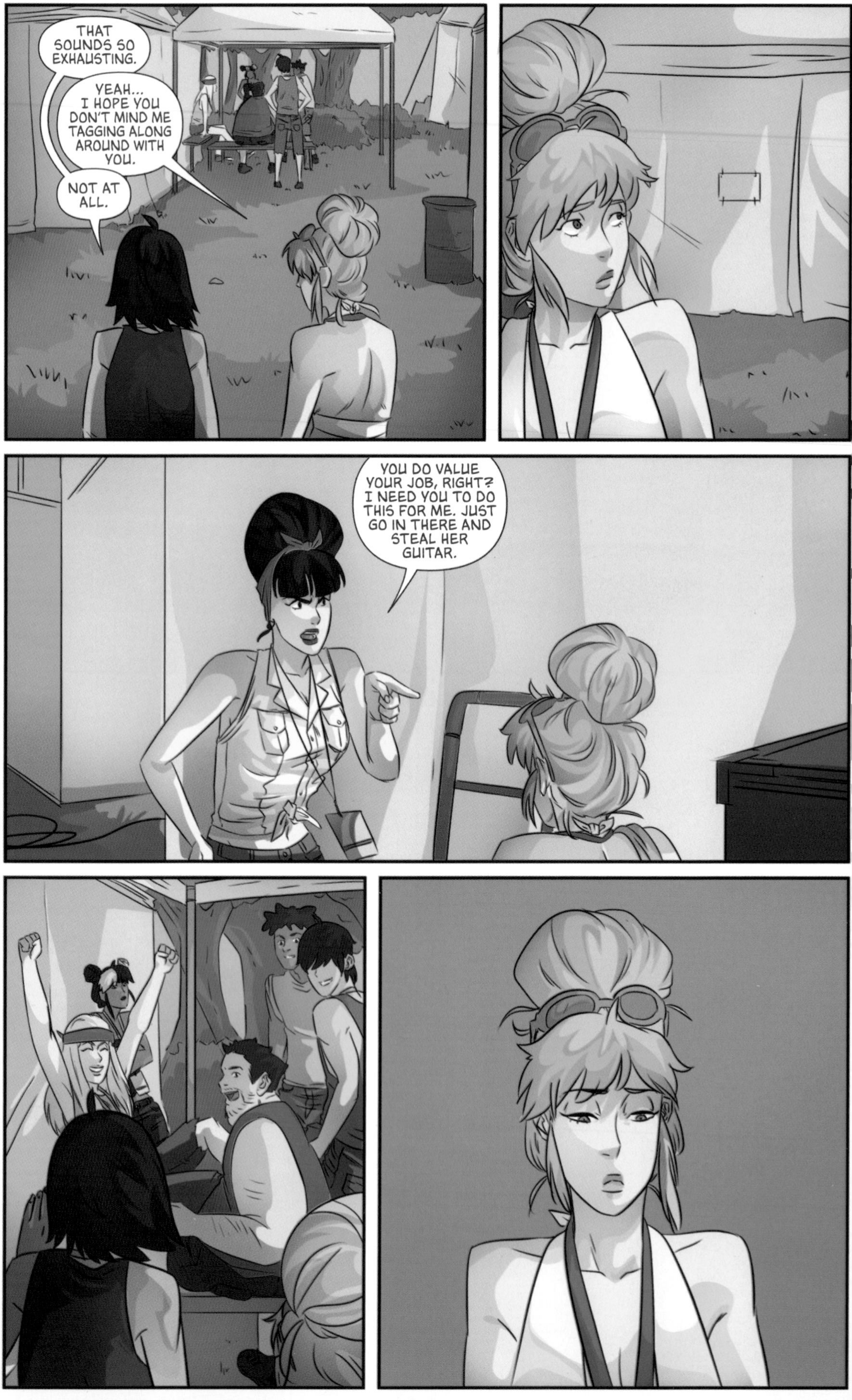
THAT SOUNDS SO EXHAUSTING.
YEAH... I HOPE YOU DON'T MIND ME TAGGING ALONG AROUND WITH YOU.
NOT AT ALL.
YOU DO VALUE YOUR JOB, RIGHT? I NEED YOU TO DO THIS FOR ME. JUST GO IN THERE AND STEAL HER GUITAR.

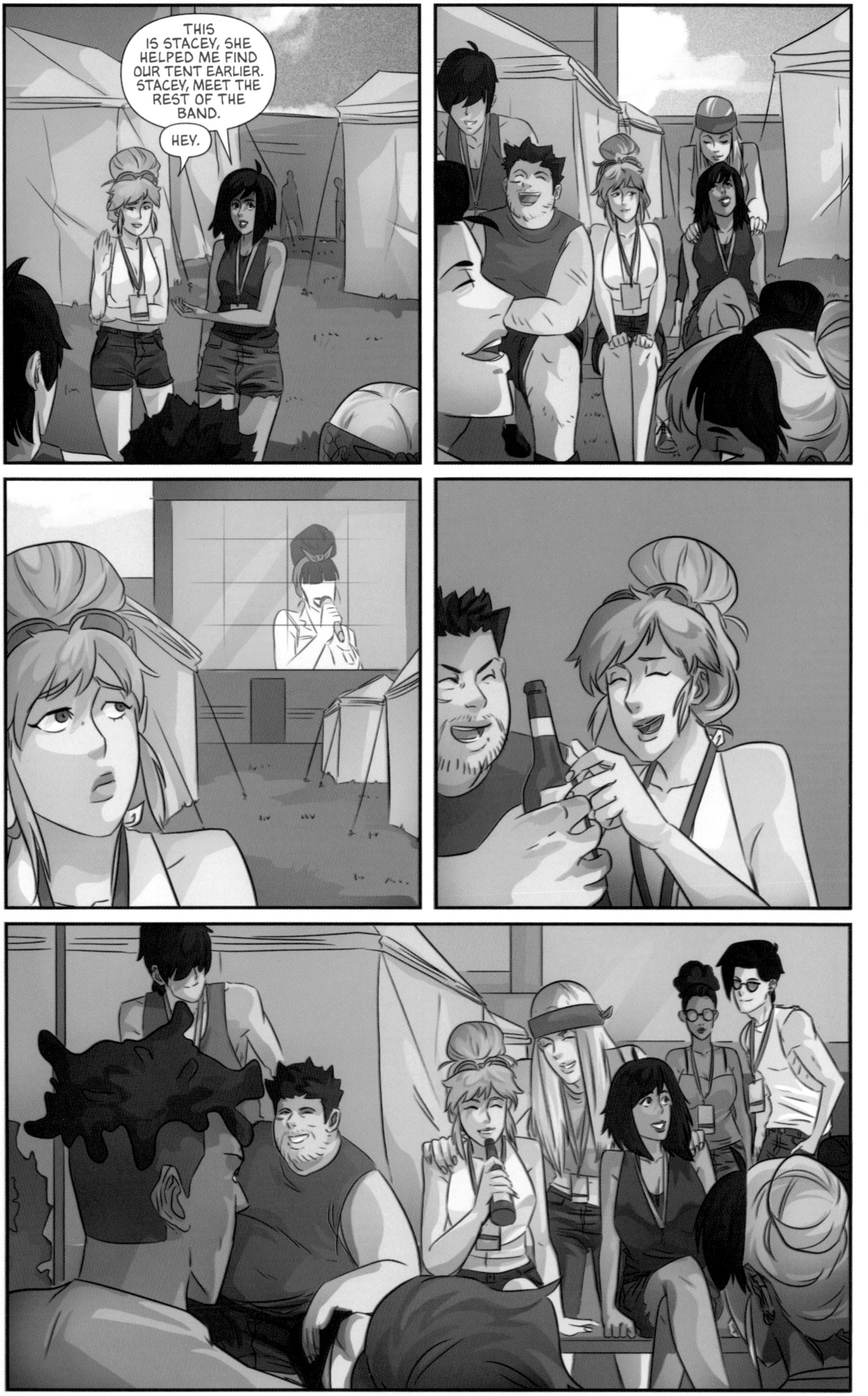
THIS IS STACEY, SHE HELPED ME FIND OUR TENT EARLIER. STACEY, MEET THE REST OF THE BAND.
HEY.

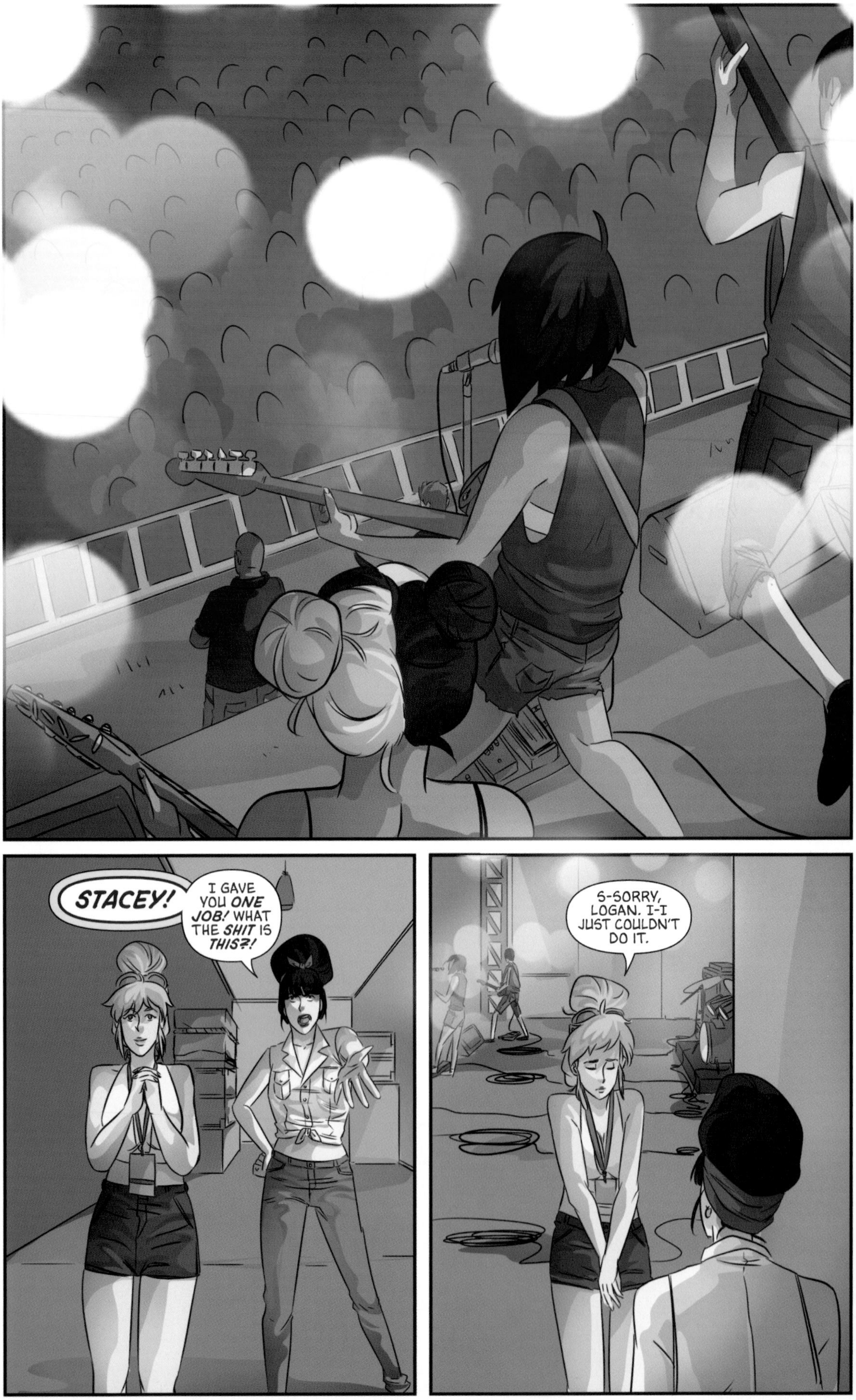
STACEY!
I GAVE YOU ONE JOB! WHAT THE SHIT IS THIS?!
S-SORRY, LOGAN. I-I JUST COULDN'T DO IT.

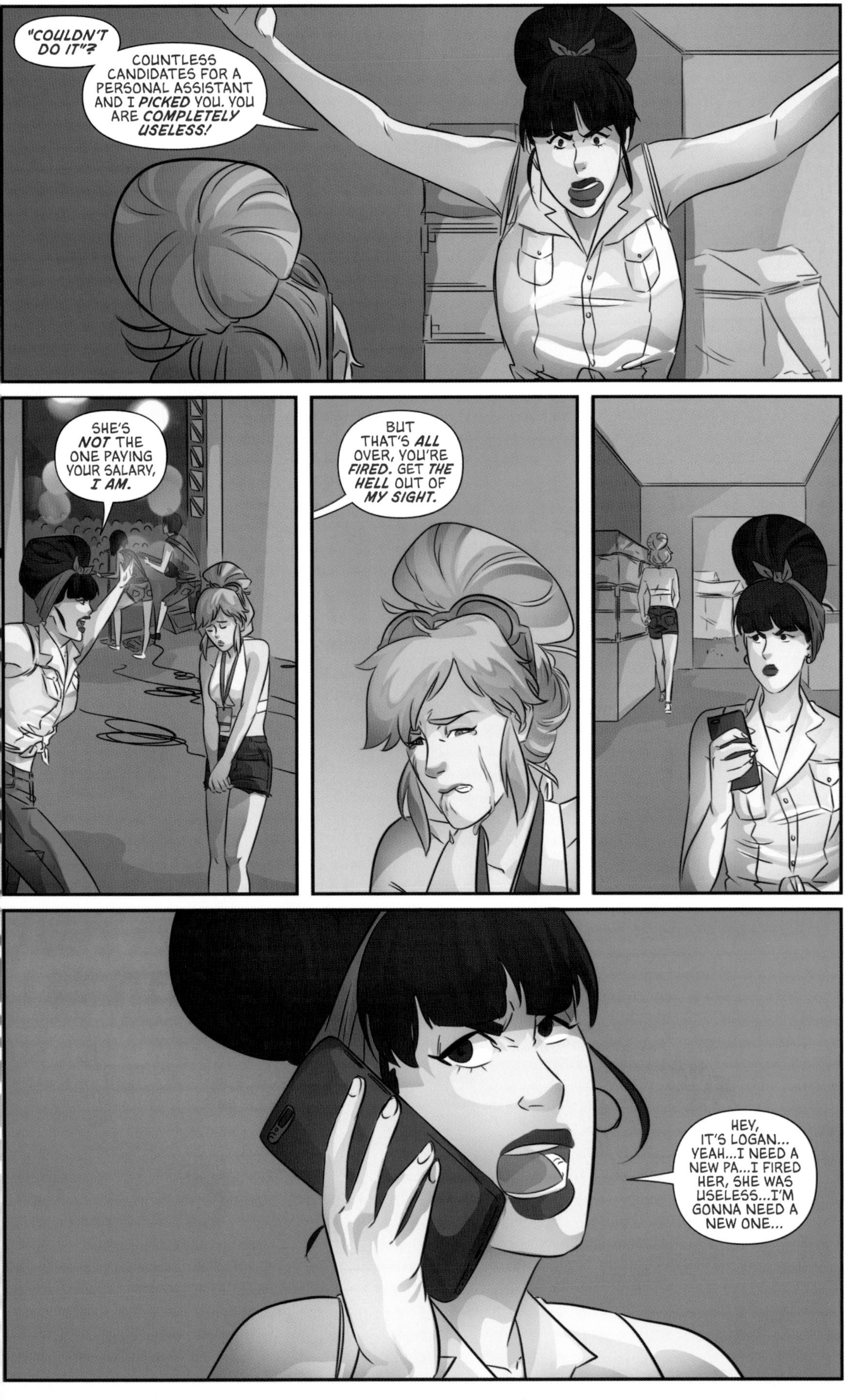
"COULDN'T DO IT"?
COUNTLESS CANDIDATES FOR A PERSONAL ASSISTANT AND I *PICKED* YOU. YOU ARE *COMPLETELY USELESS!*
SHE'S *NOT* THE ONE PAYING YOUR SALARY, *I AM.*
BUT THAT'S *ALL* OVER, YOU'RE *FIRED.* GET *THE HELL* OUT OF *MY SIGHT.*
HEY, IT'S LOGAN... YEAH...I NEED A NEW PA...I FIRED HER, SHE WAS USELESS...I'M GONNA NEED A NEW ONE...

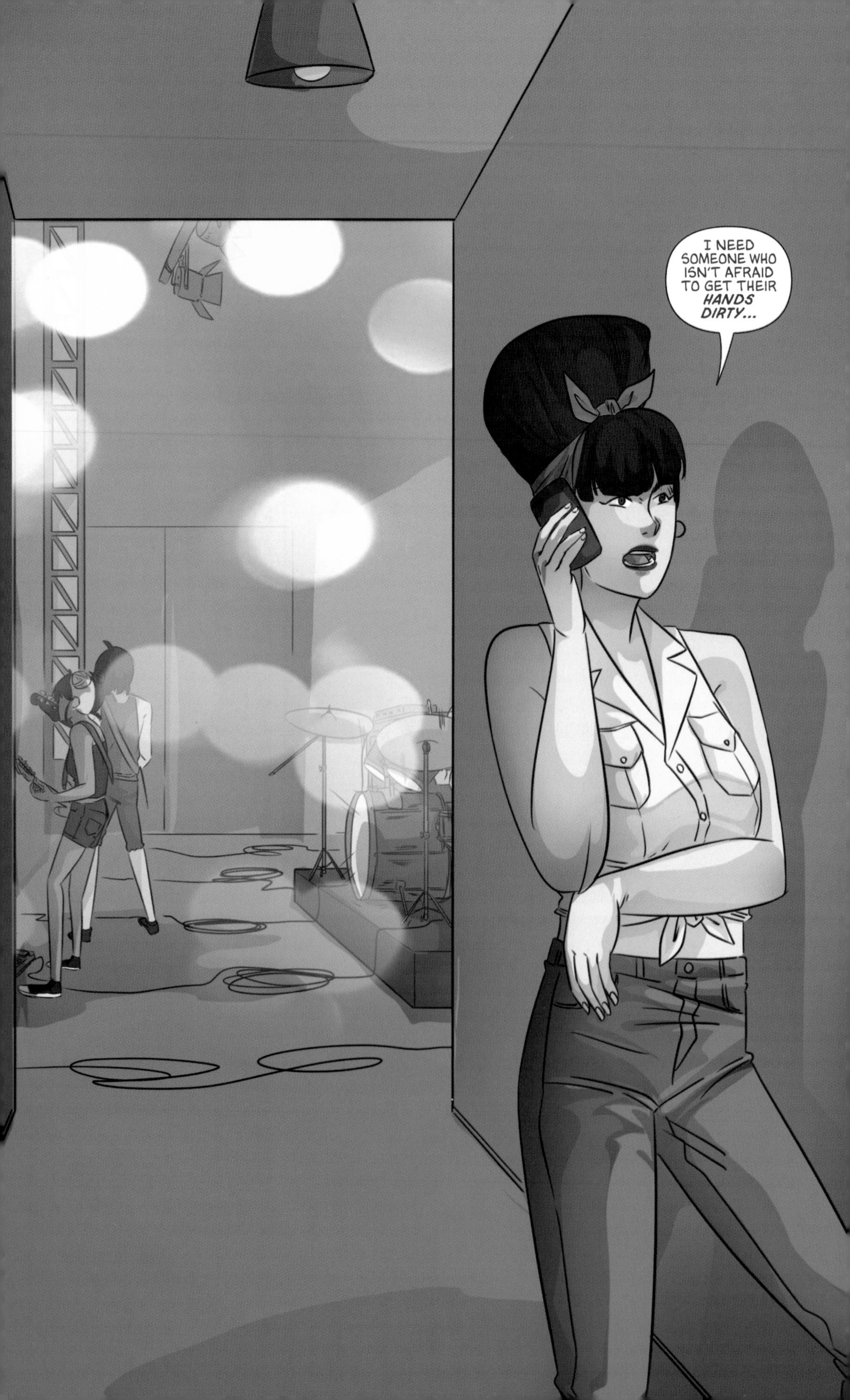
I NEED SOMEONE WHO ISN'T AFRAID TO GET THEIR ***HANDS DIRTY...***

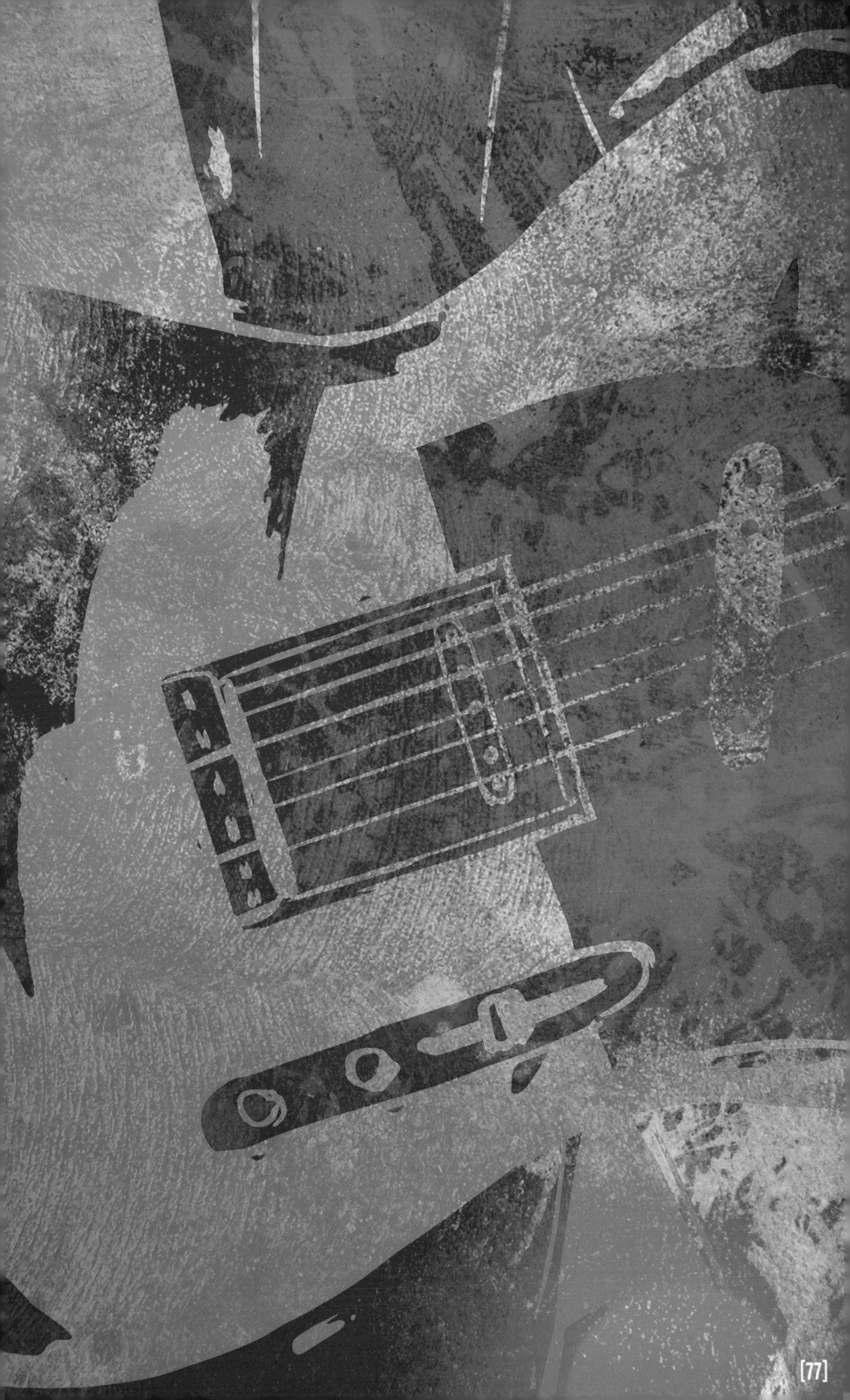

# ISSUE 4

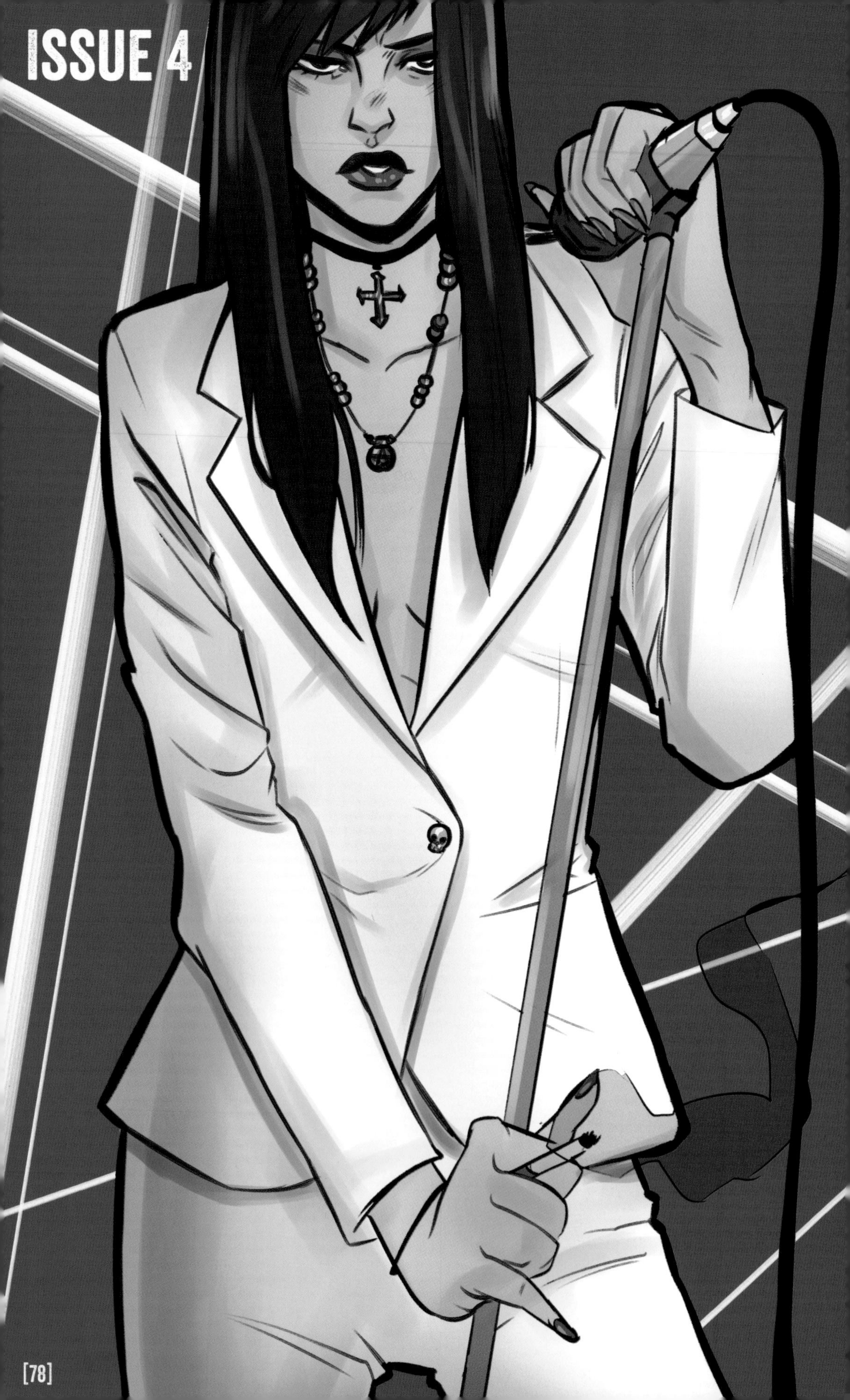

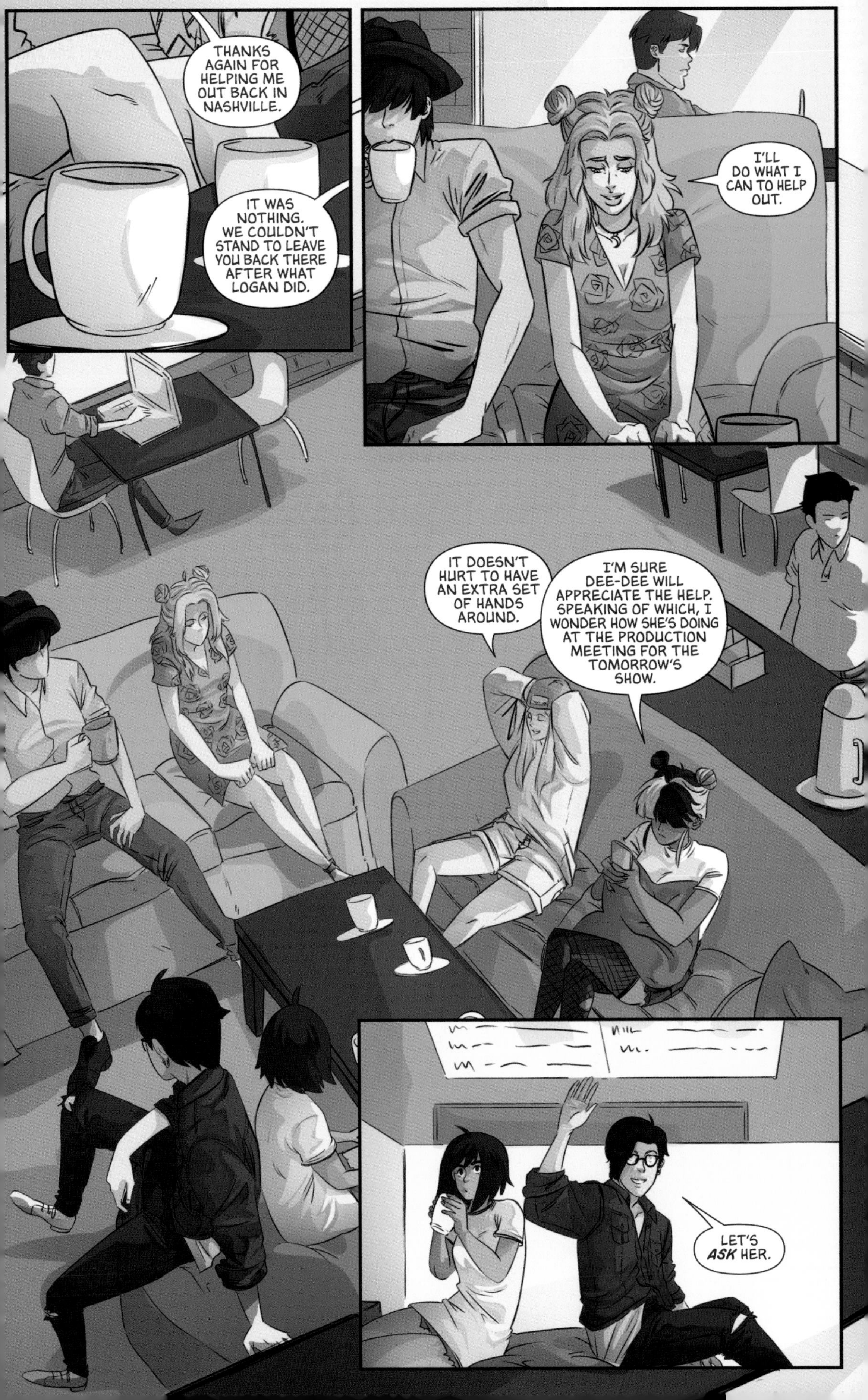
THANKS AGAIN FOR HELPING ME OUT BACK IN NASHVILLE.
IT WAS NOTHING. WE COULDN'T STAND TO LEAVE YOU BACK THERE AFTER WHAT LOGAN DID.
I'LL DO WHAT I CAN TO HELP OUT.
IT DOESN'T HURT TO HAVE AN EXTRA SET OF HANDS AROUND.
I'M SURE DEE-DEE WILL APPRECIATE THE HELP. SPEAKING OF WHICH, I WONDER HOW SHE'S DOING AT THE PRODUCTION MEETING FOR THE TOMORROW'S SHOW.
LET'S *ASK* HER.

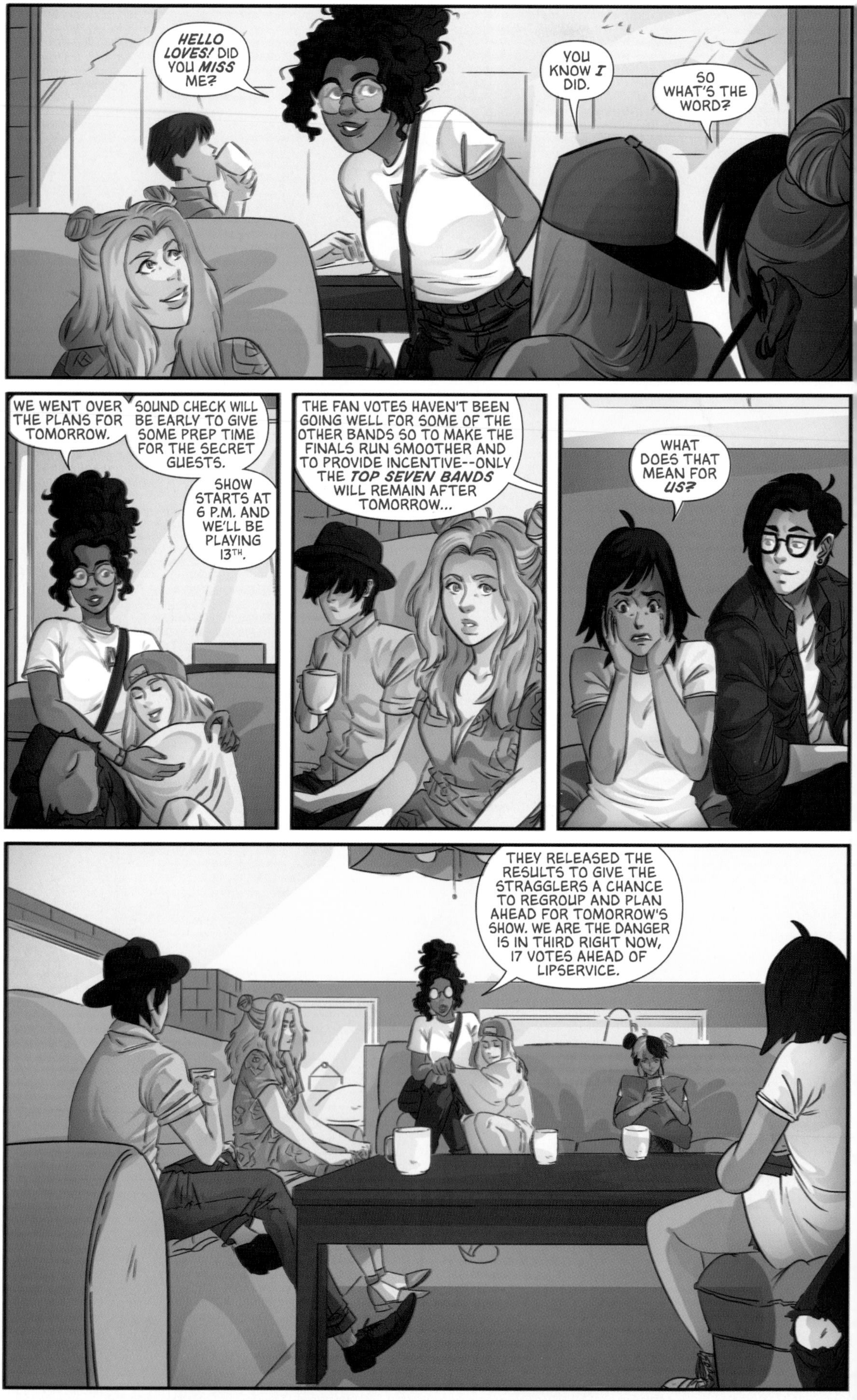
HELLO LOVES! DID YOU MISS ME?
YOU KNOW I DID.
SO WHAT'S THE WORD?
WE WENT OVER THE PLANS FOR TOMORROW.
SOUND CHECK WILL BE EARLY TO GIVE SOME PREP TIME FOR THE SECRET GUESTS.
SHOW STARTS AT 6 P.M. AND WE'LL BE PLAYING 13TH.
THE FAN VOTES HAVEN'T BEEN GOING WELL FOR SOME OF THE OTHER BANDS SO TO MAKE THE FINALS RUN SMOOTHER AND TO PROVIDE INCENTIVE--ONLY THE TOP SEVEN BANDS WILL REMAIN AFTER TOMORROW...
WHAT DOES THAT MEAN FOR US?
THEY RELEASED THE RESULTS TO GIVE THE STRAGGLERS A CHANCE TO REGROUP AND PLAN AHEAD FOR TOMORROW'S SHOW. WE ARE THE DANGER IS IN THIRD RIGHT NOW, 17 VOTES AHEAD OF LIPSERVICE.

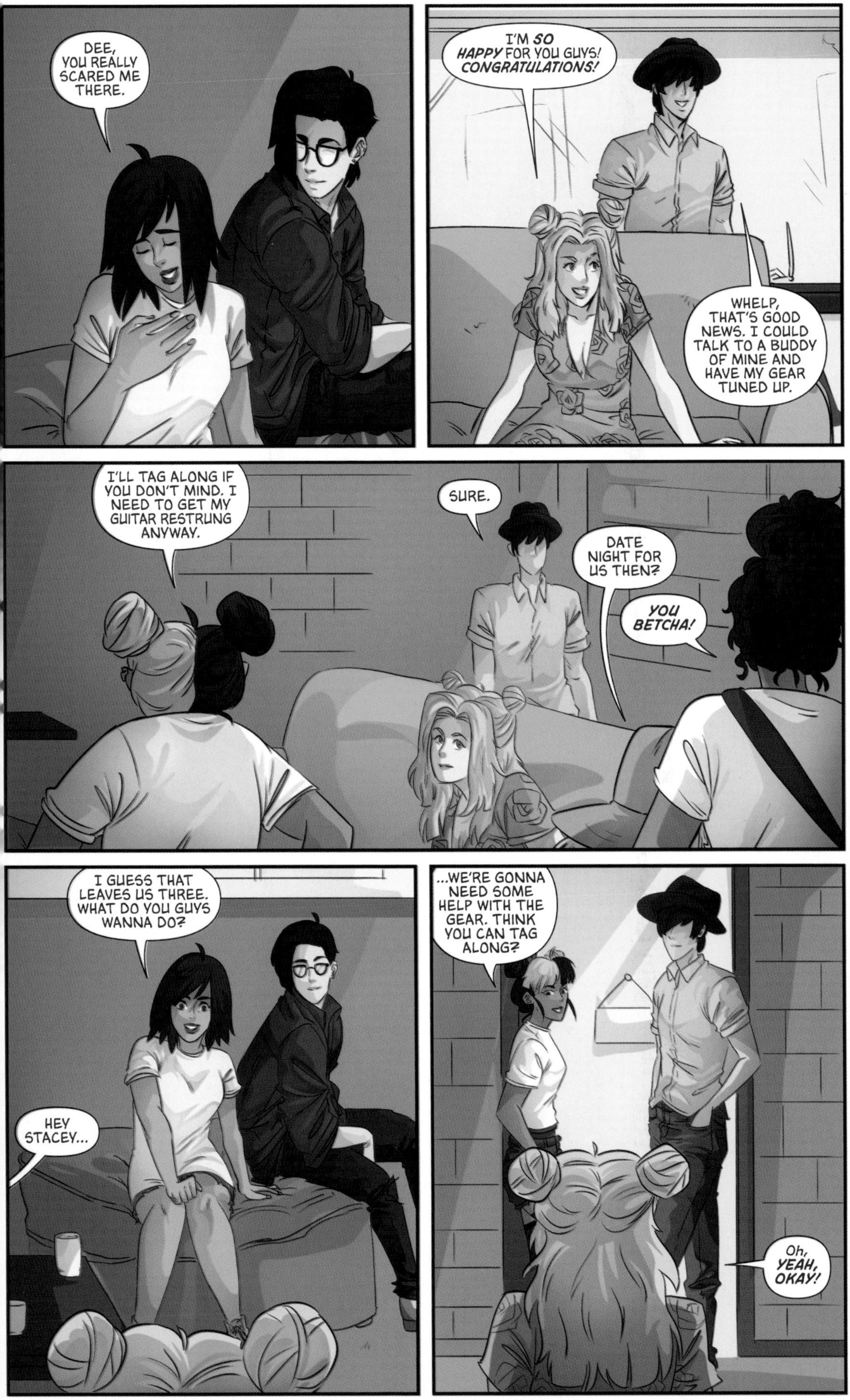
DEE, YOU REALLY SCARED ME THERE.
I'M SO HAPPY FOR YOU GUYS! CONGRATULATIONS!
WHELP, THAT'S GOOD NEWS. I COULD TALK TO A BUDDY OF MINE AND HAVE MY GEAR TUNED UP.
I'LL TAG ALONG IF YOU DON'T MIND. I NEED TO GET MY GUITAR RESTRUNG ANYWAY.
SURE.
DATE NIGHT FOR US THEN?
YOU BETCHA!
I GUESS THAT LEAVES US THREE. WHAT DO YOU GUYS WANNA DO?
HEY STACEY...
...WE'RE GONNA NEED SOME HELP WITH THE GEAR. THINK YOU CAN TAG ALONG?
Oh, YEAH, OKAY!

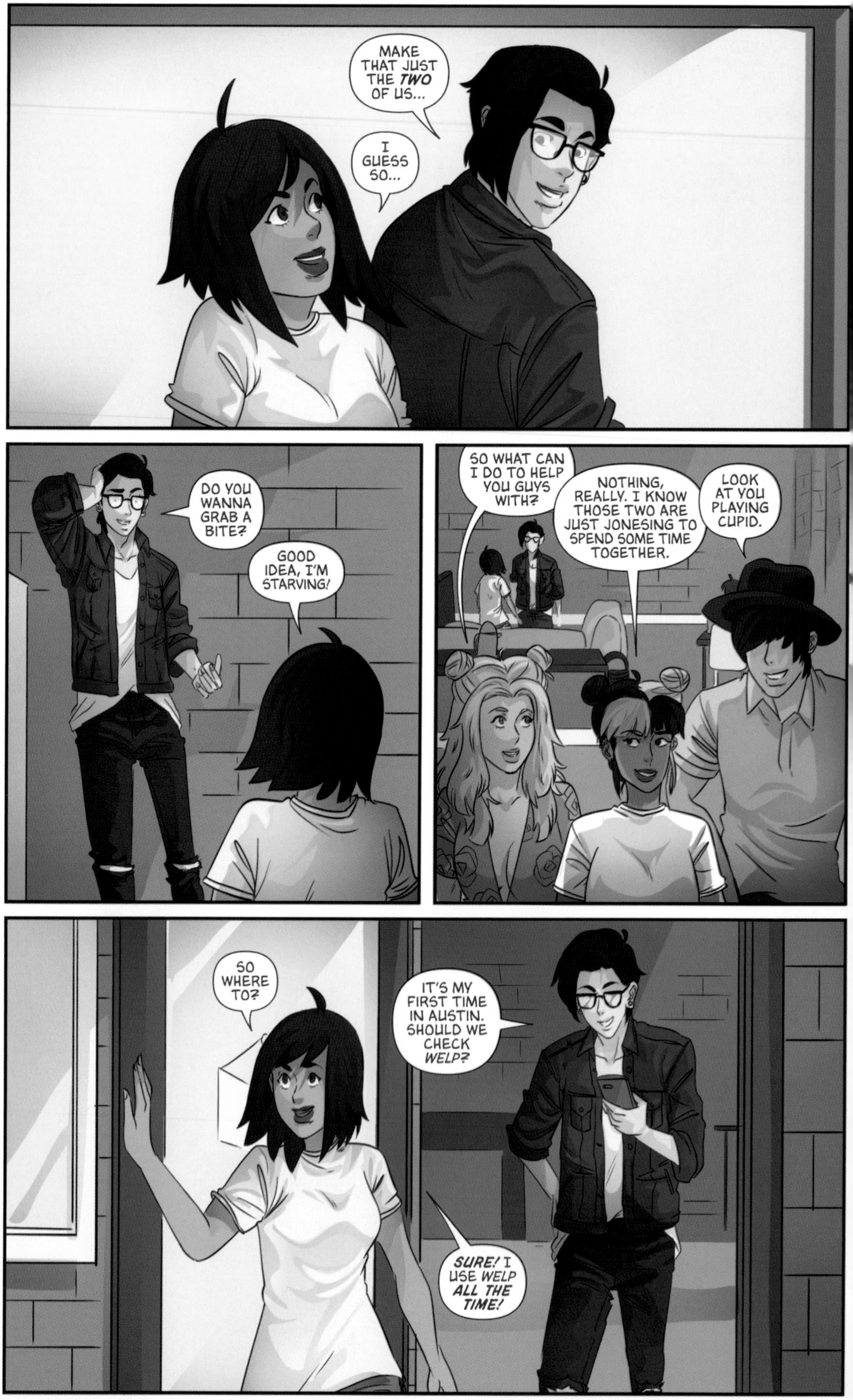

MAKE THAT JUST THE *TWO* OF US...
I GUESS SO...
DO YOU WANNA GRAB A BITE?
GOOD IDEA, I'M STARVING!
SO WHAT CAN I DO TO HELP YOU GUYS WITH?
NOTHING, REALLY. I KNOW THOSE TWO ARE JUST JONESING TO SPEND SOME TIME TOGETHER.
LOOK AT YOU PLAYING CUPID.
SO WHERE TO?
IT'S MY FIRST TIME IN AUSTIN. SHOULD WE CHECK *WELP?*
***SURE!*** I USE *WELP* ***ALL THE TIME!***

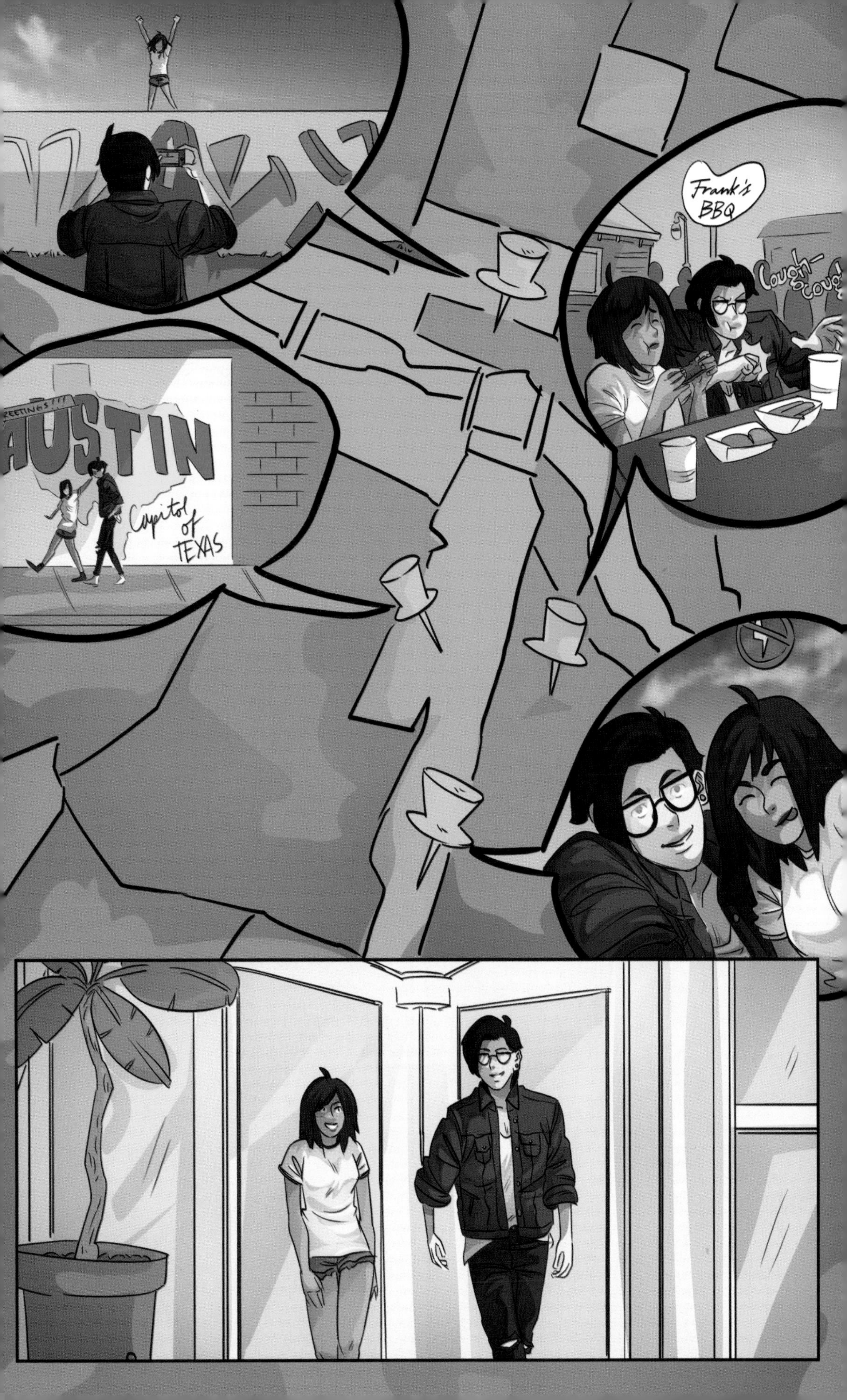
Frank's BBQ
Cough-cough
GREETINGS!!!
AUSTIN
Capitol of TEXAS

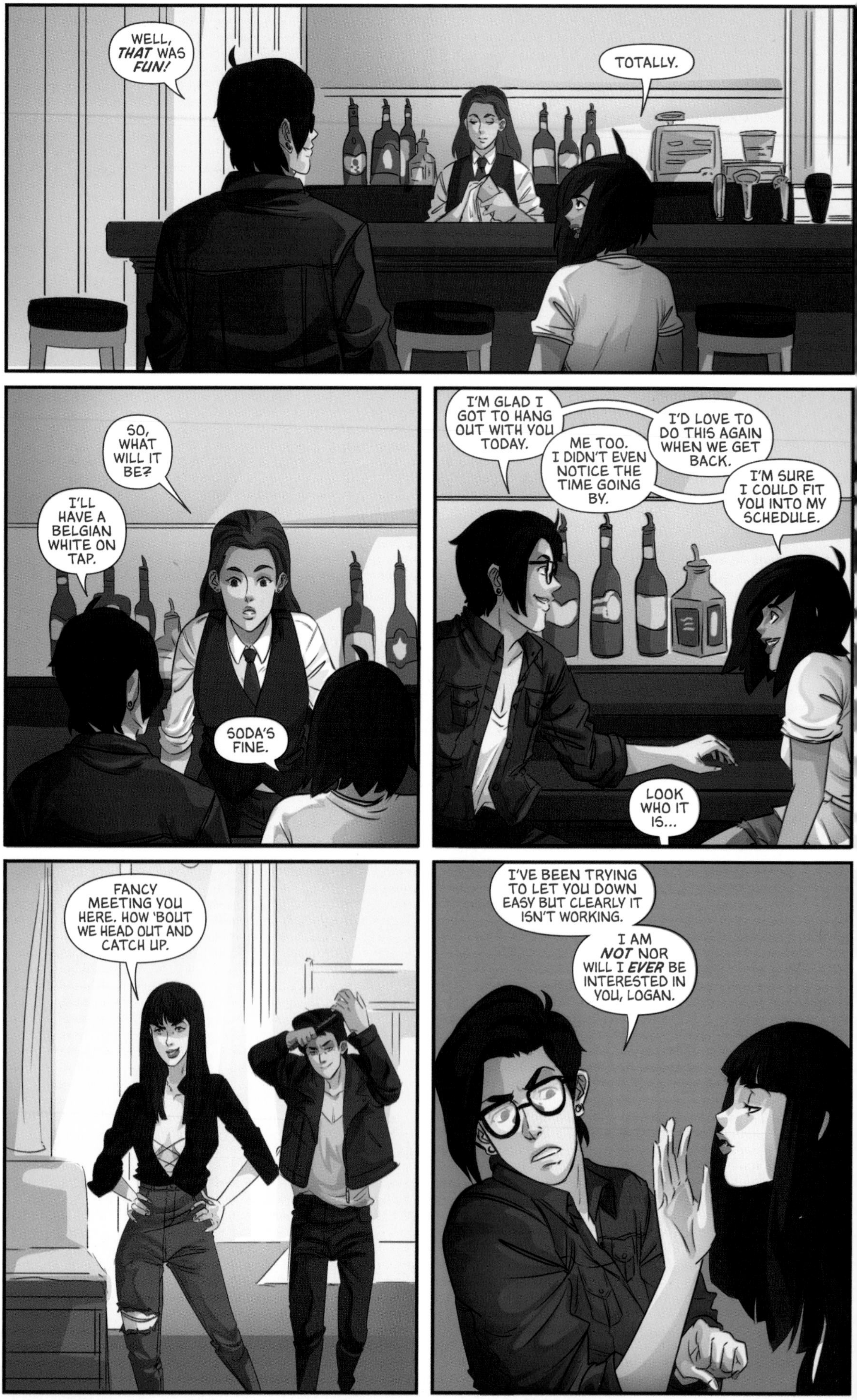
WELL, THAT WAS FUN!
TOTALLY.
SO, WHAT WILL IT BE?
I'LL HAVE A BELGIAN WHITE ON TAP.
SODA'S FINE.
I'M GLAD I GOT TO HANG OUT WITH YOU TODAY.
ME TOO. I DIDN'T EVEN NOTICE THE TIME GOING BY.
I'D LOVE TO DO THIS AGAIN WHEN WE GET BACK.
I'M SURE I COULD FIT YOU INTO MY SCHEDULE.
LOOK WHO IT IS...
FANCY MEETING YOU HERE. HOW 'BOUT WE HEAD OUT AND CATCH UP.
I'VE BEEN TRYING TO LET YOU DOWN EASY BUT CLEARLY IT ISN'T WORKING.
I AM NOT NOR WILL I EVER BE INTERESTED IN YOU, LOGAN.

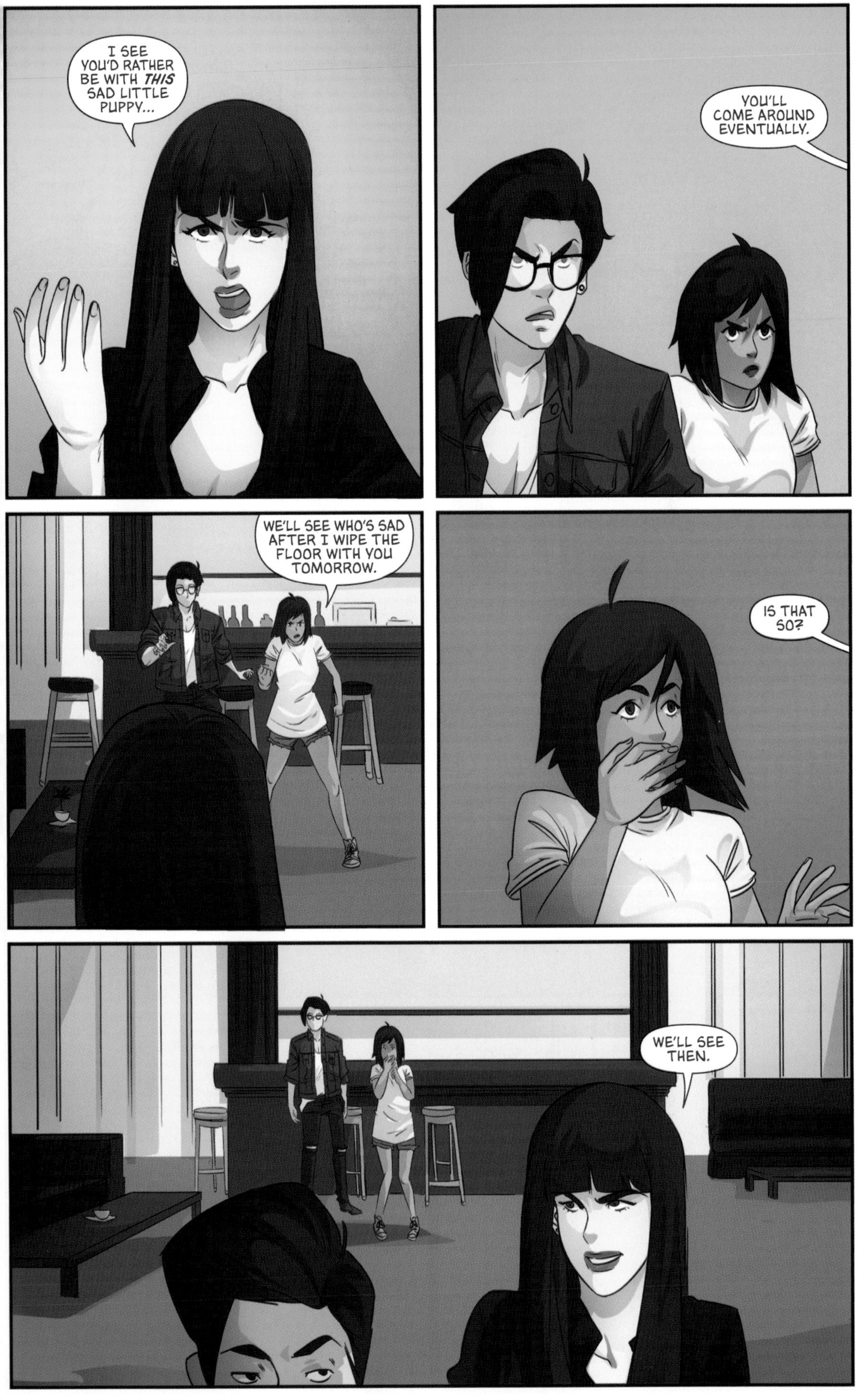
I SEE YOU'D RATHER BE WITH *THIS* SAD LITTLE PUPPY...
YOU'LL COME AROUND EVENTUALLY.
WE'LL SEE WHO'S SAD AFTER I WIPE THE FLOOR WITH YOU TOMORROW.
IS THAT SO?
WE'LL SEE THEN.

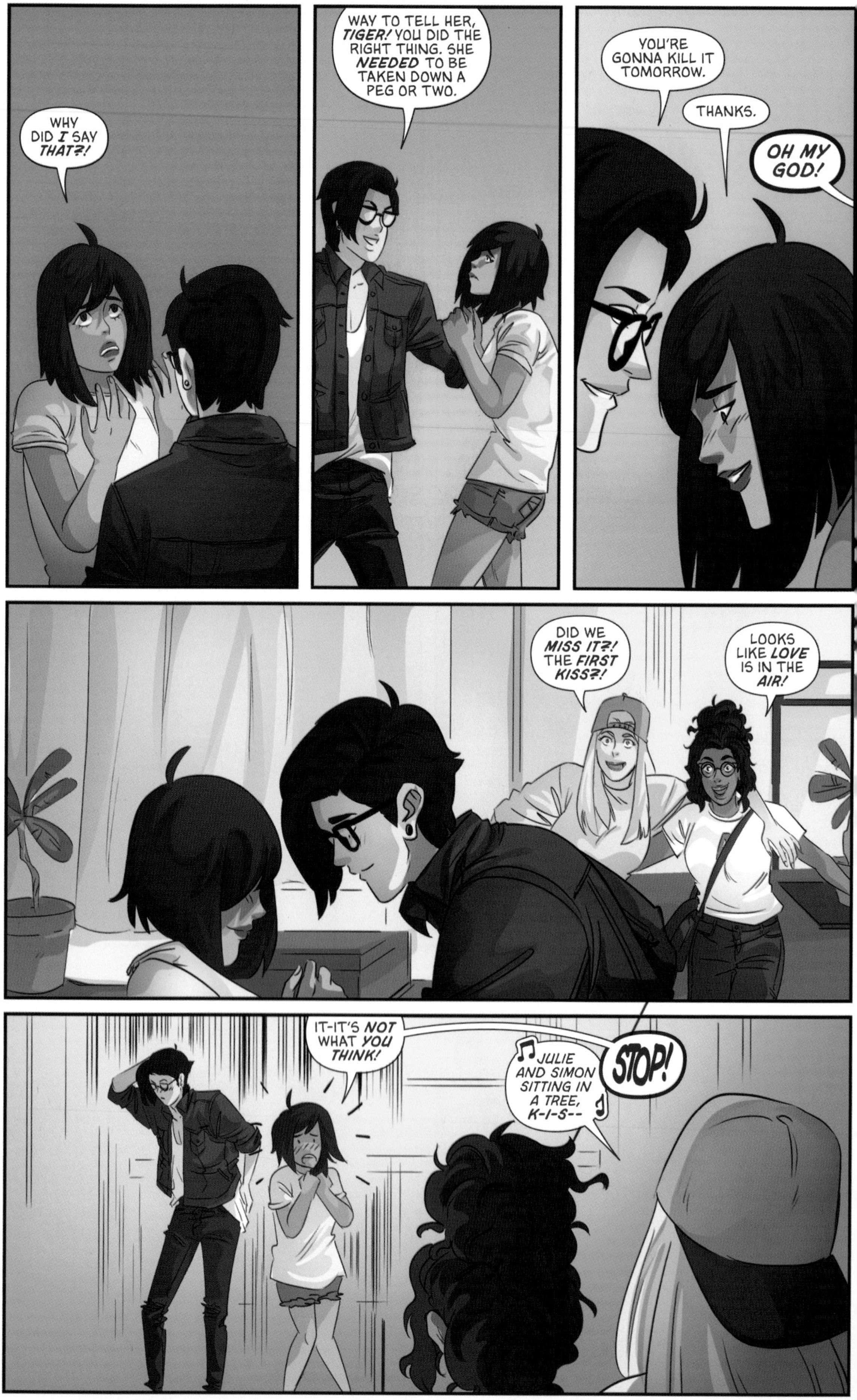
WHY DID I SAY THAT?!
WAY TO TELL HER, TIGER! YOU DID THE RIGHT THING. SHE NEEDED TO BE TAKEN DOWN A PEG OR TWO.
YOU'RE GONNA KILL IT TOMORROW.
THANKS.
OH MY GOD!
DID WE MISS IT?! THE FIRST KISS?!
LOOKS LIKE LOVE IS IN THE AIR!
IT-IT'S NOT WHAT YOU THINK!
STOP!
JULIE AND SIMON SITTING IN A TREE, K-I-S--

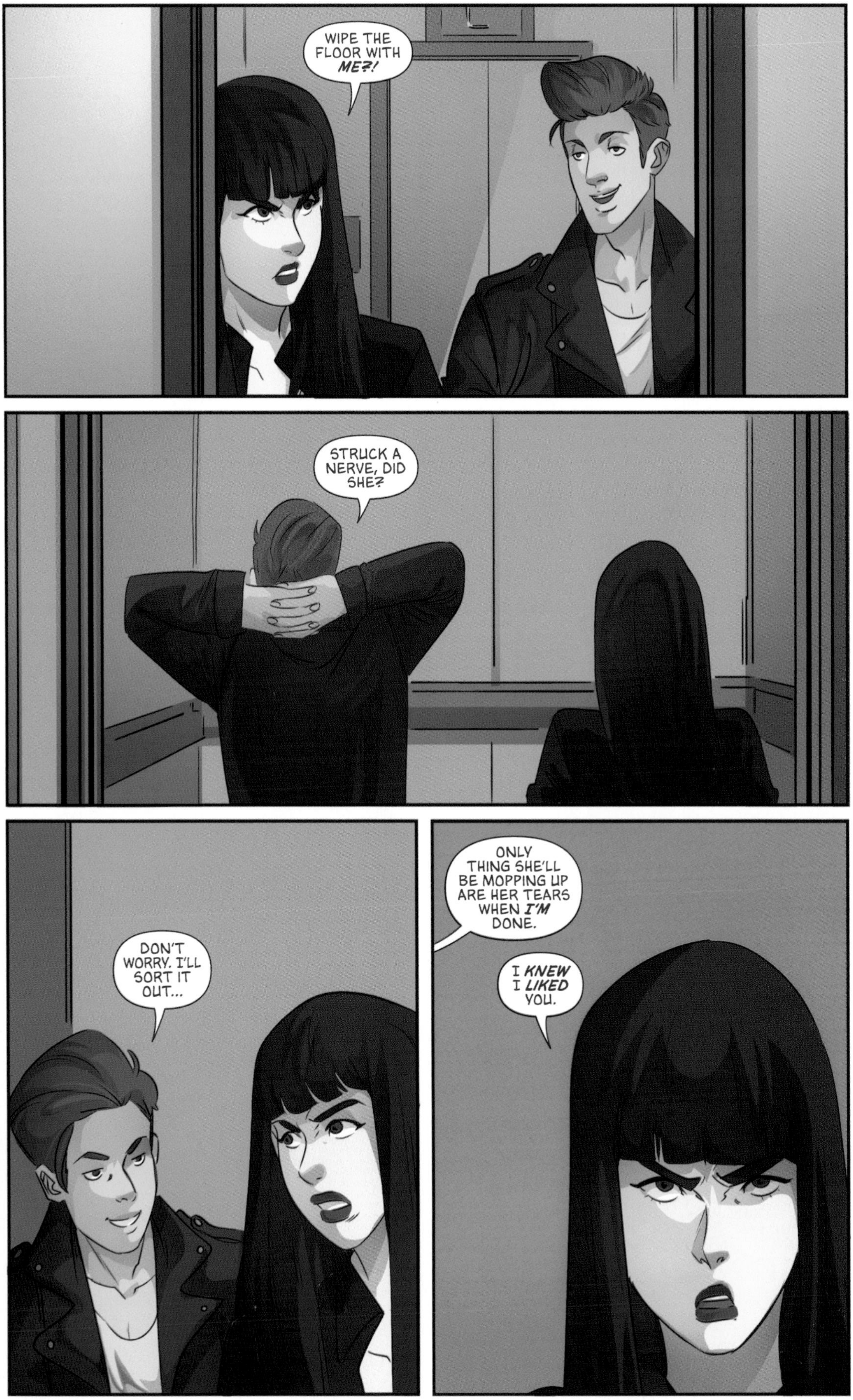
WIPE THE FLOOR WITH ***ME?!***
STRUCK A NERVE, DID SHE?
DON'T WORRY. I'LL SORT IT OUT...
ONLY THING SHE'LL BE MOPPING UP ARE HER TEARS WHEN ***I'M*** DONE.
I ***KNEW*** I ***LIKED*** YOU.

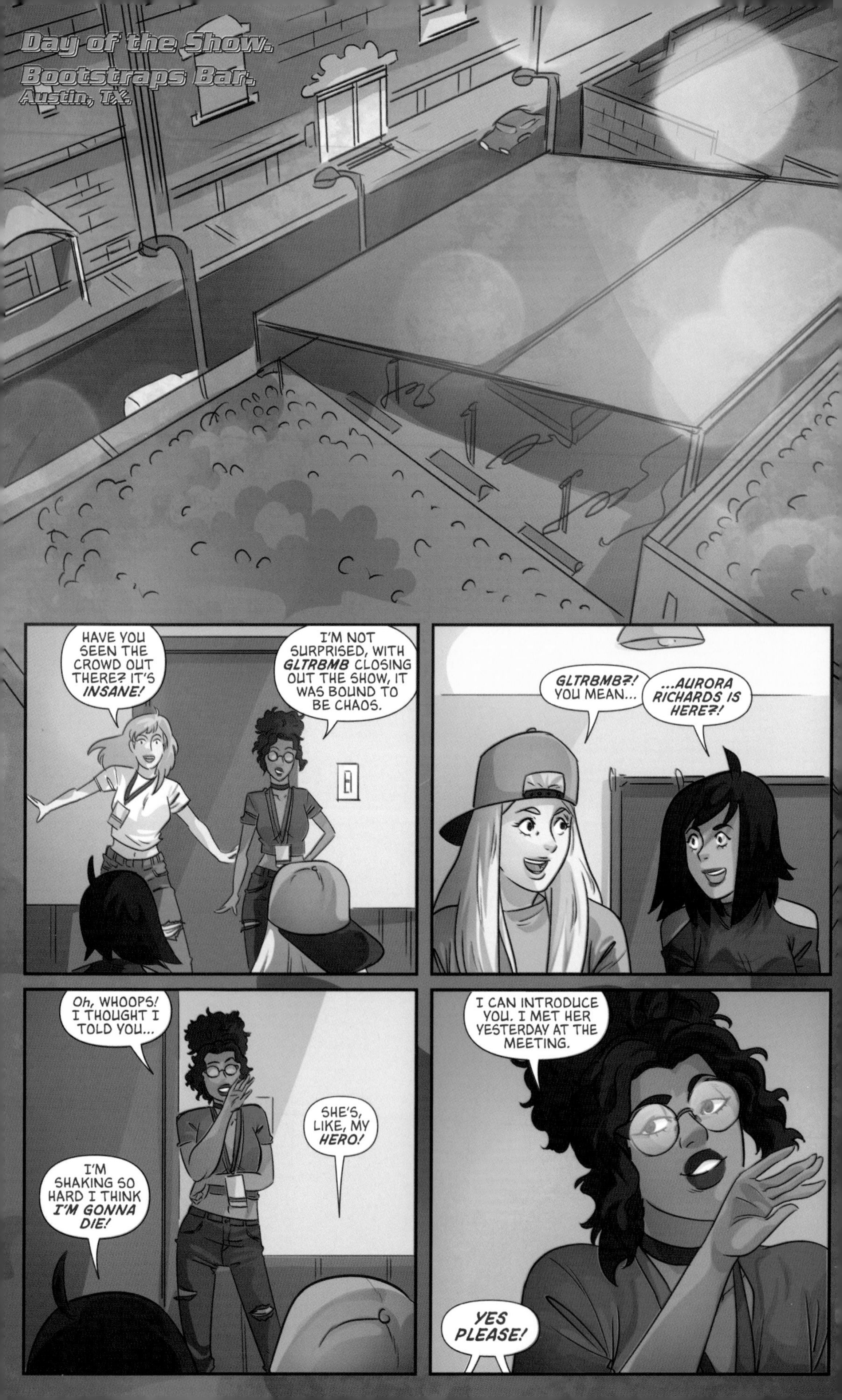

Day of the Show.
Bootstraps Bar.
Austin, TX.
HAVE YOU SEEN THE CROWD OUT THERE? IT'S INSANE!
I'M NOT SURPRISED, WITH GLTRBMB CLOSING OUT THE SHOW, IT WAS BOUND TO BE CHAOS.
GLTRBMB?! YOU MEAN...
...AURORA RICHARDS IS HERE?!
Oh, WHOOPS! I THOUGHT I TOLD YOU...
SHE'S, LIKE, MY HERO!
I'M SHAKING SO HARD I THINK I'M GONNA DIE!
I CAN INTRODUCE YOU. I MET HER YESTERDAY AT THE MEETING.
YES PLEASE!

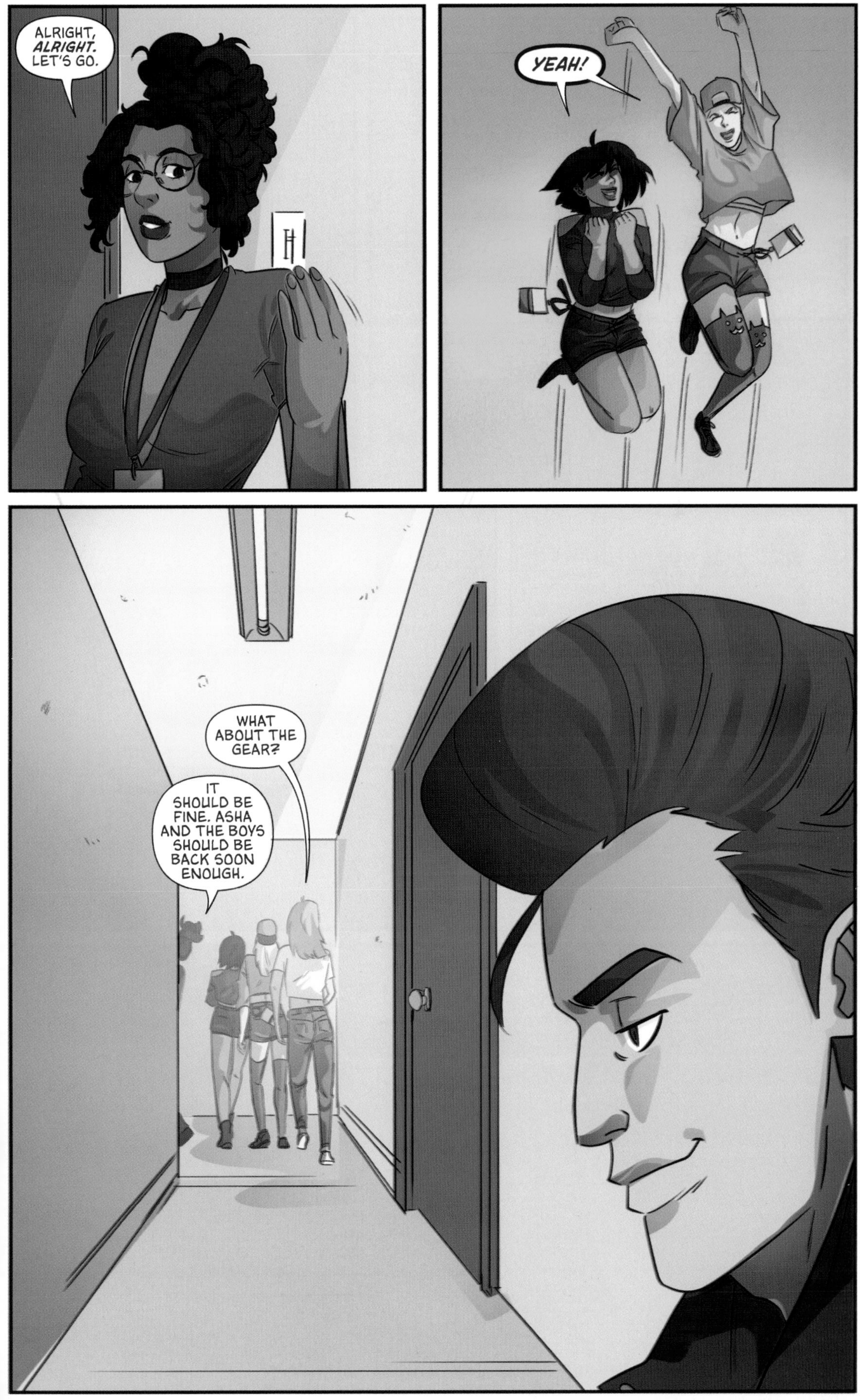
ALRIGHT, *ALRIGHT.* LET'S GO.
*YEAH!*
WHAT ABOUT THE GEAR?
IT SHOULD BE FINE. ASHA AND THE BOYS SHOULD BE BACK SOON ENOUGH.

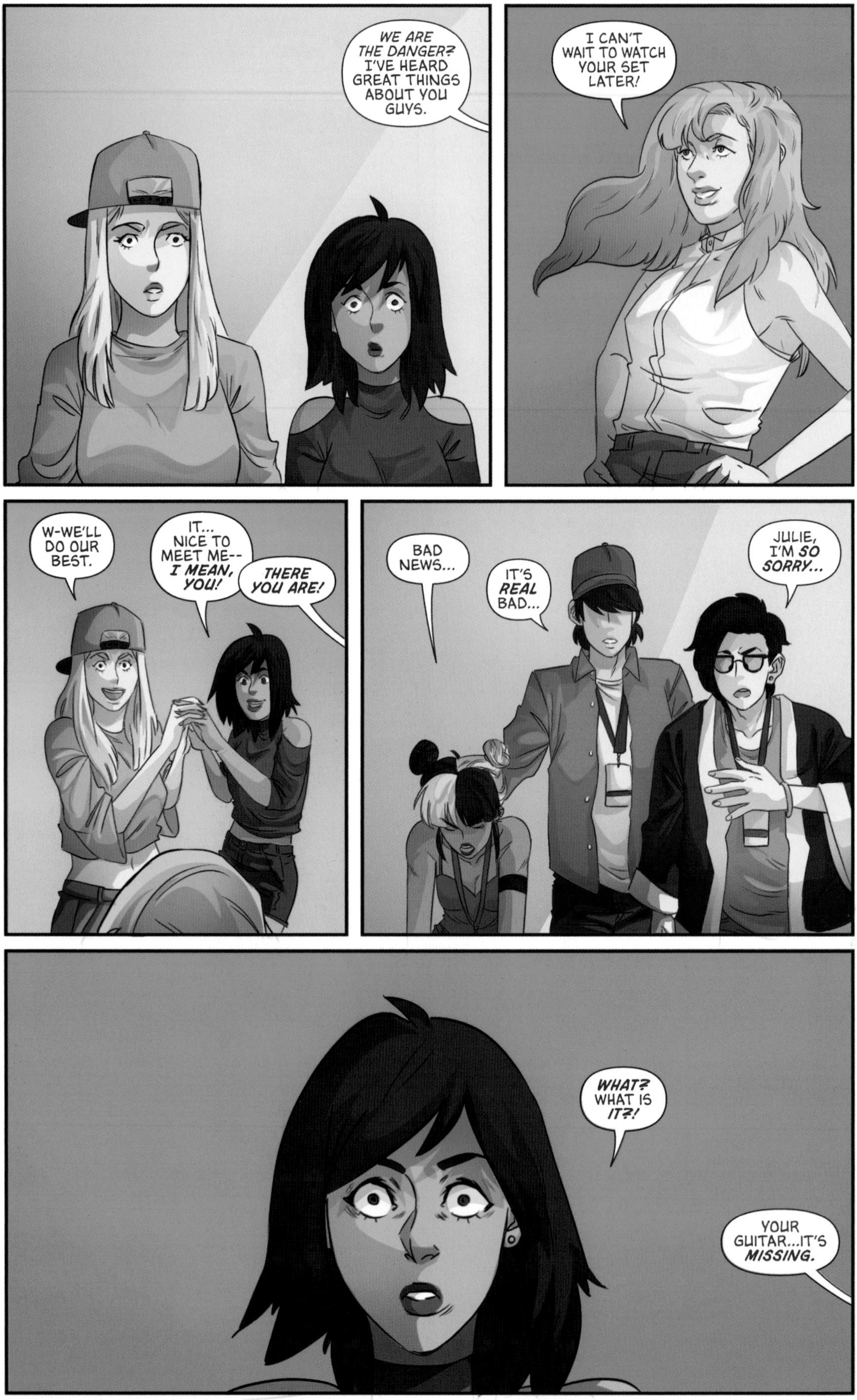
WE ARE THE DANGER? I'VE HEARD GREAT THINGS ABOUT YOU GUYS.
I CAN'T WAIT TO WATCH YOUR SET LATER!
W-WE'LL DO OUR BEST.
IT... NICE TO MEET ME-- I MEAN, YOU!
THERE YOU ARE!
BAD NEWS...
IT'S REAL BAD...
JULIE, I'M SO SORRY...
WHAT? WHAT IS IT?!
YOUR GUITAR...IT'S MISSING.

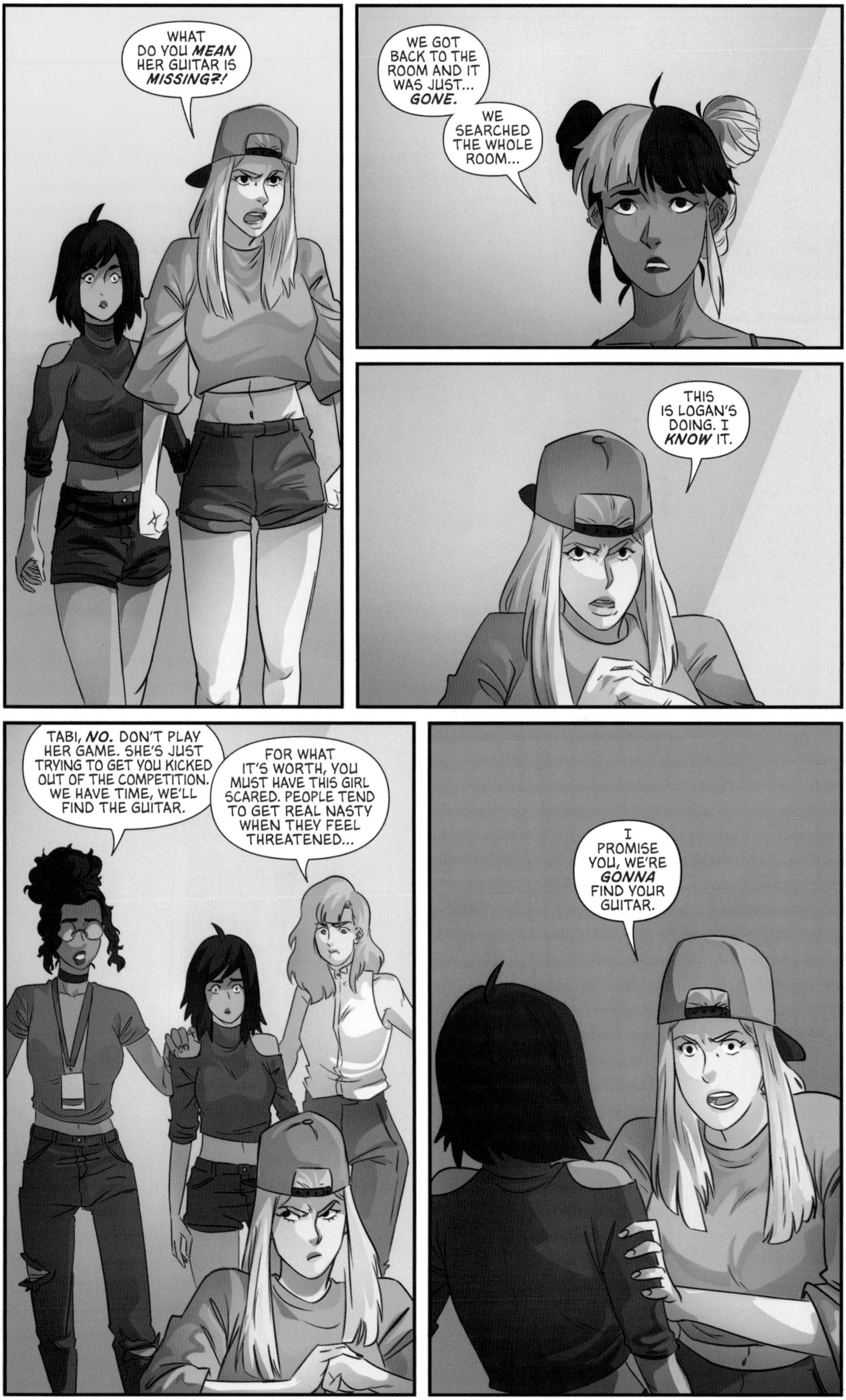
WHAT DO YOU MEAN HER GUITAR IS MISSING?!
WE GOT BACK TO THE ROOM AND IT WAS JUST... GONE.
WE SEARCHED THE WHOLE ROOM...
THIS IS LOGAN'S DOING. I KNOW IT.
TABI, NO. DON'T PLAY HER GAME. SHE'S JUST TRYING TO GET YOU KICKED OUT OF THE COMPETITION. WE HAVE TIME, WE'LL FIND THE GUITAR.
FOR WHAT IT'S WORTH, YOU MUST HAVE THIS GIRL SCARED. PEOPLE TEND TO GET REAL NASTY WHEN THEY FEEL THREATENED...
I PROMISE YOU, WE'RE GONNA FIND YOUR GUITAR.

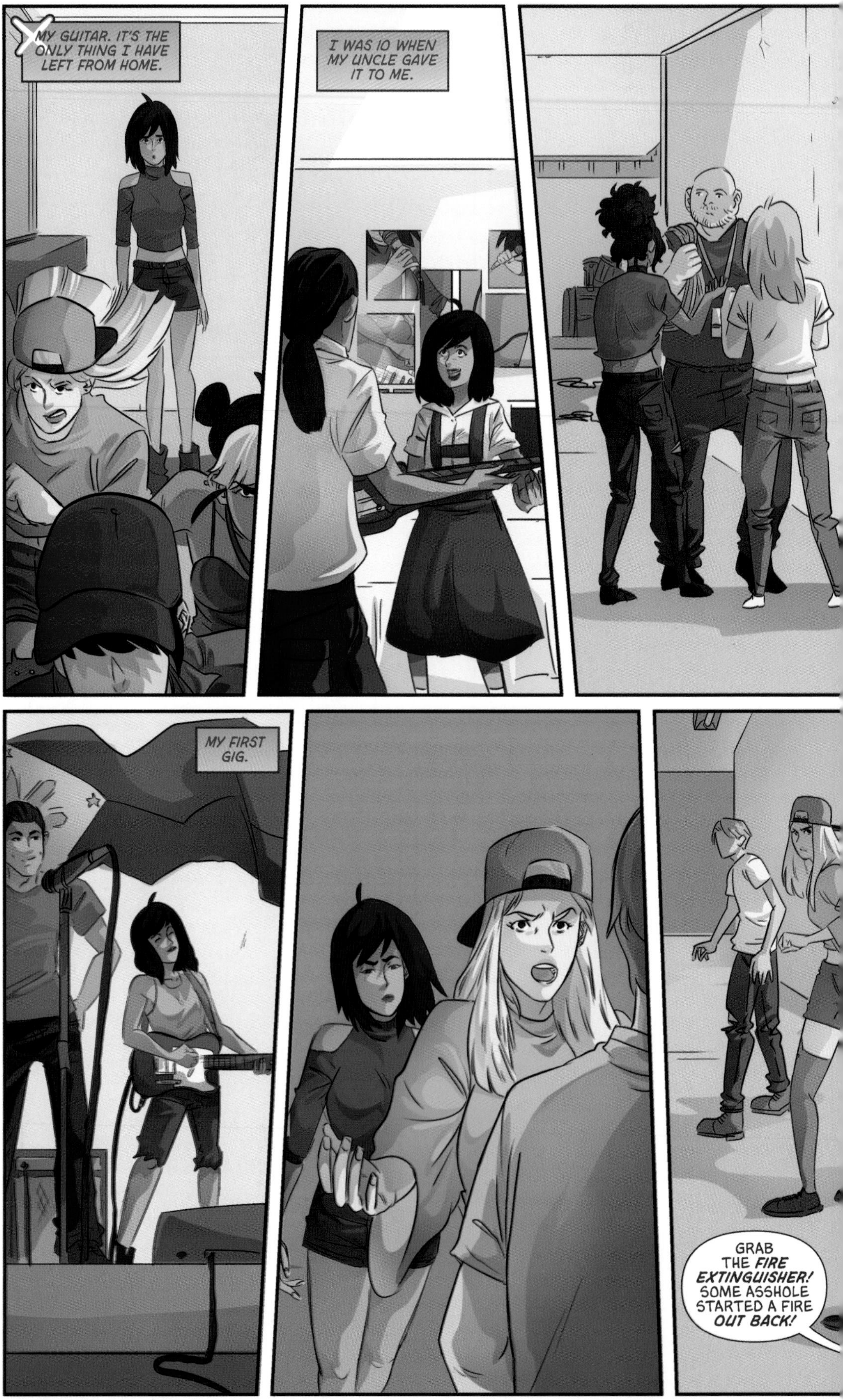
MY GUITAR. IT'S THE ONLY THING I HAVE LEFT FROM HOME.
I WAS 10 WHEN MY UNCLE GAVE IT TO ME.
MY FIRST GIG.
GRAB THE *FIRE EXTINGUISHER!* SOME ASSHOLE STARTED A FIRE *OUT BACK!*

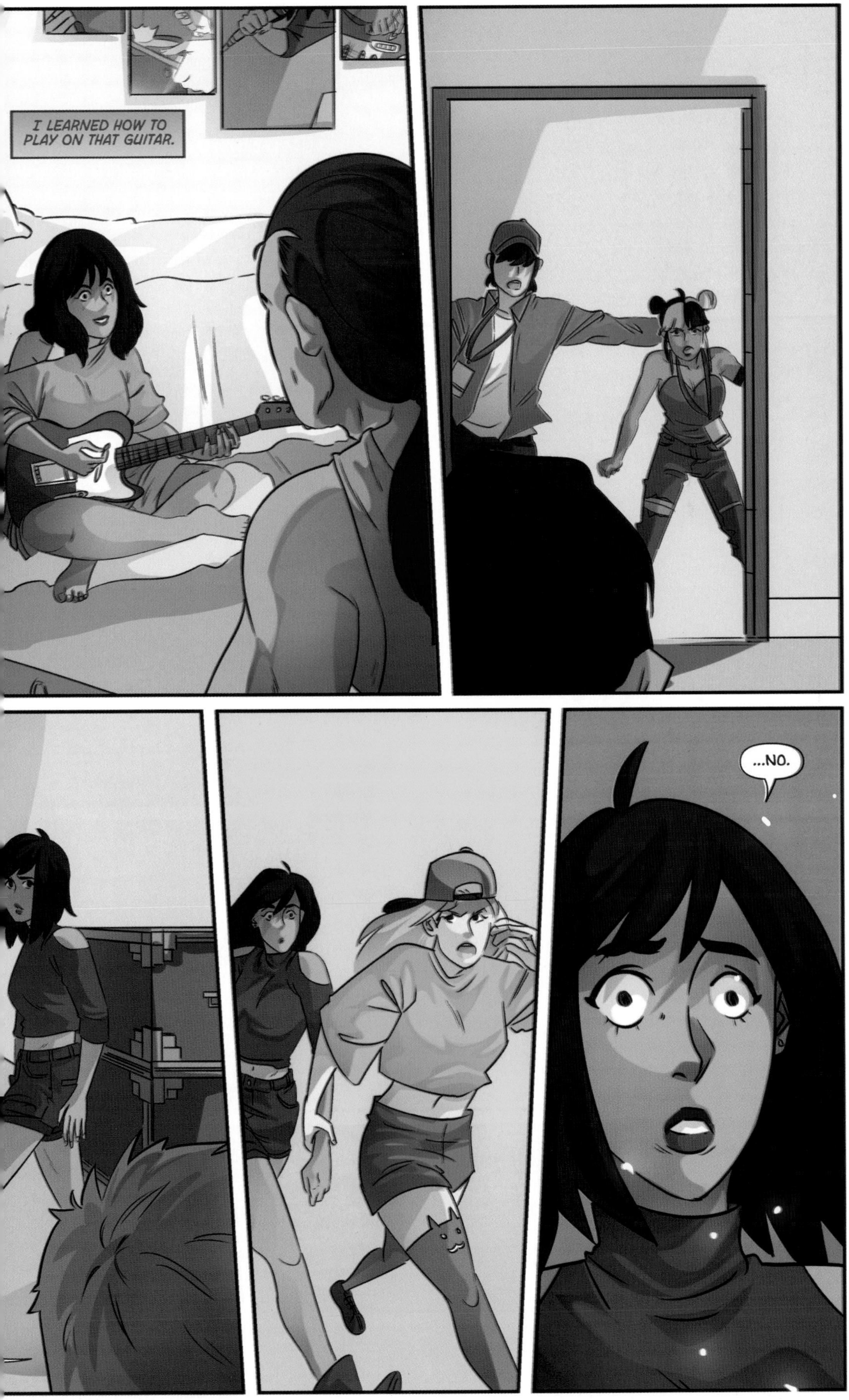
I LEARNED HOW TO PLAY ON THAT GUITAR.
...NO.

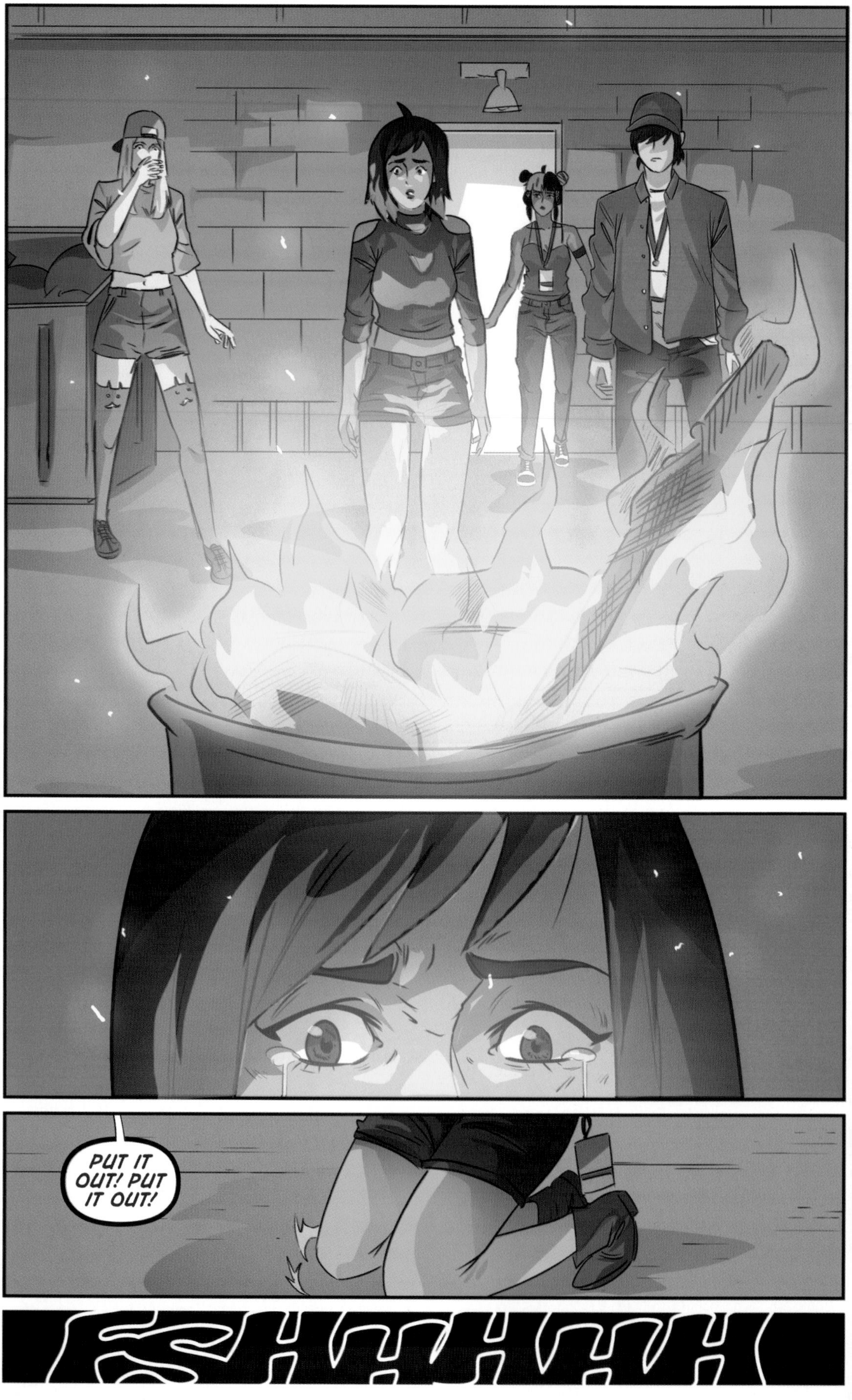
PUT IT OUT! PUT IT OUT!
FSHHHHH

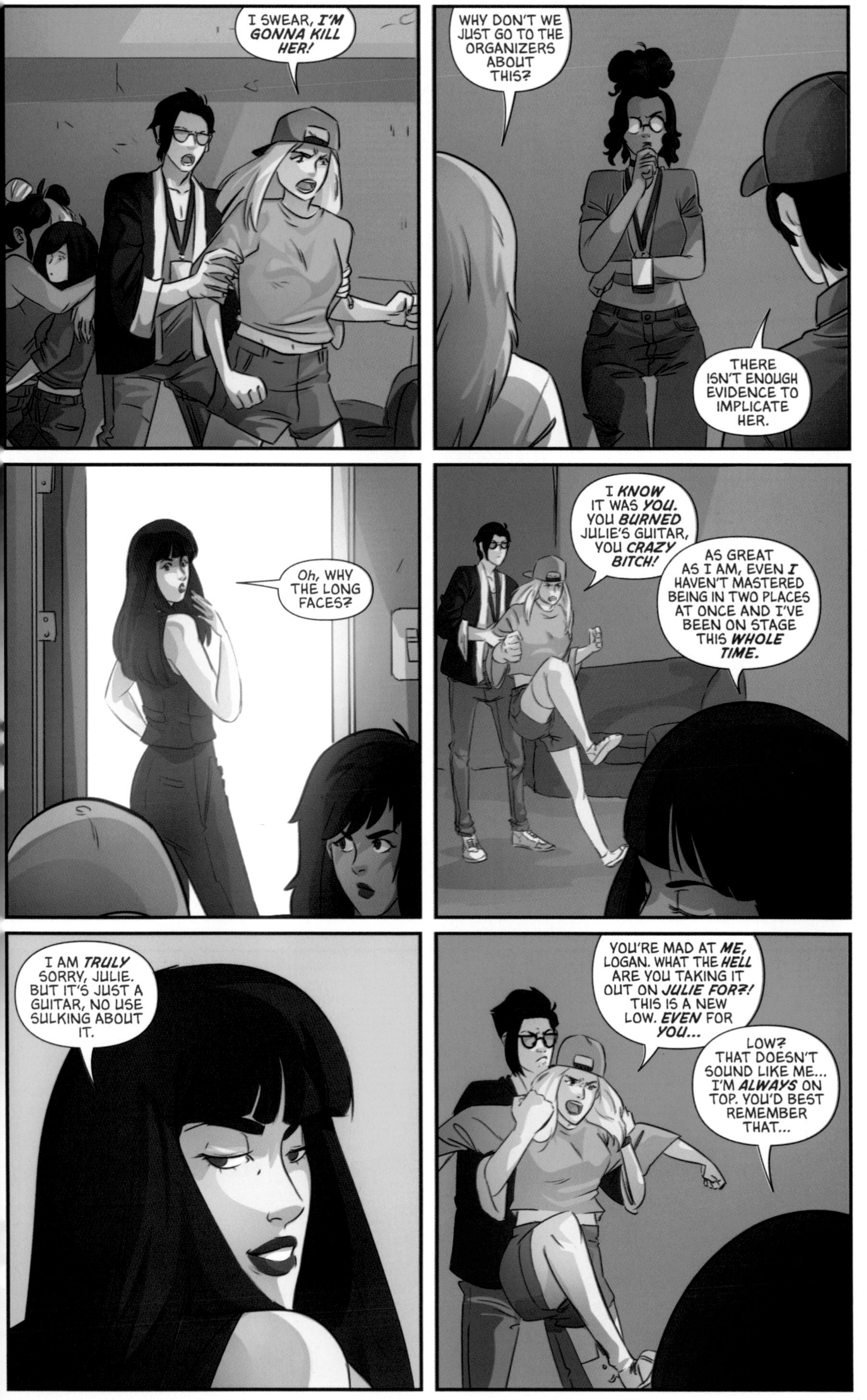
I SWEAR, *I'M GONNA KILL HER!*
WHY DON'T WE JUST GO TO THE ORGANIZERS ABOUT THIS?
THERE ISN'T ENOUGH EVIDENCE TO IMPLICATE HER.
*Oh,* WHY THE LONG FACES?
I *KNOW* IT WAS *YOU.* YOU *BURNED* JULIE'S GUITAR, YOU *CRAZY BITCH!*
AS GREAT AS I AM, EVEN *I* HAVEN'T MASTERED BEING IN TWO PLACES AT ONCE AND I'VE BEEN ON STAGE THIS *WHOLE TIME.*
I AM *TRULY* SORRY, JULIE. BUT IT'S JUST A GUITAR, NO USE SULKING ABOUT IT.
YOU'RE MAD AT *ME,* LOGAN. WHAT THE *HELL* ARE YOU TAKING IT OUT ON *JULIE FOR?!* THIS IS A NEW LOW. *EVEN* FOR *YOU...*
LOW? THAT DOESN'T SOUND LIKE ME... I'M *ALWAYS* ON TOP. YOU'D BEST REMEMBER THAT...

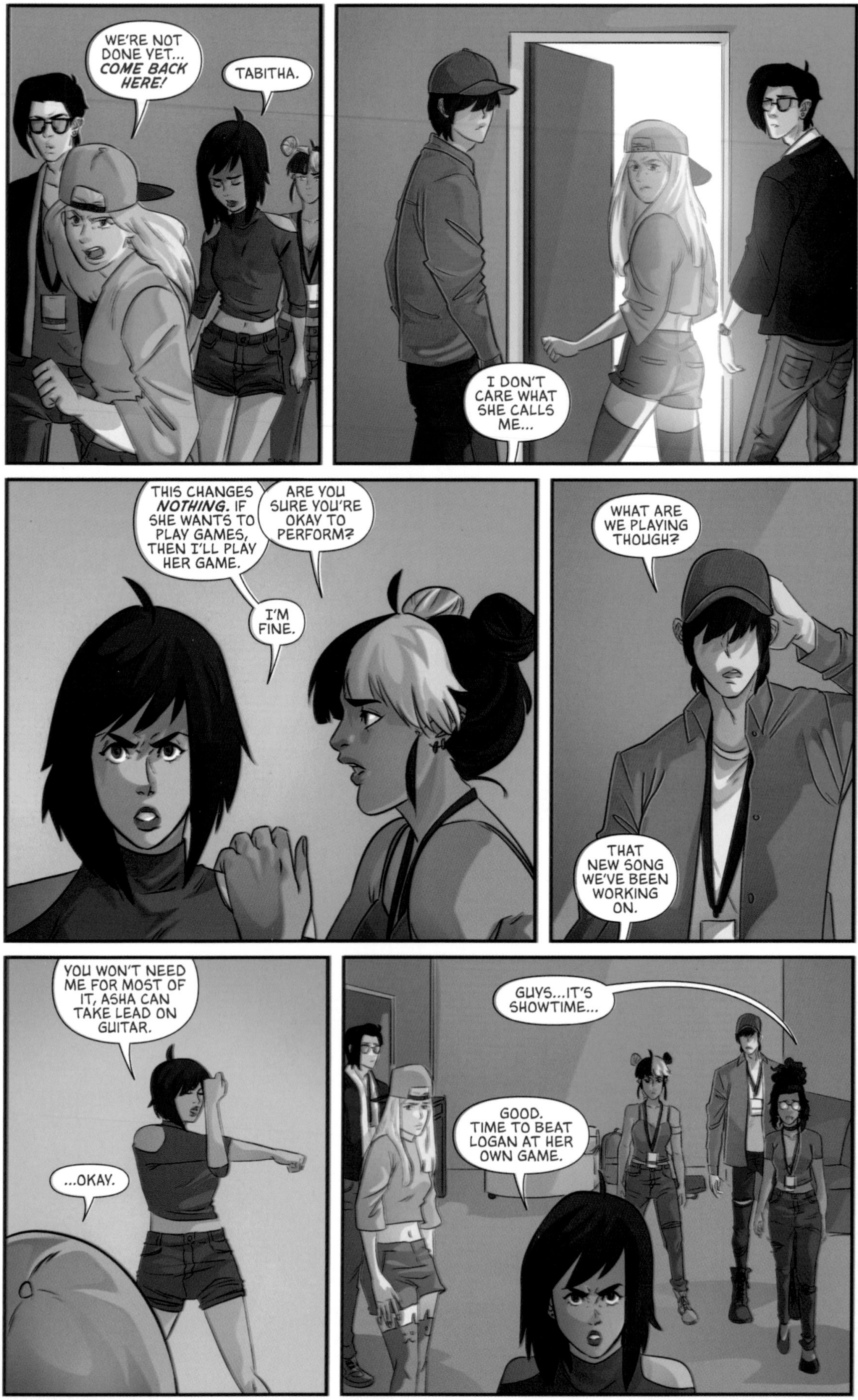

WE'RE NOT DONE YET... COME BACK HERE!
TABITHA.
I DON'T CARE WHAT SHE CALLS ME...
THIS CHANGES NOTHING. IF SHE WANTS TO PLAY GAMES, THEN I'LL PLAY HER GAME.
ARE YOU SURE YOU'RE OKAY TO PERFORM?
I'M FINE.
WHAT ARE WE PLAYING THOUGH?
THAT NEW SONG WE'VE BEEN WORKING ON.
YOU WON'T NEED ME FOR MOST OF IT, ASHA CAN TAKE LEAD ON GUITAR.
...OKAY.
GUYS...IT'S SHOWTIME...
GOOD. TIME TO BEAT LOGAN AT HER OWN GAME.

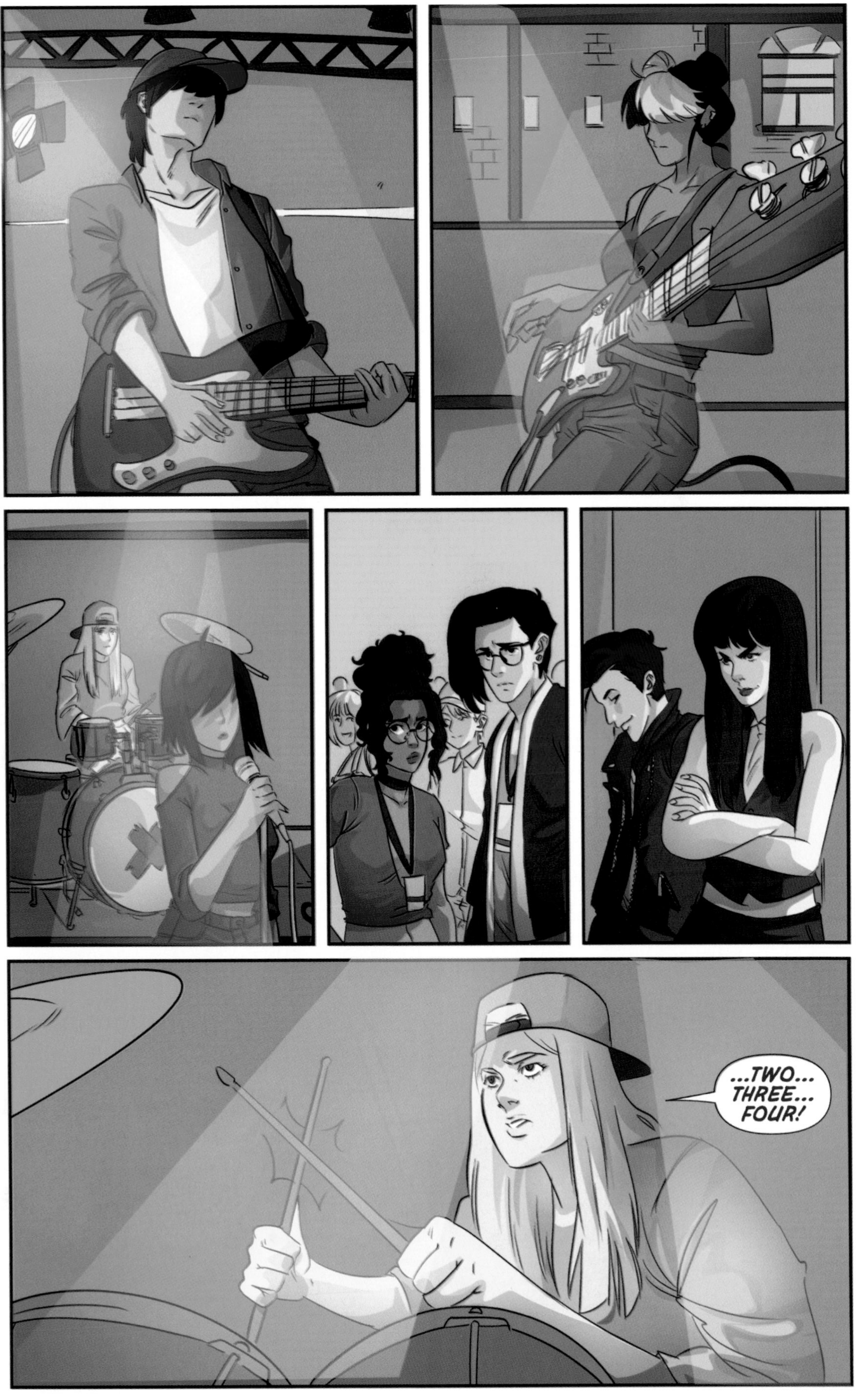
...TWO... THREE... FOUR!

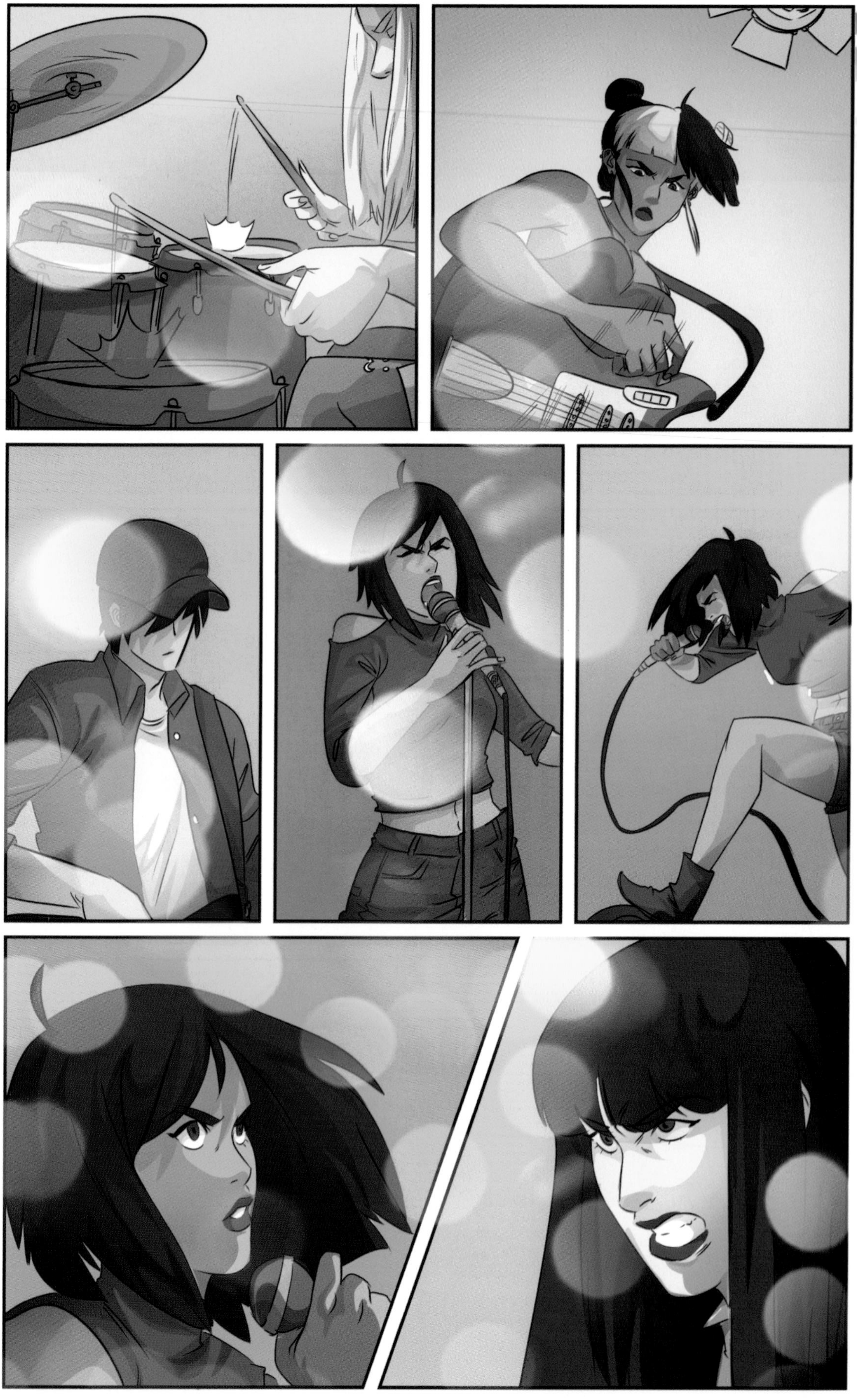

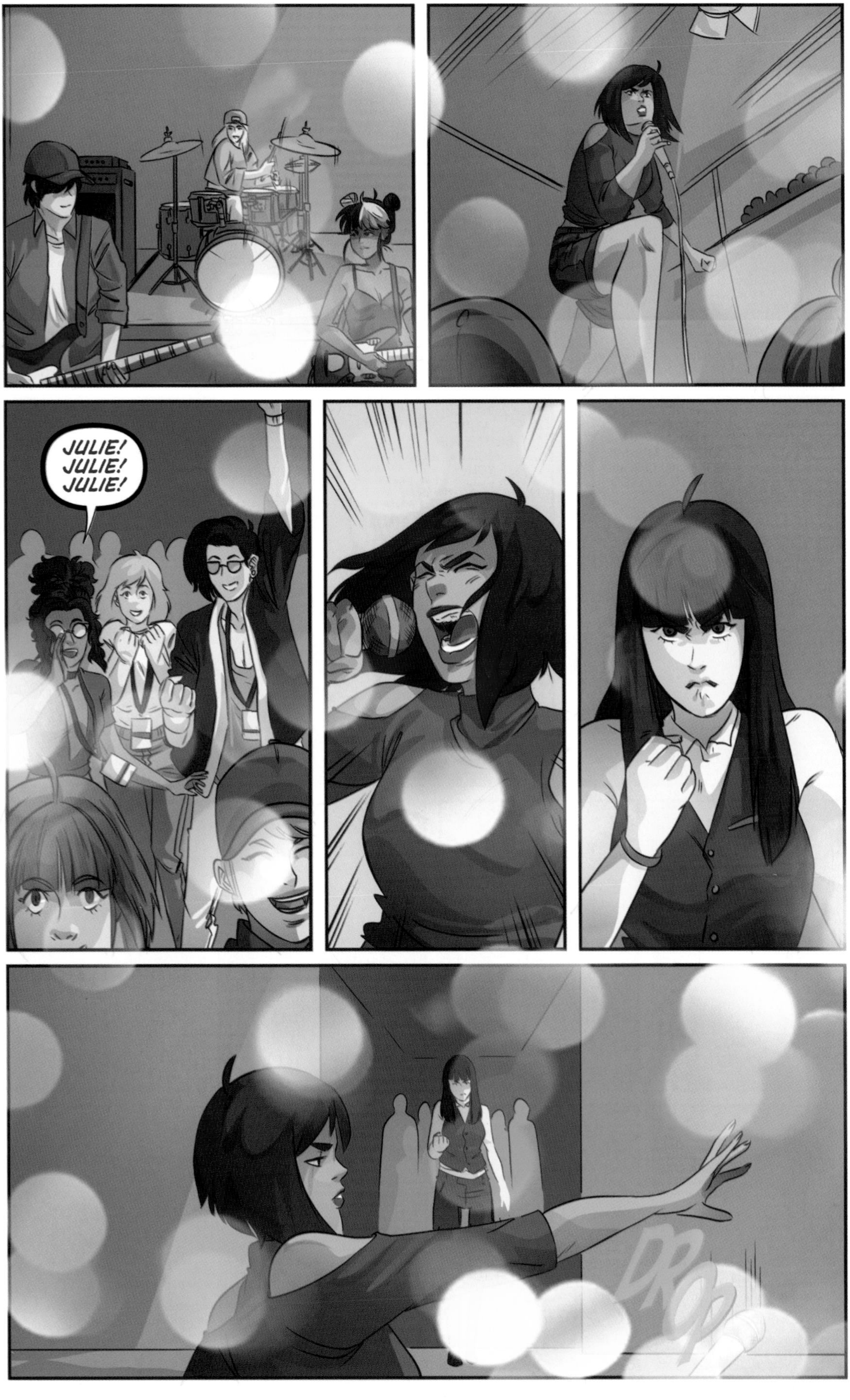
JULIE! JULIE! JULIE!
DROP

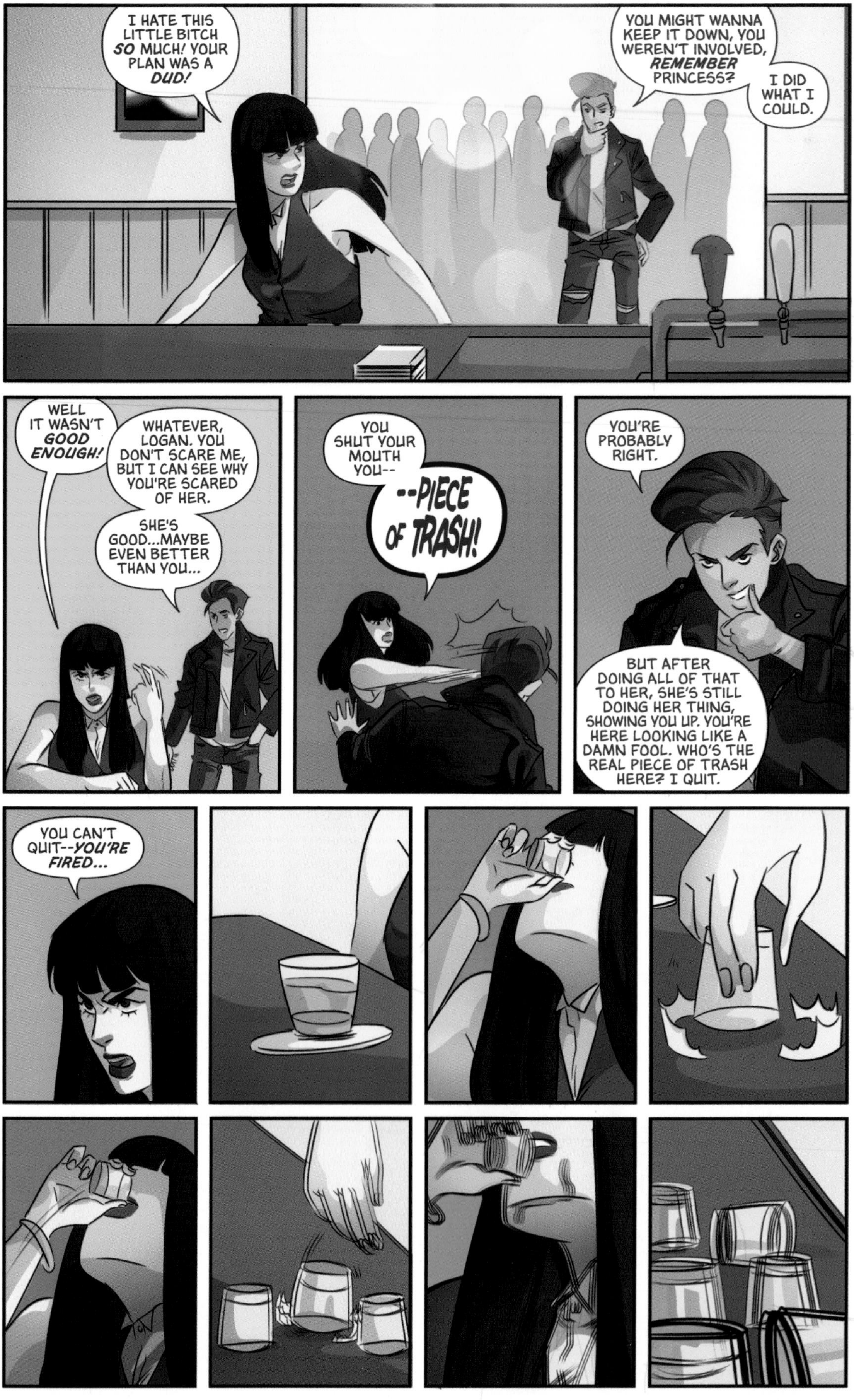

I HATE THIS LITTLE BITCH SO MUCH! YOUR PLAN WAS A DUD!
YOU MIGHT WANNA KEEP IT DOWN, YOU WEREN'T INVOLVED, REMEMBER PRINCESS?
I DID WHAT I COULD.
WELL IT WASN'T GOOD ENOUGH!
WHATEVER, LOGAN. YOU DON'T SCARE ME, BUT I CAN SEE WHY YOU'RE SCARED OF HER.
SHE'S GOOD...MAYBE EVEN BETTER THAN YOU...
YOU SHUT YOUR MOUTH YOU--
--PIECE OF TRASH!
YOU'RE PROBABLY RIGHT.
BUT AFTER DOING ALL OF THAT TO HER, SHE'S STILL DOING HER THING, SHOWING YOU UP. YOU'RE HERE LOOKING LIKE A DAMN FOOL. WHO'S THE REAL PIECE OF TRASH HERE? I QUIT.
YOU CAN'T QUIT--YOU'RE FIRED...

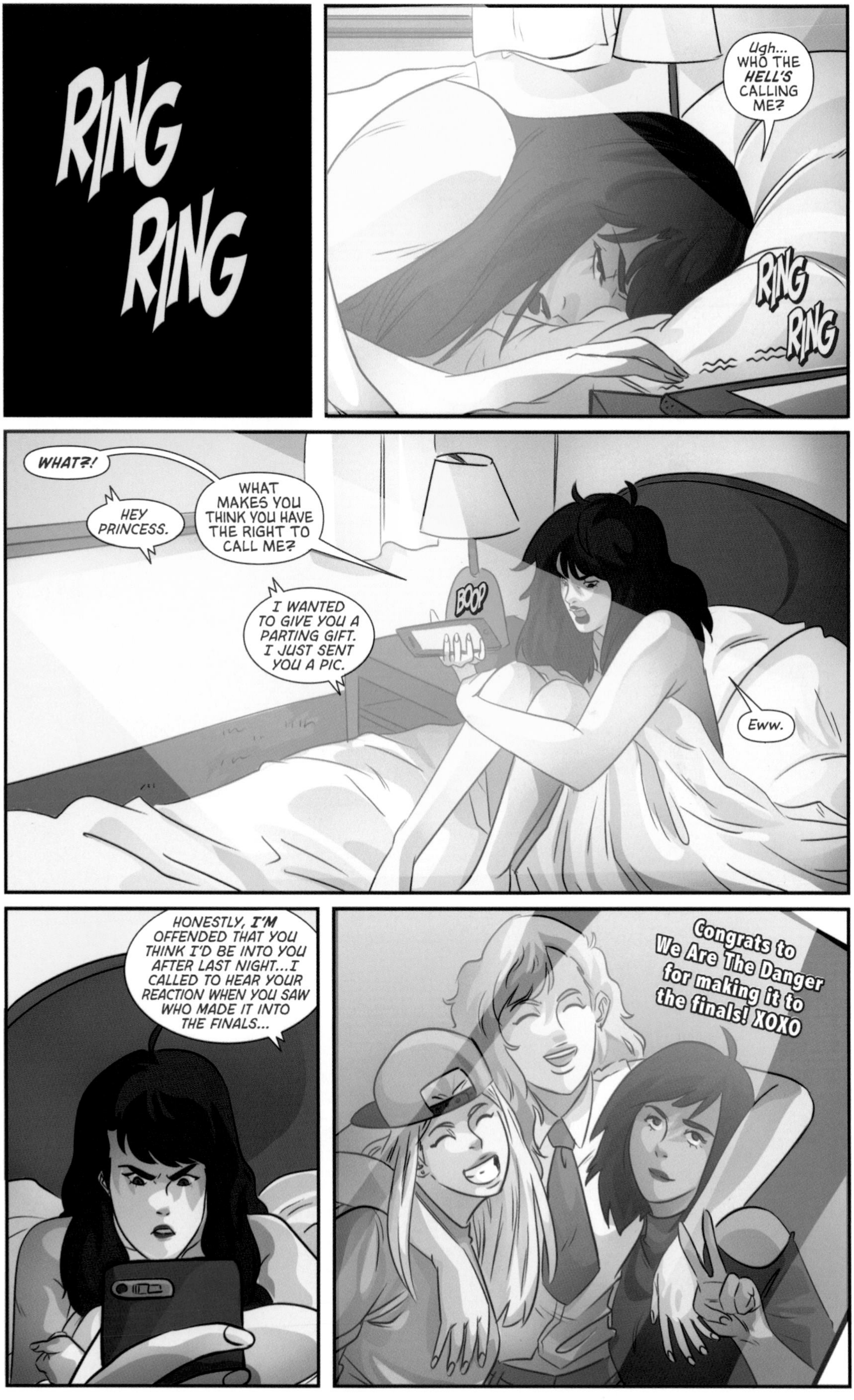
RING
RING
Ugh... WHO THE HELL'S CALLING ME?
RING
RING
WHAT?!
HEY PRINCESS.
WHAT MAKES YOU THINK YOU HAVE THE RIGHT TO CALL ME?
BOOP
I WANTED TO GIVE YOU A PARTING GIFT. I JUST SENT YOU A PIC.
Eww.
HONESTLY, I'M OFFENDED THAT YOU THINK I'D BE INTO YOU AFTER LAST NIGHT...I CALLED TO HEAR YOUR REACTION WHEN YOU SAW WHO MADE IT INTO THE FINALS...
Congrats to We Are The Danger for making it to the finals! XOXO

# ISSUE 5

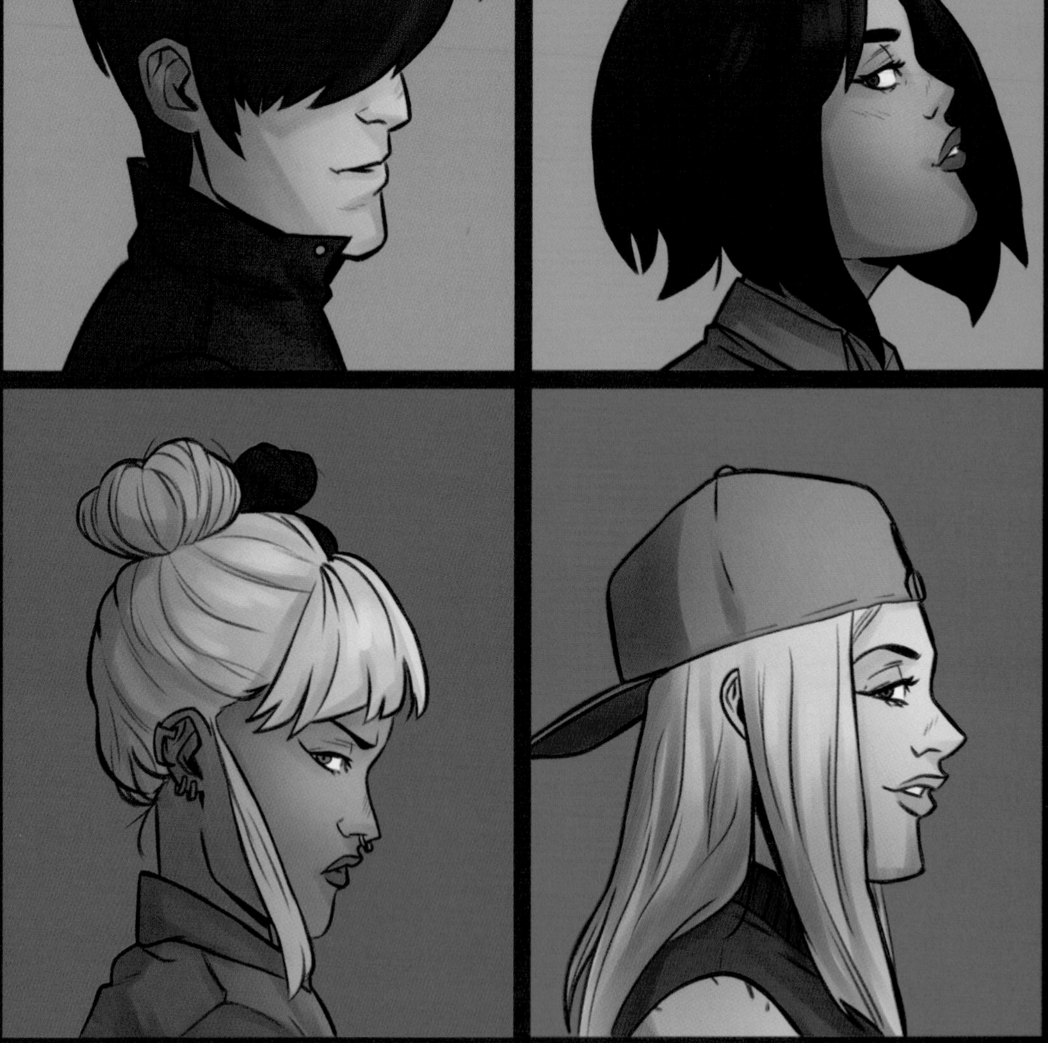

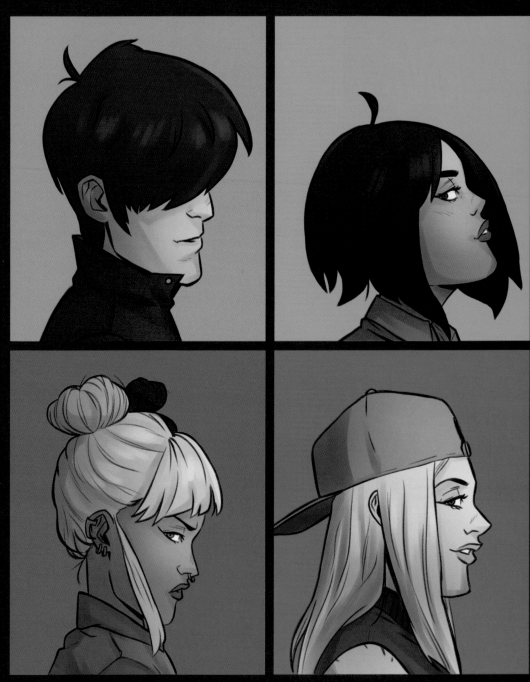

YEAH, YOU BETTER RUN

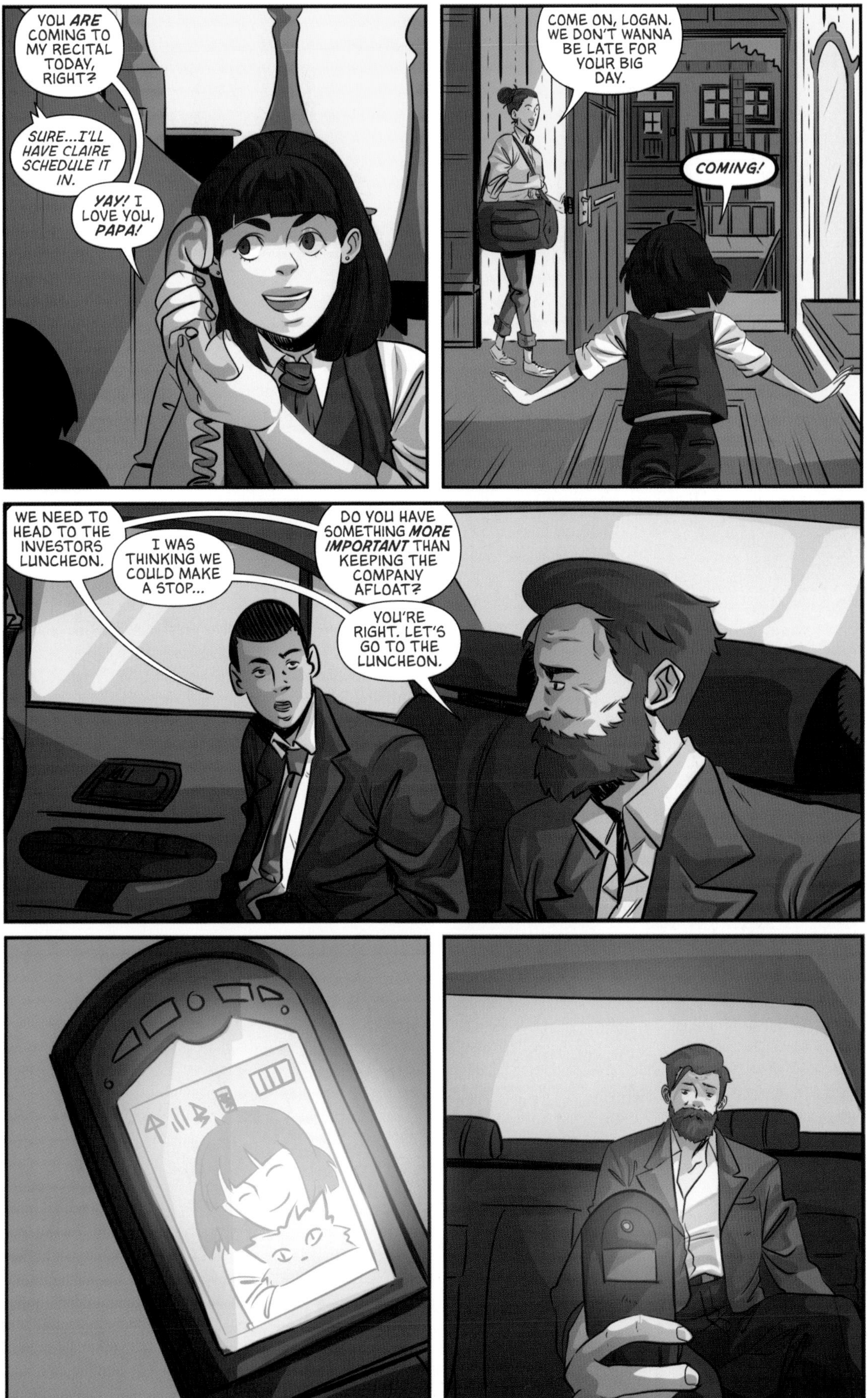
YOU ARE COMING TO MY RECITAL TODAY, RIGHT?
SURE...I'LL HAVE CLAIRE SCHEDULE IT IN.
YAY! I LOVE YOU, PAPA!
COME ON, LOGAN. WE DON'T WANNA BE LATE FOR YOUR BIG DAY.
COMING!
WE NEED TO HEAD TO THE INVESTORS LUNCHEON.
I WAS THINKING WE COULD MAKE A STOP...
DO YOU HAVE SOMETHING MORE IMPORTANT THAN KEEPING THE COMPANY AFLOAT?
YOU'RE RIGHT. LET'S GO TO THE LUNCHEON.

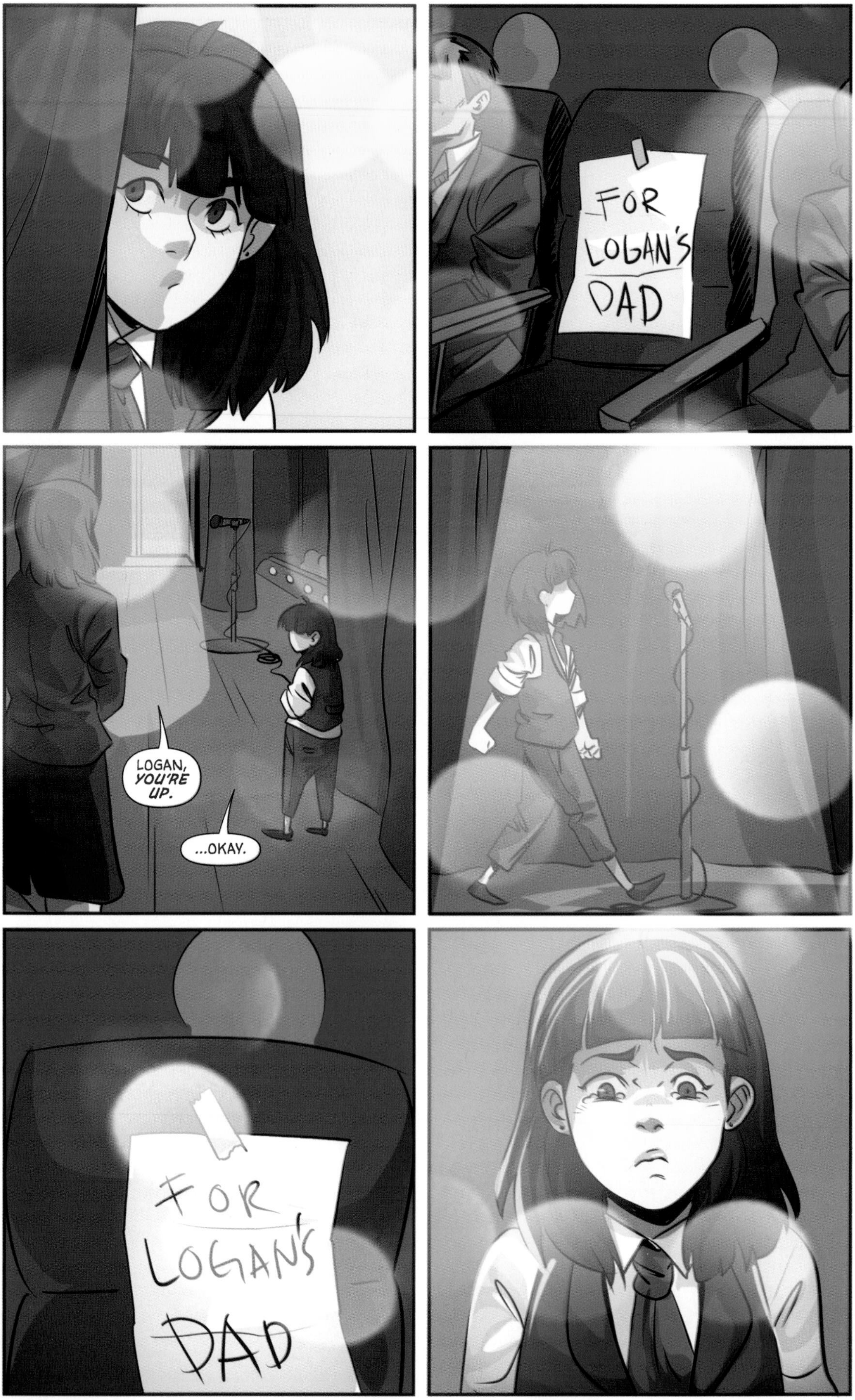
FOR LOGAN'S DAD
LOGAN, YOU'RE UP.
...OKAY.
FOR LOGAN'S DAD

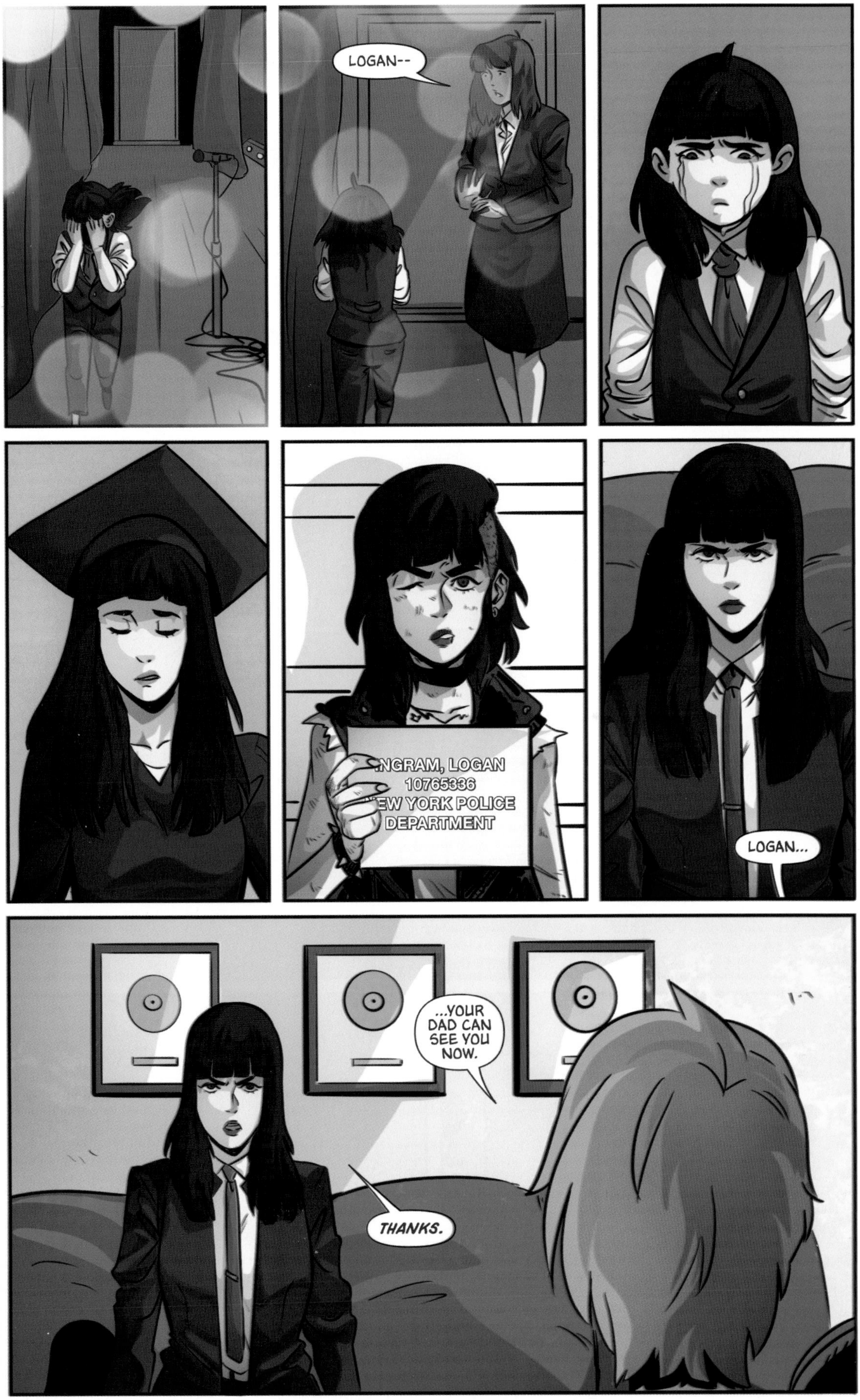
LOGAN--
INGRAM, LOGAN
10765336
NEW YORK POLICE
DEPARTMENT
LOGAN...
...YOUR DAD CAN SEE YOU NOW.
THANKS.

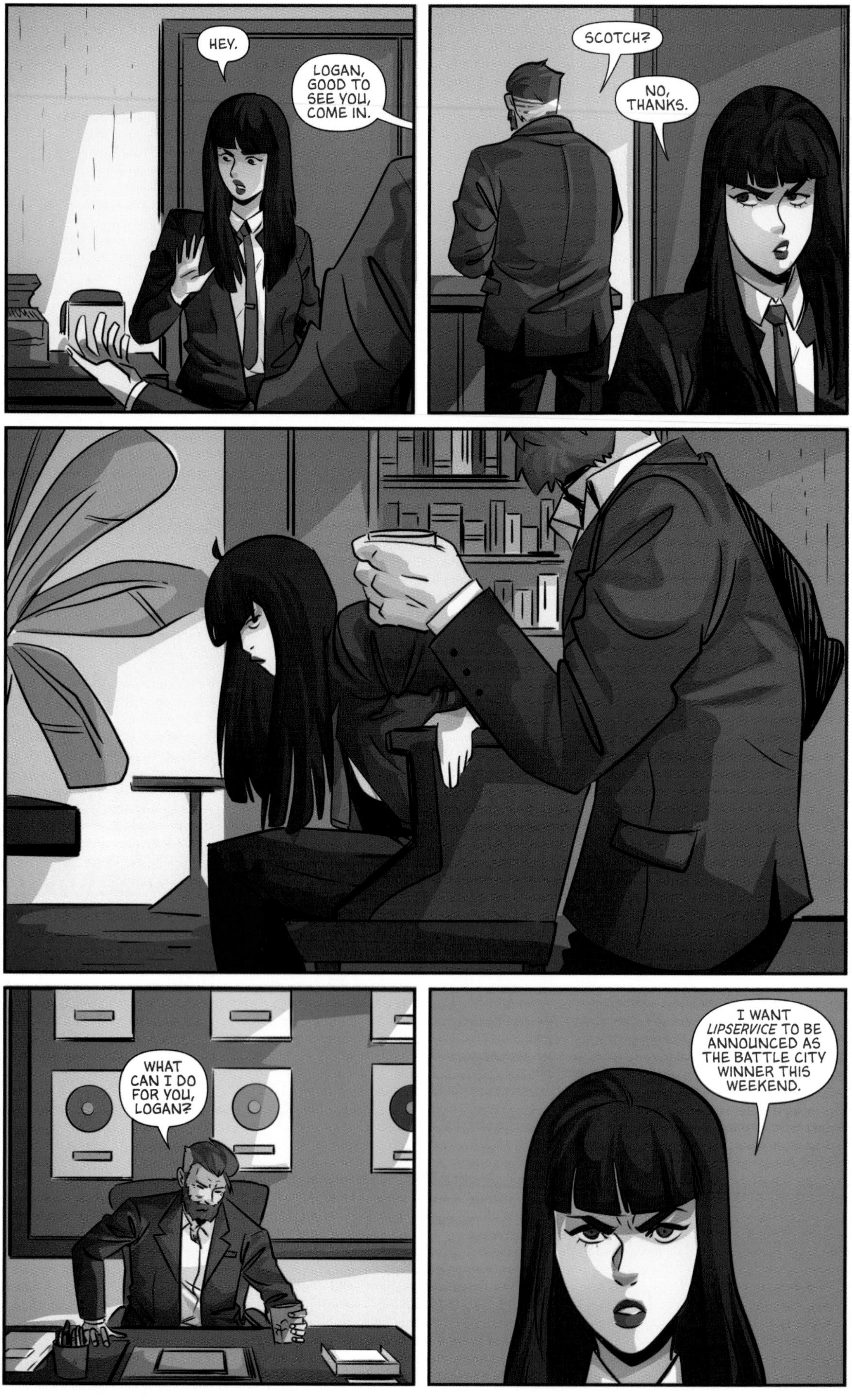
HEY.
LOGAN, GOOD TO SEE YOU, COME IN.
SCOTCH?
NO, THANKS.
WHAT CAN I DO FOR YOU, LOGAN?
I WANT *LIPSERVICE* TO BE ANNOUNCED AS THE BATTLE CITY WINNER THIS WEEKEND.

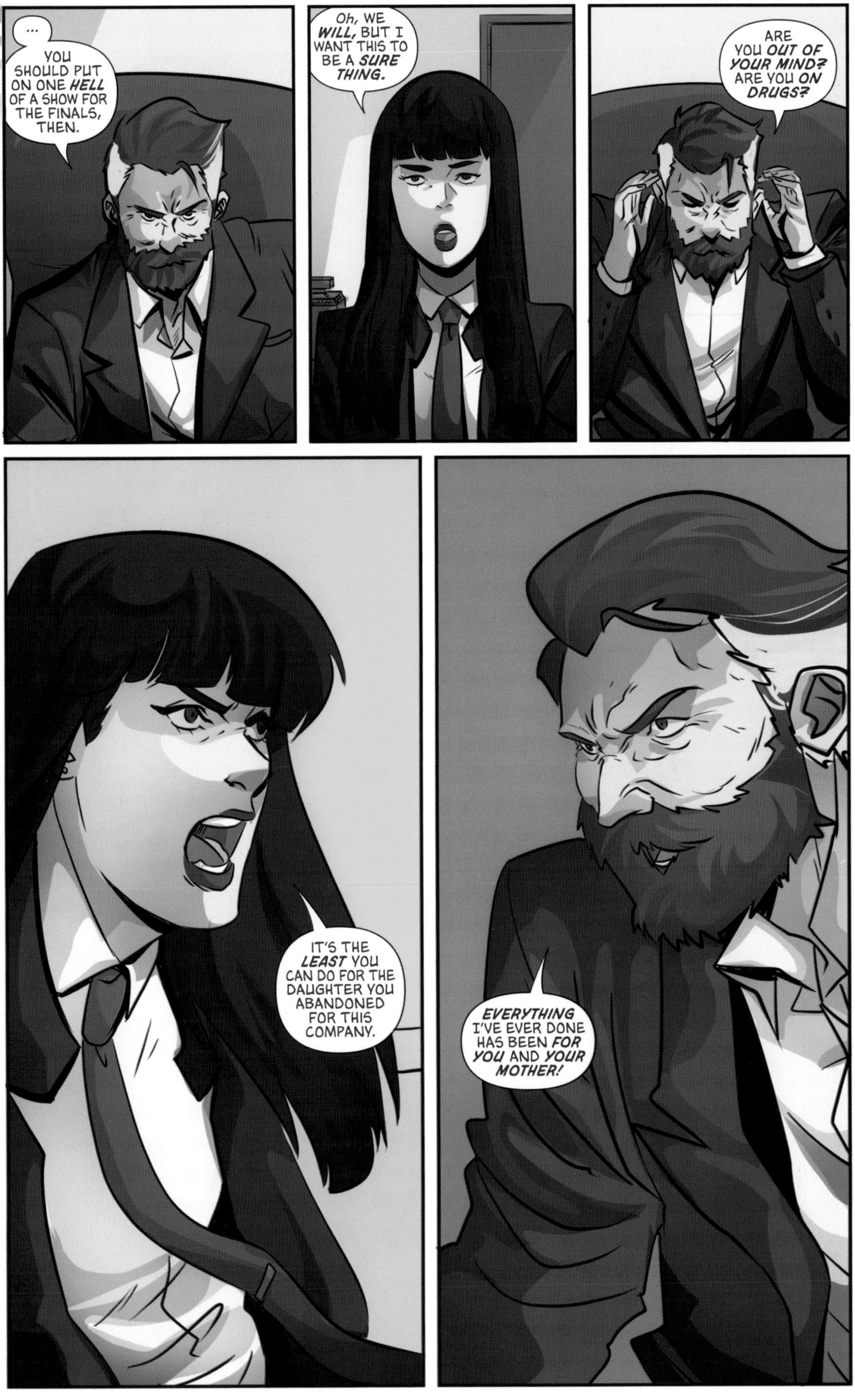
...
YOU SHOULD PUT ON ONE HELL OF A SHOW FOR THE FINALS, THEN.
Oh, WE WILL, BUT I WANT THIS TO BE A SURE THING.
ARE YOU OUT OF YOUR MIND? ARE YOU ON DRUGS?
IT'S THE LEAST YOU CAN DO FOR THE DAUGHTER YOU ABANDONED FOR THIS COMPANY.
EVERYTHING I'VE EVER DONE HAS BEEN FOR YOU AND YOUR MOTHER!

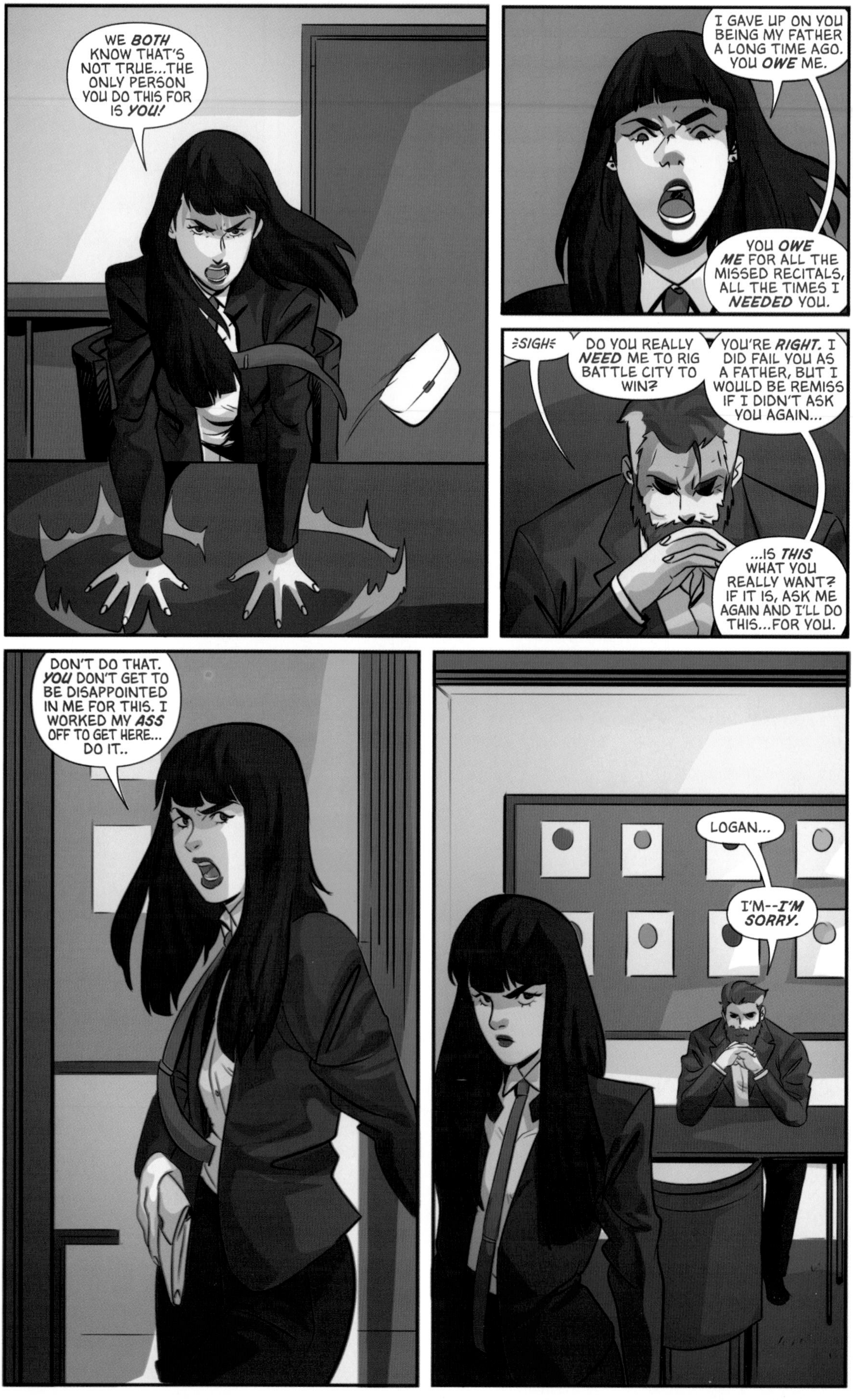
WE BOTH KNOW THAT'S NOT TRUE...THE ONLY PERSON YOU DO THIS FOR IS YOU!
I GAVE UP ON YOU BEING MY FATHER A LONG TIME AGO. YOU OWE ME.
YOU OWE ME FOR ALL THE MISSED RECITALS, ALL THE TIMES I NEEDED YOU.
SIGH
DO YOU REALLY NEED ME TO RIG BATTLE CITY TO WIN?
YOU'RE RIGHT. I DID FAIL YOU AS A FATHER, BUT I WOULD BE REMISS IF I DIDN'T ASK YOU AGAIN...
...IS THIS WHAT YOU REALLY WANT? IF IT IS, ASK ME AGAIN AND I'LL DO THIS...FOR YOU.
DON'T DO THAT. YOU DON'T GET TO BE DISAPPOINTED IN ME FOR THIS. I WORKED MY ASS OFF TO GET HERE... DO IT..
LOGAN...
I'M--I'M SORRY.

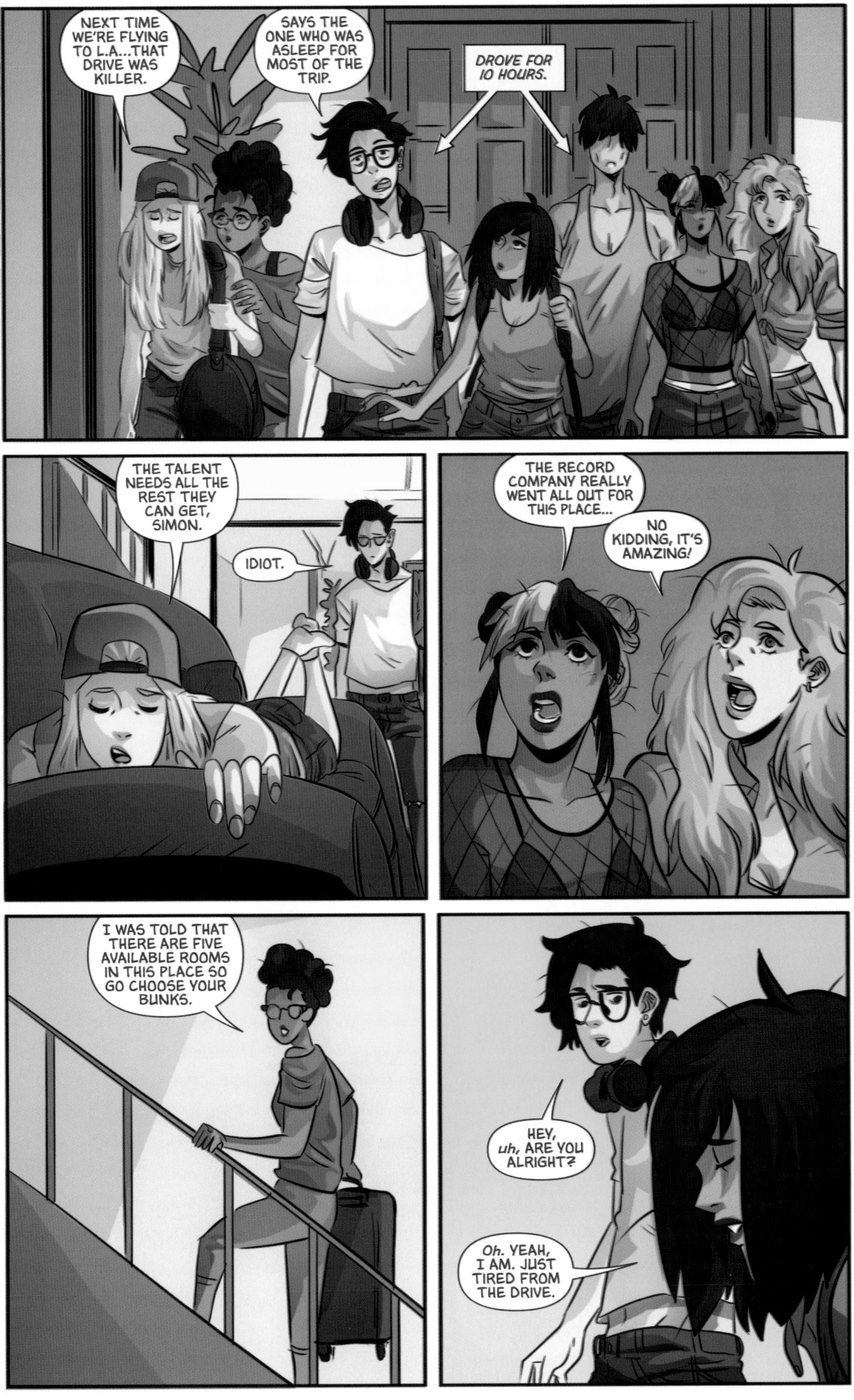
NEXT TIME WE'RE FLYING TO L.A...THAT DRIVE WAS KILLER.
SAYS THE ONE WHO WAS ASLEEP FOR MOST OF THE TRIP.
DROVE FOR 10 HOURS.
THE TALENT NEEDS ALL THE REST THEY CAN GET, SIMON.
IDIOT.
THE RECORD COMPANY REALLY WENT ALL OUT FOR THIS PLACE...
NO KIDDING, IT'S AMAZING!
I WAS TOLD THAT THERE ARE FIVE AVAILABLE ROOMS IN THIS PLACE SO GO CHOOSE YOUR BUNKS.
HEY, uh, ARE YOU ALRIGHT?
Oh. YEAH, I AM. JUST TIRED FROM THE DRIVE.

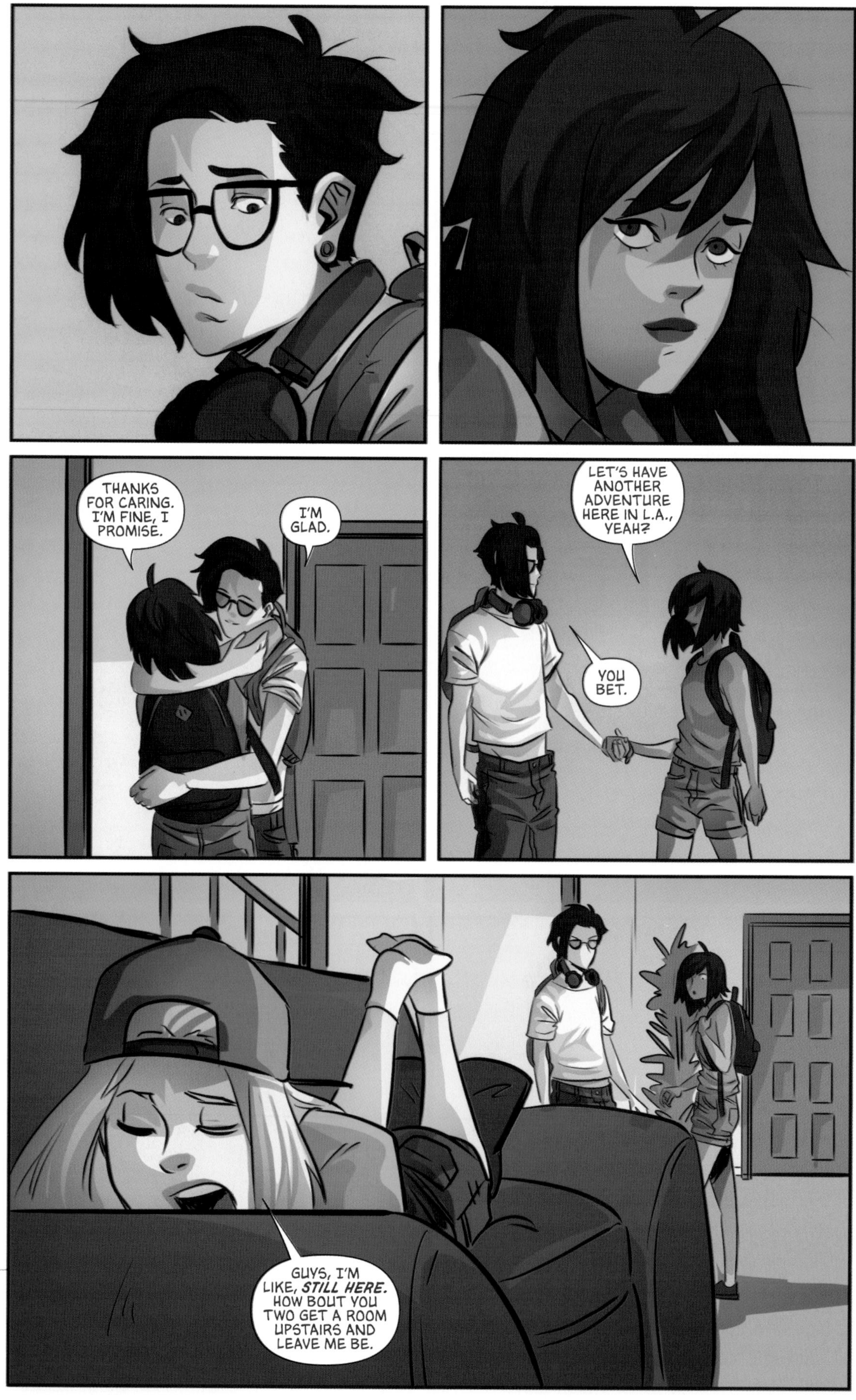
THANKS FOR CARING. I'M FINE, I PROMISE.
I'M GLAD.
LET'S HAVE ANOTHER ADVENTURE HERE IN L.A., YEAH?
YOU BET.
GUYS, I'M LIKE, ***STILL HERE.*** HOW BOUT YOU TWO GET A ROOM UPSTAIRS AND LEAVE ME BE.

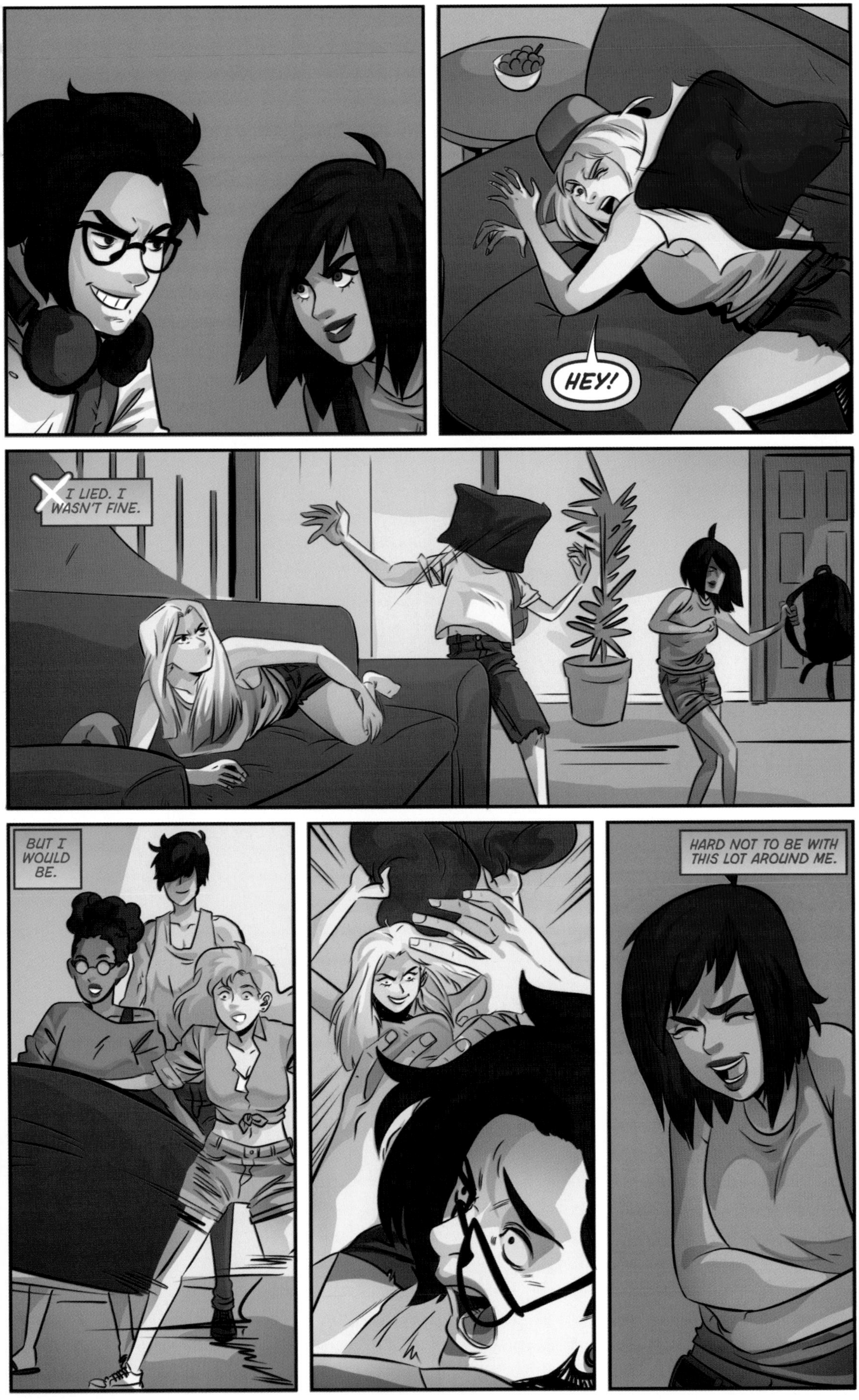
HEY!
I LIED. I WASN'T FINE.
BUT I WOULD BE.
HARD NOT TO BE WITH THIS LOT AROUND ME.

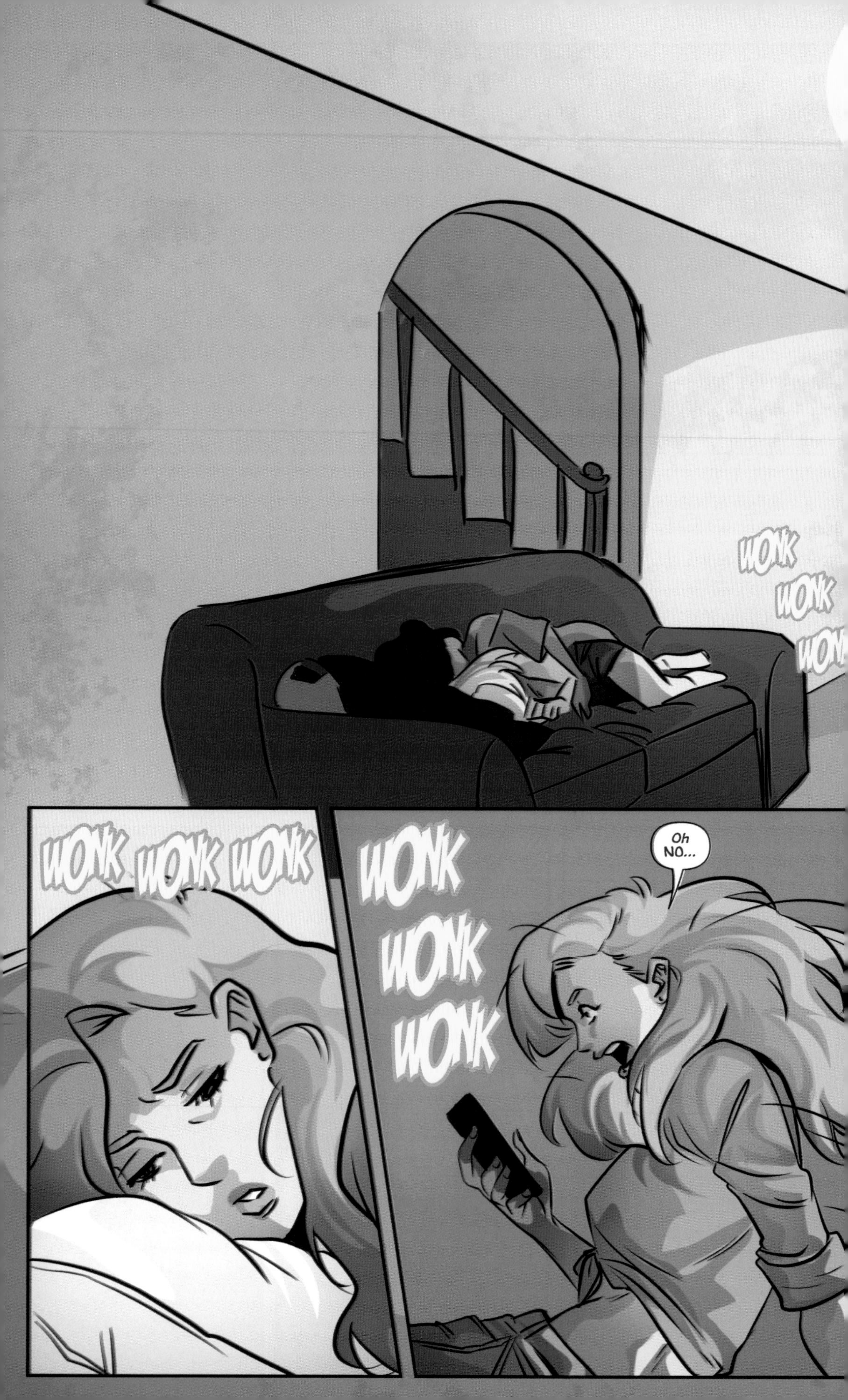
WONK
WONK
WONK
WONK WONK WONK
WONK
WONK
WONK
Oh NO...

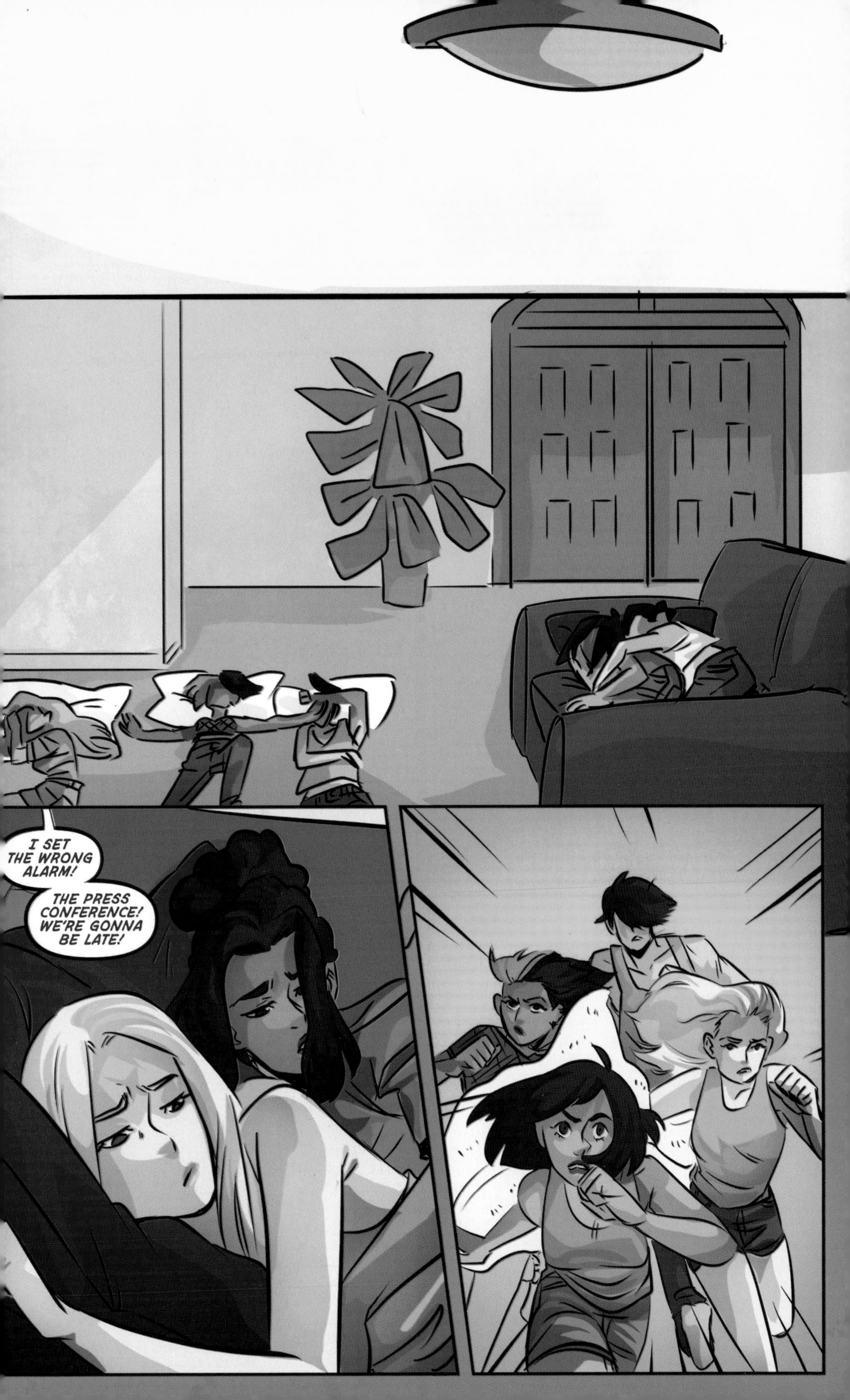
I SET THE WRONG ALARM!
THE PRESS CONFERENCE! WE'RE GONNA BE LATE!

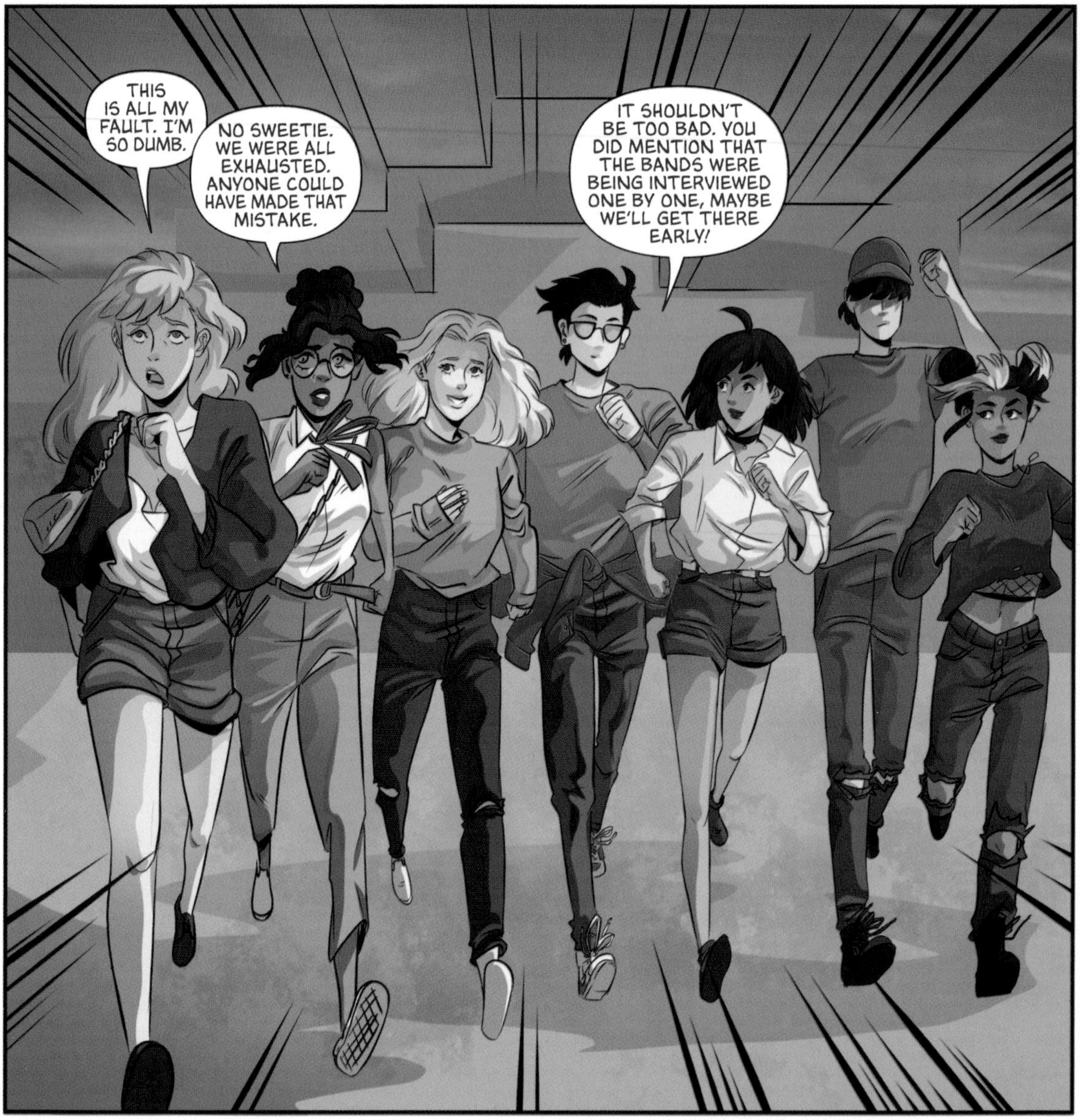
THIS IS ALL MY FAULT. I'M SO DUMB.
NO SWEETIE. WE WERE ALL EXHAUSTED. ANYONE COULD HAVE MADE THAT MISTAKE.
IT SHOULDN'T BE TOO BAD. YOU DID MENTION THAT THE BANDS WERE BEING INTERVIEWED ONE BY ONE, MAYBE WE'LL GET THERE EARLY!

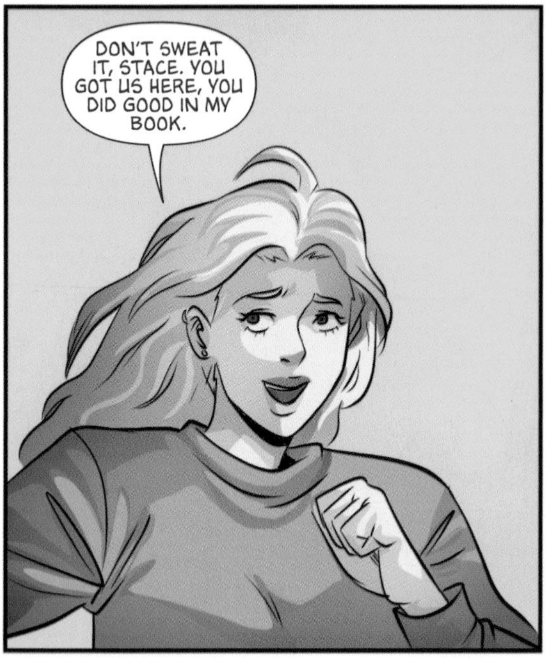
DON'T SWEAT IT, STACE. YOU GOT US HERE, YOU DID GOOD IN MY BOOK.

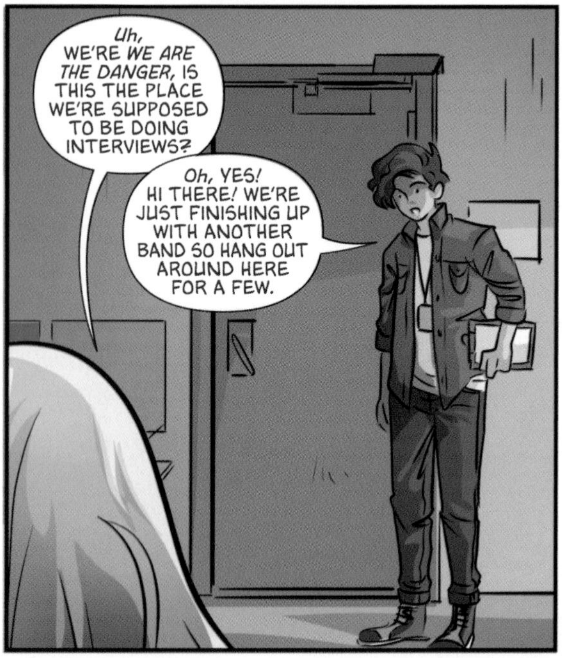
*Uh,* WE'RE *WE ARE THE DANGER,* IS THIS THE PLACE WE'RE SUPPOSED TO BE DOING INTERVIEWS?
*Oh,* YES! HI THERE! WE'RE JUST FINISHING UP WITH ANOTHER BAND SO HANG OUT AROUND HERE FOR A FEW.

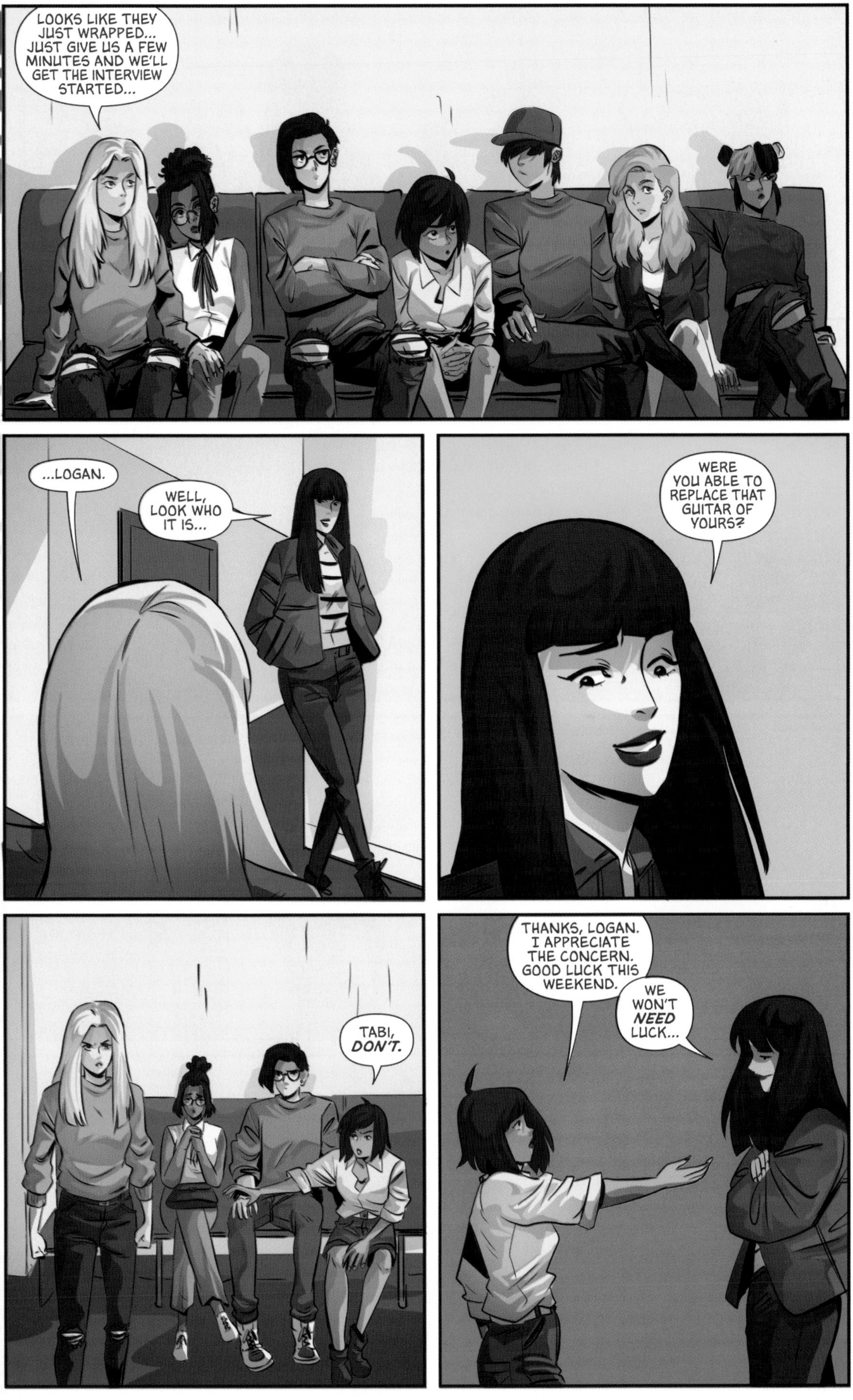
LOOKS LIKE THEY JUST WRAPPED... JUST GIVE US A FEW MINUTES AND WE'LL GET THE INTERVIEW STARTED...
...LOGAN.
WELL, LOOK WHO IT IS...
WERE YOU ABLE TO REPLACE THAT GUITAR OF YOURS?
TABI, *DON'T.*
THANKS, LOGAN. I APPRECIATE THE CONCERN. GOOD LUCK THIS WEEKEND.
WE WON'T *NEED* LUCK...

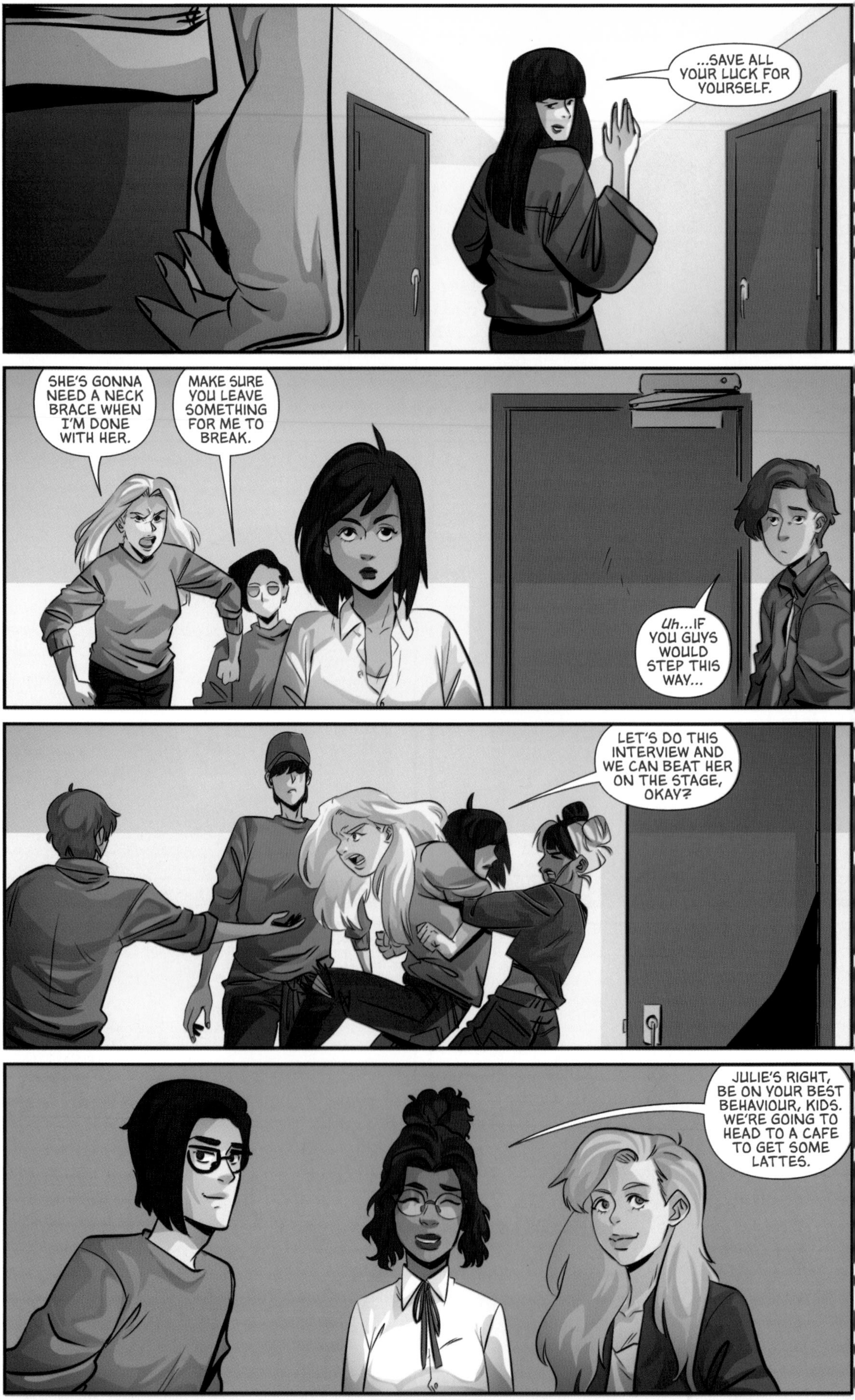
...SAVE ALL YOUR LUCK FOR YOURSELF.
SHE'S GONNA NEED A NECK BRACE WHEN I'M DONE WITH HER.
MAKE SURE YOU LEAVE SOMETHING FOR ME TO BREAK.
*Uh*...IF YOU GUYS WOULD STEP THIS WAY...
LET'S DO THIS INTERVIEW AND WE CAN BEAT HER ON THE STAGE, OKAY?
JULIE'S RIGHT, BE ON YOUR BEST BEHAVIOUR, KIDS. WE'RE GOING TO HEAD TO A CAFE TO GET SOME LATTES.

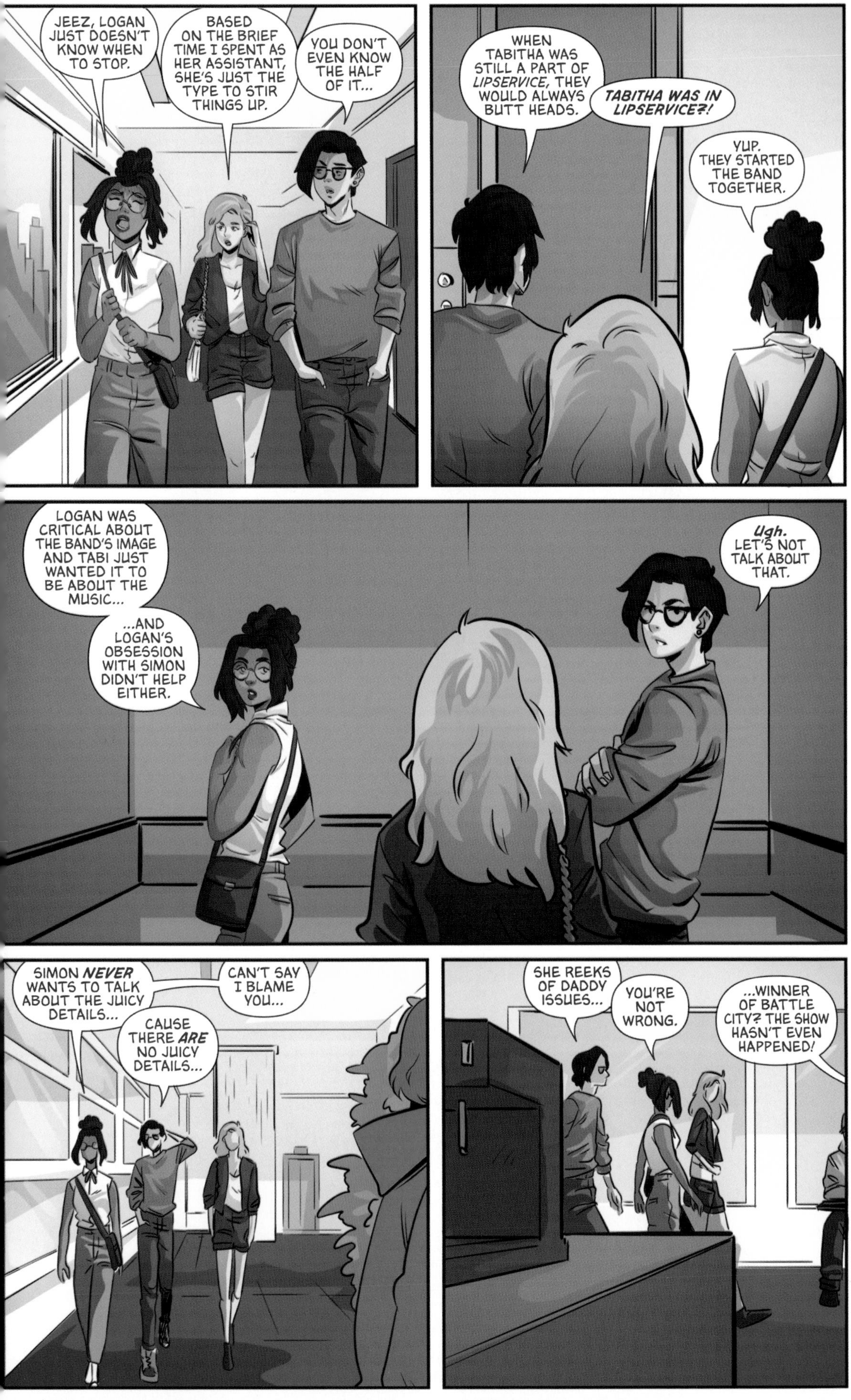
JEEZ, LOGAN JUST DOESN'T KNOW WHEN TO STOP.
BASED ON THE BRIEF TIME I SPENT AS HER ASSISTANT, SHE'S JUST THE TYPE TO STIR THINGS UP.
YOU DON'T EVEN KNOW THE HALF OF IT...
WHEN TABITHA WAS STILL A PART OF *LIPSERVICE*, THEY WOULD ALWAYS BUTT HEADS.
*TABITHA WAS IN LIPSERVICE?!*
YUP. THEY STARTED THE BAND TOGETHER.
LOGAN WAS CRITICAL ABOUT THE BAND'S IMAGE AND TABI JUST WANTED IT TO BE ABOUT THE MUSIC...
...AND LOGAN'S OBSESSION WITH SIMON DIDN'T HELP EITHER.
*Ugh.* LET'S NOT TALK ABOUT THAT.
SIMON *NEVER* WANTS TO TALK ABOUT THE JUICY DETAILS...
CAN'T SAY I BLAME YOU...
CAUSE THERE *ARE* NO JUICY DETAILS...
SHE REEKS OF DADDY ISSUES...
YOU'RE NOT WRONG.
...WINNER OF BATTLE CITY? THE SHOW HASN'T EVEN HAPPENED!

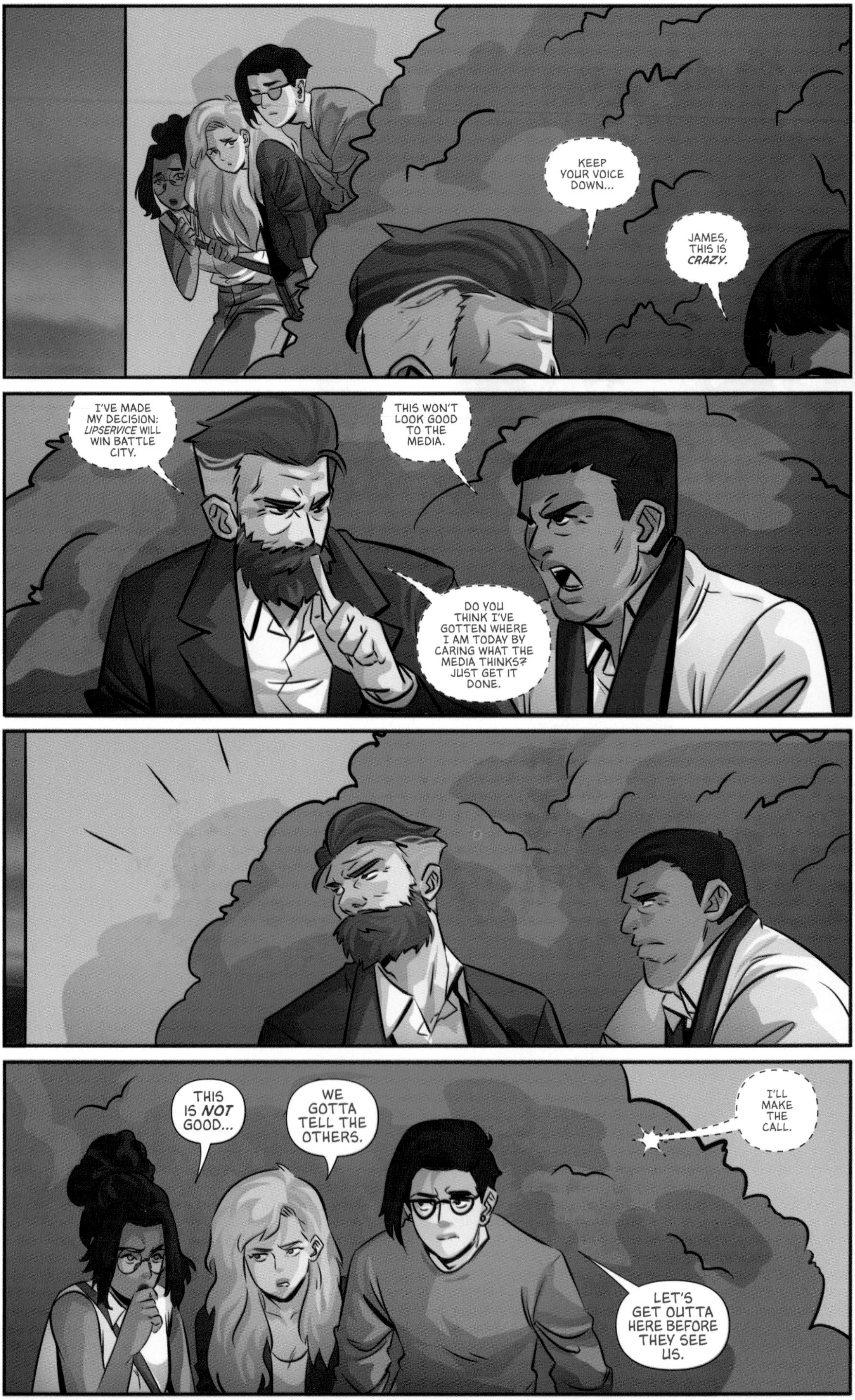
KEEP YOUR VOICE DOWN...
JAMES, THIS IS *CRAZY.*
I'VE MADE MY DECISION: *LIPSERVICE* WILL WIN BATTLE CITY.
THIS WON'T LOOK GOOD TO THE MEDIA.
DO YOU THINK I'VE GOTTEN WHERE I AM TODAY BY CARING WHAT THE MEDIA THINKS? JUST GET IT DONE.
THIS IS *NOT* GOOD...
WE GOTTA TELL THE OTHERS.
I'LL MAKE THE CALL.
LET'S GET OUTTA HERE BEFORE THEY SEE US.

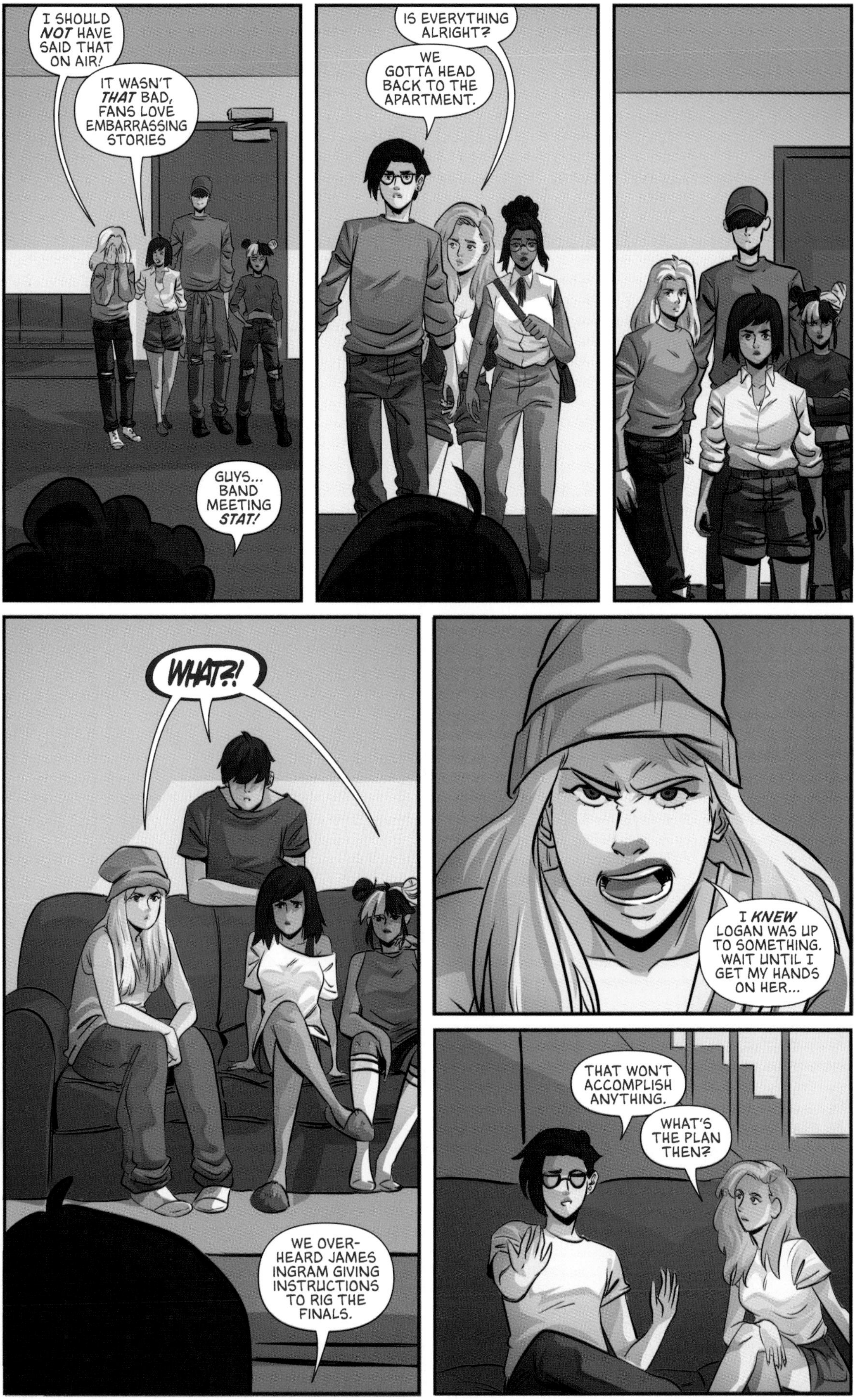
I SHOULD NOT HAVE SAID THAT ON AIR!
IT WASN'T THAT BAD, FANS LOVE EMBARRASSING STORIES
GUYS... BAND MEETING STAT!
IS EVERYTHING ALRIGHT?
WE GOTTA HEAD BACK TO THE APARTMENT.
WHAT?!
WE OVER-HEARD JAMES INGRAM GIVING INSTRUCTIONS TO RIG THE FINALS.
I KNEW LOGAN WAS UP TO SOMETHING. WAIT UNTIL I GET MY HANDS ON HER...
THAT WON'T ACCOMPLISH ANYTHING.
WHAT'S THE PLAN THEN?

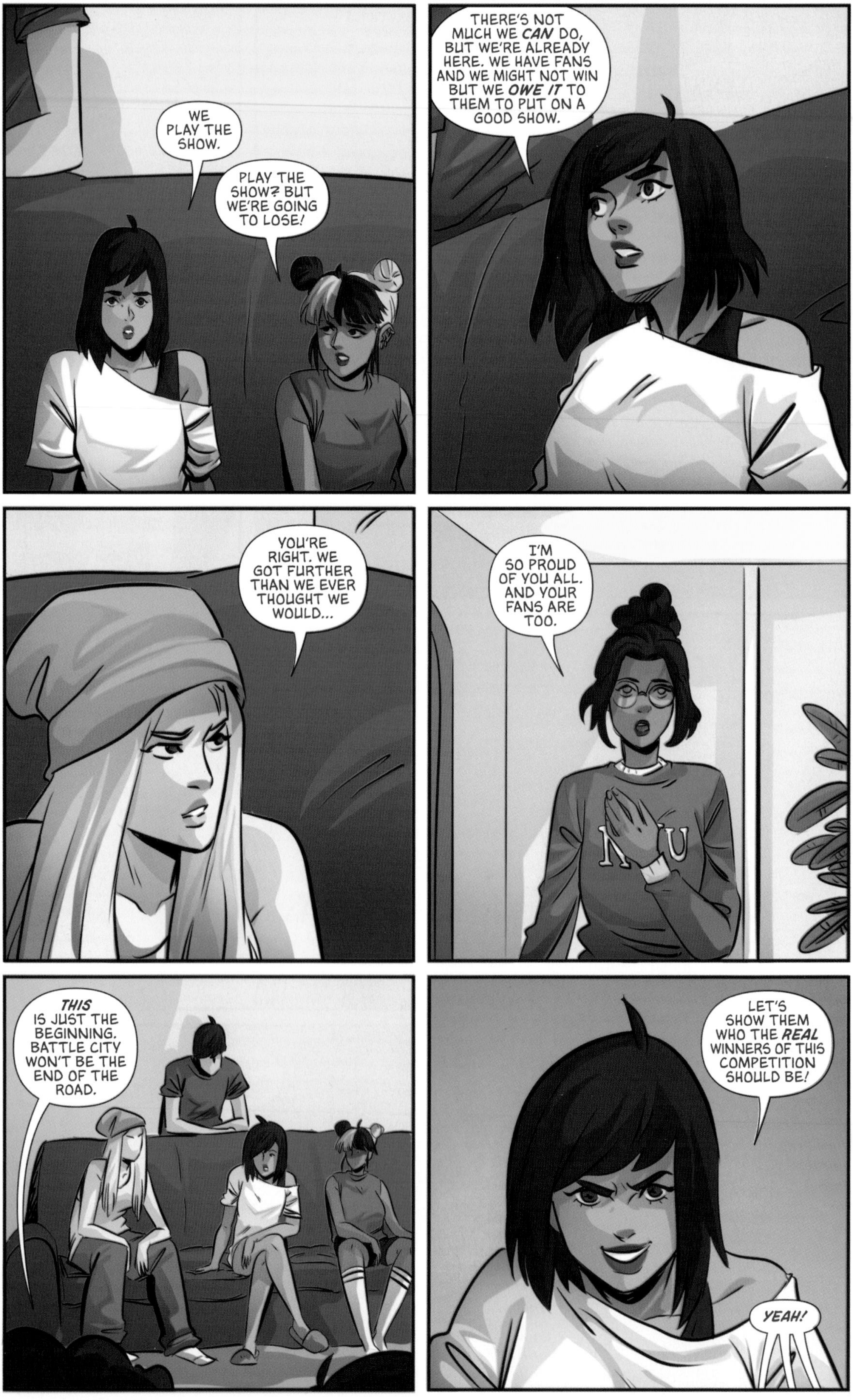
WE PLAY THE SHOW.
PLAY THE SHOW? BUT WE'RE GOING TO LOSE!
THERE'S NOT MUCH WE CAN DO, BUT WE'RE ALREADY HERE. WE HAVE FANS AND WE MIGHT NOT WIN BUT WE OWE IT TO THEM TO PUT ON A GOOD SHOW.
YOU'RE RIGHT. WE GOT FURTHER THAN WE EVER THOUGHT WE WOULD...
I'M SO PROUD OF YOU ALL. AND YOUR FANS ARE TOO.
THIS IS JUST THE BEGINNING. BATTLE CITY WON'T BE THE END OF THE ROAD.
LET'S SHOW THEM WHO THE REAL WINNERS OF THIS COMPETITION SHOULD BE!
YEAH!

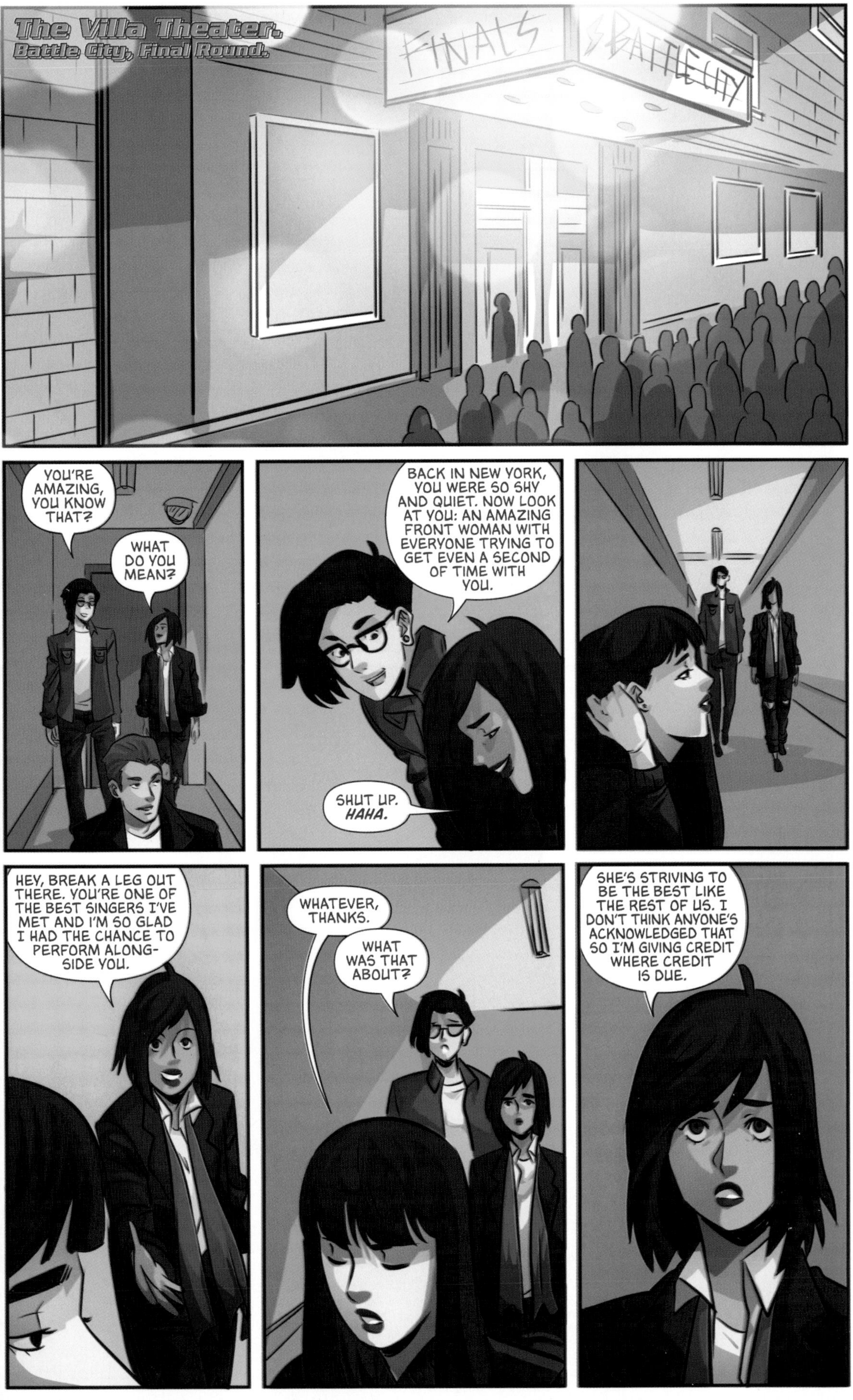
The Villa Theater.
Battle City, Final Round.
FINALS
BATTLE CITY
YOU'RE AMAZING, YOU KNOW THAT?
WHAT DO YOU MEAN?
BACK IN NEW YORK, YOU WERE SO SHY AND QUIET. NOW LOOK AT YOU: AN AMAZING FRONT WOMAN WITH EVERYONE TRYING TO GET EVEN A SECOND OF TIME WITH YOU.
SHUT UP. *HAHA.*
HEY, BREAK A LEG OUT THERE. YOU'RE ONE OF THE BEST SINGERS I'VE MET AND I'M SO GLAD I HAD THE CHANCE TO PERFORM ALONG-SIDE YOU.
WHATEVER, THANKS.
WHAT WAS THAT ABOUT?
SHE'S STRIVING TO BE THE BEST LIKE THE REST OF US. I DON'T THINK ANYONE'S ACKNOWLEDGED THAT SO I'M GIVING CREDIT WHERE CREDIT IS DUE.

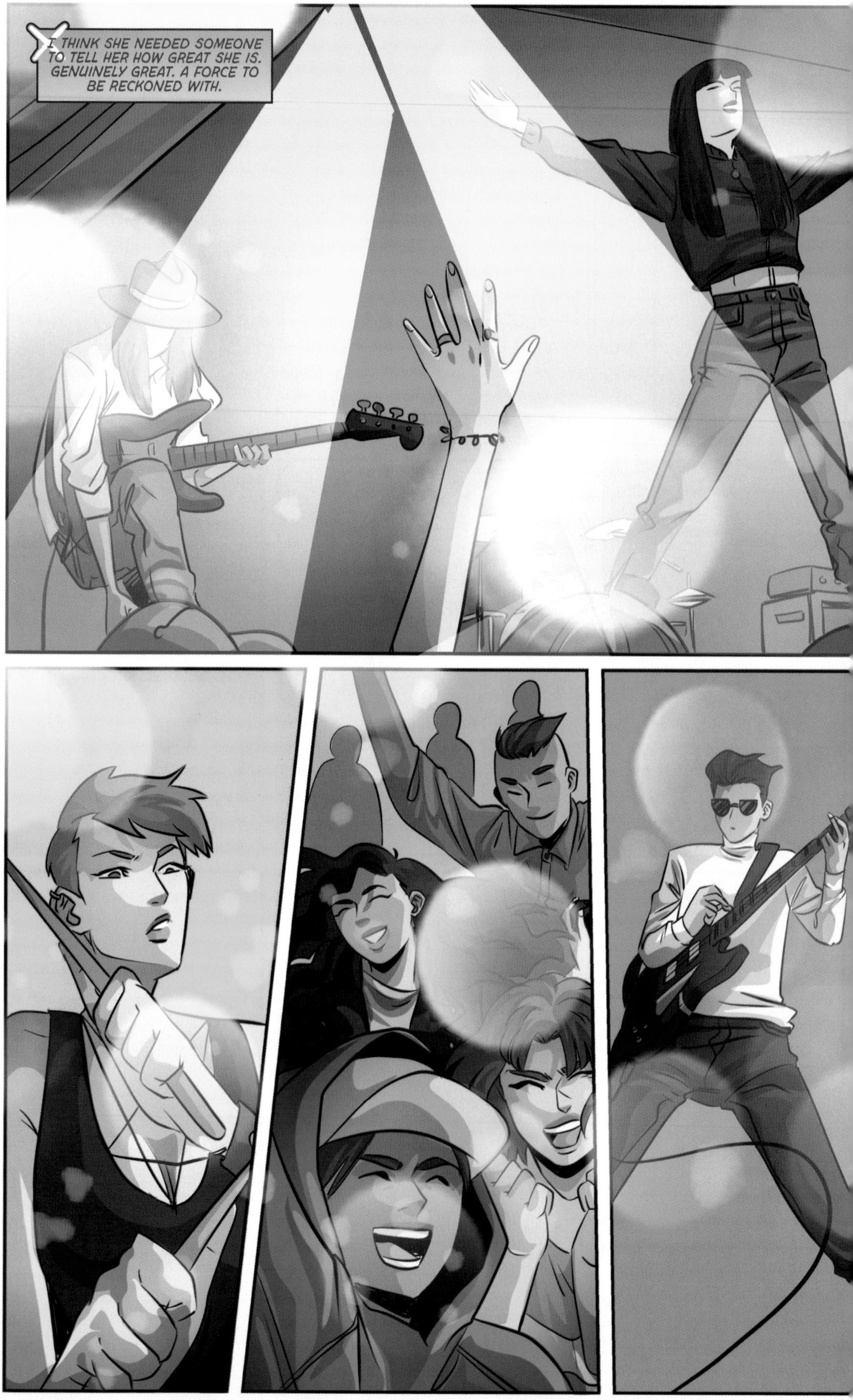
I THINK SHE NEEDED SOMEONE TO TELL HER HOW GREAT SHE IS. GENUINELY GREAT. A FORCE TO BE RECKONED WITH.

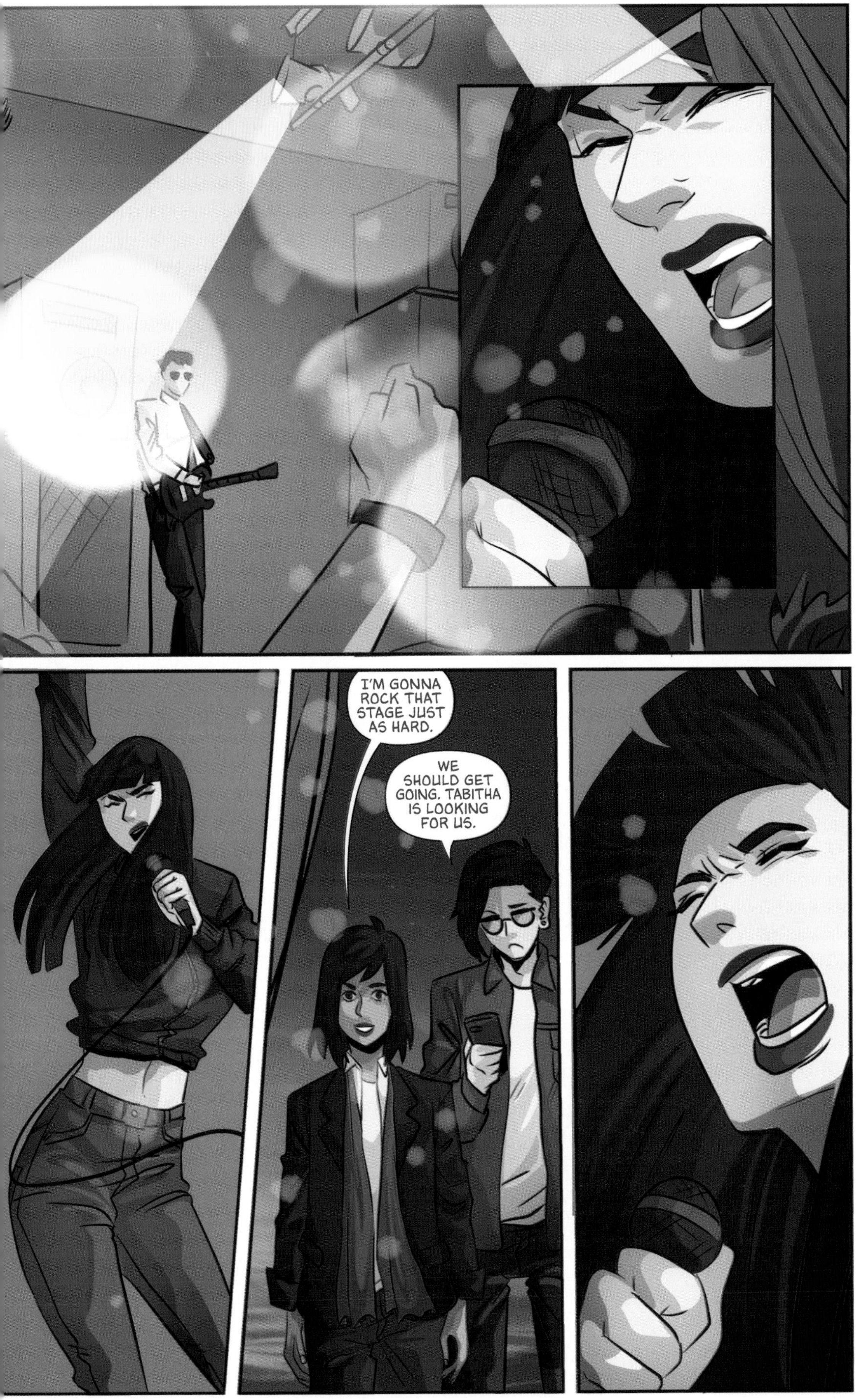
I'M GONNA ROCK THAT STAGE JUST AS HARD.
WE SHOULD GET GOING. TABITHA IS LOOKING FOR US.

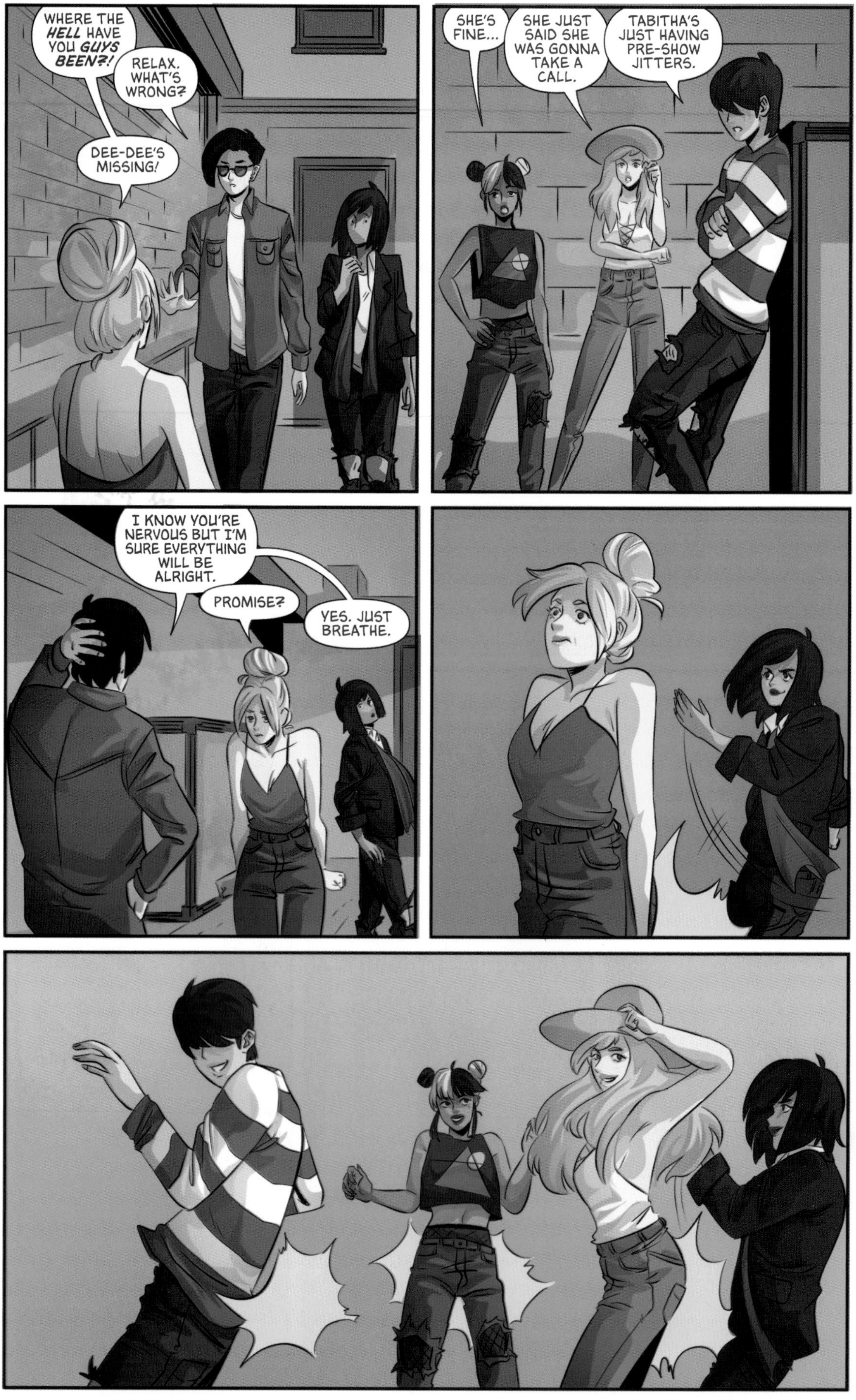
WHERE THE **HELL** HAVE YOU **GUYS BEEN?!**
RELAX. WHAT'S WRONG?
DEE-DEE'S MISSING!
SHE'S FINE...
SHE JUST SAID SHE WAS GONNA TAKE A CALL.
TABITHA'S JUST HAVING PRE-SHOW JITTERS.
I KNOW YOU'RE NERVOUS BUT I'M SURE EVERYTHING WILL BE ALRIGHT.
PROMISE?
YES. JUST BREATHE.

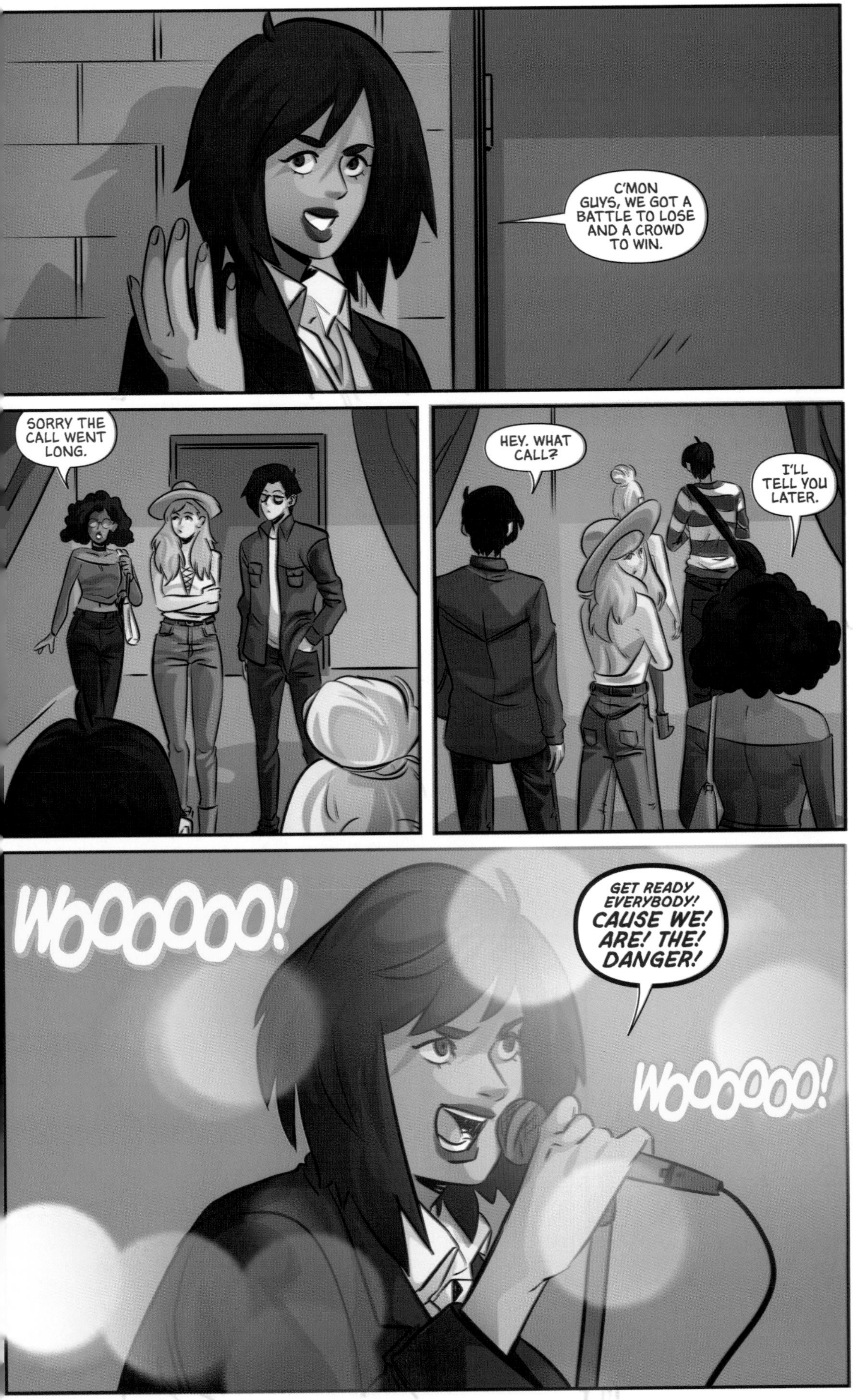
C'MON GUYS, WE GOT A BATTLE TO LOSE AND A CROWD TO WIN.
SORRY THE CALL WENT LONG.
HEY. WHAT CALL?
I'LL TELL YOU LATER.
WOOOOOO!
GET READY EVERYBODY! CAUSE WE! ARE! THE! DANGER!
WOOOOOO!

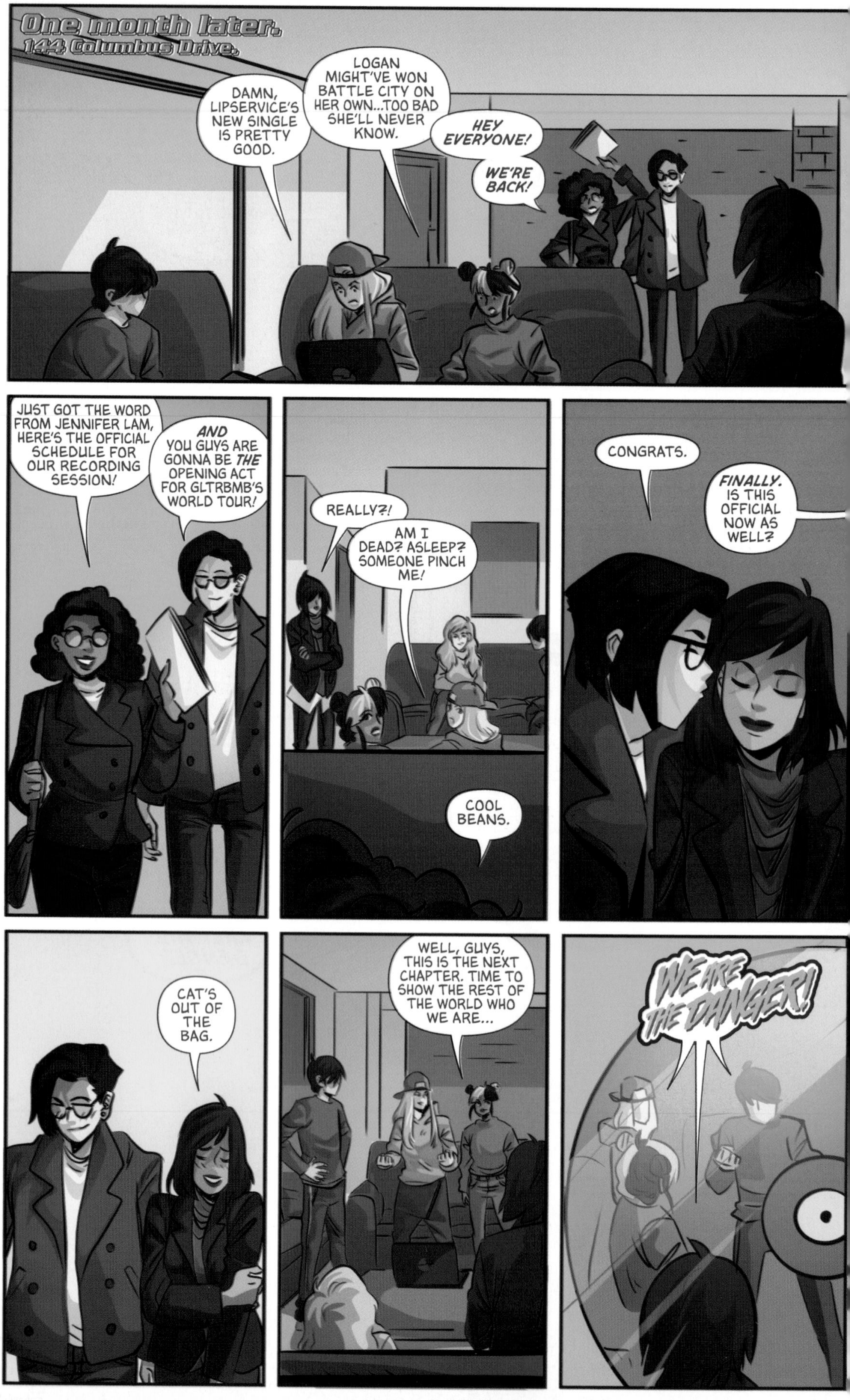
One month later.
144 Columbus Drive.
DAMN, LIPSERVICE'S NEW SINGLE IS PRETTY GOOD.
LOGAN MIGHT'VE WON BATTLE CITY ON HER OWN...TOO BAD SHE'LL NEVER KNOW.
HEY EVERYONE!
WE'RE BACK!
JUST GOT THE WORD FROM JENNIFER LAM, HERE'S THE OFFICIAL SCHEDULE FOR OUR RECORDING SESSION!
AND YOU GUYS ARE GONNA BE THE OPENING ACT FOR GLTRBMB'S WORLD TOUR!
REALLY?!
AM I DEAD? ASLEEP? SOMEONE PINCH ME!
COOL BEANS.
CONGRATS.
FINALLY. IS THIS OFFICIAL NOW AS WELL?
CAT'S OUT OF THE BAG.
WELL, GUYS, THIS IS THE NEXT CHAPTER. TIME TO SHOW THE REST OF THE WORLD WHO WE ARE...
WE ARE THE DANGER!

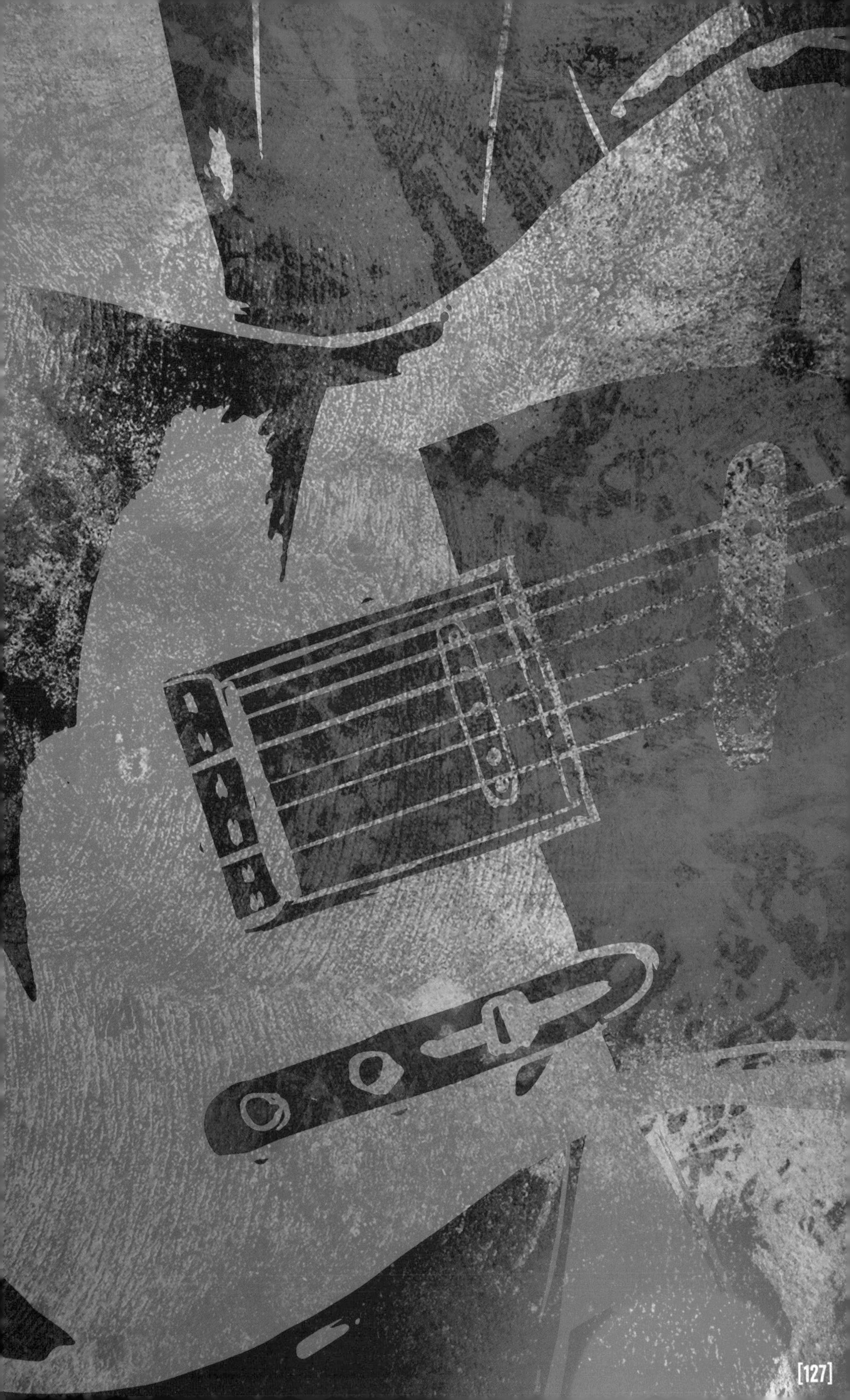

# THE TEAM

**FABIAN "SWEET CHEEKS" LELAY** - FABIAN IS A NEW YORK BASED QUEER CREATOR IMPORTED FROM THE PHILIPPINES. HE BEGAN DRAWING COMICS WITH HIS FRIENDS FROM THE AGE OF 13 AND BRIEFLY VENTURED INTO THE WORLD OF FASHION AND MUSIC WHEN HE STEPPED FOOT INTO COLLEGE. WITH EXPERIENCE AND PASSION IN THESE FIELDS, HE BRINGS TO YOU THE STORY OF JULIE AND TABITHA AS TO INSPIRE THOSE WHO ARE AFRAID TO TAKE THE LEAP IN PASSIONS OTHER PEOPLE CONSIDER AS MERE DREAMS.

FIND MORE ABOUT HIS WORK AT @ROCKETSANDPENS AND ROCKETSANDPENS.COM.

**CLAUDIA "MICHAELANGELHOE" AGUIRRE** - QUEER COMIC BOOK ARTIST AND WRITER. GLAAD AWARD NOMINEE AND WILL EISNER AWARD NOMINEE. CO-FOUNDER OF BOUDIKA COMICS; WHERE SHE SELF-PUBLISHES COMICS. CURRENTLY WORKING FOR BLACK MASK, ONI PRESS, LEGENDARY, LIMERENCE PRESS AND BOOM! STUDIOS.

YOU CAN SEE MORE OF HER AWESOME WORK BY FOLLOWING @CLAUDIAGUIRRE.

**TAYLOR "ROCK DADDY" ESPOSITO** - TAYLOR ESPOSITO IS A COMIC BOOK LETTERING PROFESSIONAL AND OWNER OF GHOST GLYPH STUDIOS. A FORMER STAFF LETTERER AT DC AND PRODUCTION ARTIST AT MARVEL, HE LETTERED TITLES SUCH AS *RED HOOD AND THE OUTLAWS, ELVIRA, BETTIE PAGE, INTERCEPTOR: REACTOR, FRIENDO, NO ONE LEFT TO FIGHT, RED SONJA AND VAMPIRELLA MEET BETTY AND VERONICA,* AND *BABYTEETH.* OTHER PUBLISHERS HE HAS WORKED WITH INCLUDE LINE WEBTOON ON *CASTER* AND *BACKCHANNEL.* FOR DYNAMITE ON *BATTLESTAR GALACTICA, BLACK TERROR, ARMY OF DARKNESS/BUBBA HO-TEP.* PLUS WORK FOR IDW ON *SCARLETT'S STRIKE FORCE.*

YOU CAN FIND HIS WORK AT WWW.GHOSTGLYPHSTUDIOS.COM.

**STEPHANIE "TRASH PANDA" COOKE** - STEPHANIE IS AN AWARD-WINNING WRITER AND EDITOR BASED OUT OF TORONTO. HER WRITING WORK IS FEATURED IN MARK MILLAR'S *MILLARWORLD ANNUAL, WAYWARD SISTERS, THE SECRET LOVES OF GEEK GIRLS, TORONTO COMICS ANTHOLOGY,* AND MORE. HER DEBUT GRAPHIC NOVEL, OH MY GODS, WILL BE OUT IN FALL 2020.

CATCH MORE UPDATES ON HER THROUGH TWITTER, @HELLOCOOKIE.